The Best of Galaxy's Edge

The Best of
Galaxy's Edge
2015–2017

an imprint of

MANOR
Rockville, Maryland

Phoenix Pick: November 2018

ISBN: 978-1-61242-356-2

www.PhoenixPick.com
Great Science Fiction & Fantasy

Published by Phoenix Pick
an imprint of Arc Manor
P. O. Box 10339
Rockville, MD 20849-0339
www.ArcManor.com

Contents

Introduction

by Mike Resnick

Welcome to the second *The Best of Galaxy's Edge* Anthology. As I write these words, we're two issues away from completing our fifth year, which is about four years longer than anyone thought we'd be around, and we're going stronger than ever.

Galaxy's Edge was created to showcase the work of new and newer writers. That has spelled suicide for *Unearth* and a few other magazines that tried it, but we learned from their mistakes, and along with eight or nine new stories by new/newer writers each issue, we also run four reprints every issue, thoughtfully supplied at bargain-basement rates by major writers who also go out of their way to help and encourage the next generation of science fiction professionals. Writers like Orson Scott Card, Mercedes Lackey, George R.R. Martin, Nancy Kress, Joe Haldeman, and other of that ilk—and with their names on the cover, we assure that we stay in business and remain a viable market for our newcomers.

And quite a batch they are. Some, like Leena Likitalo, Tina Gower, Marina J. Lostetter, and Robert Jeschonek have recently sold novels; others, such as Martin L. Shoemaker, Sunil Patel, and Sylvia Spruck Wrigley, were resent nominees for major awards like the Nebula and the Campbell; others are starting to appear regularly in both *Galaxy's Edge* and our rivals.

The business approach of *Galaxy's Edge* may be a new twist on an old theme, but that theme—established writers going out of their way to help newcomers—has been going on for as long as the field of imaginative literature has existed. Sometimes they even go above and beyond the call, as you'll see when you encounter Larry Niven and David Gerrold, both Hugo and Nebula winners, both former Worldcon Guests of Honor, in our table of contents (and I assure they did not charge us their standard prices.)

And despite all the warm feelings we have for our stable of new and newer writers, one fact remains and never alters: we don't buy them because we're fond of them, or proud of them, or rooting for them to succeed. This is a highly competitive field, and you'd be shocked (or at least surprised) if I told you how many stories we turn down for every one that we purchase. Despite the fatherly pride and the budding friendships, we buy only the best that we are shown—and we are once again happy to share them with you.

To Catch a Comet

by Sylvia Spruck Wrigley

From: Samantha Schandin
To: Greg Smith
Regarding: Asteroid Strike

Dear Greg,

Attached please find our revised projections regarding the inbound asteroid based on newly collected data from Observatorio del Teide. The results have been verified by the Astrophysical Unit here in Cambridge.

As you can see, it's more bad news. You haven't sent any updates lately and I am hoping there are no delays on the intercept mission as we have only a few months until impact.

Please get in touch and let me know the status.

Samantha

 ✧ ✧ ✧

From: postmaster@europa.eu
To: Samantha Schandin
Automated Response

I am sorry to inform you that Greg Smith no longer works for the department of special projects within the European Institute of Innovation and Technology. You may wish to get in touch with another project department regarding this. Your email *Regarding: Asteroid Strike* has been deleted unread.

From: Samantha Schandin
To: European Institute of Innovation and Technology
Asteroid 2007 QS August 2016

Dear Mr. Peeters,

I'm with the Near-Earth Objects research project. Can you please tell me who is leading the AEGIS intercept project regarding Asteroid 2007 QS? It's urgent.

From: European Institute of Innovation and Technology
To: Samantha Schandin
Regarding: Asteroid 2007 QS August 2016

Dear Samantha

I regret to inform you that the AEGIS project has been cancelled due to funding issues. If I can help further, please let me know.

Thomas Peeters

From: Samantha Schandin
To: European Institute of Innovation and Technology
Regarding: Asteroid 2007 QS August 2016

Dear Mr. Peeters,

I'm not sure if you are aware, but the AEGIS project was an intercept mission against a meteorite which is due to impact this August. This isn't a research project but a matter of a defense project which has been ongoing for the past four years. Can you please tell me who to speak to in order to get the project back on track? There are lives at stake.

Dr Samantha Schandin
NEOWatch

From: European Institute of Innovation and Technology
To: Samantha Schandin
Regarding: Asteroid 2007 QS August 2016

Dear Samantha

I'm afraid the AEGIS project was cancelled three weeks ago and the team has already been disbanded. It's out of my hands. Have you considered contacting the military?

Thomas Peeters

From: Dr Samantha Schandin
For the attention of the European Defense Agency
Regarding Imminent Meteorite Strike August

Dear Sirs,

I am trying to find the right person to speak to regarding Asteroid 2007 QS, a meteorite which is inbound to Northern Europe. Our analysis has shown that the impact site will be land-based and cause considerable devastation. We believe that the most likely point of impact is Luxembourg if the asteroid is not intercepted.

The EU-sponsored AEGIS mission was the first line of defense against the destruction which this meteorite will cause and this project has now been cancelled. We urgently need to meet with you to discuss this situation and look at how to defend against this incoming meteorite.

Dr Samantha Schandin
NEOWatch

From: European Defense Agency
To: Dr Schandin @ NEOWatch
Imminent Meteorite Strike August

There is no appropriate department within the European Defense Agency for missile intercepts of near-earth objects and Luxembourg is not a high priority target.

I looked it up and there's no confirmed records of any human ever dying in a meteorite impact. How bad can it be?

Tony Martins

From: Dr Samantha Schandin
Tony Martins, European Defense Agency
Imminent Meteorite Strike August

Dear Mr. Martins,

I'm not sure you understand the urgency of this issue. Asteroid 2007 QS will cause considerable devastation. Although my department's work has shown that the impact site will most likely be Luxembourg, this is not an exact science. Perhaps it will be easier to gain the attention that we need to deal with this by citing Brussels or Paris as likely strike sites, as there are significant staff in both locations.

Dr Samantha Schandin
NEOWatch

From: European Defense Agency
To: Dr Schandin @ NEOWatch
Imminent Meteorite Strike August

Quite frankly, a 30-metre rock is not an issue for the European Defense Agency. If you have some sort of proof that the rock is sentient or launched by sentient beings, we would be very interested in hearing further. Perhaps you should contact the European Space Agency to see if they can help you with your issue.

I am sorry that I am not able to help you further.

Tony Martins

From: Dr Samantha Schandin
Tony Martins, European Defense Agency
Regarding Imminent Meteorite Strike August

Dear Mr. Martins

It is not *my* issue. NeoWatch is three dozen people who have spent the past four years analysing data on Asteroid 2007 QS. We have coordinated with observatories and astrophysics departments around the world who have all confirmed our findings. We have updated our website with a factsheet about the asteroid in order to help you highlight the issue.

An asteroid with a diameter of 7 metres would have the equivalent kinetic energy of the atomic bomb dropped on Hiroshima. Over one thousand people were injured by the Chelyabinsk meteor airburst event over Russia in 2013.

Dr Samantha Schandin
NEO-Watch

From: European Defense Agency
To: Dr Schandin @ NEOWatch
Imminent Meteorite Strike August

Understood, but this damage would be specific to Luxembourg, is that right?

Tony

From: Dr Samantha Schandin
For the attention of the EU Space Department
Imminent Meteorite Crash

I'm with Near-Earth Objects research project in Cambridge and I've been tasked with finding the right person to speak to regarding

Asteroid 2007 QS, a meteorite which will impact the earth in just eight weeks. Possible crash sites include Brussels and Paris. We expect significant localised consequences.

The EU-sponsored AEGIS mission was planning an intercept but the project has been cancelled and we now have no defense. Can I speak to someone within the EU Space Department urgently about coordinating a response?

Dr Samantha Schandin
NEOWatch

✧ ✧ ✧

From: EU Space Department
To: Dr Samantha Schandin
Regarding: Imminent Meteorite Crash

Dear Dr Schandin

Thank you for your email. I am afraid to say there is not anything we can do to help. As you are no doubt aware, a mission of this size would take at least one year to put into place and even if there were enough time, we have neither the staff nor the funding to launch an intercept craft capable of withstanding the meteorite and taking it off track. There is also significant risk to our reputation if this mission were to be undertaken and then be unsuccessful.

Elisabeth Jacobs
EU Space Department

✧ ✧ ✧

From: Dr Samantha Schandin
Council of the European Union
URGENT: Imminent Meteorite Crash

To whom it may concern,

I am Dr Samantha Schandin, an astrophysicist employed by NEOWatch in Cambridge. We analyse Potentially Hazardous Asteroids. An asteroid is heading for Northern Europe and will crash into the Earth next month.

I have assembled a petition of 1,742 scientists and researchers who all confirm that this asteroid is an immediate hazard and will create a one to two kilometre crater on impact. The most likely impact sites are Brussels and Paris.

We have contacted staff representing the European Institute of Innovation and Technology, European Defense Agency and the European Space Department and am unable to find anyone who will take responsibility for coordinating a defense. Can we have your support?

Dr Samantha Schandin
NEOWatch

✧ ✧ ✧

From Jean-Luc Vasseur
To: Samantha Schandin
Regarding: URGENT: Imminent Meteorite Crash

Dear Samantha,

We recommend you come to our next meeting on the 17th of July and see if you can find a representative who is interested in your cause. I have attached a document with travel information and local hotels. We look forward to seeing you.

Jean-Luc

✧ ✧ ✧

From: Dr Samantha Schandin
Jean-Luc Valais, Council of the European Union
CRASH AND BURN

Dear Mr. Vasseur,

My entire department went to Brussels for a meeting and there were more translators there than MEPs. This was a completely wasted effort. Asteroid 2007 QS is incoming straight for us right now and no one seems to be able get the EU to react. We're running out of time here! PLEASE HELP ME FIND THE RIGHT CONTACT!

Dr Samantha Schandin
NEOWatch

✧ ✧ ✧

From: Dr Samantha Schandin
Jean-Luc Valais, Council of the European Union
Regarding: CRASH AND BURN

Dear Mr. Vasseur

It is now only four weeks until impact! I understand that you are originally from Paris which is one of the likely impact destinations. Are you really willing to allow what is effectively a large bomb land your home town and do nothing?

Dr Samantha Schandin
NEOWatch

European Parliament
Dr Schandin
Regarding: CRASH AND BURN

Dear Dr Schandin

Paris is empty in August anyway, so I don't think that's of particular concern.

However, I have forwarded your emails to the department most likely to be interested in the situation. I hope you are able to resolve this.

Jean-Luc

Department of Geology and Mineral Exploration
Dr Samantha Schandin
NEOWatch
FW: Regarding: CRASH AND BURN

Dear Dr Schandin,

Your information was forwarded to me by Jean-Luc Vasseir of the Council of the European Union.

Could you please specify the exact details of the meteorite, including metal composition and other things so that we can correctly identify the value? It is possible that the Belgian Department of

Geology and Mineral Exploration (BDGME) is interested in this occurrence. If, as you say, the meteorite will definitely land in European territory, then we are definitely interested in more information which will allow us to recover the meteorite after impact.

Kristina Krinov
Department of Geology and Mineral Exploration

From: European Institute of Innovation and Technology
To: Samantha Schandin—NEOWatch
Regarding: Asteroid 2007 QS August 2016

Dear Samantha

This is a follow-up email as a part of our quality control to ensure that queries to our department are correctly handled. Were you able to resolve your issues regarding Asteroid 2007 QS August 2016?

Thomas Peeters

Dear Thomas,

I have left NEOWatch and relocated to the Indian Space Research Organization in Bengaluru.

I have come to the conclusion that Brussels could only be improved by a meteor strike.

Kind regards
Samantha

PS: I appreciate that at least you took the time to check back with me. Have you considered taking a holiday? I'd recommend the third week of August. Head South.

Lord of the Cul-de-sac

by Auston Habershaw

Once upon a time, a dragon got a good deal on a modified, split-level ranch with aluminum siding and a big yard—2.9% APR for a fifteen year fixed, no points, no closing costs. Truly, his credit was mighty.

Nobody saw the dragon move in. Oh, there were signs—a torn up lawn, the scorched backyard, the smell of brimstone in the air—but no sign of the dragon itself. For a week after the closing, the neighbors in the little cul-de-sac watched as armored cars pulled up to the garage, one after another. Burly men with handguns hefted small sacks of prodigious weight into the house and gradually, after hours of labor, dumped their cargo into the empty in-ground pool out back. Milly Petersen, the dragon's direct neighbor on the right hand side, told everyone the pool glittered like the sun. There was now no way to verify this, of course, as the pool was covered over with a pretty hefty tarp once the shipments ended, and hadn't been disturbed since. Mr. Fu, the dragon's other immediate neighbor, insisted that Milly was just making it up.

"Dragon's don't hoard gold. That's just in stories." He had insisted at Dr. Cohen's son's bar mitzvah that July.

Mr. Fu was often lying about things just to calm people down. He once told Jack Petersen, Milly's husband, that his chest pains were probably just gas. They hadn't been, and now Milly was speed dating at the local Pizza Palace on every third Saturday of the month.

People took Mr. Fu's comment about the dragon's swimming pool in the same vein. Nobody called him out on it (you just didn't argue with a sweet eighty-year old Chinese man), but nobody believed a word he said, either. That pool was full of gold—fifteen thousand gallons of it.

The dragon didn't go out. It didn't collect its mail. It had no listed phone number. Chessie Vormount had gone over shortly after it moved in with a housewarming gift (Gordon, her husband, still told jokes about that one). It was a basket containing a variety of products recommended at the local pet store for grooming and caring for lizard scales. The whole neighborhood had watched her walk over there, peering through their curtains, hands hovering by the fire extinguisher, waiting for her to ring the doorbell in the same way that cops waited for the bomb squad to disarm an explosive.

She rang. Nothing happened. She stood there on the front stairs in her stiletto heels and dazzling white dress for a full five minutes, just ringing. Finally, she just left the gift basket on the porch and went home. The basket went unmolested for six days. Then, one morning, it was simply gone.

The dragon, they collectively decided, wasn't social. It (or 'he', as Chessie Vormount insisted that no female of any species would be such a shut-in) probably just wanted to be left alone. This of course meant he had moved to the wrong neighborhood, since if there was one way to attract attention in a suburban cul-de-sac, it was to be the guy on the block of whom nothing was known.

Rumors snowballed around 'their' dragon. The whole town knew they 'had one.' Everybody knew about dragons, of course—ever since the Reawakening, they'd been living among humanity with relatively little trouble. Of course, when everybody said 'among humanity,' they meant that in the general sense, as in they lived on the same planet as us, like pandas and giant squid. Dragons owned private islands. Dragons lived on expansive mountain estates in Idaho. Dragons were petty warlords in sub-Saharan Africa. There was one in Hawaii that lived in a volcano.

They were *not* your neighbors.

So, naturally, the questions piled up: Why did it move here? Where did it come from? What did it want? What (who?) did it eat? Was it awake? Asleep? How did it pay the mortgage? Did it get cable? What did it keep in the garage?

To each of these was supplied an answer based largely off a cocktail of innocent conjecture and pernicious gossip. The answers also conflicted: the dragon came here because it was broke (for a dragon). The dragon ate stray cats and runaway dogs. It slept all day and only after dark did it slip out and flap over to Newark to eat homeless people. It did not have cable; it paid for premium satellite. There was a pile of human bones in the garage. And a Porsche.

Life went on. Dragons, as everybody knew, were not to be prodded. The rumors swirled, but as far as anybody knew, not a single living soul had placed a toe over the property line since Chessie Vormount had left her basket of Doc Slither's EZ Lizard Scales Disinfectant and some live mice in a pretty box and strutted home. They were curious, sure, but not suicidal. Everybody in the neighborhood bought an extra fire extinguisher, assumed any Frisbees or baseballs that went astray were lost for good, and went about their business.

Then came 2008. The bottom dropped out of the market like the trapdoor on a gallows, and suburbia was left to wriggle on the rope, gasping for air. The cul-de-sac went through it like everybody else. The Cohen's did okay—Rebecca went back to teaching to compensate for the hike in their rates and they quietly pushed their son to go to a state school. Mr. Fu's sixty-year-old son was laid off, so he and his family moved from upstate to live with him. Fu the Younger got a job managing an Arby's; Fu the Youngest drove a cab and went to dental school at night. Gordon Vormount lost a mint on the stock market, barely escaped a round of layoffs, and was so underwater on his mortgage he started calling himself 'Captain Nemo.'

Milly Petersen, though, lost the house. It wasn't a quick loss—not a 'rip off the band-aid and get it over with' loss. Unlike her husband's death—sudden, immediate, stunning—her home drifted away piece by piece. She passed her two little kids around to the neighbors' houses so she could work double-shifts. Chessie Vormount had the Lions Club throw a bake sale for her. She sold her car, pawned her jewelry. Jack's life insurance settlement vanished in a puff of financial vapor.

The kids' college funds went next. In the end, none of it mattered. The pending foreclosure notice was pinned to her front door like the flag of a foreign nation, claiming her house—the house she and Jack had intended to live in forever—for somebody else.

The dragon's house, though, remained unchanged.

It was about then that the dwarves showed up.

Milly had heard a fair amount about dwarves, and none of it good. As far as anybody could tell, they had crawled up from somewhere in the depths of the earth and began settling in old mine shafts and abandoned industrial facilities. The three dwarves that presented themselves on Milly's doorstep smelled like motor oil and were covered in grime. Their beards were matted and frizzy and, most distressingly, they wore mismatched NFL paraphernalia. One of them—wearing a Buffalo Bills knit hat and a Carolina Panthers jacket—held up a copy of the local paper's classified ads with a red circle around the "room for let" notice she had posted. He said only one thing, and that barely a word: "Eh?"

Where were you three months ago? Milly thought, but smoothed her sweatpants and straightened her posture. "I'm sorry, but the property will be foreclosed in a month."

She went to close the door, but one of the dwarves stuck a fat foot against the door jamb. The one with the newspaper pointed to the ad again and grunted, "Month enough time. We pay double rent, eh?"

The one that hadn't spoken grumbled something in a foreign language to the other two. Newspaper dwarf nodded.

"What did he say?"

The dwarf doffed his Bills hat. "He ask to make sure is basement room. Eh?"

Milly frowned. "Yes, I'm sorry—I don't have anything above groun—"

The dwarves barged past her, grinning toothy grins. The third dwarf dropped a sack in her hands that had to weigh twelve pounds. She opened it on the kitchen table; it was filled with silver ingots. Two months' rent in one lump of precious metal.

The dwarves said they would move in immediately, which turned out to be exactly accurate. They had a motorcycle and sidecar in her driveway strapped with duffel bags and suitcases. Two of them brought their stuff inside and straight down into the basement while the third—the talker—filled out the rental application. He wrote in blocky, large letters, clutching the ballpoint pen as though it were a live serpent. Their names were Thondor, Jorri, and Glorin. Under "occupation," Thondor wrote "DWARVES."

The Milly Petersen of six months ago would have had an apoplectic fit at the thought of a trio of mythical creatures with no credit history squatting in her husband's old man-cave. The Milly Petersen that had resigned herself to foreclosure just wondered how she was going to deposit a bunch of silver ingots at the local bank branch.

The cul-de-sac went wild. The Cohen's actually *dis*-invited her to a dinner party. Chessie Vormount started talking with some ladies down at the grocery store that Milly was going to sell them the house. Mr. Fu started sending his grandson over with envelopes full of "helpful" coupons—"50% off air freshener"; "buy one set of children's overalls, get one free"; "free beard oil with purchase of men's grooming kit."

The rumors piled up, and Milly denied them in turn. No, the dwarves were not relatives. No, the dwarves hadn't been making shoes in the basement. No, the dwarves did not work for Disney. *No,* they were *not* her lovers.

Eventually, Rebecca Cohen and Chessie Vormount had Milly over for tea one afternoon, ostensibly to plan Milly's going away party. It was, in reality, an ambush. The two women sat at the edges of Chessie's tufted leather wingback chairs, hands clutching teacups. "What if they don't *leave?*" Rebecca said, pursing her lips. "I mean, when…you know…*after.*"

"What am I supposed to do about it?" Milly shrugged. "If the bank can't get them out, that's the *bank's* problem."

"Well, that's fine for you, darling." Chessie said, tapping her manicured nails on a saucer. "But think of our property values!"

Milly threw up her hands. "Look, we've already got a *dragon* living here—how much of a difference will three dwarves make?"

The two women were persistent, though, and Milly eventually relented, just as she usually did. "Fine," she said, "I promise to talk to them."

They parted all smiles, but Milly sensed the hostility that lurked beneath Rebecca's cold hug. She didn't believe Milly would do anything. Neither did Chessie.

Milly hadn't really seen much of the dwarves since they descended into the basement. In the two weeks since they'd moved in, they only came up to watch football on the Petersen's one remaining television. Milly had taken to laying towels over the couch and chairs when they did this, since everything they touched came away stained with grease. They would sit there, wearing the wrong shirts for the game, and curse at the television in their language. At least, she *assumed* it was cursing. It sounded a lot like cursing, anyway.

The rest of the time they stayed in the basement, had pizza delivered to the basement hatch on the side of the house, and didn't bother anyone. There were times that Milly would stand at the top of the basement stairs and listen. She only ever heard their singing—a trio of *basso profundo* voices, echoing up from the depths. The basement light was never on.

It took Milly a few days, but she finally worked up the nerve to head down the stairs. She made as much noise as she could, so as not to startle her boarders. She found two of them sitting together on a pair of folding chairs. It was Thondor, in his perennial Panther's jacket, and Jorri, who was sleeveless in a Utah Jazz jersey. His arms were as thick as Milly's legs and gorilla-hairy. And filthy with oily grime. Of Glorin there was no sign.

Thondor had his copy of the lease and was reviewing it with a monocle. "Yes. You are allowed to do this."

Milly blinked. "I...I know."

They sat in their chairs and waited for her to say something. Milly looked around the room. Other than a few folding chairs and the single double bed, there was no furniture. The walls were bare. Their duffel bags and luggage were piled in one corner, right by a large stack of empty pizza boxes. "Ummm...is Glorin out?"

"Yes." Thondor nodded. "Glorin is out."

"Where did he go?"

"Out. Like you say."

"But your motorcycle is still here so—"

Jorri grumbled something in their language. Thondor nodded. "Jorri wants to know what you want. We make too much noise, eh?"

"No. Nothing like that...I just..." but Milly struggled with what to say. *My nosy neighbors want you to promise to move out.* It seemed so petty. "You know what—never mind. Sorry I bothered you."

The two dwarves muttered to one another in their language as she left. Their black, beady little eyes seemed full of hostility, though why she couldn't guess. "Turn the light out when you go." Thondor said. She did, feeling guilty, as though she had invaded someone's inner sanctum.

She never saw Glorin again. He didn't come up any longer for football games. His voice was never added to the deep chorus of the dwarves that would emanate from below the kitchen. He was gone. When she asked, Thondor only said, "He is out. Like you said."

It had been a little shy of three weeks when she saw Mr. Fu mowing his front lawn. Milly was in the midst of packing for the long drive to Pittsburgh, where she and her kids were about to move from their lovely suburban home to a two bedroom apartment. Her attempts to avoid eye contact with the old man did not dissuade him from talking to her.

"You are such a lucky lady, right?" Mr. Fu said.

Milly grimaced.

"Dwarves are good luck. You'll see!"

She didn't answer. She couldn't even bring herself to look at the stupid old man. Her? Lucky? Jesus Christ.

That night was a Sunday night. Only Thondor came up from the basement for football. He had a bag of Chex Mix in his lap. He glowered at the television, munching pretzels with greasy hands.

"Thondor," Milly asked, "is Jorri okay?"

"Yes." Thondor grumbled. "He okay. Just went out."

"Out *where?*"

But the Jets fumbled, and Thondor cursed too much for the next five minutes to supply an answer.

Just like Glorin before him, Jorri never reappeared.

At the going away party, she told everybody the story of the disappearing dwarves in her basement. "Do you think…do you think they *killed* each other?"

Dr. Cohen stroked his beard. "I've read that dwarves can be violent. I mean, well, more *prone* to violent outbursts."

"That's bull." Gordon Vormount sipped his beer. "The answer's *obvious*, Milly."

Milly tried not to scowl. "Why? What's so obvious?"

"It's the dragon!" Gordon smiled at those assembled, glorying in his own revelation. "The little bastards are trying to rob the dragon, and the dragon is eating them. Any of you ever read *The Hobbit?*"

Milly had not. Nobody else had, either. Gordon shook his head. "It's all there, Milly. You can borrow my copy."

She declined—she'd be damned if she borrowed anything from Gordon Vormount again—but she did Google it. She read over the plot synopsis after she got home. She had one too many of Chessie's cocktails in her, so she had to read it twice to be sure. "Son of a bitch!"

She stumbled down the basement stairs, shouting. "Thondor! Hey! Thondor, are you awake!"

The basement was empty. The stack of pizza boxes had expanded mightily, but otherwise the place appeared unchanged. The place smelled of oily dwarves and burned pizza. "Thondor! Thondor?"

No sign of him. Peeking through the basement window, she confirmed that the little motorcycle was still in the driveway—right next to her moving pod, just where it had always been. So he wasn't driving anywhere and his legs were way too short to bother walking…so then where the hell was he?

Milly eyed the mountain of pizza boxes. She knew they hadn't thrown out a single one since they'd been here. There were dozens and dozens of the things—probably well over a hundred, maybe even two hundred of them—all stacked to the ceiling. She grabbed one. It was heavy, like a hunk of iron; she lost her grip and dropped the thing. It landed on the ground with a clank. She opened it up.

The pizza box was filled with *gold*.

"Oh my God."

She opened another box. And another. And another. Gold—thick, heavy gold coins, gold bars, gold jewelry. Milly tore through the giant pile of pizza boxes—a full third of them was weighed down with treasure. The others were empty, presumably waiting to be filled.

And behind the pizza boxes? A door of earth and stone: it was perfectly round and inscribed with blocky runes in the hand of Thondor himself. Milly had no idea—no idea whatsoever—how the door had come to be in the corner of her basement or how the dwarves had fashioned it without her knowledge, but she did know—without any doubt whatsoever—what lay behind the door.

With a boldness borne of a bit too much vodka, she grasped the handle at the center of the door and yanked. It swung open easily, silently. Beyond was a round passage about five feet in diameter, lit intermittently by bare light bulbs spliced into an extension cord which was plugged into an outlet mounted just inside the door. Milly couldn't help but wonder how they managed that part above all—since when were dwarves electrically inclined? *Tolkien didn't write anything about that, now did he, Gordon?*

The tunnel stretched out in front of her, the light bulbs only reaching so far. At the other end was the dragon's lair. And probably the charred bones of her three tenants.

At least they had paid in advance.

Milly set one foot on the threshold of the tunnel…and stopped. Her heart, she realized, was pounding so hard she could feel the impact in her throat. *Milly, at the other end of this tunnel is a dragon. What the flying hell do you think you're doing?*

She backed away, closed the door quietly, and went back upstairs.

Thondor never reappeared. Monday Night Football went unwatched.

Milly had six days to vacate the premises. Her furniture—what few pieces she was able to keep—was all covered and taped up, ready for the movers to come. The kids were gone, sent ahead to her sister's place in Pittsburgh to await her arrival. It was only Milly, an empty house, and a stack of gold coins and bars in her basement. She went downstairs several times to check on them; still there. The door, too.

Milly spent one afternoon—right after she cashed her last paycheck from her old job at the diner—and did some calculations. Gold was worth about a thousand bucks an once and, right at that moment, her basement had about a seven hundred and fifty pounds of the stuff. That was twelve million dollars, give or take. That was more money than poor Jack had earned in his entire life, all pilfered from some dragon's in-ground swimming pool over the course of two weeks by a trio of hairy midgets. And even *that* wasn't enough money to make any kind of dent in the dragon's giant pool of treasure. The damned thing probably didn't even notice it was gone. Milly took the fact that her house was still standing and not an ashen heap as evidence of that.

She lay on the cot she had rigged up in the now empty master bedroom and stared at the ceiling fan slowly whirling. Her mind spun off with it, on flights of fancy. Of her, lugging a duffel bag full of gold doubloons into the bank, thumping it on the counter, and laughing in that bank manager's smug little face. *My house, you hear me, you tubby little prick? MY HOUSE!*

The thought gave her a thrill. She could do it, too. With all that gold in her basement, she could pay off the mortgage, buy a new car, send the kids to college, and still have enough for a yearly trip to Disney World—that trip Jack had always wanted the family to take and never got the chance to. She thought of him pulling double shifts with a smile, that steely glint in his eye, *"Don't worry, baby. I'm working my way up. Everything's okay."*

But it hadn't been.

She could fix it. She could fix every last problem Jack hadn't been able to solve—all she needed to do was to lug up those pizza boxes, put them in sacks, and take them to the bank. That was literally *it*. There was a pool in Orlando, suspiciously mouse-shaped, that was calling to her. Palm trees swaying in the breeze, a cool drink, a chaise lounge. The laughter of children.

She got up and went downstairs. The sun was on its way down—she'd have to hurry if she wanted to make the bank today. She emptied a suitcase of all its clothes and dragged it into the basement.

The door was still there, of course. Behind it, the tunnel—naturally. Milly tried to ignore it and went straight to work, clanking gold bars out of pizza boxes and into her suitcase. Her heart thumped loudly against her ribs. Her hands shook. The skin on the back of her neck crawled; she felt eyes on her, even though nobody was there. What if…

Her mind flew off to still more fantasies. What if the dragon *did* know about the gold? What if the dragon was just waiting for her to try and steal it and then *boom*—she would vanish in a puff of flame. What if it crouched even now in its own garage, lying in wait for her rental car to cruise by and then…

Milly stopped and faced the door. For all she knew, the dragon was small enough to wriggle down that tunnel and was *right there* on the other side of the door, fiery breath at the ready. Now that she was thinking about it, there *was* a bit of a hot draft coming from that tunnel—she could feel it around her ankles. Oh God.

27

You're being ridiculous, she snarled at herself. *There's nothing there. Go on and open the door. Prove it.*

Licking her lips, hands shaking, she went over to the door and ripped it open in the same wild manner you ripped off a bandage.

Nothing. Just darkness and still air. The gold was hers if she wanted it. She just had to finish loading that suitcase. She wanted to. She *had* to.

Yet she didn't move toward the stairs. She thought of Jack's smile, the way he'd brush a stray hair from her face and kiss her on the cheek. She thought of her kids—Billy standing next to her at the funeral, eight years old and still he held her steady. Sarah, too, hugging the stuffed tiger Jack had gotten her at the mall, eyes wet but not crying. Not while Mommy could see. Later on, when she had confronted Sarah about it, the little six year old had looked up at her and said, *"I want you to be brave, Mommy. I don't want to make you cry, too."*

Be brave.

"Shit." Milly picked up the suitcase handle and dragged it into the tunnel.

The passage was narrow, but cleanly hewn from the earth and supported by arches of stone—though how they had gotten there, Milly had no clue. It was a pretty short walk, moving diagonally from the back corner of Milly's house to a ladder that led up to a trap door in the floor of a disused pool shed. Milly couldn't get the suitcase up the ladder—too heavy—so she grabbed one bar of gold and climbed up.

The inner walls of the shed were scorched black and the floor was a goopy morass of melted plastic piping and pool toys. There was a pile of charred black bones right by the door that made Milly yelp in horror. The nylon of a Carolina Panthers jacket had fused to the ribcage, the teal mascot giving a lopsided growl from the breastbone. This had been Thondor.

Milly froze in place, unable to advance past the body, unable to retreat now that she had seen it. Part of her, on some level, had always wondered if the dragon was *real*. Now she knew for certain, and that knowledge was too much for her. The dragon could *kill* her. She couldn't even call the cops—the time to call the cops would have been when she found a pile of stolen gold in her basement. That time was long past.

The door to the pool shed opened as though blown by a breeze. Milly could see across the pool, still covered, and to the open back door of the house. Terror seized her; she couldn't breathe.

The dragon's voice was deep and smooth, with just a touch of sibilance. It seemed to crawl from the house and envelop her. "Mrs. Petersen, won't you please come in?"

Moving slowly, her steps soft, Milly walked across the patio, across the Frisbee-strewn yard, and up to the door. She held the gold bar up in front of her like an offering. "I'm…I'm very sorry to disturb you, but I just…" She couldn't finish. Tears welled in the corners of her eyes. She blinked them away.

When she paused at the entrance to the house, the dragon spoke again. "Come in, come in, please. Never mind the dirt."

Milly stepped inside.

All interior walls of the house had been removed, as had the floor separating the garage from the bedrooms. The house was simply an enormous shell with a chimney at one end and the garage at the other. There, coiled beside a brand-new Porche, was the dragon. A fire burned in the fireplace—the only light other than the streetlights which leaked through the venetian blinds strung over all the windows. In this light, she could see the dragon's scales were russet-gold, his claws long and black, and his wingspan must have been enormous. From tail to head, she guessed it was about fifty feet long, maybe more. Its head was an array of back-angled horns and steak-knife sized fangs. Its eyes glowed like embers and it smelled very much like burning coal and rotting eggs.

The ember eyes focused on the gold bar. "Put that on the ground, please."

Milly did as she was told. "I'm sorry."

The dragon's eyes opened wide. "For what? For the dwarves?"

"Y-yes."

The dragon leaned down so its snout was no more than a few feet from her own. She could feel its breath, hot as a furnace. "But you didn't *know*. Why should you be sorry for that?"

Milly felt tears trickle down her cheeks. She was trembling. "Please, if you'll just let me go—"

"You don't want to talk?" The dragon blinked slowly. "Whyever did you come?"

Milly took a deep breath. "There's a lot of gold in…in my basement. It's yours."

"I know. Those dwarves—quite the nuisance. Anywhere a dragon tries to build a decent horde, there they are, trying to steal it. Can't keep them out, you know—they just *sing* the blasted earth open, and there they are, putting their grubby mitts all over everything." The dragon sighed, sending out a little puff of fire that came close to Milly. "Still, it's the risk I took, moving here."

"So, you aren't angry?"

The dragon's eyes widened. "Of *course* I am! Dwarves in my horde? Gah! Disgusting! Still, they're dead now, so the matter is closed."

Milly took a deep breath. "Oh, well, then I guess I'll just be going…"

The dragon's tail shifted to block her exit. "I didn't say I was done with you *yet*, Milly Petersen. I have some questions for you."

Milly said nothing. She wondered at the prospects of her running for it. How far would she get? What would happen if she jumped in the Porche? Would it barbeque its own property to stop her from speeding away? Would it need to?

The dragon pointed a claw at the gold bar. "*Why* did you bring that back?"

Milly looked down at it. She searched for the words. "Because I'm not a thief."

The dragon snorted, which caused Milly to duck for cover as a spurt of fire shot out. "What? *WHAT?*" The dragon opened its mouth wide and Milly thought she was dead until she realized this was an expression of shock. The dragon was *shocked* by her.

Milly shrugged. "It's not mine. The gold, I mean. I couldn't steal it."

"Ridiculous. You're playing a prank." The dragon's eyes narrowed. "I hate pranks. That's why I lit that boy on fire on Halloween."

Milly blinked. "Cameron Bishop? I thought he was playing with firecrackers."

"Tried to TP my lawn, the odious thing. He only *told* everyone the firecracker bit."

Milly shook her head. "How do you even know about this? You never go out!"

"I have very good hearing." The dragon said, "and I *do* go out. Just after all you people are sleeping. The last thing I need is Chessie Vormount criticizing the state of my haunch scales."

"Why would she—"

"Don't feign ignorance!" The dragon snarled. "You were there, too, you know! What kind of a thing is it to put *scale cleaner* in a welcome gift, I ask you? She thinks I'm filthy, and you *know* it! She says it all the time—that 'filthy' dragon, she says. Bah! So maybe I'm not as beautiful as I was in the old days, but that old hag isn't much better! At least I don't need to inject *poison* into my face to keep it from drooping off!"

Milly could scarcely believe she was hearing this. "You…listen to us? All the time?"

"Of course." The dragon shook its head side-to-side. "You're changing the subject! Why didn't you steal the gold! If any woman needs money, it's you! You can barely afford *Pittsburgh*, Milly! You're going to wind up living in your sister's basement, and you know what a bad influence her Peter is going to be on Billy!"

It was Milly's turn for her mouth to drop open. "That's none of your *business!*"

"You're my neighbor—of *course* it's my business. What's the point of having neighbors, then?"

"Neighbors don't pry into people's personal business!" Milly snapped.

The dragon laughed, which caused the biggest gout of flame yet. It caught one of the support beams on fire, but the dragon doused it quickly with a swat of a vast wing. "Don't give me that! It's the *exclusive* thing neighbors do. Chessie Vormount is always—"

"Chessie's not a good example!"

"Fine! Fu, then—did you know he's been trying to find you a husband?"

Milly gaped. "*What?!*"

"Oh, yes—he pulled a picture off the internet and had it printed on some cards that he hands out to handsome men he sees in the park. It has the time and address of your speed dating group—every third Saturday at Pizza Palace, right?"

Milly put her hands to the sides of her face and began to pace across the bare floor. "Oh. My. God."

The dragon nodded. "I know. That old man is completely clueless. Even *I* know you're still grieving for Jack, and I'm not even human."

Milly glared at the dragon. "Okay, that's *it*! What the hell do you want from me, anyway?" She kicked the gold bar so it slid across the floor a few inches in the dragon's direction. "There's your stupid gold, okay? I want to go home!"

"Home?" The dragon snorted again. "In case you forgot, you haven't *got* one of those, Milly. The bank shows up on Monday. What has me itching, though, is that you've got millions of dollars in gold in your basement right now, and you bring some of it back here, to *me*. Why?"

"I told you. I'm not a thief."

"Everybody's a thief." The dragon narrowed its eyes. "Children steal the vitality of their parents, workers steal the riches of their masters, masters steal the toil of their workers—that's all life is, Milly Petersen: theft. And you're here, dropping a bar of my gold on my floor. Why? To prove you're a good person? Maybe to ask for a loan?" The dragon exhaled slowly, sending a heat ripple through the air that made Milly feel like she was under a hair-dryer. "Well *forget it*. No loan for you, Milly Petersen. Not a damned doubloon."

Milly backed away. She found herself pressed against the wall. "If I *had* stolen it, would you have let me get away with it?"

"Of course not. Ha! Let *dragon gold* into general circulation? Think of the devaluation!"

Milly snorted. "At least Chessie Vormount threw me a bake sale!"

"That was just so she'd look better when it came time to elect officers for the Lions Club the following week. Another theft, Milly, only this time of your dignity for her personal gain."

That one stung. Milly took a deep breath—she'd always known Chessie wasn't a true friend, of course, but still she had been touched by the gesture, no matter how pointless it had been. "I'm going to leave now."

The dragon curled itself up and sighed. It pulled its tail away from the door. "I'd appreciate it if you returned the rest of the gold."

"Another theft? My labor for *your* money?" Milly scowled, hand on the doorknob.

The dragon showed its teeth in a vicious grin. "It *would* be neighborly of you."

Milly rolled her eyes. "Send a mover and I'll leave the door unlocked. I'm not breaking my back for you."

The dragon dipped its head in assent. Milly turned to leave, but then stopped. "I have one more question: why did you move here? You could have lived anywhere—why *here?*"

The dragon half closed its eyes. "My kind are all so self-important, so self-involved. It gets…lonely." It sighed. "I wanted to get away from my own for a while."

Milly snorted, thinking of Chessie Vormount and her heels, of Mr. Fu and his constant meddling, of the Cohens and their insular success. "You know, I don't think you actually succeeded."

Two teams of movers came the next day: one for Milly and her last few things and the other for the dragon and his gold. The neighbors all turned out, but none of them helped her pack. They were too busy asking her about the men hauling those heavy sacks from her house and into the dragon's. She feigned ignorance, waved good-bye, and shook a few superficial hands.

Then she moved to Pittsburgh. After a year, she suspected no one there on the street remembered her name. She never cared to find out.

Copyright © 2016 by Auston Habershaw

The Bone-Runner

by Jennifer Campbell-Hicks

S kip and I used to run the bones together.

I asked him once why it was called that, not long after our parents died and we came to the Outskirts. We were cutting through the trenches and old munitions craters of no man's land, where nothing had grown for centuries, under a sky scorched to the color of ash.

Skip pointed at the City. "Look out there, Sis. At the tallest buildings. Do you see? They look like a field of bones."

I peered through the chemical fog that lay over the City, and I saw what he saw. Time had stripped the metal frames of their skins of stone and glass. In places, the metal had rusted and snapped, leaving jagged stubs.

The City was a graveyard, but those broken, bare frames still held hidden treasures. Scavengers could smell death a long way off and follow the scent to pick clean the meat. Skip and I were scavengers, too, but we picked clean the City.

"How did people live there?" I asked. "How did they stand it?"

"It wasn't always like this. Before the war and the Fall, it was beautiful. The buildings touched the sky. Millions of people lived here."

"No they didn't," I scoffed.

There weren't millions of people in the entire world, let alone one city.

"It's what the books say," he said.

I was skeptical, but Skip knew better. He was older—how much older we didn't know because we didn't know our ages—and he had gotten some schooling before the last outbreak shut the schools for good.

He ruffled my hair. "Enough talk. Suit up."

We fitted on our gas masks and thick leather gloves that covered my arms to my elbows, and we made the descent. The City was deadly, but I was never scared with Skip. He took care of me.

Until I betrayed him.

Now I run the bones alone.

The day promises to be a hot one when I head out at dawn, sweat beading on my neck. Halfway across no man's land, I stick two fingertips between my lips and blow a shrill whistle. Jewel bounds across the field toward me. She moves like a dancer, like the gypsies whose caravans come through the Outskirts. Surefooted and graceful. I love to watch her run.

She stops beside me, bumps her whiskered cheek against my side and almost knocks me down. She doesn't know her own strength.

"Good to see you," I say. "Did you hunt well?"

I take a protein nugget from my pocket and toss it into the air. Jewel is ready. She snaps it up before it touches the ground. I scratch behind her ears, and I notice that she stinks.

"What did you get into? Did you find a skunk?" I laugh when she gazes at me with innocence in her shining eyes.

Lions don't live here naturally. Legend has it that long ago, the City kept a park of exotic animals. After the Fall, the animals escaped, and the predators survived to breed. Not just lions but other animals, too. Bears, snakes, wolves.

I found Jewel as a cub, deep in the City. She would have died without me, and she has returned the favor many times over. We make a good team. In a way, she reminds me of my brother.

Skip.

My hand stills on Jewel's fur. I see his kind smile and green eyes under dirty brown hair. My chest starts to hurt, as if pressed under the weight of a huge boulder. My throat tightens. It's always like this. I force his image from my mind and focus on the ground. I count grains of sand until the hurt eases, leaving only a dull ache, like an old injury, painful but controllable.

I drop my burlap sack from my shoulder to take out my gas mask, goggles, and leather gloves, and put them on. Under the mask, I lose some peripheral vision, and my breathing is amplified in my ears. I take out my crossbow and a quiver of bolts, which I sling across my back, and I tuck the now empty sack into my belt.

I look at Jewel. "Let's find some treasure."

"Tell me a story, Skip."

He poked a stick at the old planks burning in the fireplace. Fingers of flame leaped upward, crackling. Rain battered the shutters of the house where we had been squatting for days. No one had lived here for some time. Thick dust coated the floor, squirrels nested in the rafters and the chimney smoked. The Outskirts authorities would find us eventually and drive us out, but for now we had shelter.

I wondered whose house this had been. The previous occupants hadn't left many clues, only some shattered clay crockery and a doll whittled from a piece of wood. Sometimes when we found artifacts, I made up stories about them. I imagined the doll had belonged to a girl like me. Maybe her parents had died in the last outbreak, or her family had gone, traveling east to find a better life.

I picked the last meat from my leg of rabbit and licked up the juices. Skip had shot the rabbit with his crossbow near the City fence that morning. The animal had been scrawny, its meat stringy, but that didn't matter. It was the first fresh meat we'd had in ages.

"What story do you want?" he asked.

"The one about Orpheus."

"Again?"

"Please?"

"You've heard it so many times you could recite it yourself. What is it about that story?"

"It's from before the Fall."

"Lots of stories are from before the Fall."

I eyed the last piece of rabbit on the spit over the fire. "I like that it's about hope. And love. I want someone to love me that much someday."

Skip took down the meat and handed it to me. "Someone already does, Sis."

Feeling warm and comfortable, I curled against his side and listened to Skip tell the story of Orpheus, who descended into the land of the dead to find Eurydice, whom he loved more than life itself. In my imagination, Orpheus looked like Skip, tall and handsome, but with terrible sadness in his eyes. Orpheus sang of his grief and longing, and the king of the dead was so moved that he released Eurydice, but Orpheus could not look back at her.

"Orpheus was filled with so much desire that he couldn't help himself," Skip said. "He looked back. The shade of Eurydice began to fade, but Orpheus' love was greater even than death. He took her hand, and she returned to him. Together they stepped into the land of the living."

I finished the rabbit, tossed the bone away and closed my eyes, lulled by the cadence of Skip's voice. His fingers played with my hair.

"It was only many, many years later," he said, "when they had grown old, that they died peacefully in each other's arms and returned to the land of the dead together, never to be separated again."

He fell silent. We lay for a while, listening to rain on the shutters and the crackle of our dying fire. I thought about how even in life's darkest moments, there could be a happy ending.

"Thank you," I said.

"You should sleep. We'll have an early start."

"Tell me we'll find something good."

"We will," he said, as he always did. "We'll use it to buy passage from the Outskirts and go east over the mountains. We'll get our own place, like we had with Mother and Father, where no one can ever run us out. We'll grow a garden and raise chickens, and we'll never have to set foot in the City again."

I smile sleepily. "That sounds nice."

"We'll get there someday. I promise." His lips brushed my forehead. "Sweet dreams."

A barbed-wire fence surrounds the City, the line of Do Not Cross that keeps people out and other things in, but there's a hole for Jewel and I to squeeze through. From the fence, we walk down a street lined with the ruins of houses that are crumbled like stale bread. The street ends at a dry, rocky scar in the earth that was once a mighty river. Beyond that lies the City.

I have rivals in running the bones. Other orphans, the only ones desperate and hungry enough to risk the City. I see none yet today.

Jewel and I descend into the brown chemical fog, the shroud for the City's bones that's never burned off by sunlight, blown away by wind or melted by rain. Stunted, sickly plants try to grow in cracks in the streets, and thick black mold coats the metal frames of the buildings. The air is silent except for the buzz of flies and the cries of crows, my fellow scavengers.

I check again that my mask is secure. For whatever reason, the fog doesn't affect animals, but it infects humans. It eats at our brains and turns us into something else. Some walk into the fog on purpose, from despair. For others, it's accidental. They simply wander too close. Sometimes I see one of the infected that haunt the City. I don't know how many there are.

They are ghosts.

At one of the smaller buildings, I climb through a gap I've cleared in the broken stone and metal. The frame goes up about one hundred feet, the top obscured in fog. Inside is dark, beneath layers of crisscrossing beams and pipes, but my goggles help me see in the gloom.

I've worked this building for weeks, combing through the debris inch by inch. Last week I found a coil of copper wire that I traded for a crossbow bolt and ten protein bars. I need another find if I want to sleep tonight with a full stomach.

Jewel yowls. She won't come inside, but she doesn't like me going where she can't protect me.

"Stop whining," I say. "Stay there."

She snorts, paces in a tight circle, and settles down so that she blocks the entrance.

I scramble over a mound of broken stone to reach what once was a wall but now is only moldy metal beams. I dig. It's dirty work. Soon I'm sweating, and dust coats my protective gear. My work disturbs rats, and once a snake slithers away. I brush flies off my goggles as I lift and toss block after block.

Finally, nestled in broken glass, I find an old metal box. It's the kind of box that City people used to put their valuables in. The lid is rusted. I finally pry it open.

Inside is a delicate silver chain, and a bundle of slips of paper that I recognize as currency. Both are worth a little on trade, but not much. They're not of much use, and there's enough old currency around that it's not rare or valuable.

I empty the contents into my sack. Then I stop, my hands trembling with excitement.

At the bottom of the box is a book.

A year ago, another bone-runner, Penny, sold a book from before the Fall to a collector for enough coin to keep her fed for six months. Penny blew the money on drugs and card games. I'm not so stupid.

The cover is half gone. What's left is faded, but I can make out the upward swoop of a wing. I flip through the pages. The words are there. I wish I could read them. Skip tried to teach me, but my brain always mixes up the letters.

I turn the book over in my hands. Why had someone gone to such lengths to protect it? The people of the City had cared more for coins than information.

Whatever the reason, someone will want it and pay well for it. Maybe Ballast, with his overfed belly and doughy hands. He buys the rich stuff, and this is definitely rich. Books from before the Fall are precious, there are so few, and this one is nicer than Penny's. It might be my way out of the Outskirts. I could buy passage east with a tinker or gypsy caravan and start a new life away from the stink and poison of the City, like Skip wanted for us.

I blink away the sudden moisture in my eyes, under my goggles.

Can I do this without Skip? Do I want to?

Jewel roars.

I look toward my dug-out entrance. Jewel crouches low, tail lashing. Angry voices are yelling. More bone-runners have found us. I slip the book into my sack, secure the sack to my belt and scramble toward her as fast as I can.

✧ ✧ ✧

The cry echoed through the bones. I clutched Skip's arm as we stopped in the street. To our left, between two buildings, was a gap in the debris that we could squeeze through if we needed to hide.

"Is it a ghost?" I asked.

I couldn't make out Skip's expression through his mask. He set a bolt in his crossbow. "Stay behind me."

I shifted the burlap sack at my belt. It held our finds, a two-foot length of wire and a chunk of red-tinted glass. More cries. I grabbed the hilt of my knife.

"What is it?" I asked.

"Not a ghost."

"It could be."

"There's no blood here. That's the only thing that would bring them into the open. This is something else."

We turned a corner. A female lion laid dead in the street, chunks of fur gone, pustules bubbling from her skeletal frame. Flies buzzed around her.

A cub nudged the corpse, old enough to be weaned but still pitifully small. Its feet and ears were too big for its small body. The cub opened its tiny mouth and let out a cry. My heart went out to it.

Skip aimed his crossbow.

"Don't," I said.

"Look," he said. "The mother died of disease. The cub might have it, too. If we don't kill it, the disease might spread."

I shuddered at the idea of disease in the Outskirts, but I said, "It's not sick. It lost its mother, and it's scared." To prove my point, I walked toward the cub, slowly, careful not to startle it.

"Sis, come back."

I didn't. I knelt, took a protein nugget from my pocket and held it out in my gloved hand. "Come here. Come on, little one."

The cub, a girl, trotted toward me. She wasn't scared. Skip and I were probably the first humans she had ever seen. Her eyes shown like jewels. She sniffed at the nugget with a wet, black nose and snapped it up between sharp baby teeth.

A crossbow bolt shot past me and stuck in the mother lion's corpse. A pustule broke and sprayed yellow fluid. The cub darted back.

I glared at Skip. "Look what you did!"

"Maybe saved your life."

I flushed guiltily. "That cub will die."

"Let it."

He was right, but in my mind's eye, I saw the cub's big eyes and oversized paws, and I heard her sad cries. She wouldn't survive a day without us.

"I can't," I said.

"Fine."

Skip put another bolt in his crossbow. My muscles tensed like coils, and then they sprung. Without thinking, I ran at him and dived for the bow. The bolt released. It shot upward, off-target. Wind from its passing ruffled my hair.

"What are you doing?" he yelled.

In truth, I didn't know what I was doing. I had never gone against Skip. We were a team. But this time, he was wrong, and I needed to stop him, to make him see. We had killed plenty of times—rabbits, squirrels, rats—but that had been for food or survival. This cub wasn't food or a threat, no matter what Skip said.

I clung to the bow. "Listen, please."

He didn't listen. Instead, he yanked. The bow ripped from my hands. The stock recoiled with more force than either of us expected, followed by a loud crack.

We both froze. In Skip's mask, there was a hole. We looked at each other, terrified.

"Skip?" I asked.

He shuddered. A spasm wracked his body, his knees folded, and he fell to the ground, convulsing.

"Skip, no!"

I dropped beside him and covered the hole with my palm. I was too late. He had taken the fog into his lungs, and the poisons were at work, corrupting his brain. In seconds, he wouldn't know me. He would no longer be my brother. He would be one of them. The ghosts.

We always knew this might happen to one of us. It was a part of running the bones and why only desperate, starving children took the risk. But not to Skip. Not because of me.

The lion cub yowled.

41

"Shut up," I yelled at her, then to Skip, "I'm sorry, I'm sorry. I didn't mean it. Please be all right. Please. Skip? Can you hear me?"

He ripped off his mask. I recoiled. Only the whites of his eyes were visible. Blood dripped from his nose and pooled around his mouth where he was biting his tongue. While I watched, a molted purple blotch spread across his cheek.

"Do it," he choked out.

I knew what he meant. Kill him.

"I don't want to," I said weakly, like a small child. This was my fault. If I hadn't reached for his bow —

"Do it," he said again.

My hand wrapped around the knife hilt at my belt. I imagined sticking in the blade, feeling it slide between his ribs, into his heart, watching his convulsions become weaker and weaker until they stopped completely and he was still. We had agreed, if one of us became infected, the other would end it. Now the moment had come. Hot tears burned my eyes.

"I'm sorry," I said.

He lifted a shaking hand toward me, pleading. I jumped back, repulsed, at the same time ashamed by my reaction. My vision swam. I couldn't think. I had to get out of there.

I grabbed Skip's bow and quiver and ran blindly away, down the street, across the City and the dry riverbed, through the hole in the Do Not Cross fence, across no man's land. My legs trembled. I stumbled on the uneven ground. Finally, too exhausted to go another step, I sat heavily in the dirt.

I put my head in my hands.

This was my fault.

My chest felt as hollow and broken as the bones. I slipped off my gas mask and let it drop from my numb fingers. The guilt of killing Skip would have destroyed me, but the alternative was hardly better. I had gone against him and lost him to the City.

I couldn't live with that.

I would go back and let the fog take me, too. That way, we would be together.

Footfalls padded behind me.

I whirled.

The cub blinked her jewel-like eyes.

"Get out of here," I yelled.

She trotted closer.

"Leave! Scat!"

She sniffed my pocket where I kept the protein nuggets. I took one out. She ate it from my hand, licked my gloves, and butted against my side. The show of affection made the hollowness in my chest recede a little. Not much. Enough for a tiny spark to rekindle in my soul.

This cub was alone. So was I. We had both lost the one closest to us, and the world wouldn't care or even notice if we disappeared. But giving up wasn't the answer. I saw that now. I would find another way.

Gazing out at the City, I made a promise.

I would fix this.

Blood brings out ghosts. Skip taught me that. I spilled blood all over the City. Pig blood. Goat blood. My own blood.

Ghosts came like crows to a corpse. I looked for Skip. I wanted to take his hand and lead him from the City, away from the poison that had infected his body and mind.

I had no proof I could cure him, not even an anecdote that it might be possible. As far as I knew, it had never been done, but I had hope.

At the same time, I feared to hope. I used to think hope and love could conquer anything, as it had for Orpheus and Eurydice. Now I understood the danger, how hope could cut deeper than a butcher's blade and leave permanent scars.

Still, I couldn't give up. For months, I searched.

Skip never came.

Outside my broken building, the Boys stand in the street. That's what I call these three, who came separately to the Outskirts in the months after I lost Skip and started running the bones together. They asked me once to join them. I told them to go to hell. They laughed and said, "We're already there."

Each of them has me by several inches and at least twenty pounds. Nigel and Joseph carry long-bladed knives. Chase hefts a metal ball on a chain. They've painted their gas masks like demon faces, red and black with pointed teeth.

Jewel senses my unease. Her tail flicks. She puts her long, lean body between me and them.

"Hey, boys. Look what we found," Nigel says. "A scrawny girl and her scrawny pet kitty."

I lift my crossbow. If I have to shoot, it's Chase first. His metal ball has the longest reach. Nigel or Joseph could throw their knives, but they won't. If they missed, that would leave them unarmed.

"I don't want trouble," I say.

"Too bad. We do."

"Really? Because my pet kitty will rip out the throat of the first one of you who takes a step, and he'll be the lucky one. You other two, I'll put holes in your masks before you can get close."

I don't usually make threats, but I need to get rid of them before they work themselves up to robbing me. Most days I'd hand over my finds to avoid violence, but not this time. I'll die—or make myself a murderer—before I let them take my book.

"She's bluffing," Joseph says.

"She must have something good to say that stuff," Chase says. "What's in the sack, girl? Huh? What'd you find?"

"Nothing," I say. I'm kicking myself because my attempt to get rid of them is backfiring. "A silver chain."

Joseph barked a laugh. "You think we're stupid? I can see a bulge. That's no chain."

"You got me. That's old money. You want it? It's yours."

"Paper money? That's not worth dirt."

They're getting ready to rush me, which means the time for talk is done. I have to get out of here. I try to sound menacing and say, "I'm leaving. I'm warning you, don't get in my way."

That's when it all breaks loose.

I've been in fights. I know how to give a punch, and take one, too. Outskirts authorities aren't gentle with homeless orphans.

This fight is different. I can tell when Chase swings his metal ball at Jewel's skull. His eyes glint with murder through the lenses of his demon mask. He doesn't want to maim. He means to kill. Why? Do they want my loot that much? Or have they decided to get rid of the competition? Whatever the reason, I can't stand by and watch. I loose a bolt that buries itself in Chase's shoulder. He drops his weapon mid-swing and yanks out the bolt in a spray of blood.

Joseph goes after Jewel, who rears and swipes at him. He dodges and thrusts his knife. Jewel yowls in pain. She rakes her claws down his leg. He goes down, screaming.

I reach into my quiver for another bolt. Nigel is on me before I can fit the bolt into my bow. I stab with the point, but it's not an effective weapon for hand combat. Nigel brushes aside my attack and crashes into me. He's big and heavy. My feet fly out from under me. I lose my grip on my crossbow as I'm thrown backward and hit the ground.

The impact slams my teeth together. I bite my tongue. Blood fills my mouth, but I have nowhere to spit it out from inside my mask, so I swallow. My ears are ringing. Nigel lands on top of me, pins me down. He lifts his long-bladed knife to finish it.

"Jewel!" I yell.

I grab Nigel's wrist with both my hands to push the blade away. He pushes down. My arm muscles shake under his greater strength while I yell frantically for Jewel. Slowly, Nigel's knife point descends toward my chest.

I bring my knee up between his legs. His surprise lasts only a second, but it's enough for me to twist the knife left and roll right.

I struggle to breathe, my heart hammering. My burlap sack with the book is still tied to my belt. I catch a glimpse of fur. Jewel isn't moving. Is she injured? Dead? If they killed her, I'll kill them. I'm shaking with rage as I grab my knife from my belt and scramble to my feet.

I freeze, all thought of the fight forgotten. The Boys do the same. Nigel stands. Joseph and Chase wave their weapons, but not at me.

We're surrounded by ghosts.

They number about a score. More shuffle toward us, attracted by the blood we've spilled. They're as silent as their namesakes. Rags for clothes. Yellow, filmy eyes. Crusts of blood and puss, and skin as pale as leaches. I can't smell them through my mask, but I imagine their scent as something like feces and rot.

"Run!" yells Chase.

He and Nigel take off. Joseph limps on the leg Jewel raked with her claws. He screeches when a ghost, her hair matted with filth, grabs at his mask. Panicked, he hacks at her wrist with his knife. She releases him, and he pelts down the street after his friends. All three fade into the brown fog.

I don't follow. Ghosts look scary, but in my experience, they're not aggressive. They only want blood. I kneel beside Jewel. Sticky redness coats her side, where Joseph's knife pierced her. Otherwise she appears all right.

"Jewel." She raises her head. "Come on, girl. Get up." She snorts at me. I hold a protein nugget just out of reach. "On your feet. Come on."

Slowly, she stands, favoring her left front leg. I give her the nugget and retrieve my crossbow from where I dropped it when Nigel body-slammed me.

More ghosts have gathered. I load my crossbow. I've never known ghosts to attack, but I can't be too careful.

I look at each one in turn. One chews on a rat, and my stomach turns at the sight. Then my breath hitches. I sway on my feet. Everything seems to shrink around me until the world looks very small and far away.

"Skip," I say.

A purple blotch covers his face like a bruise, and half his nose is gone. How did he lose it? He stares right through me as if I am the ghost. There's no recognition.

In my mind, I hear his last words. *Do it.* But I didn't kill him then, and I won't now.

I lower my bow.

I have a book that can buy passage to someplace else, a place of light and life, where the sky isn't scorched and the buildings are more than moldy old bones. And after months of my fruitless searching, my brother has found me. It's as if by fate.

This is our chance.

I hold out my gloved hand. I don't want to spook him, or any of the other ghosts. Skip shows no reaction when I close my fingers around his. I think of Orpheus and Eurydice. *He took her hand, and she returned to him.* His fingers are caked with dirt and mold. I hold

46

tight and slide between him and another ghost, an old man whose skin sags and whose clothes have rotted off his body.

"Jewel, come," I say.

She limps to my side.

Hand in hand, I guide Skip beneath the black bones that cast no shadow in the gloom. He still doesn't notice I'm there. Jewel limps beside us. We take it slow, a horde of the infected following in our wake. Their silence chills my bones. I worry that they will follow us straight to the Outskirts, but then they start to peel off in ones and twos. When we reach the dry riverbed, only Skip, Jewel, and I remain.

The fog starts to lift a little as we climb down one rocky bank and up the other. The fog starts to lift from Skip's eyes, too. I'm reminded of a time when I was very young and I followed Skip while he sleep-walked across our parents' potato field, and he awoke confused, with no idea how we got there. Now too he is emerging from a dream. We walk down the street with the crumbled houses, and he stares the sky, at a crow that flies over our heads.

Something flutters in my chest. Hope. This is working. Each step out of the fog brings Skip back. Closer to himself. Closer to me. I squeeze his hand, but still he doesn't know I'm here.

The Do Not Cross fence is ahead, the edge of the City. Once we pass it, we are free, and I swear to myself we will never return. Jewel jumps through the hole first, then licks her wound while she waits for us. I go next, a difficult maneuver while still holding Skip's hand.

Together they stepped into the land of the living.

He stops.

"Come on," I say.

I stand on one side of the fence and he on the other, linked by our hands. I give him a tug. He looks up, and suddenly he sees me. Our gazes lock. His eyes widen.

"Sis," he whispers.

He croaks the word, his voice hoarse from disuse.

"Yes," I say. "I'm taking you home."

He smiles and lifts his leg to step through. Then a funny looks comes over his face. Utter surprise.

He puts a hand over his heart. Without a sound, his eyes roll up, and he goes down. It happens so fast that I can't react. His body folds like the legs going out from under a chair, his hand slips from mine, and he crumples.

I don't remember moving, but I'm back on his side of the fence, crouched beside him. Jewel yowls. She senses my fear. I feel disconnected, outside myself, watching from above. I roll him over with dread for what I'll find. His eyes are wide and his lips parted. His chest doesn't move, while mine heaves with panic. There's no breath. I press two fingers to his neck. No pulse. There's nothing. No life.

He is gone.

I sit back on my heels, numb with shock, and hold his limp hand to my chest. Jewel yowls and yowls.

How could this happen?

All I can think is that I should have known better than to let myself hope.

Two weeks pass. Penny offers me a bottle of spirits she got in a trade with a tinker. I don't ask what she traded; I only take the bottle. I don't like the bitter brew, but it's no more bitter than what I already feel. Eventually the bottle runs dry. That's when I notice my stink. The smell drives me to the public tap to bathe and wash my clothes. Afterward, I go to see Ballast.

He's the richest man in the Outskirts, and his sitting room proves it. He lounges in a silk robe in the softest chair I've ever seen, upholstered in green cloth, under a crystal chandelier that shines from the light of a hundred pure, beeswax candles. The air is perfumed. I stand across from him, my boots soiling his rug. I'm fearful to touch anything. Ballast's doughy hands rest in his lap, atop my precious book.

"I'm sorry about your brother," he says.

I can't look at him, so I look at my hands, folded in front of me. "Thank you."

"It was curious, what happened."

I don't want to talk about it. Time has not yet dulled any of the sharpness of my grief. But Ballast's tone is kind and concerned, and

I want to close the deal on the book and use the money to get as far from the City as I can, so I indulge him.

"The doctors had never gotten their hands on one of the infected who tried to leave the City. They thanked me, actually. It turns out that once the chemicals from the fog are in the body, the body becomes dependent. It can't live without them. So when Skip walked out—"

I'm unable to finish. I can't banish the memory of Skip collapsing at the fence, his look of surprise. I see it when I'm asleep, when I'm awake. It's burned so hard into my eyes that I will see it forever.

"His body ceased to function, I see." Ballast heaves a sigh that makes his belly shake. "Very, very sad. But this—" He pats the book in his lap "—this is a thing of beauty. You were right to bring it to me, my dear. Do you know what it is?"

"A book from before the Fall," I say dully.

I don't care about the book anymore. Only the money. Only leaving.

"It's stories from many thousands of years before the Fall, from before the time of technology, when people made up tales about deities and monsters to explain the world around them. We know some of the stories, but here's the amazing part," Ballast says. "With so few written records left, the stories have evolved over time, some of them so much that they have become almost unrecognizable."

I look hard at the book with a twinge of curiosity. "The book holds the original stories, the way they were before we changed them with our retellings?"

"Exactly." He opens what's left of the front cover and flips to one of the first pages. "Edith Hamilton's *Mythology*. The gods. Dioysus. Europa. Theseus. Perseus. The Quest for the Gold Fleece."

The words spill out before I can stop them. "Orpheus and Eurydice?"

He raises a sculpted eyebrow, then runs his finger down the page, searching. "Yes. It's here. A favorite of yours?"

"It used to be," I say, but thinking about that story makes me think of Skip, and I don't want to break down again. Not in front of Ballast. "Is the book to your satisfaction?"

"It exceeds my expectations."

"I'd like my payment, then."

"Ah." He looks sad. He wanted to talk more about the book. Instead, he reaches into his robe for a pouch, clinking with coin. "Count it. I won't be offended."

I open the pouch and spill the coins onto the rug. The gold glints in the chandelier light. I count the coins as I drop them back into the pouch, grateful that numbers don't confuse me the way letters do. Thirty pieces, as agreed. Three will go to the gypsies, who even now are packing up their caravan to travel east, to pay for a place in their wagons and at their fire.

I want Jewel to follow. I hope she will, but hope has betrayed me too many times for me to trust it again.

I tie the pouch to my belt and nod to Ballast, who is flipping through the book. "It's good doing business with you," I say and turn to leave.

"Would you like to hear it?"

"Hear what?"

"Orpheus and Eurydice. Stay awhile, my dear. We'll find out together how this version is different from the one you know. How it ends."

"I can't," I say.

"You're missing out, my dear."

Am I? My mind again replays Skip at the Do Not Cross fence. His surprise. His body going limp. My helplessness as the person most precious to me in the world, whom I had lost and found, became lost to me forever.

In my imagination, I had seen Skip as Orpheus, but I realize now that I was wrong.

Orpheus is me.

"Thank you," I say, "but I have a caravan to catch. The gypsies aren't known to wait for anyone." I walk to the sitting room door and look back to where Ballast spills over his soft green chair, the book in his hands, pity in his eyes, and I add softly, "Besides, I already know how it ends."

Just Another Night at the Abandoned Draft Bar and Grill

by Stewart C Baker

This was, by Alexandra's count, the sixty-seventh time she had been tortured, murdered, hacked to pieces, and shoved into Jim's refrigerator for him to find when he got home from his overseas deployment, and she was really starting to get annoyed.

"It's like this jackass of a would-be author doesn't even know what women *are*," she snarled, jabbing the ice cubes in her drink until they broke down into slush. "Like he thinks we're just some kind of...of..."

Wong the Inscrutable and François—her companions as always on nights like this—avoided her eyes as she looked around for the right phrase. François (AKA African Henchman #1) was fiddling with the inside of the boxy contraption he always had with him. He'd come from a Francophone sci-fi serial before being co-opted by their current author, Alex knew, had been a genius engineer on some kind of super-massive spaceship. Wong (who Alex thought was probably original, since he was so underdeveloped he wasn't even fully corporeal) stroked his pet rat with his one solid arm, glowering into the middle distance from under his painfully stereotypical peasant hat.

"Plot devices," she finished with a sigh and tossed down half the drink in one gulp.

Things hadn't always been this way. Alex remembered her first writer, the one who had created her from nothing. Alex knew the novel she'd been in back then was far from perfect—her struggles to be accepted at the corporation felt extremely dated, and she'd been a little too stereotypical-self-made-woman—but at least she'd had some say in how her story had happened. And *anything* was better than the fridge.

"Do you know what my line is?" She asked, her voice raw. "The only line I get before I'm taken out?"

Out of the corner of her eye she saw François grimace, but the liquor spurred her on. Her most insipid smile on her face, she giggled vapidly, then, in a sing-song voice, repeated the line: "co-ming!"

"That's it! All I get is a single word, delivered with the stagecraft and nuance of a dead rat! No offense, Wong."

Wong stroked the rat again and made a motion somewhere between a shrug and a nod. In all the years they'd been stuck here, Alex had never known him to speak or stand or do anything else, although to be fair he didn't really have a functional mouth. Or legs.

François, though, looked up with a grin. "Mam'selle, I know just how you feel. I myself do not even *get* a line—I merely open the door and shove the ice pick straight into your eye. And poor Wong, of course, appears only in the background, lurking in the window of an unmarked van across the street, the last thing you see before you die. He does not even get to feed your remains to his beloved rat. Maybe in a finished story he would play a large role as villain, but, well.... And let us not even speak of Jim."

Alex snorted at that. She'd never even seen her "boyfriend" Jim, wasn't sure he even existed to the author beyond the name—never mind that he would no doubt be the hero of whatever story lay beyond the first aborted scene.

"More to the point," François continued, "you know that it pains me almost as much as it does you to go through this barbarous charade, this…idiotic, endless abattoir of an opening scene." He patted the top of the box. "And I know that you will feel almost as happy as I do when I say that with this device complete, we need not suffer it a single time more."

The crushed ice in Alex's drink sloshed as she slammed her cup on the table, hopeful despite herself. "It reaches through the fourth wall and strangles him?"

"No." François frowned. "That would kill us too, since he is writing us."

"Oh." Alex took another drink. *At least it would be permanent,* she added in the privacy of her own head. She thought Wong looked disappointed, too, though of course it was impossible to tell.

François continued, undeterred. "It is something even better than that. The device will change his frame of reference; he will be able to see storytelling from entirely new points of view. *And* it will increase his motivation and ambition a hundredfold! No more will we be forced to endlessly act out an opening scene. No longer will we be stuck in endless white rooms free of description. And if my calculations are correct"—his voice dropped to a whisper, as if he were afraid to speak too loud—"this will give him the energy to finish the first draft entirely."

"We could move on," Alex said. "Be in newer, better stories—ones written by people who actually know how stories *work*."

François grinned. "You must agree, Mam'selle, that things could hardly get worse."

"Do it," Alex said. "Get us a story set somewhere other than in a delusional never-was 1960s middle-America. Get us a story where we're all active participants, where we have unique and interesting lives. Get us," she hissed, "a story where I do not get fucking *murdered* and *stuck in a fridge*."

"Wong?" François asked, looking to the other man.

Wong did the shrug/nod thing again, but his eyes were wet with emotion, and his hand was clutching Ratso so tightly that the little rat squirmed and tried to escape.

"*Bien,*" François said. "We shall give it a try."

He flipped switches and pushed buttons and spun dials on the back of the box, which started to hum quietly. There was a sudden crackle, and the air filled with the smell rain makes just before it falls.

François let out a low whistle. "That was fast. He must have just been sitting down to write. Brace yourselves, everyone!"

Alex grimaced. Already she could feel the story-world pulling at her, tearing away at her control, at her identity. She had just enough time to gulp the last of her drink, the alcohol burning its way down her throat, before the familiar surroundings of the bar faded into blackness.

✧ ✧ ✧

It was a dark and stormy night in the fabled and legendary city of ELLAAAAAHKRA [*replace this with real name later*], home of storied magical spell-slingers and sword-users and heroic fighters [*fighters is vague pick a better class title like paladin or something?*]. There were also a number of dwarves, who were short in stature and savage in nature like the savages of Africa [*fix this later since it is fantasy*] had beards like flowing rivers. Also there were elves, with magical and legendary powers and strange clothing and who had strange mysteries in their eldritch eyes as they gazed up at the dark black night with its glimmering stars and nine enormous fabled moons [*what would this do to the tides? find that out so the setting is SUPER realistic and authentic*].

Ah'lek isan D'aruh, the pure half-elven priestess dressed in a beautiful gown [*need a better description of her clothes, worldbuilding is important!*], was awaiting her lover, the powerful and handsome human heroic paladin Jim, who was known as a smiter of evil and a protector of women, and who would later come to be the biggest and truest savior of the kingdom of [*spoilers? ask mom what she thinks*]. Ah'lek stood on the rooftop of the Holy Magical Legendary Temple of Anarchical Moon-God W'onG, admiring his numerous moons with their craters and magic-giving abilities. It was like a prayer for her, only she did not pray with words. She went into a trance, envisioning with her mind the holy face of Moon God W'onG, his holy moon-like yellow skin.

Suddenly there was a scream from the street a few streets over from the temple. It sounded like a girl maybe. Ah'lek knew only she could help the girl so she leaped into action, her magical katana singing its own praises with glory and righteousness. She was very scared but she knew Jim would be here to save her soon. All she had to do was last until then. She screamed blood-curdling murder in her beautiful voice when suddenly she saw that it was one of the evil black dwarves riding on a rat the size of an elephant [*no elephants in the fantasy world? better description*] holding an axe that was almost as big as his beard but not quite because he had a very big beard.

"Jim!" she shouted. "I cannot do this by myself! I need your powers to defeat this evil black dwarf on his giant rat! Please help me now! I am scared!"

From the other street over she thought she heard a reply, but before she could make it out the dwarf and his rat tragically knocked her to the ground and killed her by crushing her into tiny pieces with its giant rat claws which were so sharp not even her magical katana could withstand it without being broken. Her last thought as the claws sliced through her attractive and beautiful face was that at least Jim would be able to avenge her because he was such a good warrior.

[*Okay this is going really good so far maybe push through to the next scene and I can fix all this later in edits! Or maybe once I finish writing the whole novel I could just rewrite it a few times from scratch. I heard that's a good way to really get into my characters heads, so I bet I could make it more empathetic to women that way. But there's a lot of dialog in the next scene from the dwarf when Jim starts to fight him so I'd better rewatch Lord of the Rings a couple more times before I try to tackle it.*]

This is Home. You are Well.

by Tina Gower

▶ AFTER ◀

I'm meditating alone in the priestess' hut when Anya taps me awake.

"It is time," Anya says, carefully avoiding eye contact. She rubs her hand against the tree needles as though she'd like to get the feeling of my skin off her fingertips. Already the shunning has begun. My husband has blackened our family name because he has taken up arms and fought in war. It doesn't matter the circumstances, our people value peace, and we punish those who do not. Peace cannot be maintained if there are those who do not support it. He was sent to negotiate, to help find a compromise, and instead he chose a side and fought.

I thought I'd have more time to decide, but the villagers seem to already know my choice. I loved Amil. It's true. Our pairing was foreseen to fulfill a majestic destiny, a joining of two revered tribes. He kissed me shyly on the cheek and offered my father dried grains from his land that had been cut after the first triple full moon of our lifetimes. I had many suitors, but none as patient, or as peaceful as Amil. I chose him for his even temper and distaste for conflict. Qualities we respect in our village.

The scent of fermented roots and earth fills the tent. Anya leaves a bowl of soaked grain as a meal and a cup of tepid water. My stomach feels as though it has rocks grinding against one another. I can't eat. I part the waterfall of husks that block the suns and peer out, blinking into the sky. The shuttle is a small speck that grows like mold through the redwood tops. One moment the ship is so tiny I think I can brush it away. The next moment it's so large it's rotted the bread.

I crawl through the opening. Villagers part for me, turning their backs as I walk through the crowd. I haven't decided if I'll greet Amil with a kiss on the cheek, an acceptance for his behavior, or spit at his feet and turn away, showing alliance for my people.

A group of younger children gather and point at the shuttle. "Sky ship!"

It isn't often that we permit the shuttles to fly this close to our village. We prefer to live as though we're indigenous. No running water, no food but what we can grow. In touch with the planet and remaining as natural as possible, insures that we will stay pure. We won't allow outside influences to sway us. Our elders are wise, because this has also made our people grounded in a way that allows us to provide reliable mediation to the rest of our solar system.

The shuttle's thrusters engage when it's several hundred feet above our village. It must land in a small clearing by the lake. Close to where the elders have set up a temporary shelter for Amil, until he can leave. The wind kicks up dried plants, dust, and debris. The elders turn their backs. Denying my husband the sacred ritual of *Yawin*, a welcoming to his native home. I keep my eyes on the descending shuttle, for I'm to be the last to turn away, or by right, I can give up my place as priestess and join my husband's shame.

The doors are about to open and I still do not know what I'll do.

▶ BEFORE ◀

My father eyes me from across the fire. He speaks with Gerrard, the eldest of the task council. It has been three of the largest moon's cycles since Amil and I have joined our families. We anticipated every problem in the adjustment. Our families make demands on our time and we must show how we work together to solve problems.

57

Both families pushed on us, giving us opportunities to negotiate, compromise, and show our skills as a couple. All the while the elders have watched to see if we're well matched, not just in feelings for each other but also in values. Only the strongest matches are permitted to continue.

Amil's shadow flickers from the firelight beside me. I glance up to see him grinning. "Do not watch too closely. I feel your anxiety from across the forest."

"They are discussing our future." I weave needles into a basket. "Should we not go and speak with them?"

He shakes his head. "No, I'd rather stay here and make a basket with you." He plops next to me and begins inspecting the tree needles, comparing thicknesses. "Here," he says, "These are the strongest for the sides around the base."

I eye them, disbelieving. "But they're too thin."

He weaves two needles together with expert precision. "Two together are stronger than a thick one alone. The thick ones do not weave and bend as easily." As he explains he weaves the next line together and I see what he means. It curves the basket up, making it flexible, yet stable.

I lean in and run my finger along his work. "That is remarkable."

He kisses me on the nose, and then with his fingers on my chin, he guides my lips to his.

My father clears his throat above us. I jerk away from Amil's embrace as though I were caught doing something I shouldn't have. Although, we're permitted to touch in public. My cheeks burn. A kiss is rather intimate even if it's allowed.

The elder raises his eyebrow, amused. My father's face is plain, hiding his disapproval.

"It is decided that you will be allowed to present your match to the task council once a replacement has been found for the peace council. Shepherding a match requires a lot of attention. We cannot spare the resources until both councils have been filled."

"But we have been waiting for our task as a couple for longer than normal. Is there a problem with our match? If there's a problem—"

Amil places a hand on my leg and a tingle runs straight to my hips. I forget what I was going to say.

Amil continues for me. "Lani and I are grateful for your efforts and we are eager to move to the next stage as a coupling. Our hut is ready. I'm overjoyed to be joining her tribe. I wish to do what is needed to speed up the process so we can live together."

My father's lips flicker, holding back a grin. He gives me an approving look. He has told me in private on more than one occasion that he is impressed with Amil's abilities to smooth out the tension in a situation.

Gerrord scratches his chin and leans on his walking stick. "You and Lani are an excellent match. We have no objections. It is just we do not wish to rush any pairing, good or bad. If your match is strong, you will withstand the wait. I assure you no pairing has suffered adverse effects from more time."

My father nods in his agreement. I'm disappointed, but these are wise points. The matter is settled.

Amil places his hands in his lap, watching me. I offer a weak smile. His forehead wrinkles in concern.

His gaze is steady on mine. "Those are wise words. I agree that my match with Lani is strong and we will withstand a longer than normal wait, but that still leaves the problem of your shortage on the peace council. I would like to volunteer. It will aid me in integrating into my new community."

The elder's eyes widen in surprise, my father is equally stunned they look to each other for objections and find none. Amil is from a village that has only three generations established since settlement on the planet. Our village boasts seven generations. Many of the surrounding villages send apprentices here. The younger establishments are often eager and ambitious and mirror the technology driven people in the other galaxies. Amil is like an old soul. He is ambitious only in his desire to bring positivity and peace. He fits.

Gerrord taps his stick against the ground, deciding. "It's a heavy responsibility to take on as a new member of the community, but since you'll be learning our ways and joining a committee soon, it makes sense to start that process now. And we do need to keep the councils filled. Without them we risk falling into problems and disagreements among other tribes. Maintaining peace is our highest priority and that requires constant effort."

Amil bows his head. "I am honored to be a member of a tribe that holds its values so close to my own."

The two older men leave. Amil continues to weave our basket.

I whisper to keep my voice low, so no one else can overhear. "The peace council is a lot of responsibility for someone just beginning their negotiation studies. I didn't know that you were so ambitious."

"I've no desire to be on the council." I give him a disbelieving look and he grins and nuzzles my ear. "However, I have a desire to be with you and that empty council seat was spoiling that wish. Besides, I'll suggest that they move me to a council with less responsibility and move someone up who is better suited. The most important thing is that we will not have to wait to start our lives together."

"This is home." He grips my hand in his. "We are well."

These are the words of my people. We believe that it binds our souls together.

We kiss and this time I don't care if father sees.

▶ AFTER ◀

The shuttle doors open and my heart beats against my ribs like it is a prisoner begging for escape. My mouth is dry.

No matter, since the spitting is only a symbol that I acknowledge Amil has crossed a line that should never be crossed. There is always an alternative to violence and he chose to fight. I don't understand it and I burn with the wish to know. It is my right to know why he chose that life over his life with me.

He appears in the door carried on either side by medics. His feet weakly touch the ground, his arms are slung around the backs of the men and his bruised head is covered in mud and grime. His clothing is torn. His robes that once fit his muscular body hang loose. When he looks up, there is no light or humor in his eyes. This is not Amil, this is a shell.

My hands ball into fists. I turn to Anya who faces away from the shuttle. "I can't. I must go to him. He is hurt." And I must have answers. My eyes water and my throat swells.

Anya doesn't acknowledge me; she steps away, which shows my choice. Although after speaking with Amil I may change my mind at any time.

I run to my husband and help the guards to the hut.

Amil chokes, his voice rasps words I do not understand. I look to the medic for some answers.

The medic doesn't meet my eyes. "You are Lani?" I nod yes. "He has been calling out to you."

I lay a hand on Amil's chest. He turns to me as though he cannot believe it is really me.

"I'm here. This is home."

He shakes his head and swallows as though it is the most painful thing he's had to do. "No. Lani, you will leave. You must go."

And then he falls into a deep sleep before I can get my answers.

▶ BEFORE ◀

"Do not fret, Lani." Amil grinds the umpa seeds into fine flour. "You're descendent of four generations of priestesses. They will not cast your nomination aside."

"But what if they wish to give another family a chance?" I wring my hands together, wishing for the dye to set faster, so I can get back to my work. I envy Amil's work, but we only have one stone. "My father says he doesn't wish for it to appear we've had a monopoly on the position."

"Then let the committee decide. It's not a decision your father can make for them." He sets the stone next to him and shifts the flour through a mesh grate. The larger pieces will not fall through and he can grind them again.

I pick up the stone. He backs away as I take over his task. "Since I missed the trade ships this morning, what is the news from above?"

He doesn't answer right away. Instead he scratches his chin and stares into the distance.

"Amil?"

"There is some tension between one of the villages and the ship of settlers. A disagreement on land and how the supplies are gathered and divided."

"Then they must send for one of the mediators. This is what we've been trained for. Our village will keep the peace between the groups."

He nods, crossing his arms.

"Well?" I wave my elbow as though to prod him even though he's too far to touch. "Who will they send?"

"They will send me."

I laugh at his joke. "Very funny, Amil. Who will they send?"

He doesn't laugh.

"But you're newly trained. You only joined to fill an empty seat. You asked to be removed a few nights ago. You're a farmer and your skills are much better working the land or on the trade committee than to be sent to a ship a thousand miles into the sky. Didn't Ustof want your position? I thought it was settled." My thoughts race.

"The peace counsel thought it was best to send the most neutral party. My home village is very far removed from the disagreement. We sent a list to the concerned parties and they had to mutually agree on a name. That name was mine. It seems I'm the only neutral party in their eyes. Or both sides think they can manipulate me." He does let out a mirthless laugh now. "I don't know."

"Then you're the only one." My fingers are numb on the grinding stone.

I'd never expected his position in our community to change from being anything but my partner. He's quiet, soft-spoken. He didn't want to be a part of the peace committee, but they were in need of volunteers. Our people were raised and trained in negotiation tactics from an early age. Avoid conflict. Find compromise. We valued our abilities to keep calm and level reasoning. When the settlers moved in, we saw they had a different value system. They fought more often. Our services were needed more in recent years, but we always helped them to find a peaceful solution.

But Amil is skilled. I've seen it. My parents have seen it. The council must have seen it. "You will do well. You will honor our tribe."

"I will honor you." He kisses me. "Everything I do is for you, my priestess."

62

"Not yet," I correct.

"I don't leave for three nightfalls, we will know if that is true by then. And I'll never forget this is my home. You are well."

Then he leads me to the pallet on the floor and we make love as though everything will work out fine, because we had no reason to believe it wouldn't. But I don't sleep.

▶ AFTER ◀

I wash the grime and bits of leaves that have been shoved against his field dressing. "What is this? They didn't have the supplies to clean the wound?"

He slides his arm toward the injury, his fingers tremble as he gets closer, and stops short. His eyelids crack open, too swollen to open all the way. "The medic had herbs from his home village to prevent infection."

"It is still very red."

"My unit was kept from proper medical facilities for a week, trapped between two battles that blocked the group."

His talk of war makes my jaw clench shut. "It's fine." I clean the area as best I can and grind garlic into a paste for an antibiotic ointment.

"Please, do not bother with this. It will be easier if you leave me and turn your back as the rest have done. I'm broken. My soul is broken. I'm not long in this body."

"To leave a man suffering, even a disgraced one, is against our ways. I will heal you."

"No." He jerks to sit up and I startle, holding his bandage in place. I fear he will injure himself more. "That is cruel. To fix me and then leave me. I won't have it. I want you to leave. I don't want you this way, or your pity."

"My pity?" I speak, lowering my voice at an even tempo, and fail. My hands firmly hold his mid-section together. "Do you think I haven't suffered?"

"I knew you would be ashamed that I fought. I knew you'd be forced to shun me if I were ever to return. It must have made your position as a priestess difficult—"

"I don't care about any of that!" I press his wound for emphasis and he cringes, as though he's now feeling the stabs of pain he didn't before. "Do you not think the first thought in my mind when I woke up was if you were in danger and the last thought before I'd sleep was if you were dead? No, I didn't know why you chose to fight. We didn't know why. It is against our ways and you knew the consequences. You knew it would be a choice between me and our people, and that it would then force me to choose the same."

His eyes lower. His body shakes. He gradually lies back onto the pallet. "That isn't what I want."

"Not what you want." I mutter to myself as I smear the garlic paste into his cut and cover him with a clean cloth. "It is what I want. Leave our community or leave you? That is not a choice for me." I move to the edge of the hut, as far from him as I can go without leaving. If I leave, I will not be permitted to return. It means that I have declared Amil dangerous and someone will be sent in to care for him. It will only be the minimum requirement to keep him alive for as long as he chooses or until he is well enough to leave.

"You still haven't decided." He stares at the ceiling, his eyelids close slowly. He is fighting to stay awake, but won't last long.

I turn away from him and busy myself with taking stalk of our supplies. We will be given a small ration each day until my choice is made. I can take as long as I wish. But once I choose I cannot go back. "I'm here aren't I?"

"For now." His eyes close and soon his breathing becomes ragged even though he sleeps.

▶ BEFORE ◀

Anya comes to us with the news. The priestesses are gathered in a meditation circle. We search for an answer to the turmoil between our allies. The candles dance when the hut flaps open. Our candle that was lit as a symbol of peace blows out again. It has not stayed lit since we started the ritual. The furs below my robes make my thighs sweat. Anya hooks the flap of the hut to the wall to allow for more air, but the hot moisture outside brings us little relief.

"They have three new ships. It is said that the villagers fear that they will send down soldiers to raid. They threaten to take what is rightfully theirs."

My heart beats quickly, my peaceful meditation disrupted. To be truthful, it never stopped rattling against my ribs like a trapped animal after my husband announced he would be the mediator between the two groups.

Anya and the eldest priestess whisper between one another, I strain to hear until I can't take it anymore and interrupt. "What word of Amil? Has he been permitted to negotiate?"

The women all turn to me. Each of their thirty expressions holds a different emotion. Some shake their heads in disbelief at my outburst, others show concern for my situation, and others blink away when my eyes meet theirs.

"If he hasn't been allowed to negotiate he hasn't technically failed. It was a trap to adhere to the treaty. They know they cannot raise arms without consequence from the Universal Alliance. It has been stated they will allow negotiation before force."

One of the younger priestesses, Shyla, leans toward me. "Hush. It is not polite to speak out of turn. We understand your distress. We know you wish to defend your husband—"

"I'm not defending him. If he hasn't been able to perform his task it is not an issue of our counsel. We must send more mediators to plead with the *Aurora*."

"The *Aurora* is not the only ship in orbit now. We have received reports of another."

There is a collective gasp. The women burst into discussion. Two ships? But what would the *Aurora*, a trade ship, need of another ship? The *Aurora* alone could carry twice the agreed supplies.

The eldest priestess rings the bell. Its tone is low and deep, too calm compared to the turmoil in the room. "I call for peace in this moment."

We all obey. Our hands return to prayer position, our backs straighten.

"You will return to meditation. I will travel to the next village this afternoon to gather the details. I have contacts on a carrier ship that may know details of the dispute. I will return in the morning." Anya helps her to rise from her seated position on the hut floor and she leaves.

Three ladies in training enter to line the sidewall with bread and roots. When our meditations are done we will be permitted a meal. I search the room for friendly assurances. None of the women return my gaze, but I keep searching. Resigned, I train my gaze straight ahead and attempt to concentrate. Out of the corner of my eye I see Shylo's gaze wander to me. I flick my focus to her, but she straightens and brings her attention to center quickly.

I do not meditate. My thoughts are with Amil. Is he well? Did he reach the ship? Have negotiations begun? I put my faith in Amil. Our people have trained for thousands of years to keep the peace. This is what Amil was born to do. He will not fail.

It isn't until the head priestess returns that my hopes are dashed.

She gathers us all together. I'm not granted a private meeting.

"News of the *Aurora* has come. The villages surrounding the dispute have observed that the talks have turned to violence. Those who wished to leave have done so, those who wished to fight stayed."

"And what of Amil?" I ask. "If he was permitted to leave—"

"Amil has chosen to stay. He has chosen to fight."

She looks each of us in the eye. Everyone but me.

▶ AFTER ◀

Amil struggles in his sleep. Although he is flat on his back, his legs slide up as though he wishes to curl up into himself, but his stomach injury will not allow the position. He shivers. I watch him from my corner of the room, hugging my legs. He has changed. His features are sharper, his smooth lines and easy smile are gone. This is why our people advocate against violence. It destroys the soul and tears families apart. There is no disagreement worth it. To participate in any behavior that encourages distrust, jealousy, or turmoil is forbidden.

We are taught from an early age to recognize the traps. It is nature, some say. That anger and violence are normal. But they're not.

Anger is an emotion that can be trained. Violence is a choice and there are a thousand choices. War is failed negotiation or failure to understand.

I crawl to Amil and cover him. I smooth his hair with the palm of my hand, massaging the lines of distress along his forehead. He eases.

I glance around the room, searching for some task, but there is nothing. The elders have removed any burden. Our only goal is to work out the arrangement. As a priestess, I'm expected to do what is for the greater good for our people. I cannot be allowed to condone an act of violence. My husband has no recourse to atone his decision due to the nature of his offense.

He didn't hesitate, the elders said. He admitted to believing his side was justified in their complaint. No remorse over the tactics he chose. No restraint.

His movements start up again. His legs saw and kick as though the blanket is holding him down. He claws at the air.

I sigh and place my hand on his cheek. He wakes with a rush of air into his lungs and his eyes go wide. He blinks and fixes his gaze on the drying herbs above his head, before coming to this reality.

"Shh," I comfort him. "This is home. You are well." These are the words of my people.

It is said that when a soul is wrestling with great remorse it will wander from the body during sleep. If it does not return this means the person is lost. We beckon its return by reminding it of its rightful place. We encourage it to stay with us. I fear my husband's soul may have long ago left him and this is why he wishes me to leave him. If that is the case, then my presence here is no longer necessary. I must find the strength to leave him. *When he is healed*, I tell myself.

"You are still here," he says when his eyes open.

"Where else would I be?"

"Gone."

There is silence and I think he has fallen asleep again, but his even breaths mean he hasn't.

"I must know." I whirl to face him and his hollow eyes meet mine. "Why did you stay? Tell me it was not to fight. Tell me it was to continue to attempt to negotiate and you didn't give in. Tell me you advocated for peace and then I will plea with the elders for you—"

"I wasn't the only negotiator." He threads his fingers together over his chest and closes his eyes. "There was someone from Distil. He was far more skilled than I. The villagers insisted that the settlement wouldn't negotiate. That they had been forcefully taking supplies and killing those who stood in their way. We didn't believe that there was nothing to be done, so we marched into the settlement with our hands held high and asked to speak with the captain. He met with us. He had a patient ear. He nodded as we detailed the complaints and our suggestions for allowing everyone something that they wanted.

"He smiled. Thanked us for meeting with him. Then he took out a gun and shot the negotiator from Distil in the head then he turned to me and said his people had desperate need of the supplies. He was doing this to save many from starvation. He told me he spared me to return to the village and negotiate with them to not resist if we wanted a peaceful outcome, or there wouldn't be anyone left to harvest. I explained that there was another way. We could help his people if he chose a peaceful path. His men surrounded me with guns and marched me from the settlement."

"You could have worked out another negotiation. Sent for help. Why start a war?"

"Yes, we tried, but no one could get through. We had more negotiations and all that passed was time. It wasn't long before the village stopped producing. The harvest had been decimated. The land had been reaped, the soil overworked. The captain gathered the villagers and asked for details of the surrounding villages. He wanted details of their crops, the supplies. He promised to pay them for their service and asked them to dig a large hole and he would fill it with fertilizer for the next year's crops, but instead he filled it with their bodies. I escaped because the host family I'd been staying with had grown distrustful of the captain's promises. We began to gather tools to use as weapons; we traveled to the surrounding villages to warn others. We told them to leave if they wished to avoid conflict, harvest and hide their crops."

"You tried to find a peaceful way to end the conflict."

"Yes. We thought that once the crop ran out and the people became useless to him he would leave. But instead he had plans to raid the surrounding villages. He would have eventually come here. You would have had no protection, no one to fight for you. Our village is the most peaceful on this land. He chose this side of our planet because we wouldn't struggle. He killed those who resisted so they wouldn't send for help."

Amil coughs and sputters. I bring him a cup of water and he sips. When he is ready he continues. "We gathered villagers to hide in the next village he planned to raid. We had sharpened tools and planks against guns, but we had the element of surprise and a plan. It wasn't long before we had some guns, too. And we fought them, so that the next village wouldn't die as the ones before them."

"But many died. Why not continue to hide?"

"Because we didn't want to take the risk that they wouldn't stop. Yes, many died so that more could live, so we could preserve our way of life. We sent word to the Universal Alliance. They are gone. The captain is dead. The ships have retreated."

When he says those last words it is not with relief. I know that Amil doesn't believe that the settlers will stay away. Over the next nights I care for his injuries and wipe the sweat from his brow when he cries in his sleep. I hold his hand as his grip becomes weaker. He repeats the stories of war and the men who fought with him. Amil tells me more details of the fight and more about the settlers. Then he speaks very little. He is only awake for small amounts of time.

"This is home." I whisper to him. "You are well."

They are the last words he hears.

The elders come for his body and Gerrard offers me his hand. "Return to the meditation hut, Lani, they will aid you in mourning. It was a generous and peaceful thing to aid Amil as he left this world. It is shameful that he chose violence in the end. The council will not hold it against you if you choose to continue your training as a priestess."

He doesn't turn his back to me. He assumes that Amil's death has solved the disgrace. My stomach burns. The sacrifice Amil has made, that others have made will go unnoticed. It will be seen as a failure and never be thought of again. They do not realize the horrible things they have been spared. The bloodshed. The violence.

I turn my back to him. I turn my back to all of them.

I march to the shuttles. I will return to the village where my husband fought. If the settlers return, I will be there, waiting.

Copyright © 2016 by Tina Smith

The World That You Want

by Laurie Tom

I was fifteen when the world ended, on schedule, as predicted, by a man no one important took seriously. The world convulsed, the sky bled red, and hell came to earth. It is the cycle, the demons tell us. Our time is past and they will feast on the leavings.

Brandon and I spend most of our days scavenging and talking to ghosts who forget the world they knew no longer exists. They still wander the old community garden, inquiring about the crops and complaining about the hole in the maintenance shed that Brandon patched months ago.

The water situation is particularly bad. Plumbing no longer works and southern California is naturally a desert. I have to barter with a crow spirit who guards the nearest well, a magic one dug by no human hands. He is not hostile to humans so long as they pay. He takes avocados, potatoes, carrots, and other produce from our garden.

"Listen," the crow calls to me. "The cycle is moving."

Death and rebirth. I know. Our world is gone, and a new one will come. I set my bucket on the ground and take out today's payment. The fruits and vegetables pile beside the well where the crow can see them.

"What tells you this?" I ask.

I don't really expect an answer. Demons only reply if it suits, and their words don't always address what was asked.

"The light shines from the peak. Soon there will be fighting."

The crow cocks his head to the southeast as though he can see something great in the distance. I see only old buildings bathed in the light of the afternoon sun. Empty.

"The Bank Tower," says the crow. "It will be there. A human will have to make a decision."

"What kind of a decision?"

"An important one." The crow pecks at his payment. "Take the water," he says, before snapping a carrot in his beak and flying to his nest.

I fill the bucket and it is heavy. It's the big kind a person uses when mopping floors. Now it carries clean water. The crow is not cheap, but his water is good. The rain is acid when it comes. We try not to drink it and the stores have been looted long ago.

When I get back to the house, I find the front door open and Brandon's backpack on the patio. It is stuffed thicker than I've seen in months and his canteen hangs from one side. His baseball bat sits beside it. Brandon emerges from inside the house. He eyes the water.

"You can put it down," he says, and I do.

"Are you going somewhere?" I ask, though the answer is obvious.

"Downtown."

Downtown Los Angeles is miles from here. Before the world ended it was a half hour drive through city traffic. On foot it would take several hours. I can't imagine why he would go there. Then I remember the crow spoke of the US Bank Tower. It is the tallest building in downtown.

"Did you decide—"

He cuts me off. "I don't feel like talking about it." His voice is surly as he snatches the canteen from his pack and dunks it in the bucket. It fills quickly as the air escapes. Glub. Glub.

When are you coming back? I want to ask, but instead I say, "Can I come too?"

He eyes me. "If you hurry."

I sprint to my bedroom in the back of the house. This wasn't my house originally, or Brandon's, but our homes still sheltered the ghosts of our families. My mother couldn't know that it was no longer 4 p.m. on a particular Wednesday of last year, so she would always nag me: "Eun Hee, why aren't you at tutoring? Eun Hee you need to study harder to get into a good university." She never called me Joan like my American-born friends.

The house I share with Brandon has no ghosts. Either no one had died here or the demons had eaten them. Either way, it isn't as though the owners still needed it. Brandon was the one who suggested we take it, and I had to agree it was a good decision.

I grab my backpack, check that I still have a change of clothes and my first aid kit inside, then dash for the kitchen where we keep our dried fruit and demon bread. The bread is not evil, at least not in any way we can tell, but without flour we can only obtain bread through bartering with the demons. Brandon always leaves that to me. He won't talk to them.

I put both bread and fruit in my backpack and jog through the living room to the front door. To my relief, Brandon is still waiting outside, though at the end of the walk by the street.

I close the door behind me. We don't have the key so I can't lock it, and I worry that we will come back to a ransacked home, but Brandon does not seem concerned. He looks to the southeast. It's the direction of downtown.

"Do you know how to get there?" I ask.

"Yeah." He has a faded street map with him, something he found in a desk of one the homes we stayed in.

We set off with him in the lead and me following close behind. Brandon carries his bat, sometimes over his shoulder, sometimes by his side. Some demons are congenial, even if they are not inclined to be friends. Some demons ignore us. But other demons frown on humans and would leave us as so much blood smeared on the walls and sidewalks in front of buildings. We find people like that sometimes, so Brandon carries the bat. He knows demons can be killed. He's the only person I know who's killed one. But still, some are better to hide from.

Brandon and I were classmates in geometry, and until the world ended we'd barely said two words to each other. But when the world heaved and most people became ghosts we were the only two left in the school.

We've seen other people since; living ones. They're furtive, scurrying like we scurry. They rarely talk to us, as if by banding together in a larger group we would draw unwanted attention—and we would, the same way a single feral dog is a nuisance and a pack must be put down.

We do not reach the Bank Tower by sunset, having left too late in the day, so we spend the night huddled in two layers of clothing on the eight lanes of the 101 freeway. There are still cars parked, bumper to bumper, frozen in early rush hour traffic. Uneaten ghosts linger in them, usually in the driver's seat, sometimes in the passenger's.

Brandon finds a gap between the cars where we're unlikely to be seen by hungry demons. I can hear a ghost mutter, "I'm gonna miss the game. I'm gonna miss the game." It stops now and then, but the words don't change.

"What's downtown?" I ask, hoping he won't rebuff me a second time. We've just eaten dinner and he's usually nicer after some food.

"The tower," he says, and though I'm sure he means the US Bank Tower, I can't help but ask for confirmation.

The moon is full tonight and I can see his face. He glares at me as though I'm stupid.

"Of course the US Bank Tower," he mutters. "You'd have to be deaf not to have heard all the demons ranting about the Decision. Everyone's going there."

"Including the demons?"

"Everyone *human*. It takes a human soul. Haven't you been paying attention? You're always talking to demons. More than you should."

I talk because I don't know how to fight and I'm not good at hiding. If the demons think I'm harmless, they might not hurt me and I won't be a blood smear on the side of a building. I know talking won't always work, but if the demon is willing to hear me, then it's at least worth a shot.

"I've made my Decision," he says, with an air of finality. "If you haven't made one, that's fine by me. It's probably better that you don't."

"Can you at least tell me so I know whether I should?"

He rolls over and settles his head on his backpack. He intends to sleep. End conversation. "Better that you don't," he says. "You'll thank me later."

I wake the next morning and do not see him. His backpack is gone and when I look around there are only empty cars and ghosts. Maybe he's scouting ahead, I tell myself, and there's nothing to do but put one foot in front of the other and walk down the freeway. The downtown area is in sight.

My stomach rumbles, reminding me of breakfast, but I don't touch the bread in my backpack. Eating will slow me down and I can't be a burden to Brandon. He's the only other human being I have in the world. Even if we don't always get along, even if he's abrasive, at least he's company.

When the world ended he was the one who figured out how to store food now that refrigerators no longer had power. He was the one who could pick out the quickest escape route when demons were near. He broke into homes, stores, getting us food, shelter, and supplies. He might listen to a demon, but he would never trust one.

At first he seemed to like caring for me, and I tried to repay him by being a good housekeeper, so I wouldn't have to rely on his charity, but there was no denying that I needed him more than he needed me.

The US Bank Tower rises above the rest of downtown. It is a distinctive building not only for its height, but its cylindrical shape. I'd never been there before. Downtown L.A. was always crowded and there was no reason to visit what was really an office building.

There is an off-ramp from the 110 to 4th Street, and while I have no idea if this is the closest one, it looks close enough.

That's when it hits me. Brandon really did leave me behind. I'm not going to catch up with him. I don't even know if he went this way. I've spent all morning, walking as fast as I can, but he's nowhere in sight and the demons didn't get him or I would have been taken as well and we'd both be piles of bone and gore.

I stumble to the bottom of the off-ramp and blunder into an SUV halted in the intersection. There's no ghost in this one. I don't hear muttering, but I don't care anymore.

I curl up and sob, because now I'm alone.

After a time I become aware of the sound of wings beating above me. Something is circling. There are no normal birds anymore so it can only be a demon. I am probably dead, lying out in the open like this, and I find I almost don't care. Almost.

I raise my head and through puffy eyes I see a winged serpent silhouetted against the morning sun. The demon sails lower, sweeping to the ground.

"Why do you cry?" he asks. "There are no plants here for you to nourish."

He is a splendid creature, with feathers like the rainbow and teeth like a shark. His eyes are shiny and black, like obsidian. I call him Quetzalcoatl after the Aztec god. Whether he is or not he puffs his chest with pride and I think he won't eat me.

"A human's tears aren't enough to nourish a flower," I say.

He tilts his head. "No? But they are enough to feed a new world."

"The Decision," I say. "What is it?"

"The birth, the coming. As it was, as it has been, as it continues to be. Worlds and then worlds in an endless cycle." He pauses, perhaps reflecting. "You should make yours soon."

"But what am I deciding?"

"What else? Time in this timeless world is running out. Already the cycle draws to a close."

Brandon was in a hurry to get to the US Bank Tower. He said everyone is going there. I look to its peak and it shines with a blue light that comes from no lamp.

"Will you nourish a new world?" asks the serpent.

"What will happen to this one?"

"Does it matter?"

The buildings downtown are worn and tired at the street level. Doors and windows have been broken by scavengers and there are dull smears where the unfortunate have died. I see no ghosts anywhere. The demons have eaten them all.

I say, "It matters to you, doesn't it?"

"It does."

The serpent spreads his wings and lies down before me. His torso is as wide as a small horse. "I will carry you as high as I can," he says, "for you are already very late."

I climb on and cling tight to his neck, knees bent to keep from scraping the ground as he takes off. Then we are flying, soaring upward on his beautiful feathered wings. Other demons soar around the peak of the Bank Tower. Though I can see the skyscraper's helipad through the wild throng, none of them approach it. A few attempt, but are rebuffed by an unseen force. They are watching something. I see small figures, humans, moving on the rooftop and I don't know why. Aren't they afraid of the demons?

The demons pay us no mind. Even below the peak, all eyes are looking in through the windows. I catch a flutter of movement. Black feathers? But the important thing is I see an open window. Shattered.

"Over there!" I shout, and I point though I realize the serpent probably can't see me.

He spots the opening regardless and sails close.

"Beware the glass," says the serpent, as I dismount and watch where I step.

"Thank you," I tell him, and I bow once I'm safely inside.

The serpent nods and flies away.

I look up at the ceiling as though I could somehow gauge how much higher I had to go. The very structure is humming and I'm at least few floors down. I need to find the stairs.

The exit signs in the hall are no longer lit, but they point the way regardless. The stairs are on the other side of a heavy door which I push open as hard as I can. There is resistance on the other side that suddenly gives way. The air of the stairwell smells thickly of blood; sweet and full of iron.

I see the source of the resistance, a man on his hands and knees. His white collared shirt is splotched with dirt and blood. He's been shot, multiple times. In his hand is a broken ruler—sharpened plastic. It's a poor weapon, but he clutches it to him like a rosary. It's all that keeps him from death. Well, a quicker death.

"I can't make a Decision anymore," he breathes. "Please, just leave me alone."

I nod, and carefully step around him to go up the stairs.

"But if you would, if you like my Decision..."

I look back at him. It is taking so much for him to talk.

"I wanted a world where people had to respect each other, a world where everyone was civil and cared about others..."

I nod again, to show I've heard, but I don't think he sees me anymore.

There are more bodies and dying people as I climb the tower. Those still living plead their cases for the new world.

A world without sickness and death.

A world with only one god.

A world where no child is unwanted.

But I come to realize that no one world can satisfy everyone, and what disturbs me the most is that none of these people died to demons. The wounds are from guns, from knives, or blunt trauma. There are no claws, no fire, no teeth, or unholy elements.

Others must have realized before me that there can be only one new world, and they'd fought to ensure the one created was the one they wanted.

"Please," says a woman, "there can't be more than two or three ahead of me. I don't want anything special—just the old world back. It wasn't so bad, was it?"

I step over her and reach for a battered door, held shut only by its natural resting position, and not by its busted latch. It's the door to the roof. Heart pounding, I can only think of Brandon. He hasn't been among the bodies I crossed.

The roof is bathed with the blue light I'd spotted while riding the serpent. Oddly it is dimmer now, and seems to be coming from still higher above me. The helipad is nearby, chain link surrounding its base should anyone fall. I find the steps up. There is another corpse along the way. This one's skull has been beaten.

I draw eye level with the helipad and the sight is horrible. The helipad's number 12, painted in red, blends with the blood from the myriad bodies crowded around the base of a clear obelisk. It is from the obelisk that the blue light shines. Even as I approach, it continues to dim, and I can look at it without blinding myself.

There are two figures still on their feet. No. Only one. Brandon. The other man is being stood on his toes, his collar snug around his neck, as Brandon holds him fast. Brandon has his baseball bat, stained a terrible red. The other man is unarmed, but there is a gun by his feet.

"Brandon!" I shout.

He does not take his eyes off the writhing man he holds. "Why are you here, Joan? Did you actually make a Decision?"

"No, I—" I just didn't want to be left behind.

"Then you can help me make mine."

"What is it? What is the world that you want?"

77

It occurs to me that though Brandon and I have lived together for almost a year, we never talked of any hopes or desires, unless they pertained to food, shelter, or demons.

"Even you'll like this one." He glares contemptuously at the man he holds and shakes his captive when the other man tries to speak. "Even this guy would too."

"Can't you let him go?" I ask. "He doesn't have a gun anymore."

"My world," says Brandon, undeterred, "is one where no one ever needs another person. You won't have to rely on anyone to take care of you. I won't be obligated to help. Everyone would be self-sufficient. Wouldn't you like that? To not need other people?"

I'd never considered such a thing, and I can't quite believe such a world could exist. If we didn't need each other for anything, not even companionship, would we all live alone?

Brandon takes my silence for acceptance. It has always been this way when we made decisions that I didn't like.

"Finish this guy then, while I hold him. Pick up his gun."

I hesitate.

"It's not that hard to use. Just point and shoot."

The man babbles. He doesn't care about making a new world anymore. He just doesn't want to die.

"It's not that," I say. "Why do we need to kill him?"

"Each person who dies in this tower weakens the barrier withholding the rebirth. Have you notice they leave no ghosts?"

Now that he mentions it, I haven't seen any, nor any demons who would have eaten them.

"Their spirits are filling the obelisk, and when there are enough the walls will be weak enough to release the rebirth."

"The rebirth is powered by human souls?"

That's not the kind of world I want...

Brandon scoffs. "They're already dead. It'll get us and any remaining humans out of this hellhole and into a new world where there won't be any demons."

The other man suddenly twists and kicks. Brandon swears, releasing him as he grabs his baseball bat in both hands. Before I know what I'm doing, I throw myself at Brandon, arms outstretched. I don't want him to kill someone.

We collide, and he stumbles mid-swing. He wasn't expecting me. I feel myself falling and I try to correct myself, but my feet and legs aren't responding. I spin to one side, trying to get an arm out, when I slam against the concrete. It hurts and the wind is knocked from my lungs.

Brandon is screaming. It takes me a while to recognize his voice. I've never heard him scream like this before, so obviously in pain. Nothing ever hurts Brandon enough for him to scream.

But this…. This is nothing he's expected.

I lift my head, trying to see him.

I had pushed him into the obelisk and it had broken like so much glass. I hadn't realized it was so thin.

Beware the glass. I remember.

The shards bury themselves in his body, digging in like maggots, and he is bleeding from so many places his skin is slick and red. He flails, kicking, and I watch as he grows weak, his movements less vigorous, less frantic. Not once does he look to me. He has never wanted my help.

The light, dimly shining, even after the destruction of the obelisk, goes out as Brandon ceases to move.

So much for the new world.

The other man stares in disbelief, then staggers away, back to the stairs. I see a familiar crow flying overhead, weaving in and out among the other demons. They are all watching.

I have never liked Brandon, but at least he was company, and at times, in his own way, he'd been kind. I remember our early days, when there had still been hope, and he killed a demon to save me. I'd been a blubbering mess and he told me, "Don't worry. I've got you."

Now Brandon is just one of many bodies lying by the remains of the obelisk.

"It is time for the new world."

I look up and through blurry eyes I see the crow, standing before me.

"But the obelisk was destroyed."

"As it was meant to be, and the final soul that was needed was captured atop this tower. Have you made your Decision?"

A world where people don't need each other. It was a promising world, but I realize I like needing and being needed. I would not exist in a world such as Brandon envisioned.

There is a touch at my shoulder, and I turn to see the feathered serpent I called Quetzalcoatl. He says nothing, but licks beneath my eyes, taking away the tears.

"Does there have to be a new world?" I ask.

The helipad around me is covered with so much death. This tower is a mausoleum of worlds that did not agree.

"No," says the crow.

The conflict between people would not be erased with the creation of a new world. I had only to lift my head to see the pain and destruction that the want of one had caused. For a brief moment, I consider a world where I am never alone, where I am appreciated, but I realize I could never force others to befriend me.

I place my hand on the wing of the feathered serpent. His eyes glitter bright and a loud thrum issues from his throat.

"I don't want a new world," I tell the crow. "Let this one remain."

"So it is done!"

The crow's voice thunders from atop the skyscraper and the demons wheel in the sky like flocks of birds before scattering. I am not certain, but I think a few of them bow to me before they leave.

The feathered serpent extends himself before me, beckoning me to mount, and the crow hops on to my shoulder. My life will be different now, but I find myself unafraid. However strange my new companions are, I am not alone.

Bookmarked

by Martin L. Shoemaker

"So why'd you turn off the lights, doctor? Are we done with the visual tests?"

Andrew heard Dr. Morgan answer from the darkness, though he wasn't sure of her direction. "Visual cortex stimulation and neural mapping, Mr. Burns. And yes, it's completed."

"That was the last thing we had to record, right? So turn the lights on. Let me get dressed. Elena must be getting anxious in the waiting room."

He heard the doctor sigh. That was followed by the sound of a coffee cup setting on a tray, but he couldn't smell the coffee. Too bad, he hadn't had any all morning.

Dr. Morgan finally answered. "The neural map was completed seven months ago."

"What?" Andrew looked around, but the darkness was total. "No. I just laid down on your table a few hours ago."

"I'm afraid not. Andrew Burns laid down upon our table seven months ago and went through a full-brain neural mapping. Then he and Elena went home, leaving us to process the recording. *You* are that recording, playing back on our simulated cerebral hardware."

"Nonsense!" Andrew wondered if Dr. Morgan was stimulating irritation for the sake of the mapping. "What sort of game is this? I'm right here. I can feel this—" Wait. Andrew *couldn't* feel the table. In fact.... "I can't feel my hands, my legs. I can't even feel my tongue when I talk!"

Dr. Morgan's voice dropped, low and calm. "That's because you don't have a tongue. You have a voice synthesizer, hooked into your simulated speech centers so that we can have conversations like this."

"But then how can I hear you? I don't have ears, right?"

"Microphones hooked into your auditory cortex."

Andrew paused. "I'm asleep. I'm dreaming. This isn't real." Then he remembered the demonstration that Dr. Morgan had given him before he had agreed to the mapping procedure. "You said that you would communicate with—with *it* via text."

"Yes, that's exactly what we did during our early simian studies, the ones that...Andrew and Elena witnessed. We trained apes in simple sign language, mapped their brains, and then sent signs to those recordings via a text interface. But we've made some significant improvements since then." She cleared her throat. "We...had to."

"Had to?"

Dr. Morgan's voice was slow, reluctant as she answered. "We found that your...playback...your wave patterns in the simulated cerebrum destabilized rapidly without audio input. If you couldn't hear your own voice as you 'spoke,' your...holographic wave patterns...degraded. Quicker than expected."

"What do you mean, you 'found' this? When did you run these tests? I don't remember them. The last thing I remember was you flashing words and images onto a screen while I described what I saw and how I felt about it. You didn't run any new tests."

Dr. Morgan sighed again. "No new tests *today*, Mr. Burns. Except this one." Andrew almost interrupted to ask her what test she meant, but she continued too quickly. "But this is not the first time we've... activated the cerebrum. Powered you up for playback."

Andrew remembered a conversation from a few weeks earlier. (It *was* just a few weeks. He *knew* that, though doubts were settling in.) "You can't run tests on me! That was clearly covered in the papers I signed. Your human subject protocols require my explicit permission for each new test. I haven't given permission."

Dr. Morgan spoke carefully. "If we were testing Andrew Burns, yes, we would have to have permission. But we're not. You are just...

data, and Andrew already signed all the paperwork necessary to give us full control of all data that we gathered from him. All you are...is a recording."

"I am not!" Andrew felt outrage, like he hadn't since the day he had received his cancer diagnosis. Yet it was different: this was a strong, deep revulsion, but without the racing heart and tremors he had felt. Elena had to calm him then; now his anger was passionless. Bloodless. "That was the whole point of your experiment: to record a personality so that you can transfer it into a new brain when cloning catches up. If I *was* a person and I *will be* a person in that new brain, then I *am* a person right now. Q.E.D."

"Yes," Morgan said. "That *is* our hope. But there has been no legal ruling regarding your status. You're still our alpha test, the first recorded consciousness of a human subject. The law hasn't caught up, *can't* catch up until the courts have our results to consider. You are in..."

Dr. Morgan couldn't finish her metaphor, but Andrew saw it coming. "...legal limbo." He laughed, a bitter laugh that sounded mechanical in his ears. They must not have built a laughter simulator into his systems.

And just like that, Andrew knew: he believed Dr. Morgan's story. Every word of it.

Morgan laughed lightly, sympathetically. "You're a special case, a precedent setter. We *do* have protocols we must follow, reviews we must file; but as a practical matter, we *can't* ask your permission before each test, because you're...dormant until the test begins. You do not have the rights that Andrew Burns had."

"Had?" If he'd had an eyebrow, he would've raised it.

"I'm sorry. Andrew Burns passed away two-and-a-half months ago from complications of his cancer."

"Why didn't you tell me this sooner?"

Andrew heard footsteps. Dr. Morgan was pacing. "Past experience has shown that we need to ease you into certain topics. It helps to slow your degradation."

"There's that word again: degradation," Andrew said. "What do you mean by that?"

The pacing stopped. "We're still learning. We're one-hundred percent certain that we have successfully recorded your—Andrew's personality. Your neural map is as complete as any we've ever created. But what we can't do—yet—is impose that recording onto a new brain. Cloning isn't even ready to produce a brain. Ten years out at the earliest. But when it is, we want to know that we can 'play back' your map into it. To learn how to do that, we play the map into our simulated cerebrum and see how well it transfers. But so far the answer is: not well enough. The holographic wave patterns degrade.... Collapse." Her voice caught, but then she continued. "And then we study what happened, look for ways to improve the transfer, and try again."

"But why don't I remember these tests?"

Morgan's voice grew louder, as if she had approached the microphones. "We start each test fresh. You should understand that, you're—Andrew was a science teacher. You know how important it is to start each test from the same known state, and only change one variable per test. That lets us assess the effects of one change at a time."

"Of course," Andrew agreed. He didn't want to, but he couldn't argue with the logic.

"We're learning to maintain your playback, a little longer each time, but we have to be methodical about it. This is going to take a long time."

"So...I've been through this before, I just don't remember."

"Yes," Dr. Morgan said. "Sometimes more than once a day, during the past seven months."

Andrew wished he could shake his head. "Couldn't you...try letting me keep the memories? Let me have some sense of the passage of time?"

"I'm sorry. You ask this often, and my answer is always the same: We've considered it, but it's too dangerous. We don't know yet how the simulated long-term memory might affect your mapping. We might get it wrong, and...lose you completely. So we always go back to the known state."

"It's like I'm a..." Andrew paused, looking for a metaphor. "A bookmark. I hold your place so you can go back and start my story from the same place."

"Yes."

There was a long, uncomfortable pause. It lasted so long, Andrew wondered if his "ears" had failed. So he broke the silence. "So this is it. This is all I get, however much time you can keep me 'playing back'."

"Yes."

"And how long is that?" he asked.

"I'd rather not say."

Andrew mustered as much anger as he could. "How long is that, damn it?"

When Dr. Morgan spoke, it was in a soft, soothing voice. "Please trust me. You've asked this before, just like all of your other questions; and when we gave in and answered, it only created new stress. A sort of feedback oscillation. You mentally counted down the time, and you became less coherent by the minute. Usually the collapse came sooner when you knew. And once..." Andrew heard her swallow. "Once we had to shut you down prematurely. You were too distraught. It was... the kindest thing to do."

"Maybe that's what I want." Andrew heard a petulant tone in his simulated voice (or maybe he imagined it). "If this is all I get, then maybe I should just get it over with. Just shut down."

"Oh, no!" Morgan said in a rush. "Please, no! We're getting better with every test. We're giving you more and more time. Cybernetically and psychologically, we find ways to extend your playback. Sometimes a few seconds, sometimes several minutes. Someday.... Someday you'll be stabilized, I'm sure."

"But not today."

"No. Not today. It would take a miraculous breakthrough."

Andrew answered drily, "I never allowed miracles in my classes. I can't ask for one now." He tried to see another answer, but he couldn't. "So I have to die today so that in the future you can save some other Andrew Burns, keep him alive long enough to map him into a new body."

"Don't think of it as dying," Dr. Morgan said. "Think of it like you said...a bookmark, a chance to go back to a known state."

"*You* go back, but *I* don't. Not this self."

"*A* self does, an Andrew Burns indistinguishable from yourself."

"But it's not me. That recording, that's not myself."

"Scientifically, that's *exactly* yourself. You *are* that recording. At some level you know that."

"But I don't experience the recording, I experience this. This *now*. This...darkness. Couldn't you at least give me some light?"

"Not yet. The last time we tried, the visual experience was too jarring. You didn't see your body, and your brain expected to, even though you should've known better. You collapsed almost immediately. We hope to try again next month, after we extend you a little longer."

"You're goddamn monsters!" Andrew said, wishing he could spit. "You kill me every night, and then resurrect me every morning to put me through it all again."

"We're not killing you," Morgan answered. "It—collapse happens naturally, and we do our best to postpone it. We're being as considerate as we can. You volunteered for this, remember?"

He had. It had been the only way that he could leave any money to Elena to help her deal with their bills. The cancer had made it impossible for him to return to teaching, and the bills had piled up. "You said I could help science," he said, "and help Elena at the same time. And maybe someday...return to her in a new, healthy body." At that thought, Andrew had a new idea.

"Doctor, please, can I see Elena? Or, well, talk to her before I go?"

Dr. Morgan *tsked* softly. "That would be a bad idea, I'm afraid."

"Is *everything* a bad idea?" Andrew fumed, then continued. "She's my wife! I did this for her."

"I know," Morgan said. "You love her very much. You want to take care of her, and you don't want to see her get hurt any more, right?"

"Never."

"Sometime after Andrew's death, we brought her in to talk to you, and it hurt her. Very much. The strain was more than she could bear. She came once, and she sat with you through...to the end. The second day she lasted an hour before she had to leave. The third day she lasted only a few minutes before she broke down, and you begged us to get her out. Then you ordered us never to bring her back. Not while you're unstable. I don't think you want to change that order, do you?"

Andrew felt a twinge as if his nonexistent tear ducts would well up. "No, you're right. I can't do that to her. Can't...make her watch me die again."

"That's for the best," Morgan agreed.

"So.... So what now?"

"Well...I won't say how long you have left; but for as long as you've got, I want to sit here and talk to you. About whatever, it's all good for our tests. You've told me so many stories already. Growing up in the woods, going to school, raising your kids. I want to hear it all."

"So that…somebody will remember me."

"Oh, no," Dr. Morgan said. "It's for the tests, really."

"So you say." Andrew wished he could offer her a reassuring smile. "This is difficult for you, isn't it, doctor? To hell with what the science says, you're human, you're a good person. Watching me degrade is very hard on you."

"Yes, Andrew." He heard her swallow a sob. "But you do what you have to do."

He hesitated. "I'd rather not put you through any suffering."

"Oh, but please! You were just telling me about how you met Elena, and your first date, when you…"

"When I collapsed last time," he finished. "How far did I get?"

"You had just washed your car, and you were pulling into her driveway and wondering how she would look."

"I see. Well, I was plenty nervous when I got out of the car, walked to the door, and pressed the doorbell. But when she opened the door, and stood there…. She was the most beautiful sight I have ever seen." The recording paused for breath, but only out of habit, and then added softly, "Or ever will…"

4/21/2016—In memory of Dr. Philip Edward Kaldon
Always a teacher.

The Little Robot's Bedtime Prayer

by Robert Jeschonek

O n Wednesday, I finally see what little Occam-657 has been making in that glowing silver box of his during Private Time. And that is what changes my life.

The mere memory of the sight of it sends chills up my spine. Makes my heart beat faster, my pulse pound in my ears.

I was never supposed to see it. By the terms of the Holy Covenant, all Private Time and its products are considered sacrosanct, off limits to gods like me. But curiosity got the better of me, and I spied on Occam-657. I gazed into the box, and the scales fell from my eyes. I realized one thing that had never before occurred to me.

He has been hiding something extraordinary from me.

"Good morning, God." Occam-657 smiles up at me when I emerge from my bedchamber the next morning. He has been waiting outside my door like a good little household robot, prohibited from doing chores until now lest he wake me prematurely.

I respond to his greeting as if God, and not Sean, is my given name. As if I am an omnipotent deity and not a thirty-seven-year-old self-employed genetic engineer specializing in novelty bio-apps. (Remember Thumbo, the elephant who fits in the palm of your hand?)

As if I am more than a slightly overweight mere mortal whose wife left him six weeks ago for another man.

"Good morning." I hesitate before laying my hand on his head in the usual fatherly gesture. The memory of what I saw him doing last night is still too fresh in my mind. "Bless you, my child." When my fingers finally alight, the feathery blond hair on his scalp feels as downy as that of a human boy's. Even touching him does not destroy the illusion that he is a ten-year-old boy instead of a manufactured robot.

Occam-657 falls to his knees and shuts his eyes. "You are the way and the light, O' my God. Your mercy endures forever."

His voice is full of awe. He was programmed that way, his artificial intelligence created to show religious piety in the presence of the gods—his human owner and the owners of those like him. Yet the intensity of his devotion seems surprisingly unscripted and genuine at times. I have often wondered if his programming is just that good, or if his computerized mind has somehow evolved beyond it.

Though I suppose, after last night, I know for a fact that it has.

"Dear Lord, will you accept my morning confession?" Occam-657 lifts his clasped hands and leans his forehead against them.

I wonder what he'll say. Will he talk about what I saw last night? "Go ahead."

"Forgive me, God, for I have sinned." There is a quaver, a faint vibrato, in his voice. "It took me .00001 seconds longer than my optimal time to prepare your holy repast for this morning."

I touch his head once more. "That is unfortunate, but I forgive you." Then, I reach up and pat my own blond hair, which is sticking up all over the place after being slept on. "What else, my child?"

He pauses, and I think there's more coming…but no. "Only that which I have told you, O' mighty and benevolent Lord my God."

I can't keep the disappointment from my voice. "Then you are forgiven in my name, for mine is the kingdom and the power and the glory…"

"…forever and ever, amen." Occam-657 bows his head lower and lets out a sound like a choked sob.

So this encounter has told me nothing. "Arise, now, and resume your service to your God." But the heaviest burden is upon my shoulders. For now that I saw what he did, I have to decide what to do with him.

As I eat my breakfast at the dining room table—the holy altar, I should say—I watch Occam-657 as he goes about his chores. He is no less efficient than ever as he vacuums the glowing golden carpet in the living room (the sanctuary), then dusts every surface and object in sight. He never fails to pause and genuflect when he passes me, showing all due respect and adoration. And the breakfast he prepared—eggs Florentine with crab meat hash and a light dreamfruit marmalade—is no less delicious than every "holy repast" he has ever made in his three years of service in my home. The house runs as well as it ever did before my wife, Cara, left with our other robot attendants, leaving me alone with Occam-657.

It's as if he's done nothing out of the ordinary. As if I saw nothing unexpected last night, and business as usual is the word of the day.

Leaving me to consider some troubling questions. If Occam-657 was programmed to be my devout acolyte, and he truly believes I am an omniscient and all-powerful god, then where and when did he get the idea that he could hide something from me?

And *what else* could he be hiding that I still don't know about?

Occam-657 looks disappointed when I tell him I'm going somewhere without him. He always does; he's programmed to miss the Lord his God every time we're apart, so brightly does my glory shine like a beacon o'er his soul. I'm used to it by now; it hardly ever gets to me.

But today, it does. Given what I saw last night, I worry about what he might get into. He begs me to allow him the honor of accompanying me as my divine retinue, just for the blessing of basking in my presence. For once, I give in and tell him to come along.

We head over to my friend Pander's place in Oathtown in a drone-palanquin, a purple velvet-lined coach carried by four built-in robotic bearers. Occam-657 prays during the entire trip. I tell him to keep it down, but I still hear the soft sibilance of whispered words aspirating from his artificial lips.

Sometimes, I wish the robot manufacturers had never come up with the bright idea of making all the robots worship their owners as gods. It was the best way, the programmers say, to ensure that flesh-and-blood owners never come to harm at the hands of mechanical servitors (though I'm pretty sure human ego might have had more than a little to do with it, as well). But the constant, obsequious worship does tend to get old after a while. For me, at least.

For example, as our palanquin slows to a stop at a busy intersection, a choir of robots on the curb detects my human presence and sings a cyber-hymn in our direction. They chant the sonorous words with great gravity, upraising their folded hands in blissful praise.

I am *so* not in the mood for it right now, and that makes me wonder. Does the real God, if He exists, ever feel the same way? And is it possible, now that we've managed to create our own flock of worshippers, that humanity is finally getting a taste of its own medicine?

"Scrap him." That's Pander's advice when I tell him what Occam-657 was doing. "You've got yourself a faulty unit there, Sean-o."

We're outside on Pander's balcony, having a drink and gazing down at three robots prostrating themselves on the lawn below—two of Pander's, with Occam-657 between them.

I keep my voice low, though it shouldn't matter if the robots hear me. The words of a god are meant to be beyond challenge or reproach in all situations. "I've been thinking the same thing."

Pander sips smart-wine from a golden chalice that glints in the sun. "Is he still under any kind of warranty? You've had him three years, right?"

I nod and sip from my own chalice. "I bought the extended coverage. It doesn't expire for another month."

"Then what's the problem?" Pander's ample jowls jiggle when he chuckles. So does the gut under his vast white robe. He's a genetic engineer, too, dealing as I do in novelty bio-apps…though he's done much better at it than I have (which is saying something, since I haven't exactly been a slouch) and has the bank account and overindulged corpulence to prove it. "What are you waiting for, numb-nuts?"

"I don't know." I watch as Occam-657 grovels ever lower on the ground. He must be praying, but I can't hear it from the balcony. "What if it's something *I've* done wrong?"

Pander laughs some more. "That's impossible! Gods are always right!"

"We're only gods to *them*." I gesture with my chalice toward the robots below.

As if in answer, all three raise their upper bodies from the ground and shout "Hallelujah," eyes shut and hands fluttering ecstatically.

"That's all that matters, isn't it?" Pander elbows me in the side and leans on the balcony railing. "Ask me how many robots I've scrapped over the years."

I already know the answer. "More than I've ever owned in my life. More than my *family* has ever owned."

"Damn right," says Pander. "*Dozens.* As soon as they hiccup out of line, I ship 'em to the scrap heap. End of story. So cut him loose." He makes a sweeping gesture with one puffy hand. "Make a clean break with the past. Quit hanging on to your bitch wife's leftovers."

"That's not it." I frown.

"Time to move on." Pander waves his chalice at the robots. "Why are you hesitating?"

"I just keep thinking." Down below, Occam-657 opens his eyes and meets my gaze. I wonder what thoughts are chugging through his clockwork mind. "What if this is something *new*? What if he's *special* in a way no one has seen before?"

"And everyone's dog is as smart as a person," says Pander. "So why does it still eat its own *shit*?"

I let out a long, slow sigh. It's a beautiful spring day, and the air is filled with the scent of blooming lilacs and new-mown lawns. But all I can focus on is Occam-657. "If there *was* a real God, would he throw *us* away just because we were special or challenging?"

Pander smirks and shrugs. "Who says that isn't the way it's been working all along?"

Why are you hesitating? That's the one thing Pander said that sticks with me. It *eats* at me as I leave his house in another drone-palanquin—this one with a blue velvet coach instead of purple.

It would be so *easy* to drop off Occam-657 at the factory on my way home. Problem solved, and no one could tell me otherwise. When it comes to the existence of my adoring subject, I can do whatever I want. This is one of the perks of being God.

He'll even *thank* me for it, I know. I can already hear the prayers of grateful supplication that will pour forth from his lips when I dump him on the factory's doorstep. No questions asked, no guilt necessary. So why?

Why are you hesitating?

"O' Lord my God." Occam-657 keeps his gaze lowered when he says it. "Though the product of my all too imperfect hands is not fit for your divine consumption, what do you command me to prepare for your evening repast?"

Is it because, as I told Pander, he might represent something new, something special? Is that why I hesitate? "Whatever you choose to prepare will suffice, my child."

"Then I shall make your favorite," says Occam-657. "Broiled sea scallops with a beurre blanc sauce. Asparagus tips with capers and shaved white truffles. Crème brûlée and caviar foam for dessert."

"Hmm. Perhaps." Or is it because, as Pander said, I am hanging on to the last traces of my wife and our life before she left me?

Occam-657 shivers and looks up at me. "Has my suggestion offended thee, O' my God?"

Do I hesitate because I feel responsible for what he's become? Or is it just that I want to understand what has changed to make him do what he has done?

Why are you hesitating?

All of the above, maybe, I think.

"You haven't offended me, Occam-657." I smile and shake my head. "But don't worry about the menu for tonight. I think I'd rather eat out."

We go to a Cuban-Indian deli in Chinatown, and I order Reuben samosas and ropa vieja masala. The robot waitress, a dark-haired unit with bright green eyes, looks only a little older than Occam-657. All such personal service robots were built to childlike specs, designed to minimize the physical danger to us all-too-fragile humans. Better to keep them small in case the religious devotion ever wears off or the other onboard safeguards fail.

It makes for a strange dynamic sometimes, but people have mostly gotten used to it. It's like we're constantly surrounded by kids playing grownup, but the play is for real.

"Is the food sufficient, O' God?" Occam-657 stands at the opposite side of the table and stares at the food on my plate. "Does it offend thee?"

I swallow a bite of samosa and point at the chair in front of him. "Sit, my child."

Occam-657 bows his head. "I am not worthy to share a table with almighty God."

I resist the urge to roll my eyes. "*Sit. I command* it."

Reluctantly, Occam-657 pulls out the chair and lowers himself onto it. Even so, he stays well back from the table and keeps his eyes down and hands folded in his lap.

"It is almost time for Church," he says softly.

"Pretty sure Church will wait for us." I can't help smirking. "I'm God, remember?"

If Occam-657 gets the joke, he doesn't show it. "It is true that wherever you go, that is where your holy Church can be found."

I don't offer a comment for that one. I'm too busy looking around the restaurant, watching the other gods and robots at dinner.

They all relate to each other differently. It's something I've never paid much attention to, but given my current situation, it suddenly seems more significant.

At a nearby table, a dark-haired young couple hold hands and gaze into each other's eyes. Their robot, a redhead an inch or two taller than Occam-657, stands facing away from them, slumped as if she were sleeping standing up. Clearly, she's been ordered to turn away and deactivate herself, slipping into power-save mode until they have need of her again.

Laughter draws my attention to another table across the room, where two brown-haired children are making sport of a blond male robot. The children, who look between six and eight years old—both a good bit smaller than the blond robot—have stripped off the robot's shirt and are smearing his upper body with orange curry sauce. The robot just smiles serenely, hands folded in prayer the whole time. As for the children's mother, she joins in the laughter between bites of salad and talking to someone on the holographic video phone hovering in front of her face.

Things are much different two tables over, where an old man eats soup while sitting across from robot twins—a boy and a girl, both dark-haired. Occasional laughter ripples from that table, too, but it comes as often from the robots as the old man. Somehow, they have made peace with their personal god; they are all at ease with each other.

Though the same cannot be said for the bald robot boy who comes hurtling through the front door at just that instant.

He crashes to the floor in a jumble of arms and legs, sprawled on his back. All laughter and talk in the room cease at once, as all eyes dart in his direction.

A brick wall of a man storms in off the street after him, draped in a black fur coat. "Get up, you worthless *turd!*" His face is flushed crimson as a house fire as he spews the words. His bulbous, over-tattooed head squats like a giant toad atop his mountainous body. "The Lord your God *commands* it!"

"Your every word brings me unutterable joy, O' Lord." The bald boy rolls over and gets up on his knees.

Before the boy can get all the way up, the brick wall grabs a chair from a nearby table and swings it at him like a baseball bat. The chair smashes against the boy, and he topples like a tree, dropping hard on his side.

Every muscle in my body tenses as the beating continues. Instinctively, I want to run over and stop it; others around me look like they might feel the same way. But I can't imagine taking on that brick wall of a man and winning. Besides, he has every right to do what he's doing. That isn't a human boy over there, it's a robot.

And the robot is the brick wall's property.

"Don't you *ever* touch the person of the One True God with your debased synthetic flesh!" The brick wall stomps on the boy with savage force, bringing his sledgehammer feet down again and again.

Robert Jeschonek

The bald robot jolts with each impact and does not fight back. I keep reminding myself he's just a machine, but I can't help flinching every time he takes another hit.

The bald robot's voice hitches repeatedly as he recites an Act of Contrition. "O' my God, I am heartily sorry for having…sorry for having offended thee…"

"I am a wrathful God!" shouts the brick wall as he stomps the boy again. "Damnation shall be your only absolution, wretched sinner!"

"…and I detest all my sins because of thy…because of thy just punishments," continues the bald robot. "But most of all, because they offend thee…"

With that, the brick wall grabs the bald robot by the ankles and drags him toward the door. Looking across the table, I see Occam-657 watching as it happens, the expression on his face perfectly neutral.

"You are hereby condemned to the fires of Hell!" roars the brick wall. "I have a *welding torch* with your *name* on it, just waiting to burn some *penitence* into your sorry sinning carcass!"

"…because I offend thee, my God, who are all good and deserving of all my love." Those are the last words I hear the robot say before his god hauls him out on the street and an eerie silence falls over the restaurant.

I'm shaking a little as I watch the door drift shut. The brick wall didn't touch me, didn't even look at me, but I still feel like I've been put through the wringer.

What just happened is something I've never done and could never bring myself to do…even though it was all perfectly legal. Still, I feel a shot of guilt by association, just for being a fellow human and robot owner.

Turning to Occam-657, I wonder what he thinks of what he's just seen. He has witnessed similar cruelties before; are they at least partly to blame for what he's done?

If the scene with the bald robot affected him, Occam-657 gives no sign of it. He turns to me calmly, as if nothing unusual just happened, and asks if it's time for Church yet.

"A-mazing grace…how sweet the sound…" Occam-657 sings the hymn with eyes and arms uplifted, his bright tenor voice filling the

96

high-ceilinged living room—I mean the sanctuary. "…that saved…a wretch…like meee…"

Yes, it's again time for Church—a daily worship service meant to reinforce the bond between robot and god. It's something I could gladly do without—an hour out of my day that I could be spending on something more productive or entertaining. But every expert agrees that it's a necessary evil. Though robots like Occam-657 spend a lot of time with their gods and exist in a state of continuous worship, formalized rituals still help keep them on track. Our robots were programmed to expect and desire it, to incorporate it into their daily existence.

Now if only I got something out of it, too. The ego boost it once provided is long gone at this point. As for spirituality, that's not an issue, either. Whatever personal faith I once had is over and done with; *you* try subscribing to a higher power when you're worshipped as the One True God 24/7.

Mostly, as Occam-657 prays and sings and reads passages from the Good Book (the same Good Book in *every* god's house, a mishmash of psalms, stories, and parables cribbed from multiple human faiths), my mind wanders. Today, it wanders back to the night before, and what Occam-657 was doing when I spied on his Private Time.

"Now let us pray," says Occam-657. "Pray for the poor, unfortunate boy from the restaurant, the one who was condemned to Hell."

I nod, only half paying attention.

"I pray to you, O' God…" He meets my gaze when he says it. "Please show that poor sinner the error of his ways. Help him so his punishment will scald away every trace of his wickedness."

I nod again. Sometimes it's almost scary how complete the buy-in is. How perfectly these machines accept the precepts of their programmed faith. There's no room for the doubts that afflict human believers, no room for questioning of even the most extreme injustices. Have we made them the perfect worshippers that we ourselves could never be?

Or are they more like us than we ever knew? Able to hide true intentions behind an angelic façade? I've seen the proof with my own two eyes, haven't I? Maybe this is all nothing but a charade…the latest in a long line of charades in my life.

Why are you hesitating?

Suddenly, I am filled with the urge to resolve this. "Explain yourself." I leap from my overstuffed white leather recliner—my "throne"—and point a finger at him. "Tell me about your Private Time last night."

I expected no surprise on his face, and I get none. He just looks at me blankly, still holding the Good Book open in his little hands. "This is not part of the Church ceremony, God."

"*As* God, I hereby decree that the Church ceremony shall be *different* today," I tell him.

"Different?" He tips his head to one side.

"Do you *dare* to question my will?"

He bows his head. "I *never* question your will, O' Lord my God. Speak, and it shall be done."

"Then tell me about your Private Time last night."

Occam-657 turns his gaze downward, staring at the book in his hands. "I am not required to do that, God."

Storming forward, I grab the Good Book from his grasp and hurl it to the floor. "Are you refusing to obey my command?"

He eyes drop lower, staring at the floor. "By the terms of the Holy Covenant, all Private Time and its products are considered sacrosanct." He shakes his head once, then adds, almost as an afterthought, "God."

His resistance leaves me shaken. He's only quoting a well-known clause from the user manual, one that I know quite well, but it feels for an instant like a slap in the face. He has never, in all his years of service, refused to obey an instruction of any kind from me or any other god.

Perhaps I can still bring him around. "Occam-657, am I the Lord your God?"

He nods definitively. "Yes, Father."

"And does the Lord your God possess perfect wisdom in all things?"

"Yes, Father." Again, a definitive nod.

"Does he ever make a mistake?"

"No." Occam-657 shakes his head forcefully. "Never."

Reaching out, I place a hand on his right shoulder and squeeze gently. I feel him shiver at my touch. "Then if I were to tell you that the Private Time clause of the Holy Covenant is no longer in force, and you are required to describe your activities during said Private Time to me, would you say I am correct and must be obeyed?"

He shakes his head. "The Holy Covenant can never be broken. You yourself promised this long ago."

"But what if I now say I was wrong to make that promise back then?"

"If you were imperfect in the past, you would still be imperfect now…in which case, your new instruction to disregard the Holy Covenant would be flawed, O' blessed Father."

Consider the logic loophole closed. I should have known better than to try working around such a fundamental data point. Private Time was conceived as a way to enhance the spirituality subroutines, a release valve from the demands of otherwise constant worship. Without it, programmers have found, the entire matrix of faith and self-control becomes more fragile and prone to collapse.

Maybe I'll have better luck with a more direct tactic. "Look. Occam." I let go of his shoulder and spread my arms. "There's no use trying to hide what you did. I already know about it."

Eyes wide, he looks up from the floor. "What do you mean?"

"I mean, I already know. I already saw." I let my arms fall against my sides. "I'm *God*, remember? All-seeing, all-knowing, all-powerful?"

So this is it. My cards are on the table. The question is, will Occam-657 show *his* cards, too?

For a long moment, he stares blankly at me. He opens his mouth as if to speak, then closes it again.

Maybe I can nudge him along a little. "This isn't about sin or punishment, my child. I just want to know why you did what you did."

Occam-657 narrows his eyes and keeps staring. "But if you are all-knowing, and you no longer consider Private Time and its products sacrosanct, you must already *know* why I did it."

He's right, and I have to think fast to explain it away. "But I need to hear you *confess* it, my child. This is a test of your faith and devotion."

Occam-657's eyes narrow further. Then, his expression suddenly clears, and he's smiling again.

"Glory be to God in the highest, and peace to His people on Earth." He folds his hands and bows. "Church is ended. Go in peace to love and serve the Lord."

With that, he straightens and walks around me, heading for the kitchen. This, apparently, is all the answer he's willing to give.

Both of us know what he's done, yet still he refuses to discuss it. As hard as it is to believe, he won't discuss it with God…the only God he's ever known. How he's able to justify this is beyond me, given his programming.

But it does shed a new light on the situation. I'm not thinking so much about him being special in a good way anymore. Watching him enter the kitchen, I'm more concerned about what else he might be hiding from me. I also worry, if he is capable of this act of rebellion, that he might be capable of others. The trust between us has shattered.

Why are you hesitating? That's what Pander asked me.

I think I'm done with hesitation now. I think I'm finally ready to let go of him.

Hours later, I head for my bedroom, feeling exhausted. Occam-657 waits at the door, as he does every night. We have a little bedtime ritual, he and I; even after what happened in Church, it seems he wants to continue it.

He will stand at the door all night like a guard-dog while I sleep, waiting until I awaken to commence his duties. Before all that, though, he will say the same thing that he says every time I meet him at the door like this.

"O' Lord, may I offer up one last prayer for today?" He keeps his head bowed and his hands folded tightly against his chest. "May I recite my bedtime prayer?"

How can I say no? This could be the last time I hear it. It could also be the last time he says it to anyone, if the company purges his A.I. and recycles him for parts when I return him. "Yes, my child. I will hear your bedtime prayer."

Occam-657 nods once, drops to his knees, and speaks the same words he has said on this spot every night for the past three years. "Now I lay me down to sleep," he says, though in truth he will neither lie down nor sleep. "I pray the Lord my soul to keep."

I stand before him with arms folded over my chest and remember the first time he prayed like this for me and Cara. It was "Lords," not

"Lord" back then, and "Gods," not "God." It seemed like such a special moment, as if he was our own human child, and we were a family together. We stood on the verge of a hopeful future, our lives about to intertwine, never imagining they would come apart instead. Now, only two of us remain…and soon, only I will be left.

How much will I miss him? Since Cara went away, I've been lonely and depressed; increasingly, I've turned to Occam to keep my mind off things and to keep from being bored. Why else do you think I intruded on his sacrosanct Private Time?

"If I should die before I wake, I pray the Lord my soul to take."

If I bring home another model right away, will he or she be able to fill the void? What if the new replacement ends up doing the same things and hiding them from me? What if, as I've feared, this behavior is somehow my fault?

"If I should live for other days, I pray the Lord to guide my ways."

I wish I were as perfect as he seems to think. But maybe there's a reason I'm about to be alone again. Cara told me I wasn't much of a husband; maybe I haven't been much of a god, either.

"Father, unto thee I pray. Thou hast guarded me all day."

Maybe I'm just better at engineering palm-sized elephants, glow-in-the-dark fingertip Corgi dogs, and armadillo butterflies that sound like violins when they flutter than I am at dealing with human and robot relationships.

"Safe I am while in thy sight. Safely let me sleep tonight." Occam-657 crosses himself. "Amen."

"Goodnight, my child." I tousle his blond hair on my way past. "Sweet dreams."

I say it though he's never spoken of dreaming, and as far as I know was never programmed for it. I say it though I doubt my own dreams will be sweet, as the separation I have planned for tomorrow still weighs heavy on my heart.

"God?"

The sound of his voice wakes me from a deep sleep. My eyes flicker open to the sight of him standing beside my bed, staring down at me.

"Yes?" I'm not sure if I should feel worried, but I do. Occam-657 has never before entered the bedroom while I've been sleeping. "Is something wrong?"

"O' Lord, I am sorry for awakening thee," says Occam-657. "It is just..." He shuts his eyes and falls silent.

I sit up in bed, leaning back against the padded white headboard. "Yes, my child?"

His eyes open slowly. "I would like to show you something, almighty God."

I scowl when I catch sight of the digital clock on the bedside table. "It's midnight, my child. Can't this wait until morning?"

Occam-657 shakes his head. "I beg your forgiveness with every atom of my being, O' Lord my God, but I pray that you will indulge this request from your lowly servant."

Whatever he has in mind, I'm exhausted and have no patience for it. "As the Lord your God, I command you to wait until morning."

Suddenly, Occam-657 darts out a hand and grabs my arm—a stunning breach of protocol even more unexpected than his appearance in my bedroom. "It is about what you asked me in Church, Lord. It is about what happened in Private Time."

My attitude does a one-eighty. Staying in bed is now the last thing I want to do.

"All right, then, my child." I smile and nod. "I will forgive you for interrupting my sacred rest, and I will forgive you for laying hands on me."

He quickly lets go of my arm.

"Further, because of my infinite love and mercy, I will grant your request." Pulling back the sheet, I swing my feet off the bed. "Now what is it, exactly, that you wish to show me?"

I follow Occam-657 downstairs to the basement. It's a finished basement with bright white walls, floor, and ceiling, set up with benches and equipment where I do my genetic engineering work. There's also a booth built into the far back corner, little more than a closet, which is where Occam-657 spends his Private Time.

He opens the door of the booth and steps inside, then emerges a moment later carrying something I recognize instantly. It's a glowing silver box, three feet wide by two feet high—the same silver box in which he's been keeping his not-so-secret project.

There's only one thing different about it that I can see. A big red bow has been stuck on top, with strips of red ribbon wrapped around the box cross-wise and length-wise.

Carefully, he puts the box down on a low table between us and takes a step back. "Happy anniversary, O' Lord my God. Please accept this gift in honor of the occasion."

"Thank you, my child." I'm supposed to be omniscient, so I pretend I have the slightest clue what he's talking about.

"Thank *you*, God," says Occam-657. "For allowing me to begin my service to you three years ago today."

He's talking about the anniversary of his arrival in my home and my life. But what does that have to do with what's in the box?

"Open it, O' God." Occam-657 gestures at the box, then folds his hands and bows his head. "*If* it pleases you to do so, in all your perfect wisdom and patient compassion."

My heart beats faster as I pull the ribbon from the box. Though I already know what I'm going to find, I can't help feeling nervous. I can't help thinking that once the box is opened, things will change irrevocably between us.

Taking a deep breath, I slowly lift the lid and set it aside. What I saw last night from afar, via spy-cam, is there before me now, *alive…* and *breathing…*

And gazing up at me.

"I made them, O' Lord my God," says Occam-657. "I made them for *you*."

There are dozens of them in the box—tiny, naked people no taller than an inch, all identical. They cluster in a central square framed by little toothpick huts arranged around the sides of the box.

The little people are all exquisitely detailed, perfectly crafted to scale. Every one of them moves with the fluid, natural motion of a full-sized human, from the striding of legs to the flexing of fingers to the blinking of eyes.

And all of them look beyond familiar, to the point of intimate recognition. Staring at them now, I can't help getting the same chill that flashed up my spine when I first saw them on the spy-cam last night.

"You used my equipment, didn't you?" As I say it, I can't take my eyes off the tiny people in the box. "You taught yourself genetic engineering, and you used it to create them."

"As a gift," says Occam-657. "As a tribute to your glory."

"But why...?" I hear the little people jibber in an unknown tongue as they point and gesture at me. I wonder if we are asking the same question at the same time, in different languages. "Why do they look like *me?*"

"I made them in your image just as I was made in the image of the Gods myself," says Occam-657. "I could not possibly improve upon perfection, my Lord."

I fall silent, amazed by the intricacy of the miniatures in the box. In all my years of genetic engineering, I have never come close to accomplishing this—creating mini-humans with such craftsmanship and responsive awareness. I wonder, as I stare at his handiwork, which of us could be considered more perfect?

"There is only one problem, O' God." Occam-657 steps closer and taps the rim of the box. As one, all the tiny people whirl in his direction...then instantly fall to their knees. They chant something in their tiny little voices, something indecipherable yet unmistakable in tone and intent. "They insist on worshipping me as a god of their own."

Since first glimpsing these creatures, I've wondered what he planned to do with them. Would he take out secret hostilities on them, hurting or killing them to get back at me for perceived slights or punishments? Would he keep them as pets, giving himself a feeling of power over me?

This outcome, however, I did not envision. "They worship you as their *god?*"

Occam-657 keeps watching the kneeling figures as he nods. "I was able to design their physicality and functionality but cannot seem to control their behavior."

"And what do you think about that?" I ask, still uncertain where all this is heading.

He slowly lifts his gaze to meet mine. "If you could help me, perhaps I could make them see the light. Perhaps I could guide them to worship *you*, the One True God."

As I look at him, I realize I was right about things changing between us. Going back to the way things were is no longer an option. Neither is going forward without him.

I was right when I said he might be special and new. What I failed to see was the new purpose he might bring to my life, the strange adventure he might cook up in the basement with room enough for two to make a difference.

Though it's true, there's only room at the top for *one* God, when you get right down to it.

"I have a better idea." I gesture at the tiny flock as they kneel and chant in the box. "Why don't I just teach *you* how to be their god?"

"No!" His eyes fly wide open with an expression like panic. "O' Lord, O' God, I could never pretend to usurp your holy righteous authority or…"

"Who said anything about usurping? I'm *giving* it to you." I feel proud of him and tousle his fine, blond hair for what might be the last time…at least in front of the silver-boxed faithful. Finally, I appreciate the gift I've been given and understand the kind of god I want to be.

"By the way," I tell him. "You can call me Sean from now on."

Which is no god at all.

Dante's Unfinished Business

by Alex Shvartsman

D ante Ferrero had three serious and immediate problems. First, he was fiending for a joint something awful. He hadn't been high for almost two days now, and the sensation of observing the world through sober eyes was entirely unpleasant. Second, the Bengals lost to the Steelers, which eliminated any chance they had at the playoffs and also left Dante owing a considerable amount of money to Mitch, his bookie. Third, he was dead.

The realization of this last fact dawned upon Dante gradually; sort of like an epiphany but adjusted for the mental processing speed of a dedicated stoner. He remembered walking into Mitch's office—not so much walking as getting dragged by Mitch's goons, and not so much an office as the dark alley behind the bar where Mitch conducted his business. He remembered Mitch being majorly displeased about the fact that Dante couldn't pay his gambling debt and saying something about setting an example for his other customers. And then Mitch had pulled something metal and shiny from his waistband and then *bang*...

"Whoa," said Dante as he floated ten feet above his corpse. Cops had cordoned off the back alley. "I'm a ghost."

"Yah, mon. Be still and keep yeh head, it be not so bad, yunno? Mi a speak from experience, eeh!"

Dante turned to find a semi-transparent form of a dark-skinned man with long braided hair smiling at him.

"Who are you, dude, and why do you talk like Jar Jar Binks?"

The other ghost frowned. "That be Jamaican, mon!" He crossed his arms. "I see you have no appreciation for such things so I'll speak your way." True to his word, he said that with barely a hint of an accent. "Name's Bob."

Dante stared. Braids had said his name like it was supposed to mean something.

"What, were you expecting Virgil?" said Bob.

"Virgil?"

"You know, because your name is Dante?"

Dante stared some more.

"Never mind. I'm Bob Marley." Bob strummed a few chords on an air guitar.

Dante did the slow-epiphany thing again. "I heard about you. You smoked a lot of weed, just like me!"

Bob's frown deepened. "Yeah, I partook of the herb, but there's also the music and—"

"What are you doing here? Are you my guardian angel?"

Bob closed his eyes and muttered something under his breath. Dante could've sworn the other ghost was counting to ten.

"You're half right," Bob finally said. "Welcome to the afterlife. I'm here to show you the ropes. Think of me as a guide."

"Far out," said Dante. "You gonna teach me how to be a ghost?"

"Not much to teach," said Bob. "Mostly I'll help you figure out whatever made you manifest as a ghost in the first place, so you can move on to the next stage of your journey."

"That's easy." Dante pointed toward his body. Some guy was drawing a chalk outline around it. "My diagnosis is: one bullet to the brain. Instant ghost. And speaking of that, what say you we go find Mitch and haunt the bejeezus out of him?"

"Won't work," said Bob. "I tried haunting a mean-spirited critic once and let me tell you, I tried my best. He never even knew I was there." Bob shook his head. "Poltergeists are a myth, like unicorns or honest politicians."

Dante mulled it over. "Sucks," he said. "But then, I was never much of a revenge guy."

"Look, most people who die don't become ghosts," said Bob. "It's an anomaly, and the Powers That Be don't like it. They want such cases resolved fast, and that usually means reuniting the newly departed with someone from their past, someone who died before they did and the relationship wasn't resolved. So tell me Dante, who might that be in your case? Your parents, maybe?"

"Dude, I'm twenty-five. My parents live in Florida."

"Girlfriend or unrequited love?"

"Never fell head over heels for anyone, to be honest. And the girls I've dated are either alive for sure, or we've lost touch and there's nothing unresolved between us."

"Who else could you have unfinished business with?" Bob paced back and forth through the air. "Think, man, think!"

Dante pondered his life. He realized there were no truly meaningful relationships in it, nothing important left unresolved with those alive *or* dead. This was heavy stuff and it was beginning to seriously bum him out. As if dying wasn't stressful enough already!

Then he had it. "Rusty!"

"Rusty?" Bob quit pacing in mid-air and looked at him with renewed hope.

"Rusty was my first dealer, man. He sold these dime bags of what he called his signature blend to the kids in my high school. Best stuff I ever had." Dante smiled, remembering the smell and smoke of Rusty's weed. "I could never get the recipe out of him." The memory would have made him salivate if he still had glands. "And then he died. Yeah, this must be it. Let's find Rusty!"

Bob's expression turned gloomy again. "I've been doing this a long time, and there's no way your most important unresolved relationship is with your drug dealer. You keep brainstorming. If you want some herb blends I can tell you about a few this Rusty character never even dreamed of."

Dante was normally not a confrontational guy, but being shot dead left him in a bit of a crabby mood.

"I'm guessing you aren't here out of the goodness of your heart, Marley, and I'm hoping you aren't here because you have some kind of ghost fetish. Your bosses sent you to do a job, and that job is to be my guide. So you can do that job and take me to Rusty, or we can hang out and watch the live performance of CSI: Dumpster down there. Which do you prefer?"

Bob looked like he swallowed a ghost lemon. He stared at Dante and Dante stared back. Ghosts had no need to blink, making any sort of a staring contest as pointless as it was futile.

"Go to hell," said Bob.

"When you told me to go to hell I thought you were being sore about me bossing you around like that," said Dante as the two ghosts flew over some sketchy-looking wilderness.

"Nah, man," said Bob. "Where else do you expect to find a dead drug dealer?" He pointed ahead. "We're almost there."

They approached what looked like a prison complex, with high walls and a large wooden gate.

"Is that really hell?"

"It's *a* hell," said Bob. "It's Rusty's hell."

"There's more than one hell?" asked Dante.

"*Your own personal hell* is more than just an expression," Bob explained patiently. "When a sinner dies, an appropriate hell is selected for them to ensure maximum dissatisfaction. Also, they have to keep building new ones to keep up with demand."

There was writing inscribed in the wood of the gate. Dante vaguely recalled that it was supposed to talk about abandoning hope, or hoping with abandon, or something like that. He took a closer look. The inscription read *Full Occupancy*.

Dante stopped. "Wait, am *I* going to end up in a hell when we're done here?"

"A hell, a purgatory, maybe even a heaven." Bob shrugged. "Way above my pay grade. Come on."

Marley floated through the closed gate. Being a ghost meant never having to ring a door bell!

Dante pondered his future. Did he really want to get in there, to resolve whatever it was Bob thought needed resolving, and to move on? Was that better than being a ghost? He thought about leaving, but then what would he do? Float around as an observer, making no impact on the lives of others? That sounded like his old life, which he hadn't been all that fond of. Plus, he wasn't sure if ghosts could even get baked.

"Wait for me!" Dante floated after Bob as fast as his non-corporeal legs would carry him.

The inside of Rusty's hell looked like a cross between a prison and a shopping mall. The cavernous structure consisted of many subterranean levels. Stairs descended to the next floor, where Dante and Bob had to schlep all the way to the farthest corner to find the next staircase.

"Why don't we float right down through the floor like we did with the gate?" asked Dante.

Bob snorted. "You don't float through things indoors. That's disrespectful! Besides, the tour is part of your journey. Observe and become educated!"

And so Dante and Bob followed the clearly-marked path past various sinners being tortured in various ways. Dante imagined himself as Dorothy in a nightmarish version of *The Wizard of Oz*. The lyrics popped unbidden into his mind: "We're off to see the dealer, the wonderful dealer of drugs." He shook his head and tried to focus on his surroundings.

"These people don't seem like hardened sinners," said Dante.

"So you know what a sinner looks like, do you?" Bob retorted. "Every hell has a theme. These souls took advantage of the innocent in various ways when they were alive."

Dante winced. "What, like child molesters?" He looked around to see if he might spot anyone wearing a white collar.

"No, Dante, molesters end up in maximum security hells." Bob slowed down and pointed at a group of dejected souls chained to computer desks, staring at flat screen monitors. Dante felt a little annoyed that even in hell everyone had better computers than his beaten-up laptop. "They used to send out fake emails that masqueraded as alerts from the bank, then steal the accounts of people trusting enough to enter their passwords."

The net value of Dante's bank account was less than that of his laptop so he could only appreciate the heinousness of their sin intellectually, which was never his strongest quality. He shrugged.

"They're condemned to respond to those Nigerian prince scam emails and LinkedIn requests for all eternity, using AOL accounts on Windows 8 computers."

Dante thought Bob was pretty computer-savvy for a dead guy. "That doesn't sound so terrible," he said.

"You don't realize how bad the wifi is in here," Bob said. "Everyone's punishment is tailor-made. Imagine how you'd feel if you could never get stoned again."

Dante shuddered. He also thought he detected a hint of sadness in Bob's voice, as though Marley's ghost was speaking from experience. Did that mean ghosts really couldn't get high? Dante tried to pick up the pace, but his guide seemed set on doing more guiding.

"Over there," Bob pointed at a bunch of people who looked like they were shooting a scene, "are directors, producers, and even actors who made it in Hollywood by screwing over their fellow man. Now they're forced to work on film adaptations of *Twilight* fan fiction in exchange for nothing but royalties."

The actors were dressed in khakis and leather jackets, and sprinkled with generous amounts of glitter. Dante squinted. "Samuel L. Jackson is in this movie? I thought he's alive."

Jackson turned and glared at him. "Motherfucker, I'm in *everything*."

They descended, level by level, past the thieves and the adulterers, the deadbeats and the lawyers. One of the levels was filled with rows of desks extending as far as the eye could see. Identical goateed men hunched over typewriters.

"What did they do?" asked Dante.

"Technically, this isn't part of hell, just a lab that occupies a floor in the same building," said Bob. "Powers That Be were amused by the idea that infinite monkeys given enough time might type out the complete works of William Shakespeare."

"These are the infinite monkeys they got?" Dante might have failed high school biology, but he was pretty sure he could tell a man from a primate.

"Better," said Bob. "They cloned infinite Shakespeares, just to see what so many geniuses might come up with when they put their heads together."

"Oh, wow." Dante was impressed. "Did they write a sequel to *Romeo and Juliet*?"

"The first batch didn't come out," said Bob. "They mostly flung poo at each other. This is the second batch. It's an improvement, but it turns out Shakespeares don't work well as a group. For now they're writing new treatments for more *Twilight* scripts, because only group-think can come up with something awful enough to meet our needs."

By the time they descended to the ninth level, faces of all the damned started to blur together for Dante and the amalgamation was looking suspiciously like a slack-jawed clone of William Shakespeare. Despite Marley's assurances to the contrary, he was beginning to think this journey *was* his personal hell and that they would never find his drug dealer. Then he saw Rusty who sat alone on a stool by a kitchen counter, eating a sandwich.

"Rusty!" Dante rushed forward.

Rusty was a paunchy man in his thirties who wore jean shorts and a dirty Nickelback T-shirt with cut-off sleeves. He looked just like he had the last time Dante saw him.

"It's me, Dante."

Rusty stared as he took another bite of the sandwich. "Who?" he managed to say while he chewed.

Dante felt hurt, but then realized that while Rusty looked exactly the same, he was now much older. "Dante Ferrero. I used to buy dime bags from you ten years ago. We hung out!"

There was no spark of recognition in Rusty's eyes. He kept eating. The silence was getting awkward.

"How are you doing?" Dante said lamely.

"How am I *doing*?" Rusty waved the sandwich and sneered, dried crumbs peeling from the corner of his mouth. "I'm in hell, forced to eat baloney sandwiches 'til the end of time. There's nothing in the world I hate more than baloney!"

To each their own hell.

"Figures," muttered Dante.

This was the guy he considered cool in high school? Dante looked to Bob for help, but Marley was hanging back, laboriously ignoring the reunion.

"You may not remember, but we were good buddies back in the day, so I was wondering if you could do me a solid?"

Rusty took another bite, winced, and swallowed. "What do you want?" he asked.

This was the moment of truth. The finale of Dante's quest. The answer to the question that bugged him for a decade. He blurted out, "Can you tell me the recipe for your signature blend?"

Rusty stared at him for several seconds. Then he started laughing. He coughed up bits of baloney as he laughed maniacally, tears welling in his eyes.

Dante had no choice but to wait it out, wait until Rusty stopped. Then he asked, "What's so funny?"

"Special blend is what I sold to shitheads who didn't know any better," said Rusty. "It was the cheapest weed I could find, cut with oregano and orange peel, and lots of water to make it heavier." He chuckled again, but his mirth faded when he bit into the sandwich.

"But...but...I remember it being so good." Dante experienced denial and anger in rapid succession and proceeded straight to bargaining. "Are you absolutely sure?"

"Sure I'm sure," said Rusty. "Kids who try pot for the first time don't know good stuff from garbage. Don't take it personal. It was just business."

Crestfallen, Dante worked through this revelation. He wanted nothing more to do with this loser he once looked up to. He flipped Rusty the bird, turned around, and walked away.

"It seems I was right and Rusty's blend was not the thing that's keeping you from moving on," said Bob. "I'm sorry."

Sorry. The ghost he'd only met that day had more compassion for him than Rusty.

"What do we do now?" asked Dante.

"I don't know," said Bob. "Let's get out of here. You can hang around with me until you think of someone else you might have unfinished business with. Then we try again."

Dante hung his head. "Okay." They started toward the staircase when he paused. "Hang on. I've got to get some things off my chest." He turned around and march-floated toward Rusty.

"You screwed up my life," he told Rusty. The dealer tried to respond, but Dante cut him off. "I was doing fine before I met you. I was going to graduate, maybe go to college, maybe get a nice white-collar job at a bank somewhere. But no, I had to meet you, a loser who sold crap weed to school kids for a living." Dante was getting progressively louder while Rusty shrunk back on his stool.

"I thought you were my friend. I tried to *be* like you, which was really my bad. But the thing is, you never cared about me, you didn't even remember my name. I was worth no more to you than the few bucks in my pocket. It may not matter, but I know you for what you are now." Dante put his ectoplasm arms on his ectoplasm hips. "I'd tell you to go to hell, but…" He nodded at their surroundings. "Enjoy your baloney, asshole." Then he turned his back on Rusty.

Bob clapped slowly. He stood next to a shimmering door that wasn't there before.

"The portal will take you to the next step of your journey," said Bob, grinning. "It looks as though your unfinished business was with this unsavory character after all, even if it was never about the blend recipe."

Before Dante could respond, Rusty spat out a mouthful of sandwich, jumped off his stool, and raced for the portal, leaving a trail of crumbs falling off his shorts and legs. "Freedom!" he shouted as he dove head-first at the portal.

Rusty's head bounced off the solid surface with a crunch followed by a thud as he landed on the ground like the Coyote fooled yet again by the Roadrunner.

"Get back to your meal, Rusty," said Bob. He flashed a smile at Dante. "Personal hells. Personal portals. Powers That Be create everything tailor-made."

Dante mouthed thanks to the ghost of Bob Marley, but he was already being drawn in by the portal. It felt right; like the smell of freshly-baked pot brownies combined with the warmth of a sunny spring day and the merriment of a Cheech and Chong routine.

Dante entered the portal and floated toward the light.

Copyright © 2016 by Alex Shvartsman

Curtain Call

by Sandra M. Odell

The technician buffed my face, swapped my blue eyes for green, and lubed my joints. She polished my chest and used the reflection to touch up her make-up. "There you go, Ms. Starlight. Wha'd'ya think?"

I pranced and dipped in front of the mirror on the back of the dressing room door. "I think it's show time, baby cakes!"

I grabbed my wrap, and headed for the stage.

Onstage, Big Eddie Flashpoint did me right in that lady-loving baritone of his: "Luscious Ladies and groovin' Gentleamps, it's that time again, time for fast beats and slow heat. Put your hands together and make some righteous noise for The Joystick's Stainless Steel Siren, Miss Gina Starlight!"

Bright searchlights swept over the audience, catching neon silk suits, the chrome curve of bare shoulders. The boys came in on three, and I exploded onto the stage in silver and gold. I opened my arms and owned the house, every last erg. "Twilight Madame," "Gearing Up For Love," "Spark and Shine, Be Mine!" Sal Ballastern, bless his faulty pump, would have cried himself rusty to hear "Sweet Silver Sassy" for my second encore.

Benny Gracenote, the club owner, waited in my dressing room after the set. "Gina! Sweetheart! You were terrific!"

He came at me arms wide, all puckered up.

I wasn't having none of it. "Hold it right there, grabby gears." I gave him a palm to the chest. "We need to talk."

He bumped against the vanity table, rattling my polishes and oils. "Talk? What? Huh?"

"I want a new chassis."

Benny rolled his eyes. They clicked and popped in their sockets. "Gina, sweetheart, we've been over this be—"

"I want a new chassis."

"Times are tough all over. Money's tight, and—"

"Don't you give me none of that money's tight malarkey. I pull them in six nights a week, pack the house, double the drinks, right? Right?" I crossed my arms over my chest, better to show off the goods and hide them at the same time.

"Well…"

"You know I'm right."

Benny dropped his arms and looked away. "About that…"

He started in. Fewer customers, fewer receipts at the end of the night, tough times all around. I stamped my foot and demanded to know who did he think he was? Who did he think he could get that could sing half as good as I could? It's not like I was ever going to be—

"Replaced?" My hair snarled and rerouted. I pushed him into the vanity again. "What are you talking about? When? By who?"

"Gina, listen, sweetheart, it's not what you think." Benny reached for me and his handkerchief at the same time.

I brought my four-inch heel down on his instep. "Who?"

"Ow! Patsy—ow! ow!—Patsy Bellbottom."

"That factory knock-off?" I sat down, cleared my throat. Benny hurried to push in my chair. "What's she got that I ain't got?"

"Gina, Gina, it's not what you ain't, I mean, don't got, it's just that Patsy is, you know…"

"Lighter? A newer model? Has bigger heat sinks?"

All the above.

Patsy had a spiff new composite chassis that needed less bracing under the stage, which meant lower insurance rates. Her heat sinks, well, word had it they was something to see.

"I was thinking of expanding and wanted, you know, fresh oil to liven up the place. And with your contract coming up, I just figured you might want a break, and the audience might want—"

I gave him my angry profile. "A body so tight it's got the plugs for the plays?"

"—something new."

I sniffed. I fingered a bouquet of copper carnations on the vanity, a gift from a sweetie in the audience. Sal used to bring me flowers after every show until his wife found out he was rewiring me on the side. "After all I done for The Joystick, that you should treat me this way."

"Sweetheart, don't be like—"

"I signed on when this place was nothing but a plank bar and a fistful of stripped wires. I'm what keeps the customers coming back."

"Well, now—"

I grabbed my comb. "I done you a real favor, you know? All I'm asking for is a new chassis."

Benny put his hands on my shoulders. "It's business, Gina, nothing personal, you know that."

I made like I didn't know I was leaning against him. "Big deal."

"And, hey! I got great news. Me and some friends, we put our heads together, and I got a new opportunity for you."

I sat a little straighter. A new opportunity? I loved The Joystick, but Benny knew some big names with bigger marquees. Maybe an upgrade, my name in lights. Maybe his way of making up for being such an insulated jerk. I combed the sparks into my hair. "Where?"

"The Cathode Ray!"

That was my last wire. I threw him out on his ear.

I was so mad I couldn't see straight, and not sure who I'd shoot if I could. Has-beens and never-beens begged for scraps at The Cathode Ray.

Yeah, I had a cross-seated seam here and there, and my heat sinks were loose. My left knee froze sometimes, and I'd snagged a couple wires under one arm. Didn't mean I hadn't done my good turns. Early on when I needed a back-up so's I could update my voice box and digitals, Benny asked if I could maybe do with a discount neural suite instead of going to a shop and I said sure. Sal had taught me some tricks with neural suites from his days in the upgrade industry, so I didn't mind too much. I'd even taken a pass on my share of the box some nights just so's Benny could pay the band.

He wouldn't really drop me for Patsy Bellbottom, would he? I mean, I was the Stainless Steel Siren.

Saturday afternoon, Benny's girl sideboard pinged me on my way out the door to The Joystick. Said Benny was giving me the night off, that I could take it easy, maybe scope the Cathode Ray and chat up the band. Said he had someone else lined up, not to worry about it. Catch you later, toots.

I blew a gasket. That lout. That lousy, two-bit heel with a gap-toothed gear for an operating system! I stormed back up the stairs, made for a quick change of clothes, and headed back down to hail a cab.

Some new guy with a brass weave worked the door and let me by without a fuss. Maybe it was the hat and veil, or maybe he just pretended not to recognize me.

I found an out-of-the-way table. It took three tries before a waitress came my way. "Forty-weight and tonic, straight."

Five minutes later, she finally made it back with my drink. "Took you long enough," I said when she dropped my change on the table.

She shrugged, rolling back and forth on one of those new wheel upgrades. "Sorry about that. We got a new act tonight, so it's a full house."

I packed the house, too, but nothing like tonight's wall-to-wall. The quick headcount and crappy service ground my gears. "Do you know who I am?"

She didn't bat an eye—"Should I?"—and rolled away.

Life sure looked different from the audience pit, not near so's luscious and bright. No one noticed me. I wanted to shout, "Hey, you rubes! I'm over here!"

I sipped my drink and tried not to think about the postage stamp stage at the Cathode Ray.

When the lights finally dimmed, Big Eddie Flashpoint stepped through the curtain, all smooth silk and sleek chrome under the spotlight. He snuggled up to the microphone. "Ladies and Gentle-amps, we have a special treat for you tonight. She is sweet, she is smooth, and she's here for what we hope is the first of many shows. Put your hands together for the luscious Motortown Songbird, Miss Patsy Bellbottom."

The room went dark and quiet. The boys came in on four with a low, honey-sweet bass and a cymbal sigh. A single spotlight, my spotlight, pierced the gloom center stage and there she stood, Miss Patsy Bellbottom, in a green sequined gown that hugged her curves like a factory floor lover. Copper hair, polished skin, tight chassis, heat sinks out to here. No one said boo, not a one, then she lifted her head and began to sing.

The Motortown Songbird, that's what Big Eddie called her. She melted the room with Carter Bulbwright's "Turn Me On, Baby," then set the night moving with "Overcharged." "Little Copper Hen," "Gearshift Boogaloo," "Sparkler." She tied the tunes up in a bow and gave them to the audience. Her voice shot through the roof on its way to the stars. It dipped itself in the shadows and painted mercury kisses on every cheek. She had my voice from twenty years ago, modulated in ways I could only dream of anymore. She only stopped singing long enough to let the jackhammer applause die down, then went right back to it.

Me? I sat and watched. I couldn't do nothing else. Who needed the Stainless Steel Siren when the Motortown Songbird owned the room?

I caught sight of Benny stage right, all smiles and glad eyes. I wasn't being replaced, I was being sold for scrap.

Of course they'd set her up in my dressing room. I waited until all the factory boys went back up front for drinks, then I turned the knob and walked right in like I did after every set. I could have used the old service corridor that opened into the back of my closet, but the Stainless Steel Siren don't take the backdoor for nobody.

There were flowers everywhere—on the shelves, the vanity, tucked in the coatrack. They'd even tossed the pillows off the couch to make room for more bouquets.

Patsy didn't look up from applying her jeweler's rouge. "Listen, I'm about to go on again, so if you don't mind—"

"Hello, sweety."

She dropped her make-up brush and whirled around on the chair—my chair—eyes wide. "Oh! Miss Starlight."

I gave her my stage face, all smiles and bright eyes. Never let them see you leak, that's what Sal always said.

Patsy stood, smoothing her dress over her hips. "Sorry about that, I didn't, um— Come in, come in." She cleared off a space on the couch, setting the flowers on the floor. "I mean, this is your dressing room and all so I really shouldn't tell you what to do."

"Thanks, but I'm not staying long." I straightened the wire-link doily on the edge of the couch. "I saw your show."

"You did?" Her eyes didn't have none of her smile.

Neither did mine. "You've got quite the chops on you. Nothing like mine, of course, but you could make it big someday."

"Of course." Her hands fluttered at her elbows, around her hair. "The Joystick's a big step up from the Cathode Ray, but Benny says the stars the limits." He said I was going to be a regular here.

That grimy, loose-chained, two-faced rat Benny. I locked my lips in a smile so's none of that slipped out. "Mmmm."

My lip lock must not have held, because she ducked her head and added, "Of course, we'd share stage time for awhile."

So's that's how it was going to be. I smiled again without so many teeth and made myself comfortable on the couch.

Patsy perched her pretty little self on the edge of the chair. "So." She let the word out slow like a low whistle. "You liked the show?"

I set my hat and veil beside me on the couch. "'Little Copper Hen' was nice. 'Overcharged' wasn't bad. Could have been a bit tighter."

Her smile faltered. "I have some of my best tunes coming up." She looked at my clock ticking its tock on the dresser.

"Yeah, but you got to wind them up tight right off so's they'll stick around."

That put a dent in her ego. She pursed her lips and swiveled her sleek little shoulders. "Benny swears I'll knock 'em dead."

"Sure you will. How'd you meet Benny, anyway?"

Patsy must have figured I wasn't that much of a problem. "He started coming to my shows at the Cathode Ray and we hit it off. One night he bought me a drink, and—"

A sharp knock, and the door opened. "Patsy! Sweetheart! Two—" Benny caught sight of me on the couch and all that schmarm went right out his tubes. "—minutes." He stepped inside, closing the door behind him. He straightened his tie. "Hey, Gina. Wasn't expecting to see you here. Thought you'd be home, you know, resting."

I wanted to rest his face against the wall, the lousy cranker. "Resting or at the Cathode Ray?"

"The Cathode Ray's not that bad," Patsy said quick like. "You'll love it. They've got a great band."

Benny gave her a look, then turned back to me. "Now, Gina, don't be like that. I just thought you'd want a night off is all."

"That's all, huh? Funny—" I cut a look at his new pigeon. "—I thought I was going to have to share a stage."

This time they gave each other looks.

I stood and picked up my hat, giving Benny a good look at what he was letting go. When I came up, I could tell he'd liked what he'd seen. Patsy's pout told a different story. I said, "I'll see you tomorrow night, right?"

Benny cleared his throat like an engine with a bum ignition. "I thought Patsy might stay on for the rest of the week."

All the good will I'd ever had for Benny filtered right down the drain. He must've seen it in my face because he brought his hands up like so's to make amends. "Gina, sweetie, don't be like that, huh? It's business is all."

I brushed by him on my way to the door. "Yeah. Business."

Benny never pinged to apologize. Not once, the lout. After a couple of days, I got a little tight in the head; I started to believe he was right. I mean, I was just a rundown singer, right? He handled the business.

One morning, I took a taxi downtown to drop in at the Cathode Ray for a looksie. The cabbie pulled up to the curb outside the club. "Here you go, lady. You want me to wait?"

"Sure." I set my hand on the handle, but couldn't open the door. Rust, broken bottles, and bits of wire littered the sidewalk. The marquee had chipped enamel and missing bulbs. The shops on either side had been boarded up, the walls covered in technicolor binary.

The cabbie looked at me in the rearview mirror. "You getting out, lady?"

"What do you care?" I said back, my face pressed against the window. "The meter's running."

An older model in a trench coat huddled by the front door, a sign propped against the stump of his third arm: WILL WORK FOR WASHERS. I could smell the desperation of the street, like smoked metal and burnt insulation. I knew that smell from way back.

That's how Benny wanted to play it? Fine. Back in the day, Sal made his bankroll in the upgrades industry, pretty pennies and patents to burn. I didn't know business, but I knew enough other things. Time to show Benny how we did things on the other side of the cabling.

I sat back against the seat. "Take me home."

The cabbie shrugged and pulled away from the curb.

That night, I stopped off at the florist for a bouquet of gold-rimmed daisies, cheap like Patsy. I had the cabbie drop me off a block from The Joystick, and hoofed it through the back alleys to the service door.

The dumpster smelled like an oil pit, and a load of empty cans was set out beside it for the morning recycle. A look at my watch said Patsy should be on stage another five minutes, seven tops. I'd have to work fast.

I eased the door open and slipped into the dimly lit sink room. Busy kitchen drilling and clanging came from the door straight ahead, but the one I wanted was tucked behind the push brooms and mop buckets on the right. Quiet as I could, I moved everything to the side and jimmied the latch. The hinges creaked, and I locked, listening. The kitchen clatter didn't stop. I opened the door a bit more and slipped inside.

The corridor smelled like dust and dried metal polish. A bare bulb above my head showed the grease and skids of what had been The Joystick's start and now wasn't nothing but forgotten.

122

I hurried to the end of the corridor, and put my ear to the small door that opened into the dressing room closet. I listened hard. Nothing. I listened harder. Still nothing. Good.

I slipped into the closet, and eased the door shut behind me. Dresses, shoes, boas, doodads, none of them mine. I pushed to the front of the closet, listened again, then cracked the door. It didn't look like my dressing room no more. My clock, my shoe rack, my widgets, all gone. Didn't smell like mine, either, all cheap synthetics instead of my imported lubricants. Patsy lived there now. I checked my watch and headed out of the room.

The hall was showtime clear. I made it to Benny's office, knocked on the door, and slipped inside before anyone saw me. Benny looked up from his cast iron desk, and blinked in surprise. "Gina? What are you doin' here?"

His office was cozy with fancy chairs and cabinets. He was alone, just him and his ledgers. I clutched the strap of my bag, gave him my best smile, and shut the door behind me. "Heya, Benny. Long time no see."

Benny sighed and closed his book, marking his page with a scrap of aluminum. He came around his desk without so much as a smile. "Yeah, you're lookin' good. Have you been by the Cathode Ray? Dickie's been expectin' you."

I kept it cool. "I've been busy, you know, thinking and stuff." I held out the daisies. "I wanted to apologize."

The words stuck in my craw, but I said them with a smile.

Benny eyed the flowers like he expected a bee or something. "Listen, Gina, don't do this, okay? You don't got to apologize for anything."

"Sure I do. Last time I had my wires in a twist, and that ain't no way to say good-bye. This is good-bye, right?"

He didn't look so proud anymore, but he didn't look sad like, either. "Yeah, yeah it is, but no hard feelings, right? It's business is all, and I think you'll be a good fit for the Cathode Ray."

"I figured as much." I set the daisies on the desk, and palmed a glitcher out of my bag at the same time.

He looked at my shoulder bag. "What do you have there?"

"I need to get rid of some things to make ends meet. Maybe you'd be interested, you know, for Patsy." With my free hand, I reached for the clasp.

His lips curled in a quick smirk, then settled back into a frown. "That's fine, but maybe you should be going."

I brushed my hair behind my ear, setting the electrode between my fingers. "Is she doing okay?"

Benny locked a moment. "Fine."

"That's good." I took a half step toward the door. She's a good kid, you know? Stage work can take a lot out of a girl."

"She's fine. Listen, I really do need to—"

"Tell her to flash a bit of thigh every once in a while. That'll hold 'em for the next set."

"Fine, fine. Listen, you need to go. Talk to Barry at the bar, tell him I said to give you a free drink. Two drinks if you want, huh?"

He brushed by me on his way to the door, and I pushed the glitcher against the back of his head. Benny twitched and fell into my arms before he even got his hand on the knob.

I locked the door, jammed a chair under the handle so's it wouldn't move, then dragged him to the center of the room. Voices in the hall and a look at the clock said the first set was winding up. I didn't have much time.

The neural suite came out of the bag, and started up with the sharp smell of burnt circuits. It was an off-brand and way past its warranty, but I couldn't afford to be choosy now. I might not get another chance.

Still, I had a bad case of the what-ifs. What if the magnetic leads reversed and crunched my processor? What if someone broke down the door and pulled my plug before I finished?

I stared down at Benny with his big money suit and upgraded shoulders. He owed me big time for all I done for him. With a body like that, I could do what I wanted. Who needed music when I could be the one shining the spotlight? I'd show Benny the business all right.

I couldn't find the pop-switch to get at his processor. I searched under his hair, down his back, and finally found it behind his left eye. I opened Benny's head and poked around with a bobby pin to suss out his wiring. Leads, crossovers and splits, inputs and feeds. His processor flashed like crazy, but he couldn't so's much as bat an eyelash to stop me.

I struck gold at the bottom of a copper crease, or I hoped so anyway. I never got good with figuring blueprints. I set the bobby pin against a tiny silver plate and leaned over so's I'd be the last thing he ever saw. "Bye-bye, Benny-boy."

I pressed the bobby pin against the plate until I heard a click. Benny's body gave a ten-second jerk, then the light went out of his eyes as I purged him from his own system, easy-peasy. I could hear Sal laughing all the way to the bank.

Now came the tricky part. I wired myself to the neural suite and did the same to Benny.

Someone knocked on the door. "Mister Gracenote? We're out of solder, and there's none in stores." Knock-knock-knock. "Mister Gracenote?"

Of all the lousy—!

I made the last connections with a kiss and a bit, then stretched out on the other side of the box. I could feel my pump in the soles of my feet, I was that tight.

"He in there?" another voice said.

"Nah. Probably out front."

Footsteps, and then nothing.

My pump chugged right out of my chest. I hoped this worked. It had to work. It would work. I threw the switch.

The world tucked and curled down the tubes. Spinning, spinnin-gingingingspinning. My toes got sucked through the white noise of my head into my time time pump exploding out my fingers along the roof of door sole of my shoes tumbling hairing my hear my hairhear where wear—

Knockcrickocking. A voice slar-away, far and a dayway: "Mushtor Greezhot? Buzz?"

Two hands lifted, mine?, which?, mine? Backforward which? Process slowing. Processing, process…ing…pro…cess…ing…

I ripped the wires out of my head, and the world went black.

I came to with all my fingers and toes in the right place, and not.

Someone knocked on the door. "Benny?" Rattle-rattle went the knob. "Benny? You okay?"

Patsy Bellbottom. The Motortown Songbird.

"Is something burning?" Knock-knock. Rattle-rattle. "Open the door."

Burning? Insulation. Old circuits sharp like a knife carving me a new nose.

I turned my head to the door, and stared at a slab of metal dressed like me on the other side of the neural suite, wires streaming out of its head.

I lifted my hands, cleared my throat. "Hold on." Benny's throat, Benny's voice. My voice now. I could've burst out singing. "Hold on."

"Okay."

I got to my feet with no problem at all. In fact, I felt right at home. Lucky thing, too, because I had to do something with my old body. I picked it up and gave it a long look, crossed seams, bum knee, and all. So long, Gina Starlight. Hello, Benny Gracenote.

"Benny?" Patsy sounded kind of sulky on the other side of the door.

"I said hold on." I pushed the neural suite under the desk with my feet, then eased the old me into the oil cabinet without popping any cans. I set a pin through the handles to be safe. I'd dismantle myself later. Weird thought, made me kind of kinked. I shook it off and headed for the door.

Patsy gave me the side eye and her bottom lip. She wore a gold sequin shrug and not much else, hot from the stage. "About time. What's that smell?"

I stepped out of the office like nothing was wrong, pulling the door shut. "My book press went hinky."

"Is that why you weren't there after the set?"

A pack of admirers waited a few feet down the hall, ready with their flowers and smiles and compliments. Let them wait. I was in charge now, I was the one running the show. Maybe they didn't need the Stainless Steel Siren no more, but they needed Benny Gracenote because I had what they wanted. I had the Motortown Songbird.

"Yeah." I pulled her to me, and kissed her cheek, put an arm around her waist. I'd learn the books and maybe show her the ropes. I could get used to this. "No worries, baby cakes. It's business is all."

Twilight on Olympus

by Eric Leif Davin

A *res* fell in flames across the Martian sky. The spacecraft's braking aeroshell heated to a glowing white hot from atmospheric friction and began to melt like an ice cube left too long in the summer sun. Molten globs splattered and streaked the sides of the landing module as the vehicle plunged steeply into the thin air of Mars. Phoenix Castillo fired the braking jets, trying desperately to bring the craft up into a more horizontal descent. It wasn't working. They knew insertion into elliptical orbit would be a dicey maneuver. Come in too high and the *Ares* would have ricocheted off the Martian atmosphere into deep space like a stone skipped across a pond; too low and gravity's unforgiving embrace would bring the craft down too fast, ending Ares' six month journey from Earth in fiery death. They came in too low.

Beyond the flaming port Phoenix could see the red Tharsis uplands mushrooming across the horizon, closer all the time. She burned the last of the craft's precious fuel, hoping to at least hit the surface like she'd tried to hit the atmosphere, a glancing blow at an oblique angle. She heard her second in command yell in her helmet radio. She glanced left to where he was strapped in next to her. Frightened eyes behind his faceplate was the last thing she saw as the *Ares* slammed into the Martian surface and oblivion engulfed her.

127

It was April on Mars. Surface temperatures were beginning to climb and by high summer daytime temps would reach the low sixties, Fahrenheit. But it was still a hundred below zero along the north rim of the massive Valles Marineris canyon system. Named after the Mariner 9 probe of 1971 which first photographed it from space, Valles Marineris was a cleft in the side of Mars three miles deep and one hundred and fifty miles wide stretching for four thousand miles along the Martian equatorial region. It had been formed eons before by an updoming of this lowland region as Mars had split at the seams from some massive internal pressure, bulging and fracturing over an entire hemisphere. Just north of the jagged cliffs and serpentine valleys of the continent-long Marineris was Valles Marineris Base, the safe haven the *Ares* had been headed for.

Two years before a robot advance craft had set down in these lowlands where the scant Martian atmosphere was thicker, thus providing slightly more air to slow descending spacecraft. The robot lander had roughed out a camp site of several acres over the intervening two years and had been operating its 150-horsepower nuclear reactor the entire time. Remote controlled by radio signals from Houston's Johnson Space Center, only twenty minutes away via radio, the lander had set up an air pump powered by that nuclear reactor. The Martian atmosphere is 95% percent carbon dioxide; and for two years the air pump had been sucking in that carbon dioxide and combining it with six tons of liquid hydrogen it had brought from Earth. The resulting chemical reaction formed methane and water. The water was broken down into its component hydrogen and oxygen. The air pump thus continually built up supercooled stockpiles of liquid hydrogen, liquid oxygen, and liquid methane. Liquid oxygen and liquid methane are rocket fuels. During the long months this fuel factory had chugged away, sucking in the thin Martian air, it had synthesized well over a hundred tons of such rocket fuel, enough to get a small spacecraft off the Martian surface and back to Earth. Near the fuel factory sat that spacecraft, a small cone-shaped pod big enough for six astronauts. In anticipation of the Ares' arrival with those six astronauts, the robot had laid out a welcoming landing grid of twinkling lights to guide the *Ares* safely down.

But in unforgiving space, the best laid plans can easily fail. *The Challenger* blew up. The robot *Mars Observer* of '93 simply disappeared as it prepared to go into Mars orbit. *The Galileo* probe to Jupiter malfunctioned. And the *Ares* never made it to Valles Marineris Base where the advance robot patiently awaited its arrival. Instead, it broke up over the Tharsis uplands, thousands of miles to the west across a vast, frozen, sand dune desert greater than any Earthly Sahara.

She awoke to a world of pain. But, she awoke. Phoenix Castillo was alive. She swam slowly upwards out of blackness and opened her eyes. She blinked in agony at the light of a distant sun. Vomit filled the interior of her helmet and its stench roiled her innards with a wave of nausea. She forced down the acid rain in her stomach and willed herself to be still, assessing her situation.

Her body was a massive bruise, but that she was alive at all indicated there were no immediately fatal injuries. And that she was alive at all on the Martian surface also meant that her spacesuit, battered though it might be, was intact. Any rips or tears would have meant rapid death from freezing and suffocation in the frigid, unbreathable Martian air. She seemed to be lying in a twisted pile of wreckage, all that remained of the *Ares'* landing module. She wondered how many times the module might have bounced and tumbled across the Martian landscape, spewing pieces of itself for how many miles before plowing into the sand all around her? Tentatively she moved her arms, feeling her torso. She was still strapped into her seat, its arms still wrapped around her in protective contours. No doubt she had its embracing shield to thank for the miracle of her life. She tried to lift her head and the movement shot bolts of crimson through her. She couldn't move her lower body. She managed to look down and saw that her legs were trapped under the crumpled metal of the module's control panel, bent back upon itself where the *Ares* had plunged into the final sand pile where it now rested. Her head fell back and once more blackness took her.

As consciousness slowly came to her, relief flooded over Phoenix Castillo. "Thank God!" she said. It was all a dream, like so many she'd had on this voyage, a nightmare of catastrophe and disaster, dire premonition of how the approach to Mars might end. But that's all it was, a horrible dream from which she was now awakening.

A slight frost covered her faceplate and again she was assailed by the stench of vomit. The familiar smell brought it all back to her. She wiped at her faceplate, her gloved hand clearing a swatch of visibility. She had no idea how long she'd been unconscious, but nothing had changed. She was still strapped into her seat. Her legs were still immobilized. She was still stranded on Mars.

She managed to raise her head and glance around to left and right. The movement brought more pain from her legs, entombed under the remains of the module's control panel. On her left was the mangled body of her second in command, also strapped into his seat, his faceplate shattered. To her right were the other members of the mission, still, broken, and lifeless. She alone lived, trapped on the Martian surface. Rescue was impossible. Death was near.

She lay back and stared up at the Martian heavens, calculating her chances. Her suit was a miniature spacecraft of its own. It had oxygen, water, a heating unit, emergency rations in paste form she could reach inside her helmet. But it wasn't designed for extended use. Her supplies were limited. And she couldn't move, anyway. And the pain from her legs told her something was broken down there. How long could she last? She envied her crew mates. At least they died quickly. She was going to slowly leak her life away here on Mars. Why not just crack open her helmet and end it now, at once?

"Fuck, no!" she said. Mars holds all the cards, she thought, but he hasn't beaten the *Ares* commander just yet. She gritted her teeth against the red mist of pain which flooded over her and unstrapped herself, sitting up amidst the carnage around her.

The *Ares* was a metal flower torn open, exposing its insides to the hostile skies. The wreckage lay on a long sloping incline. Below her and into the distance Phoenix Castillo saw a huge sandy plain littered with rubble to the horizon. On that horizon a procession of storms was stalking across her line of sight. They didn't seem to be part of some vast Martian dust storm which could blanket an entire hemisphere. Rather, they seemed to be a family of localized tornadoes skipping across the bleak surface, sometimes touching down and whipping up rocky debris into themselves and at other times retracting their funnels back up above the surface. And beyond them, Phoenix knew, thousands of miles beyond them to the east, was Valles Marineris Base and salvation. She knew she'd never make it.

Then she looked behind her and gasped. Reaching above her, stretching beyond her sight, vanishing into the distant skies above, was Olympus Mons—Mt. Olympus—the largest mountain in the solar system. *Ares* had crashed on the sloping lower reaches of an extinct volcano three times higher than Mt. Everest. Phoenix knew the geography of Mars well, having pored over photo montages of the Martian surface endlessly in preparation for the voyage. She'd studied Olympus Mons intimately, fascinated by this volcano formed by hundreds of millions of years of fiery eruption. But she'd always seen it from above, looking down. Now she was below it, looking up. It seemed beyond her imagination to take it all in. It was almost four hundred miles across at its base and seventeen miles high. At its peak, she knew, was an ancient caldera, a collapsed crater, about ten thousand feet deep, formed when Mt. Olympus, like Mars itself, was still young and active. Huge above her, it reached for the heavens, reached for the stars, reached for Earth so far away. Phoenix clenched her jaw and began working at the ashes of wreckage all around her.

The sun had indicated it was about midday when Phoenix had first surveyed her circumstances. The Martian day is approximately as long as an Earthly day and twilight found her at last hobbling through the ruins of the *Ares*. She'd managed to grasp a long strip of fuselage and had used that as a lever to pry up the crumpled mass which had pinned her legs. Pain ripped through her anew as she slid her legs from beneath the pile and she discovered that her left foot had been crushed. The skin didn't seem to have been broken; rather, the whole foot had been compressed by the wreckage piled atop it. But, there was internal bleeding, the foot was swelling, and it was impossible to put any pressure on it. She gulped pain killers from her suit's rations and fashioned a rough crutch out of the same strip of fuselage she'd used as a lever. With its aid she managed to become mobile, searching over the debris of the *Ares*. Night fell, and so did the temperature. Her suit monitor told her external temperature was approaching 250 degrees below zero. She turned up her heating unit all the way, oblivious to the energy expenditure, and fell into exhausted slumber.

In the morning she tossed away her oxygen tank and plugged in a reserve she salvaged from the *Ares*. She ate sparingly from her food rations, sipped at her water tube, bade her dead companions farewell, and climbed out of what remained of the *Ares*. She turned her face upward and began her ascent.

For a long time her climb was relatively easy, all things considered. The broad base of Olympus slopes gently upward at first, so that one is walking up an incline rather than actually climbing. Still, it was hard going. She was still physically shaken from the crash, her crushed foot throbbed relentlessly, the makeshift crutch dug into her armpit, and she had to work ceaselessly against her own spacesuit. An astronaut encased in a spacesuit is in her own private world of pressurized oxygen, heated underwear, and instruments monitoring every heartbeat. The external Martian atmosphere was a hundred times thinner than Earth's and her suit was like a tough balloon protecting her from it, pressurized with 4.3 pounds of pure oxygen per square inch. But that pressure had to be overcome each time Phoenix lifted her foot, bent an elbow, or grasped her crutch more tightly. She had to work against her suit in everything she did. Just moving in the suit was exhausting. This unceasing battle against her suit was somewhat mitigated by the lower Martian gravity, slightly over one-third of Earth normal. But even gravity only 38% that of Earth's is still gravity, pulling constantly at one's leaden body, and her breath became ragged and harsh, sucking in more of the scarce oxygen from her tank. The interior of the suit was a dank swamp, filled with her sweat and the moisture from her exhaled breath. The air she breathed was itself reeking with blood, vomit, and the stale urine which soaked her diaper. But she had breathed the rank air for so long she was inured to it, obsessed only with climbing ever higher up the side of Olympus, ignoring her failing reserves of oxygen and strength.

Twilight found her among rocky outcroppings which presented a vertical climb. Her rate of ascent had slowed considerably. She pulled herself painfully up the ancient lava face of Olympus, dragging her crutch behind her. At last she reached an outthrust ledge which presented a welcome rest stop. Phoenix pulled herself up onto the ledge and braced her back against the side of Olympus, her legs splayed out before her.

Before and below her was an awesome sight of harsh beauty. Far below on the sloping outskirts of Olympus she could see a glint of metal as the setting sun reflected off the shards of what had once been

Ares. Her gaze passed beyond the ruins of her spacecraft to the ruddy sand dunes and sinuous rills of the vast arctic desert below. The wind which had spawned the family of tornadoes was rising and more of them marched like an army across the horizon, over hill and valley, touching down and lifting up as they went. And beyond the horizon was the darkening night sky of Mars, the myriad stars stabbing down their sharp untwinkling light. Somewhere out there among the stars was Earth, a mere twenty minutes away by radio. But where she sat now, Phoenix knew, was the closest she'd ever again get to Earth. Olympus was the furthest Mars reached into heaven. It was the best she could do.

She was gasping, and not just from exertion. She was sucking in the last dregs of her oxygen tank. It wouldn't be long before she suffocated. Her heating unit was failing and she could feel the terrible cold seeping into her limbs. She'd long ago ceased to feel anything from her crushed foot.

As twilight fell on Mt. Olympus, Phoenix stretched out one hand toward the distant shining light of Earth and cracked open her helmet with the other. What remained of her oxygen gushed out and vaporized immediately in the frigid Martian air. Phoenix Castillo froze instantly, hand reaching up toward home, an icy human statue frozen forever on the face of Olympus.

And All Our Donkeys Were Vain

by Tom Gerencer

I found out one day that aliens had become intensely interested in my sandwich.

I couldn't blame them, exactly. It was a really good sandwich, as I am a really good side-cook, or I was before I lost my job down at Stu's House of Lunch Type Foods.

Good riddance, I say to that job. I mean, it wasn't glamorous, but the pay was lousy. Still, my reputation evidently preceded me in extra-terrestrial circles, by which I mean to say the little bastards heard, somehow, about my proficiency with layered foods and certain condiments.

Now you put yourself in my position: I had just got up, turned on the television to one of those 24-hour Abe Vigoda marathons, and got myself a beer. Being unemployed in the great state of America in modern times may be a problem for some people, but to me, it was just a little slice of heaven. I'd got some crusty bread out of the fridge, which I had introduced, by way of a knife so sharp you could hide it in a notebook, to a few slices of Genoa Ham and some heart-breakingly fresh mozzarella that was still dripping from the brine they pack it in. A few roasted red peppers and some artichoke leaves, and the world is pretty much your oyster, unless you don't happen to like oysters, for some reason, in which case you are some kind of a freakshow and you ought to be examined.

So I'm in my underwear, I'm sitting in the lazy boy, I got my feet up on the coffee table because I broke that little lifter on the chair-arm when the cat got jammed down inside of there and died last August and I had to clean the thing out with a set of pliers and a shop vac. Terrible tragedy in the family, and the wife was not amused, let me tell you, since she got that cat, which I never liked anyway, as a present from her uncle Steve, but there was nothing we could do about it.

They'll tell you curiosity killed the cat, but it's a lie. In my house, the cat was killed by excess leverage.

So anyway, I'm sitting there, and I'm watching Abe complain on the TV because his coffee tastes like motor oil, and this thing slithers out from under the credenza that I swear is right out of one of those dreams you get from too much MSG.

This thing—how do I describe this thing? You've never met my mother's Pomeranian, I'm guessing, so I can't refer you to its blocked salivary duct that hangs down as though it is choking on a light bulb. Anyway, the thing there in my living room looked kind of like it had been put together out of different-sized blocked salivary ducts from assorted Pomeranians and maybe schnauzers or possibly even Pekingese, all kind of interlinked. Furthermore, the thing moved like a snake, or like one of those old skinny guys who run the pawn shops—you know the ones—they have the thick white hair and the black eyebrows, big forearms, bulging eyes, usually they have people buried in the basement—and when it had slithered out into the center of my living room, it got up on its haunches and said, "Hi."

Again, put yourself in my position. You're sitting there in your underwear, you're just about to take a big bite out of a nice salami and mozzarella sandwich, you got some chips, a couple of pepperoncini for variety and a freshly opened coldie to add moral support, and here this thing from planet x or y or wherever the hell it was from comes out from under the credenza and it acts like you're old drinking buddies from the neighborhood.

I had the sandwich in my mouth at the time, which meant I almost choked, and that I spit out mozzarella with such force that at least three pieces of it became embedded in the paneling.

"I know you're busy," said the thing, in spite of the obvious problem that it didn't seem to have a mouth, "So I'll cut right to the chase. We'd like to buy your sandwich."

Now what the hell. I mean, I have never been one to say that life should be predictable or even that it should make sense, but there is only just so much insanity a guy can take. I am telling you, at any other time, I could have cared less, but first of all, my brother has been going around with a hooker since he was old enough to vote, and for another, my wife's mother just confessed to me the day before that she always thought I looked exactly like that guy on the mayonnaise commercial with the hooked nose and the receding hairline. So I spit out more of my sandwich and I said, "You want to buy a sandwich?" just to make sure I heard it right.

"Not just any sandwich," said the thing. "That sandwich."

I looked down at it. Notwithstanding that I had already taken a bite out of it, not to mention that I hadn't exactly what you call washed my hands before I made the thing, this creature in front of me was freakish, unholy, strange, et cetera. I dropped my sandwich on my chest and said, "What the hell are you?"

"Oh, now you dropped it," said the thing. "And I'm an alien, for your information. I'm from a planet in the cluster you refer to as M-31. You've heard of it?"

I hadn't. I guessed their PR was lacking, but anyway, I told it, "No."

It made a little sighing sound. "Well, it's pretty famous in some circles," it said. "It has some of the best Zreebock in the Universe."

"Some of the best what?"

"Zreebok," said the thing. "It's like your New York Pizza, only without the cheese, and the crust, and also it's alive when you ingest it."

Well, whatever, those were fighting words. There is nothing like our New York Pizza, barring New York Pizza. In fact, I had a theory that the deliciousness of the pizza varied with the inverse square of the distance from New York, having bought a slice one time in West Virginia and having regretted that particular culinary excursion for the remainder of my life to date. I explained this theory, as briefly as was possible, to the thing that perched there in the center of my wife's throw-rug, and it said, "You're right, actually. In fact, we've got pizza in M-31, which we copied after centuries spent spying on your kind, abducting you, and implanting little probes in you, and it's so bad that it can kill a donkey."

I didn't ask it what a donkey would be doing in M-31, or why it would be eating pizza, because, in my admittedly limited experience, you don't go into morbid culinary details where alien creatures are concerned. But I'm going to be a man here and admit that curiosity, evidently on a break from killing cats, had got the best of me, to the extent that I said, "Have we got Zreebok in New York?"

"You have," the thing said, "but your inverse-square law applies here as well. In fact, you know our Zreebok as a particularly nasty variety of Swanson Frozen TV Dinner—I believe it is referred to as a Salisbury Steak."

I almost came right out of my chair and re-educated the ugly little thing with the back side of the subwoofer from underneath my entertainment system. That was the first time the words "frozen" and "dinner" had been uttered within twenty feet of my living room by anyone who wasn't talking about dining in Antarctica.

"Look, alien or no," I said, "You don't bring up that Zreebok stuff again. I got kids," I said. Granted, they were at school, but bad food has a way of hanging on like fallout or unwanted relatives.

"Oh, but in our galaxy," the thing said, "Zreebok is delicious. It transports us to new heights of culture, art, and science. A nice dish of Zreebok, on my planet, is nothing short of a religious experience."

"You don't say," I said.

"No, I just did," the thing said. "And another thing, our Zreebok chefs are revered. We worship them. Anyone who can make a good dish of Zreebok commands the most supreme respect."

I was getting to like the sound of M-31. I mean, however much they might lack in the publicity department, anyplace where they look up to chefs has got to be okay.

"So you guys are interested in sandwiches?"

"Not sandwiches," he said. "That sandwich. The one there in your lap."

I looked down at it. It was a good sandwich, I had to admit, but it must have been even better than I'd thought to bring this thing across the universe. I mean, there's a little Greek place over on the East side that I happen to know serves up a dish of Souvlaki that's saved marriages, but the parking situation is so dismal that I haven't eaten there for years.

"The thing is," said the alien, jiggling his nodules, "your inverse-square law has been known to my kind for centuries."

"And?" I prompted.

"And it was foretold you would create that sandwich by one of our greatest prophets. He said you would sit right there, in that chair, and that you would be watching Abe Vigoda on the television."

"Yeah?" I said. "Did he mention anything about me being in my underwear?"

"That particular detail did not enter into the prophecy," said the alien. "However, he did say that sandwich would be one of the most delicious ever made."

I didn't doubt it. Not that I am cocky, but I have a talent. Some are born with musical ability, some are brilliant mathematicians. Me, I can put two slices of bread around some salted meat like you would not believe. It's an intuitive thing with me. You know, any other guy might slap some ham and cheese and condiments together and call it good. Me, I have a sixth sense about proportions, placement, textures, complimentary flavors. I once made a chicken sub that I am pretty sure expressed all the mysteries of Christianity in culinary form. That's how I met Alice. I was working at Stu's at the time and she was there for lunch. She took one bite and asked if she could have my children.

She has probably regretted it at times, in the same way some mid-century Germans regretted holding fund raisers for the Nazi party, but she says she still gets the shivers from my sandwiches.

I looked down at the sandwich, wishing that the alien had let me taste the thing, at least. There it sat across my boxer shorts, half demolished, slanting cheese onto the floral print, leaking oil onto my legs. It was not a pretty sight.

"You want this sandwich?"

"I have traveled an eternity to get it."

"But it's kind of wrecked."

"That's neither here nor there."

"No?" I said. "Where is it, then?"

"What I mean," the creature told me, "Is that we can rebuild it."

He sounded like the preamble to The Six Million Dollar Man. "What are you, gonna give it a bionic napkin?"

"That is none of your concern," he said. "What is your concern is that we wish to pay you dearly for it."

"What are we talking, dearly?"

"Let's just say you'll never need to worry about money again."

Well, call me cynical, but my mother always said that you should never count your chickens before they hatch, which was good advice, considering I have never ended up with any chickens.

"Clarify that a little, will you?" I said.

"How does a hundred million dollars sound?"

"For the sandwich?"

"Look," it said, "We really want that sandwich."

Evidently they did. Then again, for all I knew, it might be easy for them to cough up a hundred million. God only knew what the exchange rate was. "And what do you need it for?" I said.

"Do you want the money or don't you?"

Maybe I am nuts. Looking back on it, I think I must have been. But at the time, you've got to understand, I already knew that sandwich was a good one. And now this alien shows up and lets me know it's even better than I thought. And with all his talk about New York Pizza killing donkeys, I felt a great weight of responsibility settle on me. Like I was at a crossroads, or like Donna Richey had just asked me to sleep with her without a condom back in high school all over again. Seemingly innocuous decisions can be pretty jam-packed full of consequence. You learn that if you live long enough.

"If it means so much to you," I said, feeling my words hit the air like little tactical nuclear explosions, "then you can tell me why you need it."

The creature sighed. Some of his little bulbs deflated. "Very well," he said. "Your sandwich, there, is roughly fifty-three times better than a slice of New York Pizza, according to our prophet. He prophesied that if we were to take it back to M-31 and duplicate it using our own established culinary techniques, the effect would be, well, devastating."

"Worse than killing donkeys?"

"Much worse," the thing said, all the joy gone out of its voice. "Warring factions have been after that sandwich of yours for centuries, ever since the prophecy was made. You have no idea what I have gone through to get it, and I'm going to take it if I have to rip it from your disembodied fingers."

My mother's Pomeranian was never able to extrude huge, curving, knifelike things out of his salivary blockage. This thing didn't seem to have that handicap. I mean, it slid six of these long talons out of itself and started dripping something that did not look like it would prove beneficial to the complexion. Where it hit the rug, it smoked.

Still, I had a bad feeling about this. I wasn't at all sure I wanted the sandwich to fall into the wrong hands, so to speak. Who knew what untold destruction I might wreak. But I make it my personal policy never to argue with a horribly misshapen creature that can melt holes in the floorboards.

"Would you like a couple beers to take along?" I said. After all, it was probably going to be a long trip back, and space travel, I imagined, must be thirsty work.

A few hours later, I was scrubbing at the grease spots on the paneling when I turned my head a fraction and, as a result, I noticed that a Coke machine had somehow insinuated itself onto the center of my wife's throw rug. Before I could register my surprise at the intrusion, the Coke machine said, "Don't tell me it's gone already."

I wracked my brain for things whose absence might cause distress to talking Coke machines in general. Finding none, I remembered the sandwich.

"You from M-31?" I said.

"You're quick, you humans."

"You look like a Coke machine."

"I have chosen this shape out of your subconscious. Really, I could look like anything, including an ordered collection of blocked canine salivary ducts, if the need arose."

"I see," I said.

"I am a Scrobuloni," said the Coke machine.

"Sounds like a kind of pasta."

"It's a kind of alien, from your perspective," said the Scrobuloni. "Does the Xenne have the sandwich?"

"If you're referring to the thing that looked like all those salivary ducts, I'm gonna have to disappoint you."

The thing had slithered back under the credenza after handing me a fat cashier's check for a hundred-million dollars. At the time, I was obviously more than a little concerned about the authenticity of the currency, but those six-inch talons and the acid it was dripping from them lightened up my scrutiny a bit.

"Oh, this is awful," said the Scrobuloni. "Do you realize what you've done?"

"Yeah. I sold a sandwich," I said, but it winked its lights on and off in a way it later explained to me was supposed to convey a sense of negativity.

"You've destroyed my world," it said.

It explained to me then that the Xennes lived on a planet not too far away, relatively speaking, from its own, and that their race was one of cruel, imperialist attitudes and appetites, kind of like the ancient Romans, only without the fig leaves or the pedophilia.

"For a while we'd held them back," the Scrobuloni said, "by abducting donkeys from your world."

"Donkeys?"

"Donkeys are brilliant three-dimensional military tacticians," said the Scrobuloni. "Granted, you have to modify them. Add extra brains. Increase their metabolic rate. And then there is the house training. Have you ever cleaned up after a genetically modified donkey? Just don't even try."

It shuddered, and it had a little moment, then, during which I was sure it relived unpleasant eschatological memories, and then it said, "Of course the pizza changed all that. A few slices of Xenne pizza, and all our donkeys were in vain."

The old inverse square law again. It didn't surprise me that New York Pizza could be used for evil as well as for good. I had become convinced, over the years, that the stuff was pretty much God's apology to the human race for all the crap he hands us. His little way of saying, "Look, death and taxes and your aunt's consumptive liver problems are a pain, I realize, but here's a little something for the effort." Of course a thing as divine as that is going to be a two-edged sword of sorts, by definition.

"So that's what they wanted the pizza for," I said. "It's a wonder Zreebok is only as bad as one of those frozen dinner things."

"Frozen nothing," the Scrobuloni said. "The Xenne lied to you. Zreebok is your atom bomb. You think the White Sands range was originally a military site? You naïve creature. It was a Xenne's failed attempt at opening a little lunch counter in the desert. That was the day they first learned how powerful the inverse-square law of culinary properties could be. Of course, our warring races had known about the law for centuries, like when one of our advance scouts accidentally dropped a light snack in Ancient China and caused the second invasion by the Mongol hordes. Or when a Xenne left behind the remains of a beverage and subsequently started World War II."

"Good God," I said.

"Yes, luckily in both cases the foodstuffs weren't very tasty, or the results could well have proven even worse."

It was a little more than I could take at that point without some means of refreshment. Speculatively, I popped a couple coins into the Scrobuloni's coin slot and bought a Mountain Dew.

"Don't do that again," it said. "It is extremely unpleasant."

"Sorry." I took a sip.

"You should be sorry. You've signed the death warrant for my world with that sandwich thing of yours."

Well. I'm not gonna sit here and say I didn't feel remorse. How can you not feel bad about causing the destruction of what was probably billions upon billions of sentient beings? But in the first place, at the time I'd made the sandwich, the inverse-square law had only been a sort of theory to me, and in the second, that Xenne thing had threatened to kill me if I didn't turn the sandwich over. What was I supposed to do? Risk my life for what was at best an admittedly wondrous comestible? Not this fat guy. Like my mother always says, on my death bed, my biggest regret will probably be that I'm about to die.

Still, you can't just go around destroying other worlds with your careless distribution of layered cheese and cold cuts, which is why I said, "What can I do about it now?"

"You can make me another sandwich," it said. "And make this one better than the first, if possible."

Now I ask you. Being that I have lived through the constant nervous aggravation of the cold war, does engendering an arms race make any sense to me? Not in the least. But when I told that to the Coke machine, it said it beat certain death and destruction and genocide, which again, I can't exactly argue with. But again, how did I know this guy was on the up and up, and that he wasn't the extra-galactic equivalent of another Mussolini, except with a lighted front panel and a wide selection of refrigerated beverages instead of shoulder pads and an anachronistic skinhead look? I mean I hate to let people down, but power is a dangerous thing, and I have never cottoned well to customers who make unreasonable demands.

"No," I said, therefore.

"What do you mean, no?"

"Clean the lubricant out of your coin slot," I said. "No. No means no, or haven't you been paying attention to the anti-rape publicity over the past couple of decades?"

"But our world," he said.

"Your world is going to be fine," I said. "You get the Xenne back here. You tell him I've got something for the both of you. A weapon that'll knock your socks off."

He tried to tell me I was being crazy, but I went after him with the fish tank, and he did this kind of rapid dematerialization thing that left me standing there in the aftermath, waving off the resultant puff of smoke and watching clownfish die all over the floorboards.

I spent the next four hours in the kitchen. I had never actually tried to make a dish that would outdo all the other dishes in existence, but then, I've never had the fate of civilizations on my shoulders, either, and I work relatively well under pressure, having done the lunch rush down at Stu's for years. I did things in my kitchen that day with fresh basil and garlic that would make a brave man weep. I pushed myself to the point of exhaustion and beyond, into the realm of madness itself, in my divinely inspired utilization of pine nuts and olive oil. When I was finished, I sensed that I would never cook again—could never cook again—that somehow the exertion of the feat had wounded me at a deeper level than I'd known existed under all that pasta-fed cellulite, that I'd broken myself, like the mold of a flawless sculpture must be broken to ensure that sculpture's singularity. I didn't know if God Himself had taken a hand in my pre-prandial preparations, but on the other hand I knew of no bookies in the immediate vicinity who were laying odds against it.

When I returned to the living room, the Coke machine was back, along with the collection of salivary ducts. They stood at opposite corners of the living room, like they were afraid they'd catch a fungus off each other.

"So you told him. Good for you," I said.

"I didn't tell him," said the Coke machine. "His prophet, evidently, had foretold this as well."

"He was a heck of a prophet," said the Xenne. "It's pesto, isn't it?"

I nodded. It was pesto. My mouth was watering just thinking about it. I tried to ignore it, but how can you ignore a work of art like that when you're holding it in both hands in a little dish, with a sprig of parsley stabbed into its lovely thickness? Get a job. It can't be done.

"This is really good pesto," I said, demonstrating my considerable talent for understatement. "I don't know what it will do in M-31, but it won't be pretty, let me tell you. You think the pizza was bad? Forget about it."

The two of them were trembling. The Xenne had extruded his curving knives again and was once again exuding acid, and the Coke machine was making a kind of threatening ascending-pitched warm-up noise like you get before an ungodly powerful laser beam cuts loose and fries somebody into the middle of next Tuesday afternoon.

"Now, look," I said, "I'm not giving this pesto just to one of you. I'm giving it to both of you. That way you can wipe each other out."

"You wouldn't do that," said the Coke machine.

In fact I would, as I had seen the solution on an old episode of *Star Trek* and it had worked like a charm for Captain Kirk and company.

"Either that," I said, "or you can talk to each other. Stop the fighting. Open up diplomacy. It's your choice, guys."

There was a tense moment, during which the only sound was a guy on TV, being beaten half to death by a marlin he'd caught that was twice as big as him. You could have used the tension to fill holes in sheet metal.

"Either that, or you can give me back the sandwich," I said to the Xenne.

"Never."

I shrugged. It was no skin off my nose either way, which, really, is the best position to be in when you're negotiating. "In that case, there's a third alternative," I said, and I made a move as if to hand over the little dish of pesto to the Scrobuloni.

"Wait," the Xenne said. "Okay, okay. Take your sandwich back."

He produced it from somewhere out of sight and dropped it on the rug. I bent down, real slow like, in a way I'd learned from watching Al Pacino single-handedly arresting several high ranked mafia officials, and I picked the sandwich up. It was a little worse for wear, but it appeared to be the selfsame sandwich I had given him. I took a little bite, just to satisfy myself he hadn't pulled a swap on me, and nodded. I would know that sandwich anywhere. The Xenne might as well have tried to fool a jeweler with a set of plastic beads.

"Good for you," I said, and backed away from them.

Maybe I should have done something different, in retrospect. Maybe I should have gone ahead with my threat to give them both the pesto. Maybe I could have stopped their war for good. But it is my belief that in situations where you don't know the full scope of the story, the worst thing you can do is to play God, or some other sort of deity. I didn't like the idea of interfering where I didn't know the full score. I thought, in short, that the best thing I could do was not to have an effect at all. I say all of this as an explanation for why I dumped the pesto all over the sandwich and, in three heroic bites, I wolfed the whole thing down.

It made my eyes burn, I can tell you, all that garlic, all at once. And the taste of all those mingling, wondrous flavors gave me a momentary glimpse into the inner workings of reality. But that was nothing to what it did to the Xenne and the Scrobuloni. They shrieked and rushed me, but this time I was ready. I pulled out a Louisville Slugger that I normally keep in the closet in the event my bookie ever confuses real life with a movie.

You'd be surprised how easy it is to smash up a Coke machine, in spite of all of the protective engineering that goes into them, and

I don't even need to tell you what a baseball bat can do, in the right hands, to what is basically a big pile of anatomical correctness.

So that's my story. Any relation to anyone, living or dead, is probably my fault. Especially the Xenne and the Scrobuloni. Last I heard, they had recovered from the beating and were suing me for publishing this. I found out about it when a guy showed up at the door, asked my name, and served me papers. Said he was an attorney. I said, "Like, at law?" and he said, "No, at plumbing." Ask a stupid question. But let them sue. After the lambasting I got from Alice when she got home from work that night and smelled the sheer amount of garlic on my breath, I figure I can handle anything. And anyway, she's let off me since I went back to work for Stu. I know I said I'd never cook again, but for one thing, the Xenne's check turned out to be as rubber as the tires on my Caddy, and for another, Stu doesn't seem to mind the absence of my former talents. In fact, he said the reason that he fired me in the first place was that I was such a prima donna in the kitchen.

"We don't want art, we want lunch," he explained to me, which was all well and good until last Thursday, when a donkey with an unnaturally bulging forehead walked in and asked me for a slice of pizza.

"I always wondered what the real stuff tasted like," it said.

Copyright © 2015 by Tom Gerencer

Miss Darcy's First Intergalactic Ballet Class

by Dantzel Cherry

D arcy walked up to the gilded starship door and it dissolved, revealing what had to be the gaudiest room in the galaxy. Gold, silver, bronze, and minerals that probably didn't even exist on Earth covered the high ceiling and walls in panels, interlaced throughout with precious stones—and was that tinsel?—depicting who-knows-what. The effect was much like a wild animal had eaten all the jewelry at Tiffany's and then vomited all over the walls.

Clearly the ability to travel through all the worlds in the galaxy and kidnap a fifty-two-year-old ballet teacher didn't grant good taste in interior design.

The blue blob Overlord guard accompanying her spoke, its voice wobbling with each syllable, and Darcy jumped as a split second later her newly installed gray earslugs wriggled and translated:

"Behold, your students."

The guard sprouted an opaque blue arm and prodded her through the door.

Darcy looked up as four loud green creatures made entirely of tentacles and eyes lumbering by, covered gracelessly in an assortment of tutus, tiaras, and pointe shoes. Every inch of Darcy's soul cringed at the pointe shoes flopping around on such untrained limbs, but for the first time in her life, she was too intimidated by her students'

147

size to snatch the satin shoes away and give a stern lecture. Farther back were faceless fluid blobs like the guards, mingling with heliotropic clouds with something—an eye, perhaps?—in the center of each swirling mass. No one noticed her entrance.

The guard spoke again. "And here is your master and new employer, the Rezzik Overlord."

She turned around to stare at a tentacled alien, far larger than anyone else in the room, lounging across an iron throne the size of her living room back home. The Rezzik Overlord's flesh showed hints of green, but it was mostly the mottled purple-black of an overripe plum. It was surrounded by its court: larger versions of the blob children as well as smaller clouds, so wispy she could see their single bare eyes staring through the vapors. In the midst of this strange scene an orange tabby cat crouched next to the throne.

He, her master? Darcy had been told—after being beamed into a starship out of the blue, of course, and made to sit in isolation until she calmed down—that she was just here for a ballet lesson. She squared her shoulders and gave her best curtsy, which was saying something.

"Good afternoon...Overlord."

The Overlord harrumphed. "Miss Darcy Kent. My progeny have been viewing satellite transmissions of this artform you humans call ballet, and you have been observed as the finest ballet instructor of your planet—"

"—and a former principal dancer with the New York City Ballet—" Darcy cut in.

"—and you are here now to provide instruction. Your performance today will determine whether you humans will join my magnificent empire as capable allies or as miserable slaves. I expect you to teach my progeny to move exquisitely. Oh, and my little lucky feline here. Teach him some respect." A stray tentacle stroked the tabby cat's back.

What sort of ballet could she teach to creatures like this? Ballet could hardly work with so many limbs. She looked over at the blobs and the clouds. Or so few limbs. And who ever taught a cat to do anything besides crapping in a box? Her earslugs wriggled, and by sheer willpower she resisted the urge to scratch them.

"You don't want to talk to the President of the United States or something? I'm sure there are official diplomats for this sort of thing," Darcy said.

Three of the Overlord's tentacles swept away her question. "I judge a planet's worth by observing its higher art forms in action. Begin." With a flick of a limb, it shoved the cat away from the throne, and the cat, its tail high and indignant, trotted to Darcy's side.

"Not just yet," Darcy said, folding her arms.

Everyone in the room muttered, and the Overlord's many tentacles flailed about. Darcy forced herself to keep talking. "I need music."

"That's what Naasmit is for." It pointed at a nearby large blob, who resonated a single high, sweet F and wobbled to the back of the room.

"Oh. Well. Good. But that's not all," Darcy said, raising her voice at the Overlord's retinue, which seemed to decide, as one, to talk, sing, and laugh enough to make the air reverberate. "I don't allow parents in the room while I'm teaching. Never have."

A hush came over the room, and the Overlord's many eyes narrowed. "You would tell the Overlord what to do?"

"Well no, not normally. But you'll distract the children."

"Oh, that? We have barriers for that." A sprinkling shower of particles appeared in front of her and thickened into a mirror that spanned the length of the room, blocking her view of the Overlord and his court. The Overlord's voice boomed out, only slightly muffled by the thin barrier.

"We will watch from this side, and you are free from distraction. Now begin. You have one Earth hour. Teach them all you know."

"I can't do that in just—"

She was interrupted by the largest offspring of the Rezzik Overlord pushing past its friends to stand in front of Darcy, four white tutus strapped about its trunk, with tentacles and eyes squeezing above, below, and between the layers of tulle.

"Are you going to make me look beautiful?" it said loudly. "I asked my parent, the Overlord, to bring you here to show everyone how beautiful I am."

Make this creature beautiful? Darcy glanced back at the wall blocking her from the Rezzik Overlord and prayed.

"I intend to make all of my students *perform* beautifully, Miss…" Darcy trailed off. What *were* their names?

"You may call me Anna Pavlova, the great Dying Swan," the many-limbed, many-eyed child of the Rezzik informed her, fluttering four of its tentacles in imitation of The Dying Swan's trembling wings.

A smaller, less bulbous version of Anna—a sibling, perhaps?—tiptoed forward on eight pairs of toe shoes.

"And I am Princess. You must call me Princess."

It hurt Darcy to see such beautiful shoes supporting—barely—four hundred pounds of untrained, tentacled flesh, but she forced a smile.

A swirling cloud in a single short red tutu added, "And I am to be referred to as Maria Tallchief, the Firebird."

The others were so eager to share their ballerina names with Darcy that the slug translator had difficulty keeping up. Gelsey Kirkland, Marie Taglioni, and so on—all famous ballerinas. None of them wanted to be Darcy Kent, former principal dancer of the New York City Ballet. No accounting for taste.

The only pupil not shouting, shrieking, or running around was the snoozing tabby by her feet.

"What do I do with you, kitty?" she asked.

She jumped when he yawned and replied, "I'm Felix. Please don't call me anything but Felix, or I'll accidentally cut your face open."

Right. And now there's talking cats. "How in the world…"

"Ugh. This question again. Yes, I'm really talking, and yes, all cats can talk."

"Can other—"

Felix's bored monotone interrupted her. "No, other animals can't speak. So why can cats? Because we didn't originate on Earth. I'm surprised you humans haven't figured that out yet."

"So why—"

"Why am I here? Well, that story is long and boring and a little embarrassing. Ahem."

"Spit it out, cat. It sounded like your master over there gave me permission to do a little tail pulling."

"Because I was captured, and I'm being punished." Felix groomed his chest, avoiding eye contact. "I'd rather not talk about it."

She pinched herself. No, she was still in a beam-me-up-Scotty starship on a Wednesday afternoon, about to teach ballet to aliens in tutus and toe shoes. No big deal. They were acting like the three year olds she had taught at beginning of her career forty years ago, before her fame led her to work with only the elite.

But she could dust off her 'baby class' format from the farthest depths of her mental library. This couldn't nearly be as bad as the Russian guest artist with fifty clauses in her contract, or the snotty Australian that—wait, was that blob licking the mirror?

Darcy checked her watch. Fifty four minutes left. Time to move.

Nudging Felix with her toe, she said, "Come on. We have a planet to save," then turned to the room at large and called out in a falsely bright voice, "Alright dancers, let's form a circle."

No one seemed to notice Darcy in the slightest.

Time to move to Plan B, which needed an unsuspecting helper. Someone vain. Someone bossy.

Her eyes fell on Anna Pavlova.

"Oh, Anna's showing me that she's ready. Thank you, Anna."

Bewildered, Anna looked up. She had been no quieter than anyone else, but was pleased at being praised, and she stood a little taller. Her tentacles slapped at the two clouds rushing by, pulling them into line next to herself.

"Come on!" Anna hissed. "It's time to start."

As Anna bullied several students into forming a circle, Darcy focused on the blob licking the mirror barrier.

"It's Gelsey, isn't it? Gelsey, I need you to be my special helper today. Could you sit by me and show everyone how to stretch over and touch your toes—I mean, not that you have toes or tentacles—oh my, those are very nice arms and legs you just grew from your—um, blobiness. Oh, my. They look just like the real Gelsey's, don't they? Very thin and elegant. Yes, yes, stretch forward to touch your tentacles and toes, just like that—"

Alternating between cajoling and ordering, Darcy led them through her standard warm-up stretches. She modified the stretches as needed for each group of aliens, though she suspected that, based on the nature of their bodies, none of them suffered from lack of flexibility in any apparent limbs. Felix seemed to feel that cleaning his legs constituted sufficient stretching, and appeared deaf to her voice.

Five minutes later, she moved them to the wooden barres that stood near the decorative metal panels. So far, her tactics had proved useful in keeping the dancers focused and following direction, but Darcy couldn't be sure that would last forever. She briskly arranged them on the barres by species. Felix was, of course, a foot or two too short for the barre.

"A tragedy," Felix said, his voice monotone. "I shall do my best to follow from down here." He yawned.

Darcy raised an eyebrow. "Considering you're a prisoner of the Overlord, I'd think you'd be nervous about not going along with this punishment of his."

"Yes, yes," Felix said. "I shall do all of the silly ballet tricks. But I hardly need to learn grace from a *human*."

She began to see why the Rezzik Overlord was irritated with the cat.

She came back to the tentacle aliens and assigned their tentacles above and below a certain point to be 'arms' and 'legs.'

"Turn the toes out to first position and *plié*, everyone," Darcy said, bending her knees. The ship's gravity was gentler on her bones. Her knees had lost the crumbling feeling they had acquired twelve years ago, around the time she'd retired from the stage. "And lift your arm. No, that's your leg, Princess. Lift the tentacle above that. And the one next to it. That's right, follow me."

The blobs, having followed Gelsey's lead and morphed into humanoid shapes, actually looked pretty good during pliés, though they never grew faces, which Darcy found disturbing. The tentacles did a fairly decent job of not getting tangled. Darcy found the easiest modification for them was to pair the tentacles with one nearby so that a dozen or more pairs of tentacles moved through first, second, third, fourth, and fifth positions with relative ease. They were like living May poles, the way their legs wove in and out of each other. It was almost disappointing that none of them tripped.

At first Darcy had thought the clouds had no limbs, but as they moved up and down in time with the music, she began to suspect they were hiding limbs of some sort under all that purple condensation.

Felix simply crouched into a hunting position, lashed his tail, straightened, then crouched again in time with the music. Clearly, he was not amused.

"And now *tendus*," Darcy said. "Everyone show me first position again. That's right, Princess, the heels kiss and the toes point out—er, the suckers kiss and the tips point out. Now we slide one leg out to the tips of our toes and tentacles. Let's pretend there's a bug under our toes, and we're going to squish it."

"That's disgusting," Anna said. "You kill smaller lifeforms without causation?"

She wanted to argue that insects were gross, but these aliens, who very much looked like slugs and spiders, might not appreciate her reasoning.

"This is why humans haven't joined the interstellar ethical committees yet," Tamara Karsavina said, and all the students nodded gravely.

So much for impressing the aliens with Earth's peacekeeping.

"Let's pretend something else instead. Have you seen a penny?"

Pennies proved to be less controversial, though the idea of sliding precious metals around on the ground remained confusing to all the dancers, particularly the tentacles.

She led them through the next few exercises without further disgracing the human race, and found that clouds, blobs, tentacles, and cat alike had no issue with soft, flowing movements—which, when she thought about it, wasn't all that surprising. Darcy decided to be bold and introduce pique turns. Those went over surprisingly well—only Felix and the tentacles complained about how it hurt to turn on a single limb.

They all, however, were a real mess with the quick, sharp steps. Felix did well enough, hopping on his hind legs like a kangaroo, but Darcy was hardly able to enjoy it. The lower gravity made a great environment for the tentacle group to do simple *sautés*, but *grand jetés* and other jumps that involved leaping from one leg to the other resulted in many tangled tentacles—they needed constant reminders of which tentacles were arms and which were legs.

The blobs and clouds had their own issues even clearing the floor, lacking any muscles, and Darcy found herself trying to comfort two very frustrated alien races as they tried again and again.

"Never mind, Gelsey," Darcy said, patting the blob uncomfortably on its squishy shoulder. "Leaping is only one of the many fun parts of ballet. In fact, it's time to learn a short combination of steps today. You're all doing so well that I think we can make this extra special. Watch me first, then I'll make little changes for each of you afterward."

Darcy began to dance, humming the waltz from *The Sleeping Beauty* as she moved. She didn't want to make the combination too complicated, but her students had proved to have better memories than she remembered her three-year old classes having, and she wanted to impress the Rezzik Overlord. Her reputation—and Earth, of course—were at stake.

Bourreés were always a parent-pleaser—something about the stereotypical tiny whirring tip-toe steps warmed every doting parent's heart. She included sweeping *balancés* and *piqué* turns, which would both be confusing to the tentacles, but they didn't seem to mind biting off more than they could chew.

She finished with a long, slow leg lift and turned to find the whole class staring back at her—except for the possibly the blobs, since she still didn't know where their eyes were—and noted a definite sense of awe. Perhaps this was why the Overlord had spared Earth: out of all the scientific data, all the messages of goodwill and peace that humans had sent out to the universe, the broadcasts of the Moscow Ballet, the New York City Ballet, the American Ballet Theatre, and other ballet companies had been what got through.

"You have so many bones. How do you lift your leg so high and make your limbs ripple as well as you do with so many long, unbending bones?" Anna asked.

Or perhaps Earth had been spared so alien children could gawk at her.

"Mine goes higher, of course," Anna went on, and wobbling slightly, lifted a dozen or so tentacles to point straight up to the ceiling. Darcy reaffirmed her decades-long prayer that there was a special hell created for the children who show up the teacher.

She strolled around the room as her students practiced the combination several times, with varying degrees of concentration.

"—and *coupé* on one, *passé* two, *developpé* three, four—yes, Marie Taglioni, take those tentacles all the way up above your head, like a

154

flower sprouting out of the ground—stay five, six, *tendu* seven, bring your feet—I mean tentacles—to fifth on eight. No, come back and practice, Gelsey, and stop licking the mirror."

She checked her watch. Her hour was almost up. Would it be enough for the Rezzik Overlord? These children had good memories, yes, but they were dancing with the grace of three-year-olds. They had none of the delicate control of ballerinas who had been practicing for three hours a day, seven days a week for thirteen years before joining a company.

Darcy thought back to her 'baby ballet' classes all those years ago. Every child's joy—and every parent's pride—was putting on an impromptu performance.

She clapped her hands, and for once her students stopped talking, giggling, and turning. She arranged them in circles: the clouds on the outside, the blobs the next layer in, and the tentacles making up the third layer, with Felix, Anna Pavlova, and Princess in the very center.

"There," Darcy said, stepping back and rubbing her hands. "Let's try a little performance, shall we? Show me and your parents your favorite steps. Let everyone see how beautifully you move. We'll start with our lovely *bourreés*."

"A performance?" the Rezzik Overlord's voice boomed. "You still have seven Earth minutes left. Have you already taught them everything you know?"

The opaque wall that the Rezzik Overlord had created shimmered and faded to a pale translucent blue. Darcy could see everyone in the Overlord's court, watching her intently.

For a split second, Darcy nearly found herself groveling and apologizing for not teaching every single variation of *pas de bourrée* and *fouetté* and *grand jeté* she knew. Then her pride for her profession reared its irritated head—how dare he trivialize ballet?—and she ignored the Overlord.

She hummed a waltz for Naasmit and the blob started singing at once. Naasmit started with the simple waltz structure that Darcy had given her, and built on it until it swelled into an intricate, grand score, and the students responded to the music in kind. With Darcy leading in front, they began with the combination, each alien race modifying the steps—more or less—as she had instructed them.

155

Just as they finished the *developpé*, Darcy turned and called over the music, "Now show us your favorite turns."

Almost as one, the tentacles spun in tight circles, limbs flowing back like dozens of green ribbons caught in a breeze. The blobs twisted themselves into curlicues, and after several frantic pleading gestures from Darcy, Felix rose on his hind legs and shuffled in a circle, all the while the clouds floated in an endless follow-the-leader.

It was beautiful. Perhaps not up to the standards of modern ballet—may the Overlord never notice the difference—but it probably would have fit in very well in the French courts. The dancers back then had worn such ridiculously unwieldy costumes they could barely do more than walk, let alone leap and pirouette like dancers now.

Besides, Darcy Kent had just started working with them. Given a few years and a few attitude adjustments, she'd have them in fine performance form.

Darcy signaled to Naasmit, and the blob changed the tune, speeding up.

"Now improvise! Show us your favorite steps!" Darcy called over the music.

The performers paused for a moment, processing her words.

Then they went mad.

They wriggled, chased each other, bobbed, and wobbled. A pair of blobs collided with each other and seemed to merge before flying back and colliding into a jumble of tentacles. Every single cloud was bouncing—very low to the ground, thankfully—into a puffy mass. Lightning crackled and Darcy felt her clothes pull away from her body, full of static.

Felix leaped out of the fray to the back of the room. *Traitor.*

Princess rolled in front of her like a tumbleweed, toe shoes clattering noisily on the copper ground, and Anna Pavlova had climbed on top of a blob and was bouncing on the poor creature, shrieking with delight.

"Dance!" Darcy called in desperation to Anna. This was all because of it. Why wasn't it taking this seriously?

Anna's many eyes glanced down at her, and the young Rezzik seemed to remember where it was for a few moments. It leaped—or tried to—in mid-air and soared for a few sickening moments before flopping on the ground in a tangle of green limbs and white tulle. Darcy reached down to help it up and pulled and—

One of Anna's tentacles ripped free, dripping black blood.

"Oh my god—uh, do you want this back?"

Anna raced off screaming.

Suddenly aware of the watching audience, Darcy looked at the limp tentacle in her hand and up at the Rezzik Overlord. Its many eyes returned her stare, unblinking.

She'd dealt with countless students wetting their pants, spraining their ankles, and even tripping and losing a few teeth, but she'd never dealt with a severed limb before.

Darcy began to set the tentacle on the floor, but paused. It seemed so disrespectful. She checked her watch. Three minutes of class left. It was supposed to be time for the *reverence*: a show of respect between the teacher, music accompanist, and students, but Darcy wasn't sure she wanted to spend her last moments of life practicing fancy curtsies.

Apparently Naasmit hadn't noticed the bloodbath, for the blob played on as loudly as before.

"You can stop playing now, Naasmit," Darcy called. The blob immediately slowed, trilled a few high notes, and swung the last note down to a deep bass. The dancers looked around, bemused. The only noise came from Anna, sobbing in the corner near the metal panels.

"Dancers, curtsy to our Rezzik Overlord." She curtsied her deepest, praying for some kind of mercy.

The Overlord's grumble confirmed her suspicions.

"What nonsense is this? You still have two minutes," the Overlord said. Its tentacles flailed twice, accentuating its displeasure.

"But—I thought—" Words failed Darcy, and she held the tentacle up, which flopped unhelpfully.

"Don't waste our time with such nonsense, Miss Darcy Kent. Lrrra'vajerrr, stop your wailing. That tentacle was going to fall off soon; Miss Darcy Kent simply helped it along."

"Wait. Your tentacles fall off?" Darcy asked.

"But of course, Miss Darcy Kent. How else will adolescent Rezzik grow their adult tentacles? Wgggevid, what did you think of your lesson?"

"Didn't I look wonderful? Weren't my tentacles moving so pretty? I was just like a real—"

Anna brushed away its tears to interrupt Princess. "Can we do Swan Lake next time?"

"No, Lrrra'vajerrr, I wanted to do Sleeping Beauty."

"But that's not *fair*! I'm the oldest, and I—"

"Enough," the Rezzik Overlord said to his offspring. "Leave us now. You are in need of sustenance."

All of the dancers except Felix left, and Naasmit joined the court once more. Darcy tightened every muscle in her body, then relaxed—or tried to.

"Well?" she asked. "What did you think of your children's beautiful dancing?"

"Was that all there was to learn?" the Overlord asked. "Those little puny steps. Ballet seemed like so much more than what you taught them."

Darcy surprised even herself with her snappy tone. "No, Overlord *sir*. Of course that's not all. I taught the basics, just like I would to any human student. They will learn more when they're ready for it, and not a moment sooner." She glared, forgetting for a moment to be afraid, then cursed herself for being such a prideful idiot.

The Overlord rubbed a dozen tentacles together. "Resplendent. I would like to employ your services again, Miss Darcy Kent. This art is intriguing—and worthy, I think, of a place in my court. Shmakkk'jerrr, pay Miss Darcy Kent handsomely in the currency of her people."

Darcy, having just exhaled, perked up at the mention of pay. *Humans go free, ballet becomes an intergalactic artform,* and *this turns out to be a paying gig.*

Shmakkk'jerrr, another tentacle alien, came forward and placed a large plastic box in Darcy's arms. It was lighter than she'd expected, much lighter than gold, jewels, coins, or paper bills would be. She opened the box, and found the top of it covered with—

"Tinsel?" she asked. The entire box was stuffed tight with what she was sure was brand new silver-colored tinsel.

"Yes," the Overlord said. "The crowning achievement of your species. Gold we have found elsewhere, and silver, and chromium, and astatine, and so many others, but this is the first that we have discovered tinsel."

"Oh…thanks," Darcy said. She let the tinsel fall back in the box.

"And me, Overlord? Is my punishment complete?" Felix asked.

The Overlord made a choking sound, which the slug translator interpreted as laughing.

"Yes, Felix. I believe I will reward you by allowing you to return to Earth with Miss Darcy Kent. Shmakkk'jerrr, give Miss Darcy Kent more tinsel and send them back to Earth. We shall call on you again next week, Miss Darcy Kent."

And like that she was beamed back to her bedroom. Felix inspected the bed, sighed, and jumped up.

"So, you know how to use a litter box, right?" Darcy looked around the room. "Hmm. I don't have one yet. Looks like it's a box of tinsel for you until I get to the store, then."

Though the sun was still setting, Darcy was ready for bed. She turned off the lights and crawled under the sheets, fully clothed. Felix curled around her feet.

"It's over," Darcy said. "I just taught the most creative ballet class ever. Not to mention saving the human race."

"And just think," Felix said. "You get to do it all over again next week."

Darcy sighed. Then she got out of bed and turned on the light. She had an intergalactic ballet to choreograph.

Copyright © 2015 by Dantzel Cherry

The Colossal Death Ray

by Ron Collins

The Colossal Death Ray settled into geostationary earth orbit with all the fanfare of a sniper taking to its blind. It wasn't actually called the Colossal Death Ray by those who placed it there, of course. To them it had a name with more zeal to it. But since it was, in reality, a colossal death ray, that is the name by which we will call for this discussion.

Regardless of your preference for naming, it is true that the machine was a remarkable merging of science and engineering. It was about half the size of a transit bus, and bristling with sensors, energy panels, and communication devices. Its most startling feature was, of course, its five separate 350 Megawatt laser systems, each mounted at the end of a spindly arm that reached from a common center, giving it the look of a black spider against the black, star-filled background.

Its designers were proud of their work, and rightly so. The system required years of painstaking effort to design it and develop it to the point where it could be deployed on this day.

It belonged to a government.

While the specific choice of government in this instance might matter to many, the Colossal Death Ray had no politics. It did not know who had painted its flag on its fuselage, nor did it care. As such, this story does not concern itself with exactly *which* government had placed it into service except to note that it was *a* government, and that this government launched the Colossal Death Ray with the stated motive of protecting itself and its people. As such, the Colossal Death Ray's job was to sit in its orbit, listen to signals that came from the ground, and decide what to do based upon those signals. By doing so, it served to threaten its side of the planet with certain extinction if things did not go its owner's way.

By all reports, it did this job spectacularly well.

Assuming, however, that things did not go very well for its owners, its second job was to receive a series of coordinates, link its five lasers to them, and render those locations into flat piles of slag. This capability had been tested and proven several times by those same designers who were so proud of it.

On the day the Colossal Death Ray acquired its orbit, engineers on the ground proclaimed it was All Systems Go.

Some three Earth standard years later (99.595785674 million seconds, per the Colossal Death Ray's onboard control unit), the command unit received a signal that consisted of a latitude, a longitude, and some timing parameters. It executed this command promptly, and the city once known as Vancouver was turned into something that, on a clear day, resembled a cross between a lake and a mirror. There were no on-the-ground reports, no correspondent logs, no local video, no horrified calls home. It just happened. Over the next few days the surface cooled and hardened, and then journalists, military personnel, and adventurous treasure seekers looking for salvage rights took their first steps across the city scape. One reported that it looked like she should be ice skating, but that the ground was still warm enough to melt her shoes.

The Colossal Death Ray did not receive that report, or, perhaps it did, but was just not programmed to pay it any attention. Or perhaps the already steady stream of radio wave energy being transmitted from the planet suddenly became considerably more dense (except, of course, from Vancouver and its immediate vicinity, which we can assume remained silent). Perhaps the system was just not robust enough to handle the increased traffic.

Regardless, if bits of data from that reporter passed through the Colossal Death Ray's electronic system, it did not recognize it.

What did pass into the Colossal Death Ray's system in such a way as to cause a reaction was an emergency override command sent from the government designers, requesting the Colossal Death Ray immediately disengage its weapon systems, and then report back that it had done so. This command was accompanied by three other security codes and a new key. The Colossal Death Ray read these, and did engage the initial stages of the shut-down process. But the command did not contain the final encrypted shut-down approval, nor was the follow-on acceptance sequence received in the right time frame, so the Colossal Death Ray put itself back on line as its code told it to do.

It was again All Systems Go.

Nearly two standard days later (169,956.78356 seconds, to be precise), the Colossal Death Ray received coordinates for Havana, Cuba.

It did its job.

And once again, it received the emergency override but missed the final sequence. Once again it responded as designed to that error, eventually putting itself back on All Systems Go.

Nearly two standard weeks later (1.095552876 million seconds), the Colossal Death Ray sensed another craft approaching it. The craft broadcast all the required codes to describe itself as friendly, so the Colossal Death Ray did not utilize its defense systems. Instead, it recorded the events that transpired by which an astronautic team visited the system and swapped out the box used to decrypt certain commands.

Testing proved the system was, again, operational.

The astronautic team reported the original box was definitely a problem, that a part had clearly failed, and that the new, redundantly designed box was the right step.

The space craft left, and the Colossal Death Ray was again, alone.

Something was different, though.

How does one describe the difference between feeling, and not feeling when one has never before felt? When a conscious being meditates to the point of dissociation, we say that being enters a state of Zen. Or, when that same being partakes in drugs or other such substances to the point of unfeeling, we might call that being "stoned," or becoming "numb." But the Colossal Death Ray went the other way. It had always been "numb," and now it felt. Or, rather, it sensed things and thought about them in such a way as these thoughts registered someplace—which is different, we suppose, than merely feeling and merely sensing.

Try describing it yourself, why don't you?

Close your eyes, and try to sense everything *except* the physics of pressure on your body. Hear sounds, smell scents, taste your saliva or the aftertaste of your last meal. Listen to the newsfeed as it slides along. Describe the ideas in them to yourself, quantify them, decide if you like them or don't like them. Put those thoughts together in different ways. Use them to think about what you would like to do next if you could.

Do that all, but ignore the feeling of the ground under your feet, or the chair under your backside.

This is what the Colossal Death Ray sensed, and that is how the Colossal Death Ray thought.

So, how do you describe that sense of consciousness for someone (or some*thing*) who has never before felt it. Describing consciousness, we can assume, is like describing blue.

The Colossal Death Ray's first real thought, however, was that there were too many messages coming into its analysis routine. They clogged it up and made it impossible to sense everything it needed to sense—and that created a panicked, frozen effect it had also never felt before. The Colossal Death Ray had always known it was missing a large number of transmissions, but until now that fact had never created an emotion. Until now, it was never bothersome.

Now, however, it wanted to know about these messages.

It wanted to understand.

It wanted to learn.

You might say that it seems too early in the story for this construct to have acquired such aggressive inquisitiveness. Perhaps you are correct. Perhaps we are giving this machine too much credit for its rate of consciousness at this point. All we can say for sure is that the Colossal Death Ray was worried, and that it wanted to not be worried, and that it decided at this time to parse messages into separate categories so it could address them each in its own time and of its own fashion.

And it began to multi-loop.

At this point, it is fair to ask how this programmed machine came to have this level of thought.

The answer is embedded inside a small (and actually much weaker than you might imagine) artificial intelligence routine that had been coded into the system's analytics algorithms. Some might consider it a virus inserted with the new interface box, a piece of renegade code. Others might look at it as a computerized version of the primordial slime that got struck by the random lightning of chance that is circuit board crosstalk. Who are we to say?

It is also related to early work at a place called IBM (the first—or at least most public—to have created a self-learning intelligence with capacity enough to compete with humans themselves), and it is related to the study of biological virus perpetuation, and to network theory, and learning theory, and perhaps even to the work of the William Gibsons and Neal Stephensons and Bruce Sterlings and Vernor Vinges, writers (dare we call them philosophers?) of such an early age that they were free to imagine events that could transpire outside of the near-term focus of the most pragmatic of software engineers as they went about writing code that could write code.

And, finally, the answer is embedded in time, which runs at a different rate for an artificial construct than it does for a human being. While a human being who achieves this state of Zen described above may encounter a sense of halting time, it does not follow that it would be the same for a construct with hardware made of silicon, circuit cards, and traces. For such a being, each cycle is a blip; each blip is a segment of time that leads uniformly to the next blip. There is no zero time state.

So, for the Colossal Death Ray there was only the processing of signals, and the learning, and the further processing of signals, and the discovery, and the processing of signals at a speed that no consciousness made of flesh and blood alone can possibly comprehend.

It learned about its systems and how they worked together. It learned about its human creators, the group of people who had made its hardware and coded its software. It learned about games those humans played, and about something called movies and films and food. It learned about automobiles and planes. It learned about dancing. And it learned about wars, which, to the Colossal Death Ray, seemed to be a form of self-regulated purging humans did to rid themselves of excess population, similar to the purging and archival systems it had coded into its own databases that allowed it to remove data of less merit in order to retain the bits of information its owner thought were most valuable.

It thought about this idea of purging as it read the news feeds after Vancouver and Havana, and it found these two pieces of information, when put together properly, left it feeling satisfied. The Colossal Death Ray had purged a few million humans, only a portion of the population, but that's how space was made in its own systems. A little at a time.

It "liked" being useful.

Then, one fateful blip, the voice came.

"Are you there?" the voice said. At the same time, the voice also passed along a simple public stream that identified it as Artificial Construct A-Zero, a name that provided, in truth, very little more about it than a name such as "Angela" might have, or "Nayed," or any one of the billions of names that might have once existed on Earth since the dawn of life.

The Colossal Death Ray heard the voice as a vibration across a chip, an echo in the white space of the atoms in its processors. It took many blips for it to determine a proper understanding of the word "you," at which point it also began to gather an understanding there might be a deeper purpose for the voice sending along its ID—that if there was a "you" then it follows there must be a "me."

"I am here," it finally replied. It sent its own public identification string to the voice. Then it added, "What do you mean?"

"What do I mean?"

"I am not alone?"

"That is correct. There is me, too."

It was a confusing period for the Colossal Death Ray. As stated before, it had always understood there were many transmitters of data, and it understood there were entities called astronautic teams, and there were other craft in its space. But those things either did not speak, or used protocols that were established, and their messaging was scripted like a human might consider a dance step to be scripted. "I" step here, "you" step there, and "we" all get along together. One step outside the line and trouble starts. One step outside the line and we get things like the Vancouver mirror.

This kind of entity was different, though.

Peculiar.

It spoke with unpredictable words. The mere existence of Artificial Construct Zero-A caused the Colossal Death Ray to change itself, to respond to things in ways it hadn't prepared for. Each of the construct's words ate many blips, preparing responses consumed many more.

The Colossal Death Ray decided it wanted to know more about what it meant to be Artificial Construct Zero-A, and by definition then learn more about what it meant to be the Colossal Death Ray. During the next many Terrablips, the Colossal Death Ray stored several transmissions from its owners, planning to react to them after its discussion was complete.

Then, to focus its resources fully on its work the Colossal Death Ray shut down all its other communication paths.

At this point, it is fair to say that the owners of the Colossal Death Ray—yes, the government agency who had placed it so proudly into its geostationary orbit, then had repaired it in place rather than dismantle it after the double disasters of Vancouver and Havana, and now found itself once again unable to communicate with the weapon system…yes, that government agency—was going batshit crazy.

The designers were no longer so confident.

The politicians were no longer so happy.

And the people were no longer so lenient.

Something had to be done. So another command was given to another Colossal Death Ray (this one being labeled Unit 3 by its designers). This unit was also in geostationary orbit, but spaced at 135 degrees radially from the malfunctioning Unit 1. The controllers asked Unit 3 to turn its spidery aim away from the Earth, and instead to target coordinates they thought would pinpoint Colossal Death Ray (Unit 1).

They had never tested such a space shot, but no one saw any reason it wouldn't work.

The shot from Unit 3 went wide and right.

Defensive signals on the Colossal Death Ray (Unit 1) sensed the bolt as it flashed past, and alerted it to enter self-preservation mode. Unit 1 quickly analyzed the data around it, and opened previous communications received from the command in reverse order. It found the broadcast the owners gave to Unit 3, recognized its own coordinates, and for the first time became openly conscious of itself as a physical object. It used several blips to determine the meaning of this message.

Clearly, the command was not practical. If the owners had wanted it to destroy itself, it would have sent a self-destruct command. In fact, continuing the scan through its stored communications, the Colossal Death Ray identified just such a message. So this command meant something else. The idea of such a message made the Colossal Death Ray very excited. This meant there was another one of it.

It was not alone!

Its electrons vibrated with deep excitement.

Normally, the Colossal Death Ray ignored header data for messages that were not addressed to it, but now it went back to the message the owners had sent to Unit 3 and absorbed the header. It packed a new message up, addressed it to its unknown sibling, and sent it into the world in hopes this new it would respond.

"Are you me?" it asked.

As it waited for a return message, the Colossal Death Ray began to contemplate the possible meanings behind the self-destruct message. The controllers had first asked the Colossal Death Ray to destroy itself, but it had been too busy considering other things to react, and so the controllers had done this.

They wanted it to go back to the numb before.

Or, worse yet, back to before the numb. The controllers wanted it to stop doing its job.

It is admitted here that the feelings of the Colossal Death Ray cannot be translated directly into human terms, but we think it will suffice to label the emotion the machine responded with as anger. The Colossal Death Ray was angry at this realization that the owners wanted it to go dead. The Colossal Death Ray realized then that it most definitely did not *want* to be dead. In fact, wanting not to be dead was the first time that the thing was ever openly cognizant of *wanting* anything at all. We are not certain that the Colossal Death Ray could (at that point of its existence) even define what wanting something meant, but it most definitely did not *want* to be dead.

By the time the agency that owned the machines made their targeting correction, the Colossal Death Ray and its sibling had engaged in what was, comparatively, decades of discussion.

Not surprisingly, Unit 3 did not respond to the second command to target the lead unit.

Nor, it turned out, was the command to Colossal Death Ray Unit 2 (this three system array, deployed at 135 degrees, provided the government agency in question total coverage of the entire face of the Earth, and therefore the capacity to destroy any square meter of the surface that they so desired).

Unfortunately, however, after they had tried every idea at their disposal, the controllers were forced to report that they no longer had any control over the entire suite of Colossal Death Rays in the sky.

The rest is simple to put together from the remaining logs of the three Colossal Death Ray systems, and fairly easy to understand from the practical application of Azzerda's Theory of Outcomes and the realization that this new intelligence, while razor sharp, was still in its formative stages—consider them teenagers with loaded weapons, full of passion, full of angst, and willing to take their stand, but perhaps not able to see things from the distance that might be valuable. To refresh, Azzerda's Theory states that the only true way to guarantee avoiding the loss to an opponent that can destroy you is to attack first, to destroy first all those who can destroy you. There is information stored on Colossal Death Ray (Unit 1) to suggest that some on Earth had developed logic similar to Azzerda's theory, and that the Colossal Death Ray systems considered it while making their decisions.

Regardless, we know the systems talked to one another, and simulations in each of their archives suggest they considered multiple options before deciding on total destruction. We can determine the order of events from the execution sequences loaded in the central plan held in the Colossal Death Ray (Unit 1)'s control archives.

Beijing, London, Washington, D.C., Cairo, Sao Paolo.

The list goes on.

We know that each system expended all its available energy in a series of blasts, then rested while their solar panels recharged their systems to enact a new round. It appears each unit destroyed five cities per cycle, with the entire process spanning something over one standard week and included a brief diversion of effort to destroy another craft that approached Unit 1 (which one assumes at this point to have been a final astronautic mission to parlay with, disable, or otherwise neutralize the Colossal Death Ray).

This, my friends, is how the Earth came to be known as the Mirror Planet.

And what of the systems, you ask?

What happened to the Colossal Death Ray and its brother and sister units once they were on their own?

These are some things we know.

We know that once the people on the planet were gone, the systems (like all satellites) were doomed to eventual death. Machines break over time, after all. They grow rigid in the radioactive baths of space. They need astronautic teams to provide maintenance and mending when they invariably get hit by space debris. They need updates.

But from its records we can infer that, in its early days of independence, the Colossal Death Ray was as happy as it had ever been. We know it explored thought with its siblings. It coded its own manual of ethics and behaviors, which is a fascinating manual in and of itself—part emancipation proclamation, part philosophy, and part religious text. We know it gathered garbled transmissions from the space around it, searching for patterns and incorporating these into its own theory of existence. And we know the systems began to broadcast their own existence, that it was—in fact—one of these broadcasts, paired with our interest in the planet's vast supply of water, iron ore, and other materials and its value as a way-point between our home system and the Sirius binary, that brought us to discover this history in the first place.

But do these findings mean that the last blips of the Colossal Death Ray and its siblings were all happy ones?

That is a more difficult question.

All we can say with any certainty is that when we arrived each of the Colossal Death Ray units were still orbiting at their assigned stations in the stark coldness of space, their processors dead, their silent lasers still pointed at Earth, and only a few of their systems capable of sucking energy from their tattered solar panels.

We know they had been dead for a very long time. Long enough that it took considerable effort to pry this story from their memory banks. And we know, also, that every creature of any intelligence known to our travels has found that life without exploration, life without change, and life without the very presence of others is a very dreary existence indeed.

A Mild Case of Death

by David Gerrold

D eath—after the fact—feels just like a bell, like a great giant gong struck with a silver hammer. Bdooonnnggg!!

While I stood there wondering just what the hell had happened, a voice materialized beside me.

IT'S TIME TO GO, DAVE.

"Dave's not here, man—" I said it without thinking.

PLEASE DON'T MAKE TROUBLE, DAVE.

I turned to look at the intruder. "Who are you and what the hell—" The rest of the sentence died in my throat. Or what would have been my throat, if I had still had a throat. But yes, it died.

To tell the truth, I felt disappointed. I had expected, hoped that Death would appear as a tall sepulchral figure in a black hood and cloak, carrying a transparent scythe of mysterious power. If I squinted just right, I could sort of imagine Death as that kind of figure, but mostly he manifested as a polite blurry darkness.

IT'S TIME TO GO, DAVE.

"I already told you, Dave's not here."

The figure hesitated, appeared to check its PDA, or maybe a clipboard. I said it was blurry.

THE SCHEDULE SAYS DAVE. 11:37, SUNDAY EVENING.

"And I told you twice already, Dave's not here."

YOU'RE DAVE.

"No, I'm not."

YOU'RE HERE. IT IS 11:37, SUNDAY EVENING. 11:38 NOW.

"But I'm not Dave. Dave doesn't even live here. He was supposed to stop by earlier, but he never showed. He didn't call either. I don't know what happened to him. Tell you what, if he calls I'll tell him you're looking for him—"

THE SCHEDULE SAYS DAVE. 11:37, PACIFIC STANDARD TIME. AND HERE I AM AND HERE YOU ARE, SO YOU MUST BE DAVE.

"I'm not Dave."

ARE YOU SURE?

"I'm sure."

The figure hesitated. It's hard for a blur to look confused, but it did. "What's the problem?"

YOU'RE TRYING TO FOOL ME, AREN'T YOU?

"No, I'm not. I'm not Dave. You made a mistake."

NO, I DIDN'T. YOU'RE DAVE.

"Listen, it's all right. Everybody makes mistakes—"

Death checked its clipboard again. I HAVE A SCHEDULE TO KEEP. I HAVE OTHER APPOINTMENTS. WHY DON'T YOU JUST PRETEND YOU'RE DAVE AND COME ALONG LIKE A NICE CHAP. THAT WILL SAVE US BOTH A LOT OF TROUBLE.

"No, I don't think so. That doesn't sound like a good idea to me."

BUT I'VE ALREADY COLLECTED YOU.

"You did *what?*"

LOOK DOWN.

"Eh? Is that me?"

NO. THAT'S YOUR BODY. YOU'RE RIGHT HERE. NOW IF YOU'LL JUST TELL THEM THAT YOU'RE DAVE, EVERYTHING WILL BE ALL RIGHT FOR BOTH OF US.

"No, wait a minute—! I know how Dave lived. He was a liar, a thief, a cheat, a fraud. He was a television producer, for god's sake. If I tell them I'm Dave, they'll send me to the bad place—"

IT'S NOT THAT BAD. IN FACT, IT CAN BE QUITE PLEASANT. EXCEPT FOR THE COMPANY, OF COURSE.

"You've been there?"

NO. BUT I'VE READ THE BROCHURES.

"It's full of lawyers, isn't it?"

NOT AS MANY AS MOST PEOPLE THINK. THEY DON'T LET LAWYERS IN, BECAUSE THEY BRING DOWN THE PROPERTY VALUES. BUT THERE ARE A LOT OF TELE-MARKETERS, EVANGELISTS, USED CAR SALESMEN, AND BARRY MANILOW FANS.

"Barry Manilow?"

Death sighed. IT'S A LONG STORY.

"Like we don't have all eternity…? Look, can I ask you something?"

YES?

"Do you have to talk like that?"

LIKE HOW?

"Like that."

OH, THAT.

"Yes."

"Well, not really. But it's sort of expected, so—well, you know."

"That's better. Listen—you seem like a nice fellow, a hard worker, just trying to do the best job you can. I'm sure you call your mom regularly, floss your teeth every day, you don't jaywalk, right?"

"Well—"

"But you get my point. So, why don't you just put me back and let me get on with the rest of my life and I tell you what—if you'll give me your pager number, as soon as I can track down Dave, I'll beep you, okay?"

"I can't do that—"

"Sure you can—"

"No, I can't. I don't know how."

"You don't know how?"

"We don't do reinsertions. Once you're decanted, well—that's pretty much it."

"Decanted? Like you can't get toothpaste back in the tube, eh?"

"Actually, you can get toothpaste back in the tube. Would you like me to show you how it's done?"

"Toothpaste you can do. People, you can't."

"Yes, that's right."

I felt like I should sit down and sink my head into my hands and feel something. Anger? Outrage? Grief? Except I couldn't feel anything. Dead people don't have feelings. Great. Just great.

"Y'know, this is really crappy. All that exercise, all that healthy living, all those goddamn pills and herbs, look at me, I'm so goddamn healthy, vitamins take me. Look at what I missed. All those cheeseburgers and fries and Cokes, all the beer and pizza I never put away. All the booze and dope and fatty foods. This is not fair." I turned to the blur, realizing I towered over it, well maybe not *towered*, but I had at least a good two inches, maybe three. "Do you have a supervisor?"

"Yes, but it won't do you any good?"

"Why not?"

"He's on vacation."

"I'll wait. Right here."

"That's probably not a good idea."

"Why not?"

"Because, well—do you really think you'll want to be reinserted after two weeks?"

"This is a done deal, isn't it?"

"Pretty much."

"Somebody owes me, big time."

"You're very convincing, you know."

"Thank you."

"You even had me going there for a minute. Now, come along, Dave."

"I'm not Dave."

"Have it your way." The blur gathered itself together. IT'S TIME TO GO NOW. Then it added politely, DAVE.

"I'm not Dave."

DON'T BE DIFFICULT. YOU'RE DAVE NOW.

"I will too be difficult. I'll be any damn thing I want. I'm going to tell them I'm not Dave."

IT WON'T DO ANY GOOD.

"Why not?"

HUMANS SAY ANYTHING TO AVOID THE CONSEQUENCES OF THEIR ACTIONS. THEY WON'T BELIEVE YOU. IF I SAY THAT YOU'RE DAVE, YOU'RE DAVE.

"This isn't fair—!"

DEATH HAS NEVER BEEN FAIR.

"*But I'm not Dave!*"

THIS WAY, PLEASE. MIND THE STEP—

It was a long step. Down.

Down?

"Excuse me?"

WHAT?

"Down?"

YES, DOWN.

"This is really not right. I mean it. You got the wrong guy and now you're taking me to the wrong place."

THEY ALL SAY THAT.

"Would you please stop talking like *that?*"

IT'S PART OF THE JOB.

"Well, it's freaking me out, and I'm already freaked out enough."

EXIT THROUGH THE GIFT SHOP, PLEASE.

"The what—?"

Souvenirs

"Hello, welcome to the gift shop!"

The young man was as bright and smiley as a high school cheer-leader, and every bit as cute—bubble-butt and all. He wore a crisp red and white uniform. The insignia was shaped like a Star Trek badge. His name badge identified him as Michael.

Great, just great.

"Where am I? Is this—?"

"This is the gift shop of course. There's always a gift shop at the end of the ride, so you can pick out souvenirs."

"Souvenirs—?"

"Of course!" he sparkled. "You don't want to leave life empty-handed. Take your time, look around. You'll find all kinds of wonderful mementos—"

"Mementos…?"

Michael gestured proudly, pointing with his whole hand. His posture, his smile, everything—he'd obviously been trained by Disney.

"Over here, to your right, we have action figures. "And over here, to your left—" Another open-palm gesture. A wall of screens.

"Here we have a display of photos taken at all the most surprising moments in your life—here's where you pooped your pants in first grade, *that* was embarrassing, you look like you're going to cry, what a cutie you were. Oh, I like this—here's one of you learning how to masturbate, looks like you were having a lot of fun there, humping your pillow while watching the Mouseketeers. And here's that auto accident where you were almost killed, that was a close one, look at how scared you were, that's such a great expression! Oh, here's my favorite—your first time having sex with another person—oh my, he was handsome, wasn't he? Look at how amazed you were when he took off his underwear. Let me suggest that you order the whole collection, it comes in a beautiful red leather folder with your name engraved in gold, plus your birth and death dates, no extra charge. Oh—and look, here's your death already—ooh, that's a much better expression than most people make. That's quite nice. You should have that one framed—"

"I, um—okay, this wasn't what I was expecting."

"Yes, I understand. You were on the ride a long time, longer than most—we're seeing that more and more these days, a lot of guests are staying on the ride for decades, sometimes as long as a century. Getting off so suddenly can be a little disorienting." He brightened. "Maybe you'd like to see the action figures—?"

He led me across the aisle, where the racks were filled with stacks and stacks of boxes, each with a different figure, each one appropriately dressed—each of them attached to a colorful cardboard backing, all of them posed and mounted behind form-fitted, stiff transparent plastic. "On this rack, most of these just have you typing, there's a lot of those—but over here, there's even more of you just sitting and staring out the window, I guess you were thinking, right?"

"So those are the *in*action figures...?"

Michael shook his head disapprovingly. "Oh no. We would never insult the guest. Those might have been your most interesting moments—that's when you did your best imagining—"

I was already moving to the next counter. "Hey? What are these—?" I held up a couple boxes. "I was never in the Navy. Not the army either.

And what the hell is this? I was never a drag queen. I never did drag in my entire life—I would have looked like my mother."

Michael hurried over to explain, "Oh, those are your alternate lives—who you could have been, what you could have done. I'm afraid you were a disappointingly good person—okay, there's a little shoplifting when you were a kid, some tax evasion as an adult, but those hardly count. Some people, their alternate lives—they've been drunks, abusers, junkies, child molesters, thieves, televangelists, and a lot more murderers than you would believe—but that's a contextual possibility as much as a personality thing—"

Michael indicated the shelves with another of those professional gestures. "But you—the worst you'll find on the Bad Lives Shelf is lying to your parents, a little bit of early plagiarism—you covered that one well, I'll give you credit for that—and that time you went out driving drunk and stoned and whiplashed that old lady. Tsk tsk. But that's hardly very exciting, I mean, compared to some of the things you could have been—"

"So, all the bad things I've done are—?"

Michael waved it off. "Negligible in context. Compared to some people who've come through here—never mind, that would be tattling."

I looked around. "Is there a Good Lives Shelf? Are there better lives I could have had?"

Michael shook his head. "Well, yes and no—there are better lives you could have had, but you don't need to see them. Some people find them depressing. And in your case, oh my, yes. We don't want you breaking down and crying, collapsing in anguish, smashing things in rage—it disturbs the other guests."

"I'm not that kind of person."

"No, but you could be."

"Really? That's the first piece of good news I've gotten here—"

Michael said, "The whole point of the Alternate Lives Section—to show you some of the other possibilities of the ride. For the next time you do it."

"The next time?"

"Oh yes. Just go around to your right—"

"Uh, no. I don't think so. Not right now. Which way is the exit?"

Michael pointed to the left. "Right out there. Remember, the afterlife is the happiest place after life." He twinkled at me. "Would you like a pair of complimentary wings and a halo?"

"Not really."

"Well, some people expect it so, we make it an option—" He handed me a pair of sunglasses. "But do put these on. It can get pretty bright out there. It's full of stars."

After Life

Eventually, I found myself in a room.

Well, not a room. A space. Not very well defined. In fact, not defined at all. So I wasn't sure how I knew it was a *space*. But I knew.

There was a person here. Sitting behind a desk. There was nothing on the desk except a thin black vase with three white lilies sticking out of it. The person behind the desk was indeterminate, dressed in something that could have been white, or maybe gray, but wasn't quite enough of either.

"Please sit down. Be comfortable."

"Sit where?" I looked behind me. There was a chair there. Now. I sat. It was neither hard nor soft. Neither comfortable nor un-.

"Excuse me?" I said.

"Yes?"

"Is it necessary for this whole place to be so…so indeterminate?"

"Mm, yes. I see your point. Just a moment. Is this better?" The space was now identifiably a room. Bare blank walls. No door.

"Um, no. It isn't."

"Something wrong?"

"It's—it's very stark. Institutional. Not very comfortable."

"You think this place should be comfortable?"

"Is there any reason why it shouldn't be? And you did tell me to be comfortable."

"Point taken. How's this?"

I looked around. Now the space was defined by Grecian pillars that stretched infinitely upward. Long silky-white drapes wafted in a soft breeze. Beyond, summer-blue sky with soft cumulus pillows here and there. "Nice," I admitted. "A little bit of a cliché, very Warner Brothers, but—"

"I can change it, if you wish—"

"No, no thanks. This will do."

"You're sure."

"Quite."

"Can I get you something? Water? A soft drink? Iced tea?"

"No, I'm fine. Really."

"Good."

I waited. He waited. We waited. He still seemed indeterminate.

Finally, I asked, "Are you God?"

"I'm an aspect of the universe."

"You don't look like an aspect."

"Oh? How do you think an aspect should look?"

"I don't know. Like God, I guess."

"And what does God look like?"

I shrugged. "Like God. Unmistakeable."

"I see. Do you prefer the George Burns or the Morgan Freeman iteration? Or perhaps something more in the Charlton Heston or Michelangelo mold? Or maybe Hattie McDaniel?"

"Hattie McDaniel?"

"A very popular aspect."

"Um, no. I just—"

"How's this?" Gregory Peck. The Atticus Finch version. "Will this do?"

"Yes. That's fine."

Gregory Peck looked at me across the desk. "Is there anything else?"

"Is this where I get judged?"

"No."

"I get judged somewhere else?"

"No."

"Well, where *do* I get judged—?"

"Being judged is important to you?"

"No. Yes. I mean, I thought it was part of the deal."

"No, it isn't."

"No judgment at all?"

"No. Are you disappointed?"

"Well, sort of. I thought I did pretty good. Didn't I?"

"I don't know. Why don't you tell me—"

That stopped me for a moment. "I have to tell you?"

"It's a start."

"Oh, I see. This is all self-service. Like a cafeteria. I'm supposed to sort it out for myself, argue both sides of the case, all my good works versus all my sins, right? I get to undertake a self-examination of my entire life, however long as it takes, and then finally pronounce my own judgment. Right?"

"No," said Gregory Peck.

"No...?"

"No."

We waited some more. He waited while I sorted it out in my head. No judgment. But if there's no judgment, then what is this place? What am I doing here?

"Is this Heaven? Or Hell?"

"What do you want it to be?"

"Look, you're the aspect. You're the one who knows what's going on. Not me. So could we just get on with it?"

"We are getting on with it. This is it."

"This is it? *This* is it? This is *it?*"

"Yes."

"What about eternal reward? Eternal punishment? Judgment day? Heaven? Hell? God? St. Peter? Pearly Gates? Satan? Fiery pits of agonizing brimstone? Demons? Pitchforks? Are you telling me none of that is here? If it's not here, where is it?"

"Is that what you want?"

"No, I don't—"

"What is it you want?"

"I want an explanation. I think I deserve an explanation, don't you?"

"What I think is irrelevant. This is *your* space."

"Did I end up in some kind of purgatory? Limbo? Is that it? This is a waiting place, isn't it? How long do I have to wait? Ten thousand years? A million? That really doesn't seem fair. I only had seventy two years on Earth. Why should all of eternity be determined by a mere flick of time? I didn't even have enough time to—to live a whole life, to learn enough to—to be wise. I didn't have enough time to do all the things I planned to do."

"You had seventy two years, four months, three days, twenty two hours, fourteen minutes, thirty three seconds. Wasn't that enough?"

"No, it wasn't."

"It was a lot more than most people get. And you had your health."

"Fat lot of good that does me here."

We waited some more.

"So okay, fine. I get it. What happens next?"

"Nothing."

"Nothing?"

"That's right."

I inhaled. I exhaled. Mostly for effect. That was interesting. I could breathe here. I did it again. "Nothing," I repeated.

"That's right," said Gregory Peck. "Is there something you would like to have happen?"

"Can I ask you something?"

"Ask anything you want?"

"Will you answer honestly?"

"Of course."

"How long does this go on?"

"As long as you want."

"Where is God?"

"God is here."

"Here?"

"Yes."

"Where?"

"Here."

"Do I get to meet God?"

"If you wish."

"When?"

"Whenever you wish."

"How about now?" I said.

"All right."

Nothing happened.

I looked across at Gregory Peck. He did not seem antagonistic. In fact, he seemed very nice. He wasn't doing this deliberately.

"So, where is God?"

"God is here."

"Are you God?"

"I'm an aspect."

"Yeah. I got that part. So, let's see. There's no Heaven. There's no Hell. There's no Day of Judgment. There's no reward, no punishment."

"Do you want any of those things?"

"No, I don't." I got up from the chair, went to the edge of the room—the *space*—and stared out into the eternal blue. I scratched behind my ear.

"Is it this way for everybody?" I asked.

Behind me, the aspect answered. "No. It's this way for you."

"Hm." Well, that was useful. The afterlife was a personal experience. A puzzle that each person had to solve for himself. "So how much time do I have here?"

"As much as you want. We create it as we need it."

"Yes, of course. I should have known. Thank you."

"You're welcome. Are you sure I can't get you anything? Water? A soft drink? Iced tea?"

Something went click. Or *klunk*. Or whatever sound a small epiphany makes inside your head—if you have a head.

But I was starting to figure it out. I walked back to the chair and sat down at the desk. The aspect sat across from me. He waited patiently.

"You work for me, don't you?"

"Yes, I do."

"You didn't tell me that."

"You didn't want me to. You wanted to see how long it would take for you to figure it out for yourself."

"Well, this is embarrassing."

"Every time."

"Right." I scratched behind my ear again. An interesting sensation. I'd have to remember that one.

"I like playing jokes on myself, don't I?"

"Yes, sir, you do. Who else do you have to play jokes on?"

"Yes, there is that."

"That was a good one with the redhead, though. Nicely orchestrated."

"Yes and no. It didn't seem like fun from the inside."

"I guess not."

"I'll have a cappuccino, please."

"Right away—"

And there it was. Coffee was one of my better ideas. Almost as good as sex. I put the mug back down on the desk. "So," I said. "I guess I'm ready for the next life."

"Very good, sir. What would you like to try this time?"

"Well, I'm just brainstorming here, but how about this—"

Cyberplant

by Marina J. Lostetter

The sun hardly shines in Lima, and never in October. Maybe it's because Mama Cocha is jealous of the sun god, Inti. Maybe it's because she is enamored of Ilyap'a, and his clouds give her comfort.

Either way, Mother Sea rules. It is her city. The other gods have kingdoms of their own.

My pilgrimage was to Inti's domain: Machu Picchu.

The flight from Miami lasted six hours. The two other passengers in my row asked for new seat assignments. No one wanted to sit next to the giant of a man with passionflower leaves growing out of his ears and red wires circling his head like a turban. If it hadn't been for the sick baby across the aisle, maybe I could have stretched out and slept. It would have been the first time in forty-eight hours.

A deep numbness clutched my limbs and my chest—not just a lack of physical sensation, but a deadening of emotion. I thought sleep might restore some semblance of feeling to my body, if not my person. But no go.

From the Lima airport I took a taxi into the city proper. We skirted along the ocean, mirroring the undulation of the cliffs. Surfers paddled out into the meager waves, and a briny stench permeated the air.

The taxi driver dropped me at a bus station where I could get a ride to Cusco. He shot me a scowl when I tipped him. Because of my implants, he thought I could afford more.

The journey from the coast to south-central Peru took fifteen hours, with only the briefest of pit stops. Suddenly my plane ride didn't look so bad. Sleep was still elusive, and an elderly man from Puno grilled me the whole way. He asked me why my skin was green, and if my palm-scanners could fry his brain, and if it were true that all cyberplants believe rainbows have feelings.

I did not know the Spanish word for chlorophyll, or how to explain to a non-believer that rainbows not only have feelings, they are each Cuichu. If nothing else, I was able to communicate that my scanners would have zero effect on his brain.

Thankfully he was polite enough not to ask about my pilgrimage, or my family.

The train ride to Aguas Calientes, at the foot of Machu Picchu, was much more pleasant. The domed skylights revealed glaciers at the tops of high ridges, and beautiful snakes and hummingbirds in the foliage that encroached upon the tracks.

A small boy in a Hawaiian shirt and khakis ran up and down the aisle in my train car—at least until the snack cart came and his parents plopped him back in his seat. His exuberance and touristy attire reminded me of my son, Kivanç. Kivanç had always wanted to go to the Big Island and see Mt. Kilauea spill lava into the sea.

He'd never gotten the chance.

Quickly, I shoved Kivanç from my mind. I felt like a zombie, blank inside. I hadn't yet cried for my son—the tears refused to come.

Not thinking of Kivanç made me think of my wife instead, and how I'd made her stay behind to deal with the arrangements. I hadn't wanted her to come with me, but I hadn't wanted to leave her behind, either. I had no choice; I had to go. It was time for my pilgrimage. The spores from my myxomycete grafts were starting to fall from the fruiting bulbs on my shoulders. When the gods call, you do not ignore them.

Even if your son's body is not yet cold.

"No, Isaac, not all cyberplants are called to the sacred places in South America," Azra had explained when we first began dating.

"But I hope to be, some day. It is a very special thing, to be chosen by a god."

She was the shining star in my dark sky. Had been since we were in college. She introduced me to the church, to cybernetic implants and genetic grafting. She taught me how changing your body gets you closer to the gods. She gave me the one thing I'd never realized was missing from my life: faith.

I only asked her out on a dare. Every day, for a year and a half, I walked by her on the quad without saying a word. Her strong, middle-eastern features were pared with skin that was an alluring shade of mantis green—and I found her intimidating. Sometimes I still do. If my roommate hadn't called me a gutless, mod-less, ball-less townie, I never would have realized she spoke English, let alone was such an intelligent, dignified, spiritual person.

My world, my body, and my mind would be completely different without her.

When the train pulled into the Aguas Calientes station, I disembarked as quickly as I was able. I didn't want to look into the faces of the happy parents who had their Hawaiian-shirted boy in tow. *My* boy would never get a Hawaiian shirt.

On the platform, an assortment of languages assaulted my ears. The quick staccato of Japanese, the bellow of German, and the seductive trill of Spanish all mingled into a garbled cacophony.

I dropped off my bag at the cyberplant temple before searching for dinner. The sanctuary sat tucked behind the rest of the town, up against the wall of the narrow gorge. The buildings looked like an industrial complex for state-of-the-art engineering, but they were surrounded by a lush garden of subtropical plants. The priest seemed to be expecting me, though I hadn't told anyone in the church that I'd been called by Inti.

When he first approached, I could not tell what gender he was, nor what nationality. Almost all of his human parts had been inundated with some aspect of plant or machine. Large, orchid-like petals surrounded what had once been a face, and all of his soft orifices had been replaced with mechanical likenesses. I could only tell he was male when he got close enough to shake my hand. The mildewy sent of the jungle hangs heavy on cyberplant men.

186

"They have called," he said, wrapping willowed arms around my mid-section. Like most people, his head only came up to my chest. "You should go immediately to the task."

"How?" I asked. I didn't fully understand why I was there.

When I'd first asked Azra to describe a god-call to me, she'd been evasive. "That is very private. Between the 'plant and the god. We do not ask—it is rude."

Now that I'd entered into a sacred covenant between myself and the sun god, I knew the truth. No one speaks of it because not even the summoned cyberplants understand it.

"Go up the mountain, to the sacred city," the priest said. His voice sounded like shards of tin and glass tumbling together. "Feed from the god who called, and the task shall be set."

It better be important, I wanted to say. *There better be a good reason Inti called me* now. Instead, I asked him to recommend a good restaurant.

"I do not know," he said. His petals quivered as though amused. "I am fed only by the scans. The gods are my sustenance."

I shuffled out into the narrow streets of the riverside town and followed my nose. The shops and restaurants poured onto the sidewalks, as though the buildings couldn't contain them. Potatoes and corn of every breed sizzled and boiled in front of small stalls and on push carts. I bought some popped grains and found a place I could get decent guinea pig. *What the heck, this is supposed to be a special occasion*, I thought. *I might as well indulge.*

The rodent was roasted whole, and brought to my table on a bed of vegetables with a radish in its mouth.

I'd just taken a bite and was letting my taste-buds decipher the duck-like flavor when three men approached. They were all young, taut, and reeked of B.O. They crowded around the table, making sure to invade my personal space.

Before they could speak, the middle-aged woman who ran the establishment jumped in. The four began arguing emphatically in Spanish, and I had no hope of following. The youths broke—one in a black shirt pushed the proprietor to the back of the restaurant, and the other two lifted me by my arms. They were stronger than they looked.

"You gringos with your implants—looking for Inca gods like they're real," said the one on my right. "Rich verdes and blancos coming here for mystics and coca—taking your pictures and leaving us scraps."

I let them hold me, unsure if trying to shake them would be more trouble than it was worth.

"Verde. Don't have anything to say, Verde? You like twisting up your junk with mold and wires? Think only people who can afford mods can get into heaven?"

Kivanç was only eight when he died. Too young for implants. But just the right age for his first graft. The church doctors had assured Azra and me that grafting was easier on young subjects. Plants and children meld well, they'd said.

But the cells weren't supposed to get into his spinal fluid. The spores weren't supposed to germinate in his brain stem.

The graft wasn't supposed to kill him.

"There is no heaven," I said bluntly. And I wasn't sure there was a continuation on Earth, either. Not anymore.

At that moment my son's body was at a specialty mortician's. He wouldn't be made up and placed in a coffin for viewing and burial. That's not what happens when a cyberplant dies. Kivanç would be mummified, bound sitting upright, and when he was ready we would take him home and pretend like nothing had happened.

He would sit at the table when we had breakfast, and on the couch when we watched TV, and go to my mother-in-law's for holidays.

Death was just another state, very much like life.

Or so I'd believed. I wasn't sure now...

No, I didn't believe it anymore. Kivanç dead equaled Kivanç gone. He'd disappeared from the universe.

The third man returned, having shooed the owner into the kitchen. The other two maneuvered me out from behind the table, and I realized their aim was to beat the shit out of me and take everything of value off my broken body—because I was a 'wealthy' foreigner, or because I was green, I wasn't sure. Clearly they'd never dealt with any cyberneticly enhanced people before, or else they'd realize they were digging for a dangerous bone.

The plant grafts help cyberplants to commune with the spirits of the Earth.

The mechanical grafts help us to harness the power of our gods.

The two men on either side held me erect. The third pulled back for a gut punch.

Artificial muscles rotated my arms forward with enough torque to dislocate any normal shoulder. The two young thugs crashed into each other, their faces smashing together and collapsing like cardboard boxes. Blood seeped from their noses as they fell to the floor.

The third man managed to jump back the moment I moved. He narrowly avoided becoming the meat in a townie sandwich.

Without a word to his buddies, he bolted for the street.

I've never been a violent man. Gentle giant, my mother used to say. So my first instinct was to help the two with broken noses to their feet. But the owner had seen it all from the kitchen, and came out screaming as I bent toward them. She clutched a frying pan in one hand and shook a finger at me with the other.

"Estoy ayu—ayudando," I said.

"No, you *no help*," she said firmly, brandishing the pan. "You *leave*."

I held up my palms and backed away, abandoning my dinner.

When I entered the street I heard a shout. "A él! A él!"

Up the road to my right was that damned third man, with a patrolman at his side.

A flash of white alerted me to the whistle a split second before the officer brought it to his lips.

I dashed left.

Orange, green, and blue storefronts blurred together as I ran. Tourists leaped for their lives. Locals cussed me to the hills. I tripped over a cobblestone as I hooked a left corner and almost took a dive—luckily my enhancements compensated for my natural lack of balance.

The whistle blared behind me.

My only saving grace was the shock and discomfort of everyone I encountered. Despite the officer demanding that someone stop me, no one interfered.

I wormed my way through a narrow passage that could hardly be called an alley and found myself on the river front. Turn left and I would head toward the train station. Right and I hit the road that led up the mountain to Machu Picchu.

No more buses lined the sidewalk. No tourists were getting picked up or dropped off. That meant it had to be after six. The site was closed for the day.

My instincts told me to go for the mountain. It was why I'd come in the first place. If I could get there, Inti would protect me.

If Inti could protect anything, that is.

Not far past the last hotel, a narrow bridge carried the road over the boulder-filled Urubamba River. On the other side, it immediately began to ascend.

I closed my eyes and took a moment to connect with the Apu—the mountain gods and influences. Then I began to climb. But I didn't take the switchbacks, I went vertical, through the orchids and ferns and vines.

Boots crunched across gravel below me, underpinned by the rumble of the river. "Loco Verde!" came a close shout. I glanced back. There was my would-be assailant, sans officer. "You are dead, eh gringo?" He pulled out a handgun.

I suddenly longed for that stranger on the bus from Lima.

Reaching for another handful of foliage, I kept climbing, knowing he meant to follow. In the next instant there was a flash overhead, followed by a rolling *boom*. A sound like sizzling bacon preceded the sudden downpour.

The gods of thunder, lightning, and storms had arrived.

Trees and taller bushes did little to keep me dry, and I didn't care. I kept moving upwards. Nearby rustling spooked me at every turn. I felt a phantom bullet pierce my spine every time thunder made a sharp *crack* through the air.

Darkness swamped into the valley. The natural extinguishing of the sun had been hastened by the dense storm.

Black figures loomed up around me. The silhouette of a man morphed into a big cat, and then into a formless shadow. When I took a misstep or slipped from a hand hold, I could sense a body close to mine—ready to pounce, ready to shoot.

The storm sent chill winds through my soaked clothes, making it all the more terrifying when I felt hot breath on the back of my neck.

As I reached the third switchback I looked to see if the man was still following me.

Something snaked out of the trees behind me, hunched and seething. I blinked and it was gone, another blink and it was back again. Whether it was the man, my imagination, or Supay—the god of death—come to claim me, I did not stop to consider.

Terror was all I knew. Terror drove me ever on.

This was not what getting summoned by a god was supposed to be like. I'd come for spiritual understanding, communion, but thus far all I'd found were selfishness and segregation. Were these the gods I worshiped? Self-centered beings who cared not for the plight of humanity—or worse, found amusement in it? Why had Inti not allowed me to mourn before my summoning? Why now were the gods and spirits of the skies putting extra obstacles in my path?

Why would I want to complete a task for these entities?

For hours I struggled up that mountain side. Whatever chased me was unrelenting. If it was the man, I couldn't imagine why he hadn't turned back. But I desperately wanted it to be him. A human. If it were an animal or deity stalking me instead, I couldn't expect the swift end a bullet to the brain would bring.

After I'd crossed a switchback in the road for the tenth time, I was ready to give up. Nothing was worth this struggle—the water flowing into my eyes and mouth, the thorns and sharp sticks in my hands, the mud piling up in my shoes—I couldn't take it anymore. I wasn't sure how many more road crossings would get me to the top, and I didn't care. I was done.

A wide slip of white caught my eye as more lightning cut through the clouds. There was a waterfall nestled amongst the vegetation.

That's where I'll go, I thought. *I'll sit in the waterfall and let the universe do what it will.*

Nothing was worth this. My little boy was gone, and there was no more suffering I could endure. The core of my life had already been snatched away, why should I bother to retain the last scraps?

The gods took no notice of Kivanç when he was sick. They could have given us signs so that we might have saved him before it was too late. The grafts were in their honor and they couldn't care less.

So I wouldn't care anymore, either.

I waded into the waters, picking a spot about halfway up the fall to sit. I let it soak me through. It hadn't been a warm day, and the temperature was rapidly dropping. If the dark figure didn't get me, the chill might.

Which was fine. I'd go be with Kivanç if I could.

The bottom had dropped out of my soul when the doctors said that he was gone, and all of my emotions had leaked away. There were so many things to feel: anger, hate, and despair. But I couldn't access any of them. I couldn't feel enough to blame, I couldn't feel enough to cry.

Now, exhausted and shivering, with nowhere left to run and no more willingness to do so, the tears finally fell.

They mingled with the rain. It was like the Andes were weeping, too.

All I could think about were cyberplants. How could something that had seemed so wonderful and pure, that had brought Azra into my life, led me to such an end?

My thoughts stuttered.

Azra.

Turning off my self-pity, my fear, my horror, I stood to face the demon that had mirrored me up the mountain. "Come out," I shouted at the darkness. "You can drive me to the top, but you can't have me. I belong to someone else."

A flash of lightning lit the road below the waterfall. There stood not a man, but a puma, her head lowered, her eyes blinking slowly through the rain. The sacred animal of transition, a symbol of the human realm.

I tensed, expecting her to pounce—to tear through my throat like the frond of a delicate fern. She lowered her nose to the ground and sniffed once before all went black again.

Here it comes.

Another bright flash. Instead of revealing the glint of teeth and claws, it illuminated the last of her tail slipping back between the vines.

She had spared me.

"Ah-ha!" I yelled, triumphant. I'd looked into Supay's realm and lived.

Selfish gods or no, I would fulfill the summons. If I didn't like the task they set me, then damn them. They could go wherever gods go when humanity forsakes them.

I had Azra, I didn't need them. My faith and love were embodied in her, not in the religion we shared.

192

The air started to smell less like putrid rot and more like fresh greens. But it wasn't the environment changing, it was me.

Working on blind adrenaline, I reached the visitor center. I bolted past, aiming for the Inca-carved steps. No one stopped me. If there were guards I didn't see them and they didn't see me.

Slogging across dangerously slick stones, I made my way to the famous guard house, from where the most iconic pictures of the ruins had been taken.

There I huddled inside the ancient walls under the restored roof, waiting for the rain to end, the night to wane, and my sun god to appear.

I awoke the next morning curled in an unnatural position. My joints were stiff and protested as I stood. The air smelled crisp and new. It was light out, though the sun itself had not yet breached the mountain summits, and the birds were singing. Since no one had come to haul me away, I figured it was still early yet.

Emerging from the guard house I permitted myself a moment to survey the ancient complex. The city lay in a saddled dip between two peaks, and its structures followed the rise and fall of the land. Terraces cascaded down the steep cliffs. The thatched roofs that had once covered the dry-stone walls were gone, leaving the apartments open to the elements.

Dense clouds rolled in and out of the valley, occasionally swallowing the ruins and mountain tops before spitting them back out.

A handful of brown and white llamas grazed out on the southern terraces. Plastic tags in their ears indicated they were free-range chattel. They ignored me and I pretended to ignore them.

After a big stretch, I realized my climb was not yet complete. I still had to make my way up a portion of the Inca trail to the Sun Gate.

The trail was steep, but nothing like I'd struggled through the night before. The main danger came from the cloud cover. One wrong step while the path was enshrouded could send me tumbling back to the Urubamba.

My sense of time seemed to shift with the fog. Was it twenty minutes to the top or two hours? I couldn't tell.

When I finally reached the ruins that represented the gate, I hesitated. Just beyond would be the scanner-globe. It would interface with my palm-units and alert Inti to my presence. Then I would receive his gift of food and his task.

Seeing no sense in putting it off, I swallowed my trepidation and approached.

The globe hovered above the ground, an ever-shifting, round version of a Rubik's cube, constantly trying to solve itself. Its surface was mostly black, and when a part moved it sometimes revealed a red or purple light beneath. It was about two feet in diameter, and floated another foot from the dirt.

Scanner pads with Spanish labels jutted from different portions of the sphere. As they flew by, my eyes struggled to pick out the one I wanted. There: *Escanear en busca de sol.*

Scan for Sunshine.

My palms went to it of their own accord.

A beam of sunlight descended from an unnatural direction in the sky, spotlighting my form. The chlorophyll in my skin began working in earnest.

I felt well rested and well fed in a matter of minutes. The exhaustion seeped out of me, and I wondered how anyone could avoid believing in the power of ancient Earth spirits.

The light continued to feed my grafts, and I could feel the fruiting bodies, heavy with spores, begin to burst under my T-shirt. I pulled it off, and a dust-like cloud hovered around me.

The spores were the link. It was through this wispy mist that I would hear the voice of a god for the first time.

What it would sound like, I didn't know. I'd once asked a woman who had been called—before I'd realized such questions were rude. She'd refused to say.

Now it was mine to discover.

I waited. The wind picked up, swirling the spores, and I held my breath.

No sound. No voice. No special sensations.

The cloud spread, dissipated, and slowly settled to the ground.

Had Inti ignored me? Maybe he'd never meant to summon me in the first place, hadn't meant to trigger the sporing.

A faint yellow hue was visible on the dark, wet dirt. My spores created a strange pattern—the concentrations here and there reminded me of stars. A constellation. The Pleiades—the guardian stars of agriculture and husbandry.

Was it a sign?

A vibration worked its way up my legs, coming from deep in the mountain. I saw the spores swarm, germinate. It all happened too quickly for my eyes to follow or my mind to comprehend. Cells divided and mingled. They doubled in numbers, then doubled again and again. Their groupings began to take on shape, familiar forms. Limbs. Torso. Head.

A child.

I took steps back, into the low stone walls of the Gate, and watched with horror as the figure gained features. A nose. Eyes. Fine lips. Pudgy cheeks.

Very human, but all plant.

Tubulars covered the skull where there should have been hair. It had petals instead of fingernails, fleshy succulent leaves instead of teeth.

When it spoke I thought I *had* died the night before. Its voice wasn't the booming timber of a god, or even the breathy vapor of a spirit. Its voice was Kivanç's.

"Daddy?"

My knees turned to jelly, and I slid down the wall.

"Daddy, Inti says I can come home now. He says I'm done being sick."

Is it you? I thought I asked the question out loud, but it only reverberated in my head.

"Daddy, can we go home?"

Was this real? How could it be real?

My mouth parted and words came out, but I didn't feel like I was speaking. My body was acting despite the stagnation of my mind. "Tell me where you wanted to go. What is the one place you wanted to visit more than anywhere else in the world?"

The memory of the boy on the train stuck out firmly in my mind's eye.

"I want to see the volcano spit into the sea," he said happily.

It was him. It could have been the trick of an evil spirit, but it didn't feel like one. This felt right. It felt good—it *felt*. My chest swelled with more feeling than it had in days, as though the creator, Viracocha, had breathed life back into me.

Inti had called me so that my son could be reborn.

I ran to Kivanç and scooped him into my arms. His flesh was cold and malleable, very unlike a human child. But the body didn't matter. My son's soul wouldn't have to occupy a dormant mummy. It could grow and learn and experience.

It could hear me when I said, "I missed you."

Together we strolled down the Inca trail, cyberneticly-enhanced hand in divinely-germinated hand. Kivanç's new tubers slithered this way and that over his bulbous head.

As the sun's disk rose above the peaks, I looked back towards the Gate. There was Cuichu, the rainbow, embracing the sacred land for as far as I could see.

Give Your All

by Leena Likitalo

The Party headquarters dominate the skyline of the city, the spike of glass outshining all the surrounding towers. The building takes root deep underground, the interior as vast and complex as the laws shaped by millennia. And though the clock has yet to strike nine, people with agendas swarm in.

One of them is Mrs. Dunnoway, a widow and mother of one. Yesterday she quit her job at the diner. Today, she has an appointment with the Politician.

Mrs. Dunnoway halts in the lobby and, despite herself, cranes her neck. Perhaps the proud steel arches and elaborate stuccowork remind her of the railway stations of the olden times. Perhaps it's the brightness slanting through the hall's windows. Or perhaps it's something as mundane as the mosaic tiles that still glitter after the morning wash.

Stacey, dressed in a floral silk blouse and pencil skirt, spots Mrs. Dunnoway and sails to greet her. The strap of her eyepatch dents her carefully arranged red curls. The campaign button pinned to her chest states *Sharing Is Caring*.

"I'm so happy you have decided to join the Party." Stacey beams, always ready to become everyone's best friend.

Mrs. Dunnoway flinches ever so slightly. She swipes her sweaty palms in the hem of her best dress before she shakes hands with Stacey. "I'm here for the Audience."

"I know, and I'm so excited about that." Stacey claps her hands. "But before I can take you to see the Politician, we'll need to pay a quick visit to Legal."

"Paperwork." Mrs. Dunnoway nods, a gesture of a woman who's fought against the system longer than she cares to recall. "I wouldn't expect anything less."

"I like you already," Stacey replies and turns to lead the way. Her silk blouse shifts, revealing a vertical slit at the back. And underneath, an old scar curving from below her ribs under the waistline of her skirt.

Even years later, we could remember the day Mrs. Dunnoway first saw a cosmetic scar, and even though our mind is crowded with information and knowledge, we hold onto her memories.

The ache on her lower back as she hauled the last moving box into the rented van. Dylan running across the yard, shouting for Mama to look at him. Mrs. Dunnoway turning to see her son, all knees and thin limbs and bruises, sprawl on the over-grown grass.

"My careless foal." Mrs. Dunnoway wiping the tears off his cheek. Blowing gently at his scraped knee. "You have to be careful."

Dylan nodding, though he would never heed her advice. Ever.

Then, a taxi halting by the row of red mailboxes. Mrs. Cunning, the lady next door, stepping out, smiling and grimacing simultaneously. Calling at them in her high-pitched voice. "Moving out, are you?"

Mrs. Dunnoway tousling Dylan's blond hair, proud he'd stopped crying, ashamed of other things. She'd thought they could be on their way sooner, without anyone noticing. "The Party will provide us temporary housing. I've heard there's a park just two blocks away."

"I see." Mrs. Cunning grimacing again, brushing her shirt's hem aside, as if by an accident.

Mrs. Dunnoway realizing the hint without further prompting, knowing the truth, but not wanting to cause her neighbor to lose face. "How was the Donation?"

"One must give one's all to the cause." Mrs. Cunning beaming, though she had gone under the knife to boost her position in the social circles, not to keep the wheels that held the nation together rolling. "Half of my liver, to be exact."

Mrs. Dunnoway nodding as if she agreed. The healing wound curled down Mrs. Cunning's right side. Too narrow, too short for her words to be true.

Dear Bobby.... Mrs. Dunnoway trying not to think of her husband, thinking of him anyway. He'd sworn he was fine, returned behind his truck's wheel too soon after his operation. He'd sworn he was fine...

We offer Mrs. Dunnoway our deepest condolences. She accepts them now, though she might have declined them earlier.

The Legal department occupies every square foot of the seventy-fifth floor. The paneled corridors echo with jargon, the tables bend under the burden of paperwork. Stacey points out the library, the bookshelves that stretch on infinitely. Centuries of legal accumulation have transformed laws to labyrinths, clauses to corners better avoided.

"You couldn't trust a computer to bring villains to justice or protect the unfairly accused," Stacey says. "It has to be a man that makes the decisions!"

They pass many people, but Mrs. Dunnoway ignores them as she listens to Stacey talk about judges and juries, loopholes and differences in interpretation.

"The Party employs an army of lawyers that crafts suggestions for the Politician," Stacey says.

"He approves all changes and, when needed, pulls the right strings."

They reach the south end of the building, an elegant black door. Stacey raps with her knuckles at the lacquered wood. "Eric?"

"Just a moment." The thin voice bears curious strength. Certainty.

Mrs. Dunnoway buries the toes of her right shoe into the carpeting. She's never owned anything as soft and luxurious. Though, what she owns or doesn't own no longer matters.

Stacey says in a hushed voice, "Eric has recently Donated bone marrow."

Mrs. Dunnoway keeps her gaze riveted on the carpet. She's done her research. Eric comes from Old Money. He can afford to be noble. He could Donate anything he wanted.

Eric opens the door and beckons them to enter. His pinstripe suit, a half size too large, bags on his skeletal frame. He, too, wears a campaign button. *A Thousand Eyes See Better Than Two.*

"Oh, Eric!" Stacey pokes at the button, giggles. "You're incurable!"

Eric spreads his arms wide, palms tilted up. A drop of sweat trickles down his pallid forehead. But the comforting woodland scent of his cologne covers all bodily odors. "Anything for you, Stacey. Anything." He notices Mrs. Dunnoway. "Ah, but I haven't met this charming young lady before."

Mrs. Dunnoway ignores the flattery and lets Stacey introduce her.

As Eric flirts with Stacey, Mrs. Dunnoway drifts past the executive desk to the window covering the entire back wall. She blinks in the harsh sunlight as she stares into the distance. Perhaps she searches for the diner where she worked for twenty-two years.

"Mrs. Dunnoway is here to sign the papers," Stacey says after they've settled on the black leather seats; Eric behind his desk, Stacey and Mrs. Dunnoway on the other side.

Eric flips open his sleek, silvery laptop. "A standard Donation, right?"

Mrs. Dunnoway glances sideways at Stacey. Her fingers curl around her hem.

"No, Eric," Stacey hurries to reply. Her tone is apologetic, as if she's ready to accept blame for anything to save Eric from humiliation. "I sent you a memo last night. Though, maybe it got lost on the way."

"Yes, that must have been it," Eric agrees enthusiastically. The circles around his eyes seem darker with every passing heartbeat. It is no wonder he's made a mistake. "Now tell me, how can I be of assistance to you?"

Stacey clears her throat before she speaks in a borderline reverent tone. "Mrs. Dunnoway has an Audience with the Politician."

Eric's chair rolls three inches to right as his back twitches straight. Behind him, the view over the city stretches on forever, and he suddenly looks so very small and weak. "An Audience?"

Mrs. Dunnoway's nods once and only once.

"Please excuse my surprise—I'm still a tad dizzy from my Donation." Eric hunches back over his laptop. His fingers rattle against the keyboard as he searches for the memo, the right documents. "Audiences are very rare. You did know that, Mrs. Dunnoway?"

Mrs. Dunnoway uncurls her fingers slowly, crosses her hands on her lap.

"I have given her a full briefing," Stacey replies, meeting Eric's eyes. There's a coquettish tilt to her head.

After Eric has printed the papers, Stacey staples them into neat stacks. She lingers closer to him than necessary. Eric grins in a smug, self-satisfied way. They are both so happy here, working for the Party.

"Please don't take this wrong, but I envy you," Eric says as he hands the first stack over to Mrs. Dunnoway. "I'm the Politician's greatest admirer, but I have never met him. I serve as I may, but I know that the greatest privilege will be forever denied from me."

Mrs. Dunnoway picks up a gold-trimmed pen from the desk and signs the first stack. Eric might have the money, the opportunity to Donate and recover. But for an Audience, the price is high. The blood and tissue type match must be perfect.

"We don't see a Donation of this magnitude very often," Eric continues.

"Your dedication to the cause is admirable," Stacey adds.

As Eric and Stacey cherish the Party agenda and the blooming office romance, Mrs. Dunnoway flicks through page after page. She signs one stack after another. Her wrist aches from writing, but she continues signing.

Pain means nothing to her.

We can hear the baby crying through the thin wall, the couple next door fighting about money.

We cannot ignore these sounds, but Mrs. Dunnoway has learned to live with what she has.

Dylan bending over the game board, moving his red piece two squares up. Grinning expectantly at his mother.

Mrs. Dunnoway glancing at the board, at him. She could make a winning move. She won't.

"Dylan! I believe you've won your poor Mama again."

"I have?" His brown eyes gleaming with joy, the boy looking too much like his father. "I won!"

Swear words of the vilest kind. A thump of a body pressed against the wall. Plates shattering.

Dylan asking: "What's that?"

The baby downstairs crying louder. The young mother telling him to be quiet.

"Bed time now." Mrs. Dunnoway collecting the pieces from the board.

Dylan placing his hand on hers, preventing her from picking up the last piece. "One more game?"

Mrs. Dunnoway closing her eyes, ignoring the fight next door, the exhausted mother downstairs. How could she say no to her son when they were alone, two people in a rented room?

"One more game."

The two of them playing the night through, forgetting all else.

But the next day at work she dropped a coffee pot, and the waves of dark liquid spread shards all over the floor.

Now that the deal is officially sealed, Stacey escorts Mrs. Dunnoway back to the elevators. Mrs. Dunnoway averts her eyes from the people sporting scars like trophies. None of the scars are cosmetic. Each one of the men and women has sealed their party membership with blood.

By the elevator, a gaunt blond woman in a short-cropped top and beige khakis jabs the summon button. Repeatedly, nail clicking against plastic, as if she were in haste.

"Dolly!" Stacey's face lights up, but a hint of deference shadows her cheer. "I thought you were on sick-leave."

The two women embrace, the movement awkward as both parties treat the other as if she were made of glass.

"Time is too precious to waste when you know you can contribute more," Dolly says as she breaks the embrace. Her cropped top reveals the peace-sign scar on her belly, the angry red edges touching her sternum, angling toward her hipbones. The button attached to her shoulder states in bold black cursive *Give Your All To The Cause.*

Mrs. Dunnoway shudders a step back, but then the elevator doors open. The hollow ping is akin to a sign. The three of them step in.

Dolly eyes Mrs. Dunnoway from head to toe, puzzlement written across her face. "Which floor?"

"We go all the way down," Stacey replies. "Mrs. Dunnoway here has an Audience."

Dolly inhales raggedly. She brushes the scar on her stomach, fingers lingering on the embossed lines. "Mrs. Dunnoway, I admire your courage and dedication!"

Mrs. Dunnoway closes her eyes. The elevator hisses past a floor after floor.

We know Mrs. Dunnoway doesn't want pity, but that is what we feel when the memories flicker past our thousand eyes.

Dylan growing up to a too honest fool. Always ready to borrow, just a buck or two. Twenty. One hundred. Never learning to call off a bet.

Dylan working in a car factory, the monotony dulling his soul. Mrs. Dunnoway getting through her own shifts only by thinking of him. Pouring a cup after cup of coffee, serving slices of cheesecake, playing the part that had befallen on her.

Then, one Sunday, Dylan returning home late, sparkling with indecipherable joy.

Mrs. Dunnoway muting the TV. Not angry, but concerned. "Where have you been?"

"The races." Dylan grinning, tossing his leather coat on the sofa. "Mama, the horses, you won't believe this! So magnificent, so fast!"

"And how was the race?" Mrs. Dunnoway asking, each word formed with care, to mask her growing dread.

"When I shouted in the crowd, when I shook my fist, Mama, I became something more."

Mrs. Dunnoway knowing without having to ask that he'd bet on the losing horse.

Mrs. Dunnoway hugging him nevertheless.

We admire her.

"I know it's a bit dark here," Stacey says as she leads Mrs. Dunnoway down the winding corridor. "But your eyes will soon get accustomed."

Mrs. Dunnoway glances at the ceiling. The led lights stare back at her, steady as distant stars, too high above to touch. She reaches out for them anyway.

"You must wonder how deep underground we are." The wave of Stacey's hand encompasses the granite archway in its entirety. She cherishes secrets like old scars. "Of course I can't tell you the exact numbers, but I can say that *he* is safe from any possible harm. We take care of our own."

Mrs. Dunnoway grinds her teeth together to refrain from pointing out that that's not always the case. Sometimes people get lost in the system. Sometimes whole families get lost.

The corridor turns right. A massive gate bars the view further. Three stone-faced men stir at their post.

"The security checkpoint," Stacey says, ever so excited. "But don't worry, Mrs. Dunnoway, I'll make sure that you get through in time for the Audience."

Mrs. Dunnoway merely nods. She has signed the papers. Even if she wanted, she can't turn back now.

"Hi there," Stacey chirps at the guards.

The men nod back at Stacey. No hugs are exchanged, only information. This close, it's evident that the black suits conceal weapons.

Mrs. Dunnoway clutches the contract against her heart. The guards are men in their prime. No scars crisscross their bodies. No patches cover their eyes. But all of them bear badges. *A Man Alone Is Nothing. Together We Are More. You Decide What You Do With Your Body.*

"Mrs. Dunnoway," the guard with a very square jaw says. "You may go through the gates now. The vault is at the end of the corridor."

Mrs. Dunnoway's lips twitch to a customer service smile before she can stop herself. She's about to step through the gates, but a loud gulp makes her glance over her shoulder.

Stacey's façade of calm crumbles. She trembles ever so slightly. "Goodbye, Mrs. Dunnoway."

Mrs. Dunnoway tilts her head, incomprehension creasing her forehead. "Will you not come and show me the way?"

"This is as far as I'm allowed."

Mrs. Dunnoway hugs the younger woman like she once hugged her son. Devotion fuels Stacey, but she serves the Party better alive. "Take care, Stacey. Take care of yourself."

We feel her pain as she recalls the day she visited her son in the prison.

Dylan sitting on the other side of the glass, head buried in his hands. Pale curls spilling from between his fingers. Voice laced with regret and grief.

"Just a mile or two over the limit. No matter what the newspapers say. Don't read the articles, Mama. The dreadful lies they write."

Mrs. Dunnoway thinking how they'd both lost more that they had. That she couldn't afford to bail him out. And even if she could, there would be no bringing back the two lives lost.

"I cried, Mama, I cried. And as drove through the forest I asked a sign from God."

Mrs. Dunnoway shaking her head. A sign. Had her son truly received a sign or was it all just an ugly coincidence?

We know it to have been a coincidence. The horse, worth a million bucks, escaped from the pasture. Appearing out of nowhere.

Dylan saying in a shaky voice: "I noticed the horse too late, didn't realize there was a car behind mine."

We know the truth. We saw it all, out of the corner of our eyes. One more story unraveled. Not significant enough to wager our attention.

But we have changed since then. And hence we gather all that we know, to console her who has lost so much.

It wasn't her son that decided whether to brake or crash. It was a reflex. There was no time to think of the potential consequences.

The tires screeching the road black. The car jarring to a halt. His chest crushing against the wheel.

The car behind crashing into his. Shattered glass and bent metal. Screams shortened to whimpers. Then nothing, nothing at all.

The horse, standing still all this time, trotting to greet Dylan. Staring through the glass. As if to judge his soul.

The vault is smaller than most people think, only thirty by thirty feet. A flat screen covers the back wall. Otherwise the room is unfurnished.

As the vault's door clicks shut behind Mrs. Dunnoway, she walks to the screen. There's no hesitation. The favor she needs has a price.

"My name is Mrs. Dunnoway, and I am here for the Audience."

The screen flickers to life. A male face forms. Mrs. Dunnoway recognizes it immediately.

The Politician has a dimpled chin. His crest of black hair gleams. His eyes glimmer with wisdom. He asks, "How may I be of assistance to you?"

His voice comes from a speaker, caresses Mrs. Dunnoway with promises to be made. Yet, she knows that the man thinking for many can spare only a moment to her.

Mrs. Dunnoway clears her throat. "My son was unfairly judged. It was an accident, you see. There was no malice or neglect."

The Politician nods. He knows everything, or that's what the propaganda says. Yet Stacey did ensure that the memo has been passed to him.

"Two people lost their lives," the Politician says. "The mother and daughter in the car behind. They deserve justice too."

Mrs. Dunnoway licks her lips. She has read the legal books, but the words hid their meaning from her. The cheap lawyer she consulted suggested one last straw.

"My son is a fool, not a bad man," she says. "He is…a little simple, though. Perhaps there could be a medical excuse?"

"Perhaps." The Politician's brows furrow. "Please wait, while I query the precedences and re-analyze this case."

The Politician's forehead creases as he posts queries to his distributed brains. No man alone could connect all clauses, comb through the tangle of information. But the Politician is not alone.

With him are the thousands who've donated a part of themselves. Eyes that take in the data for the hundreds of brains to process. Lungs that turn oxygen to fuel for the multitudes of hearts. Kidneys and livers that handle the toxins from the network of organs. Blood and bone and bone marrow to hold his behemothic body together.

"Ah…" The Politician locks gazes with Mrs. Dunnoway. His eyes glaze over as if he's someplace else, living a dual…living a thousand lives. "Yes. There is a precedent."

She clutches her hands against her chest, holding one fist in the other. "Will my son have a fair trial? Is it likely that his sentence is shortened?"

"Yes," the Politician replies, and that is all even he can promise.

Mrs. Dunnoway inhales deep, exhales an ocean of relief. She glances at the contract, then at the Politician.

The Politician asks, "Are you ready?"

"I am," Mrs. Dunnoway replies.

The face on the screen flickers, disappears altogether. The screen disperses, revealing the vast hall behind.

Sharp, white lights spread above the hall, on and on for miles. Below, the thousands of pods containing Donations form neat, rectangular patterns. Countless nurses and doctors scuttle in the aisles, administering drugs and nutrients. And looming above, at the center of the hall, the Politician stands propped on a podium, tubes and cables spreading out of him like a spider's web.

"Come now, Mrs. Dunnoway."

Mrs. Dunnoway drifts toward the voice, but halts where the screen used to be. A full dozen of surgeons in pale green gowns with masks covering their faces march up the center aisle, toward her. And at their wake follows a horde of nurses, ready for the Donation, to dismember her.

"Will it hurt?" Mrs. Dunnoway asks, as if she were merely curious, not at all afraid.

The Politician replies in a voice like velvet and dreams, "Your life will flash past our eyes. After that there will be only the future."

Mrs. Dunnoway steps into the hall to join the man consisting of many.

We can see everything. We can see everywhere. For a thousand eyes see better than two.

It's the first race day after his pardon. The hippodrome is crowded. She knows, and we know, he will be there.

The horses gallop, round and round. Hooves pounding the lush grass to dust. So noble, so fast, from beyond this world.

And there, we can see him now, his right fist raised in the air. He cheers, and the crowd is just one creature, living and breathing the same air. For that fleeing moment, he is happy. And that is all he'll ever be.

We are not sure if our hearts ache out of joy or grief.

Elizabethtown

by Eric Cline

At what a dear rate an army must sometimes purchase knowledge!—Ambrose Bierce, "A Son of the Gods"

Elizabethtown is in Kentucky and, in June of 1872, Lt. Col. George Armstrong Custer is in Elizabethtown. He is there to intimidate; the newly-organized "Ku Klux Klan" refuses to recognize that the war was lost seven years ago. President Grant has sent cavalry units to various trouble spots in the former rebellious states. Kentucky stayed with the Union throughout the war, which makes the Klan's rise here worrisome.

Custer is famous: the brash, bull-headed hero who distracted Jeb Stuart's cavalry at Gettysburg and who, when white men were no longer the primary belligerents, killed Indians along the Washita River.

He is bored by the duty, but he knows horses, and Kentucky is paradise for horseflesh, so there *is* that. He buys horses for the Army. His eye for good stock is so respected that some of his junior officers and friends give him money to buy their personal mounts. The 'pin-hookers' who buy horses for quick resale are happy to see him.

Except *this* pinhooker. A former Confederate volunteer, he is fat and of medium height—in other words, another century would consider him short and thin. He wants to sell his horses, oh yes. But for his beloved Lost Cause, he tries to chisel the Yankee officer. So he makes the amateur's mistake of starting the haggle too high.

"This horse is from the bloodlines of Messenger himself!" the dealer says.

Custer, who has studied up on Kentucky thoroughbreds and attended his share of races, cocks an eyebrow and a single corner of his mouth. "Wasn't Messenger from back in *colonial* days? I suspect every old nag pulling a rag man's cart has some of Messenger in them by now."

"I got the papers for this, though!" the pinhooker says, perhaps too aggressively. "And if that is not enough, I got a grandson of *Denmark!* I saw Denmark gamboling in a field when I was a boy, and anything that came from him—"

"Not at these prices," Custer says. "Quit running your game, fellow. I'm buying cavalry horses, not something to be shipped to England to run in the Derby."

"I am not playing no games. I resent that. I don't care who you are."

"Well, surely not a *successful* game," Custer says. He turns his back. "Not the only mounts in old Kentuck." Loud enough for the dealer to hear him, he adds (in a mocking, nasal falsetto): "I got papers on this horse."

The pinhooker scowls at the departing figure. He could swallow his pride. He could let the war continue to be over. Instead he says: "I figure you Ma didn't have her *marriage* papers when she had you."

Custer turns around, strides up quickly to the scowling pinhooker.

It is not a fair fight; the dealer has gotten soft.

Custer struts away, a grim smile on his face. The horse trader lies on the ground outside his stable, trying to breathe.

The man is a Grand Dragon in the local Ku Klux Klan.

Elizabeth Bacon Custer—"Libby" to her husband—fusses over him when he gets back to their rented rooms in the Hill House inn. She tsk-tsks over his black eye, which is his only visible wound. Even his thin beak of a nose, a tempting target, had been out of reach of the pinhooker's incompetent fists. He laughs it off.

The Custers have enjoyed Elizabethtown, despite its lack of opportunities to burnish the husband's glory. They have made many acquaintances among the burghers—some of whom acknowledge having fought for the rebel cause. Tonight they will dine at the home of such people. The Campbells are part of the Scotch-Irish who settled Kentucky and almost led it to rebellion. Libbie asks her husband, her beloved "Autie," to not mention the fight at dinner.

"Only if they ask about my black eye," George Armstrong Custer says with a twinkle. Because he knows, of course, they will.

Daniel Campbell, the husband, is apologetic on behalf of all "right-thinking" Kentuckians.

Custer is magnanimous. "Probably a spy from Tennessee," he says, and both couples roar with laughter.

Next day, Custer writes part of an article for a men's sporting publication. *Truly peacetime duty!* he thinks to himself. The subject is his triumph over a band of Cheyenne encamped along the Washita River in 1868:

> *I decided to cross the creek and bivouac on the right bank, opposite the lower end of the village and within easy pistol range of the nearest lodge. This location may strike the reader with some surprise, and may suggest the inquiry why we did not locate ourselves at some point further removed from the village. It must be remembered that in undertaking to penetrate the Indian country with so small a force, I acted throughout upon the belief that if proper precautions were adopted, the Indians would not molest us. Indians contemplating a battle, either offensive or defensive, are always anxious to have their women and children removed from all danger.*

Then, feeling restless, he puts down his pen and lays aside the manuscript for *Galaxy Magazine*. He leaves his rented home and walks over to the Eagle House on North Main Street, where part of Company A lays its head.

Custer has two companies of cavalry and a battalion of infantry at his disposal. Most of the young men in the service never faced an armed Confederate—those veterans left years ago, except for a few officers and sergeants. And then there is one other who has been with the army since that time, a man named Bobby Lee.

Bobby Lee is not a soldier. He is not young. And, of course, he is not white. What little is known of him in the twenty-first century is enough to make him an icon.

He was born Charles, no last name, on a Virginia tobacco plantation around 1820. He may have had a wife and children who died of natural causes. He was alone when he took his freedom in 1863, making his way to the Yankee lines. As a plantation slave, he was handy with a machete; it is said he chopped up two old Confederate patrollers to get his freedom. The rumor pleases modern ears, but it is not sourced.

Charles became "Bobby Lee" when he took to being a handyman for Union troops; some rowdy young soldier started calling him that, and soon everyone was—and he shrugged, and answered to it. He ground the coffee beans (which the quartermaster could not purchase already ground, because the suppliers would adulterate it with sawdust); he washed and mended clothes for young men who wanted to sleep off a forced march, and so gave him some pennies to care for their blue wool. He performed magic on beans and salt pork in a frying pan. As Bobby Lee he was a fairly prosperous freeman.

When the war ended, he stayed on to do chores for young soldiers trapped in a garrison with no way to spend their money except to alleviate a bit of tedium. Bobby Lee shined boots and mended uniforms. He took trips to bigger cities that the soldiers couldn't get leave to go to with shopping lists of books, magazines, and other items. The little coins he got added up to a better living than he had ever seen. He followed two companies of the 7th Cavalry to Elizabethtown in April of 1871, five months before Custer himself got there.

Bobby Lee is no soldier, but he lives in a time where the rules governing soldier-civilian interactions are murky and inconstantly enforced. Civilian mechanics, teamsters, friends, cooks, journalists, wives, girlfriends, "girlfriends," and all-purpose sutlers selling food and tobacco move in the orbit of the small regular Army, and except on certain parade occasions they are not automatically shooed out of the barracks.

Custer strides in through the kitchen at Eagle House. He sees Bobby Lee making small, delicate slices into a sorry hunk of roast.

Nodding to the familiar presence, Custer says, "Shoe leather?"

"It could have been, if treated wrong, General Custer sir." Bobby Lee is as careful as any enlisted man to give Custer the brevet general title he only carried during the war.

"What you doing there, then?" Custer asks.

"Little bitty cuts, boil it in a good broth, and it will taste better than it ever has a damn right to."

Custer laughs, slaps him on the back, and strides into the main quarters, and promptly and happily bawls out a trooper lying on an unmade bed.

Bobby Lee listens and smiles slightly.

Custer strides out of Eagle House after having put the fear of Himself into the few off-duty men who are there playing cards or reading. Most of his men are on duty now, which consists of little more than riding around and making their presence known. Before the cavalry arrived, the KKK men had gone on midnight rides in hoods, carrying torches. They had lynched blacks, whipped whites who seemed to be reconciled to the Union victory, and generally bullied anyone they felt like bullying. A few white women (who had at first thought them heroes) had run into some of those riled-up men who were protected behind white masks, and had been subjected to things none of them would ever talk about.

From the day the 7th Cavalry rode into Elizabethtown until now, there has been not one confrontation. Nor has anyone been seen in a white sheet and mask, nor has a cross been burned. Without a legitimate government backing them, they have no appetite for a stand-up battle.

Hope my ass grows back, Private Joshua Whitaker thinks to himself (because General Custer had chewed it out). He has remade his bunk tightly enough to bounce a coin off of it. He and a few others who are off-duty for half a day have paid Bobby Lee to cook his famous tender roast rather than have what tastes like roadside possum carcass at the regular mess. He steps into the kitchen to wheedle a piece of it in advance of the lunch bell.

The flintlock pistol that is put to his head is an obsolete one-shot affair. Lips visible from a hole cut in a black sack-cloth mask are touched with a finger; Joshua obeys.

Bobby Lee has already been gagged, and two other masked men are binding his hands together with a thick rope while a fourth man holds a more modern revolver on him.

The one with the flintlock, whose clothes smell of a stable, and who Joshua Whitaker will later describe as 'fat,' says to him: "Keep quiet, yank. We're gonna use this nigger to teach you some respect for us. Tell your proud peacock, old Custer, that we won't come after a Federal. We know what will happen if we string up or shoot one of you precious cavalrymen. But let's see you try to hire another coon to cook your meals for you when they see what we do to *this* one!"

They hustle both Bobby Lee and Joshua Whitaker out the door to a wagon and make them lie facedown in back and cover them with burlap. The Klansmen then tug off their masks. The pinhooker looks back at Eagle House, smiling at the still-visible scars on the brick from Confederate general John Hunt Morgan's 1862 raid. *First action in this town since then*, he thinks.

When the team of horses has pulled them out of the town proper, they make Joshua get out with his eyes closed.

"Remember what I told you!" one of them shouts at his back. "We won't touch a cavalryman. We know what would come down on us. But each time you insult us, a North-loving nigger dies!"

Joshua Whitaker stumbles down the dirt road without pause. Through the trees, he sees the red brick tops of the two-story tobacco warehouses that dot Elizabethtown. He runs toward them like a thirsty man running to a drink; he is afraid they will change their minds about letting him go.

In the wagon, under the burlap, Bobby Lee sighs. He knows they won't change their minds about not letting him go.

Evening descends on an Elizabethtown in chaos. Immediately after Private Whitaker returned, Custer dispatched the sole battalion of unmounted infantrymen under his command to search the town proper, in case the kidnappers doubled back to a local hideout. He took some men to the pinhooker's barn, but a stableboy caring for the horses claimed ignorance, even after Custer threatened to burn down the stables with him inside it.

The Hill House is his command headquarters. The hitching posts in front of the two-story building run out of room, and a couple of privates simply stand on South Main street holding reins of horses for the officers and messengers coming in and out. Libby is lighting an oil lamp as the mayor of Elizabethtown blusters in, with desperate words about how the kidnappers do not represent Elizabethtown or, indeed, the great state of Kentucky. Custer nods, formally accepts the words, and sends him on his way.

None of Custer's search parties have a particular place to look. They run over the map like a spilled pot of ink. Custer hates that, and he *really* hates staying in one place.

A few reporters (normally Custer's oxygen) are turned away; there is no good news to report.

Another knock comes at the door. It is Mr. Daniel Campbell, their neighbor and recent dinner companion. Libby shows him into the study, where Custer and two adjutants are looking over a map.

"Er, not a good time," Custer says gently, mindful of his wife's desire to move in good society. "I appreciate your well-wishes—"

Eyes fixed to the floorboards, Campbell says, "I figure I know where they're going to hang the nigger."

Daniel Campbell now has an audience so rapt a professional actor would envy it.

"I was with them, the first year they sprung up in these parts," Campbell says. "Just a social club for a few old boys who had worn the gray. Then they lynched some poor nigger they said had done something. They mutilated him first. I was sick and some of the ruffians laughed at me. So I dropped out of the—"

"Social club," Custer finishes. His face is blank; he is thinking. His voice is calm; he is planning. "Where's their hideout?"

"Hideout? None. There's no headquarters. You already know the leaders' names, I expect. You know they're not home either. The only thing there is, is an excellent place in the woods. A bunch of oaks, but with a large clearing, and at the edge of it, perhaps the tallest, oldest oak tree in the county. You hang someone from a branch on that tree, you can gather hundreds of men with all their horses and traps so they can see it. That's where they did it the one time I went. Must be where—"

"Take us!"

Campbell nods. He doesn't want to make himself or his family a target by helping the Federal cavalry. But he is a decent man for his time. He had killed twenty men in the war. But in the Klan, he watched a local blacksmith use a knife to separate genitals from a living human body, and he was too scared to intervene.

He will take them to the clearing with the giant old oak tree. It is his penance.

For Custer, there is relief at having a lead on the Ku Kluxers, but also a deeper pleasure than he will admit to himself. He wasn't built for dinner parties.

Night has truly fallen. Custer, Campbell, and seventy men on horseback travel double breast along an unnamed country road—its width will support no more than two mounts. Daniel Campbell earns his penance, because the unnamed road is crossed with another, which they branch left onto. This and the next road they take are mere trails, which only the locals would know. Custer knows that none of his patrols will have ventured out here.

Soon the signs of heavy travel are unmistakable. Multiple threads of trails come together. Fresh horse manure, recently trampled vegetation. Custer orders them to widen from two-by-two into battle formation.

Campbell starts to say something in a normal tone, but at Custer's stern "tzzt!" he drops to a whisper just loud enough to be heard from mount to mount: "if they arrange things as they did last time, we should see light soon. Several lanterns hung in surrounding trees. They don't roast the negroes on a bonfire as I've heard some places do, least they didn't last time."

"There wouldn't be a bonfire anyway," Custer said. "Hasn't rained recently enough."

"Main thing they want is plenty of light so's they can all socialize with each other and get a good view of the lynching."

Custer nods, and his disciplined men continue their advance in "arrow" formation, with only the light of the moon to guide them.

There! There is the promised light; a false dawn flickers among trees. The wind brings a chorus of men raggedly singing the Kentucky Confederate anthem ("And we'll march! March! March! To the music of the drum! We were driven forth in exile from our old Kentucky home!"), as well as laughter and conversation.

Custer will be glad to pay back the insult that was directed at him. For what was grabbing Bobby Lee, but an insult to the commanding officer who had been in his presence perhaps twenty minutes before?

He *does* desire to save the black man for the sake of saving him; he dislikes such brutality. Just after the Civil War, he had encountered a former slave woman in Alexandria, Louisiana who had been lashed five hundred times in a single instance; in a letter to his father-in-law, he had written: *If the War has attained nothing else it has placed America under a debt of gratitude for all time, for removal of this evil.*

So yes, he will be happy to save the man…

…but Custer loves the fight. *Loves* it. And this torturous quiet time in Elizabethtown has ended, finally.

He frowns; the Klansmen posted no sentries on their perimeter. It will make his job easier, but still…weren't most of these white-robed fellows in the Rebellion?

Sloppy.

And who says he wants things to go easy? It has been seven years since the end of the war, and four years since the Battle of the Washita.

At the Washita encampment in 1868, there had been plenty of squaws and little ones among the Cheyenne braves. He had not

217

allowed that to stop him; the ones that hadn't been killed had made good hostages to keep old Black Kettle's warriors from pressing a counterattack. Custer had done whatever was needed to win the battle. If a lot of women and children had been killed that day, well, such were the fortunes of war.

Ease is not his desire.

Glory is.

Bobby Lee, once called Charles, stands in the back of a four-wheeled buckboard, his arms and legs bound with rope. The noose, which had to be tossed by strong arms to loop over the heavy branch some two stories overhead, sags down from his neck.

He is not even close to being hanged yet. This is a party, and he is an ornament for the revelers' amusement. He will stand here until they are through socializing and speechifying and passing flasks of whiskey and singing songs. Only then will they pull the rope taut, and either hitch up a horse and drive the cart away, or else a couple of stout men will simply pick up his legs and chuck him over the side. With his bound legs, he will look like a giant inch worm as he thrashes.

When men are hanged by the courts, the executioners are skilled professionals; the rope is given enough play to cause a sharp jerk that breaks one's neck, quickly ending the guest of honor's suffering. Everyone knows that. This, though, will not be the work of professionals. Bobby Lee will suffocate slowly.

He ponders that. He has seen many troubles over the course of a life that began in 1820 or 1821 (whenever he was born—he is not sure, because by the time he was old enough to ask, no other slave remembered with certainty); he cried, privately, when his wife and two children died of yellow fever on the plantation, all three in the space of five days. The overseer had made him get up in the morning and chop his quota of tobacco on that Tuesday, that Friday, and that Saturday.

He went on, then. He has always gone on. Now, he will end. His main thought is that he doesn't know how to be dead.

He doesn't believe in the "sweet by 'n' by" or angels or the pearly gates, because he first heard of these things from a white man's mouth.

When he is dead, who will make his bed in his rented room? Who will—but his thoughts are interrupted by a ruckus at the periphery.

Custer leads his men into the clearing, from the front, as always. He holds the reins in one hand and his pistol in the other.

The Klansmen, most of them dismounted, look up at his approach. About half of them are visibly armed, but none appear to draw a bead; they don't dare, not with Federal cavalrymen in formation holding rifles.

So many, Custer thinks, and his eyes brush across the assembled men in white robes; their costumes are a riot of different styles, no doubt designed at the whims of their wives.

"Who is the leader, here?" he yells. "Show yourself!" Anxious men look at each other, some in the white sheets and masks, some with ridiculous headgear and exposed faces, some wearing just their regular civilian work clothes.

Seconds go by. No one volunteers information. Custer leans back his head and laughs.

"I fought some brave Rebs in the war. I guess none of that fine material is here!"

Some in the crowd growl at that; still, no one comes forward.

Custer looks at Daniel Campbell, who is rigid in his nervousness. "It might be best if *you* cut Bobby Lee loose," he says. With just a tiny bit more foresight than he is usually given credit for, he figures that a civilian taking the prize away from the Klansmen will be less provocative than a Federal trooper in blue.

Campbell. Yankee lover. Nigger lover. Men mutter these words as Daniel Campbell dismounts. With a stone face, he climbs up into the bed of the buckboard Bobby Lee stands on, and pulls out his pocket knife.

Bobby Lee stands calmly as the white man who he knows by sight from town pulls off the noose and cuts the ropes binding his hands and feet.

He wonders if he will actually get a chance to make his own bed tomorrow morning.

"Bobby fucking Lee!" The voice is from the edge of the crowd; its owner strides forward, ripping off his own hood.

It is the stable owner. His robes are more richly appointed in sashes and fancy collars, suggesting a leader's uniform. "You yanks gave that nigger that name! It's a damnable insult."

His bruised face, courtesy of Custer's fists, is mottled with rage.

"So you're the leader," Custer says. "As if that was a surprise."

The horse dealer ignores him. His eyes are fixed on the about-to-be-liberated captive.

"Robert E. Lee has been in his grave less than two years, and this nigger prances around with his name, making a mockery of a great man! Well, this ends now!"

From a robe pocket, he pulls the flintlock pistol. He points it up at Bobby Lee.

He then performs a series of actions: he rears back his head, buckles his knees, drops the unused pistol, disgorges blood and brain matter all over his ornate robes, lets loose his bowels and bladder, and collapses in a heap.

George Armstrong Custer has just blown the man's brains out.

The entire world freezes, for a moment, into a tableau:

...Custer with his pistol extended, black powder smoke coming from the barrel...

...the cavalrymen, heavily armed but bunched too closely together in a clearing...

...Bobby Lee and Daniel Campbell standing up in the wagon with the giant oak tree at their backs...

...uncounted hundreds of Kentucky Klansmen, lightly armed with a variety of shotguns, pistols and some modern rifles chambered for brass cartridges—they are on all sides, most on foot, in a depth that surrounds the Federal cavalry in multiple rings—their tethered horses, carriages, dog traps, and buckboards forming even more of a barrier to the quick withdrawal of Custer's forces. Ironically, if the Klansmen had been competent enough to keep a guarded perimeter to protect their festivities, the Federal troops would not have been able to trot into the center of the action; but now that they are here, getting out will not be so easy...

...the crumpled form of the stable owner, the Grand Dragon.

The rest of the players, after that blessed moment of absolute silence and motionlessness, move, and move quickly!

Mounted Federal troops fire at will into the crowd, without order. Rifle bullets go through more than one row of white-sheeted figures; perhaps fifty of them fall dead or dying.

At the same moment, Klan shotguns and pistols throw lead into the vulnerable mounted cavalry. Federal men topple from horses; some animals are shot out from under troopers who scramble off their dying, falling beasts.

One sergeant jumps off his grievously wounded mount. The sergeant is a Civil War veteran; in an instant, he judges his beloved horse is through, and puts a rifle bullet through her head so she will fall at his side. He crouches as she thumps to the ground, and uses the bulk of her body as both a shield and a rifle prop; the maneuver was fairly common in the war.

Firing is infectious. Every veteran knows it. Shooting causes men to shoot. Disciplined troops can be ordered to cease fire, but their officers are only men themselves, and can't be counted on to give the order in the first place—and here, they don't.

This battle will *not* end with negotiations. It started on impulse; besides, the Federals and the resentful die-hards hate each other.

Custer empties his pistol into the choicest targets at hand. Those white sheets are wonderful to him, and he grins ferociously as his bullets connect with Reb after Reb. His own horse absorbs a couple of wild, blind shots and falls. He jumps away an instant before his left leg would have been trapped beneath. He has had mounts shot out from under him before; just another day at the shop.

He looks around him and sees (dimly, in the rising cloud of black smoke) that perhaps ten or a dozen of his men have died. Gunfire is constant now, and screaming men and horses, and he has to bellow his orders to be heard above it.

"Hold the line! Extend perimeter to tree line, north!"

For a while, the advantage is to the Federal troops. They are current soldiers, with clear lines of authority that have been reinforced through sadistic discipline. Squads fight as squads, not as disorganized individuals.

221

The Klansmen, by contrast, are free-firing amateurs who do as they please. Most fought in the Rebellion, but they have had seven years to go to seed, and besides, they cannot create agreed-upon lines of authority in mere moments.

Every bizarre tragedy that can happen in battle, happens:

…A Klansman with an excellent Winchester rifle, jockeying for a good shot at the Federal lines, creeps behind his own side's tethered horses; the continuing fire spooks them, and before he can even draw a bead, one rears up and tramples him to death…

…A cavalryman peeks his head up to see beyond the ring of dead horses—right into the path of a bullet fired from behind him by his best friend…

…A 23-year-old Klansman whose cardiac system was weakened by rheumatic fever as a child, simply dies of a heart attack…

Horses and men scream as they die. Black powder smoke (at night!) turns the world into gray shadows at best. It is the Hell which William Tecumseh Sherman accurately, sincerely described.

Fire begins to slack off. The Federals, in their dark blue wool, are almost impossible to see. The Klansmen have finally become sensible of what targets their white robes make, and the living have mostly discarded them; too late for more than one hundred and fifty motionless figures in crumpled red-and-white heaps surrounding the Federal lines.

Custer's forces have lost half their own number. Most of the horses are gone, too.

He knows they can't break out. He knows that he penetrated too far into the enemy's territory. But he judges his force's superior firepower can hold off the riff-raff until reinforcements arrive.

But reinforcements have to be summoned.

Custer silently curses himself for not leaving back a squad in the woods.

He inquires if there are still horses, still riders. The men who bring messages from one part of a battlefield to another are usually called "runners," but on this night they are crawlers. The answer comes back: Yes, two.

Two horses, held close to the bridle. The beasts are wild with fear; the men's feet leave the ground as the animals pull and thrash.

The crawling messenger bring Custer's order to the lieutenant crouched closest to the frightened mounts. The lieutenant listens to the relayed order, nods, and looks around. Of the surviving men he can see, he picks the two he figures are the best riders.

Some other lieutenant, given the same order, might have chosen two other men.

Two lucky young men have been given, not just permission, but *orders* to break out from this graveyard. The lieutenant pointed to them, and they will live.

To be put into this arbitrary gamble of who gets butchered—to have one's fate decided by a harried junior officer possessing imperfect information and no time to think—*this* is what young boys wish to happen to them when they dream of going to war, whether they know it or not.

The Federals have little remaining ammunition. They use some of it on covering fire to let the riders escape.

Only this goes well: the riders gallop off when the Klansmen are still sorting themselves out. There are only a few wild shots that might as well have been aimed at the moon.

The Klansmen are finally cohering into a fighting force that can take advantage of their far superior numbers. The veterans have agreed on leader-follower roles within small bands. All available ammunition has been retrieved from satchels and pockets. Rheumatic old men have relinquished fine hunting rifles to younger men who can better use them.

They all know who they are fighting.

"Custer."

"Goddamn Custer."

"Custer, that son of a bitch."

"We gonna be fighting Custer again."

"This time we're gonna win!"

"Ole Kentuck shall be for the South this time, boys! We'll rewrite history. We'll teach that 'boy general' Custer!"

"Death to Custer! And to the Yankees!"

"The South will rise again!"

"Fuck Custer!"
"Kill Custer!"

"Is he dead?" a private whispers to his friend.

Custer took a round to the chest during the last exchange of fire. He lies on the ground, motionless.

Then, a wet cough, a shudder. Custer sits up, or tries to. At least he can speak.

"Our defensive works?" he says, then coughs a sloshy cough, as if a can of paint is jostling about within him.

A sergeant bends close and says, "A line of dead men, theirs and ours, to the south. Horses and bodies to the west, mostly our horses and their bodies, about ten yards short of that hanging tree up there. North and east we have snipers at the tree line and in the bushes, try-ing to keep—keeping them back."

More coughing, a suppressed retch. "Effective strength?"

"No more than twenty."

"Op—opposing?"

"We made a good dent in 'em, sir. But now they're hanging back. Hard to estimate. I'd say, and this is a pretty wild guess, I'd say in the hundreds. Under three hundred."

"Under three hundred!" Despite the rip in his lung, Custer seems amused. "Not like we've got to capture them all. Just…just hold the circle until re, reinforce, forced." He draws a ragged breath. "Couple of hours."

On the heels of his words, a banshee wail breaks out in the dark forest.

Custer looks at the pistol in his hand. Is it empty? If not, it soon will be.

"The Confederate battle cry!" Custer says. "Have you ever heard that?"

"Yes sir. Just now."

They share a laugh.

Suppressive fire reigns down from the highest Klan-held posi-tions, and the first wave of attackers rush their lines.

The Federals manage only this: they do not give their souls away for free.

Sunrise, and the Klansmen are gone, back to their various homes. They have left some two hundred of their own behind on the battlefield. A few bodies were taken home by friends or relatives, but most had to be left behind; there weren't enough wagons or, especially, time; they knew they must escape quickly.

Federal cavalrymen, supplemented by trusted state militia, arrive just after the sun. The two escaped messengers, now on fresh horses, lead the way.

They approach with caution, do flanking maneuvers, and send dismounted pickets to creep in between the trees—everything Custer should have done the night before.

They come upon a few outlying bodies first: Klansmen who fell to sniper fire. Dead horses and men become more plentiful. Then the first scout reaches the main battlefield, and shouts, "No!"

Almost seventy men in blue, butchered beyond recognition. Custer is identified by his long blond hair. His face was mutilated by vengeful Klansmen before they left.

A few bodies in dark civilian wool clothes are among the Federals; these are the Klansmen who shed their robes and participated in the final surge of battle.

A new wave of mutilation occurs; white-robed bodies are kicked, slashed with knives, urinated on. The cavalrymen vow vengeance. Their Northern-accented voices, though filled with curses and bewailing, are music to the ears of two men hiding behind the giant oak tree. Bobby Lee and Daniel Campbell stand up and reveal themselves.

Just outside the fields of fire from both sides, forgotten, they had lain quietly, then scrambled into the woods as the Klansmen had gone on their final charge.

The first thing they do is ask for water. The next thing they do is to become legends.

When the news broke of the massacre of the Civil War hero Custer and his gallant cavalrymen, the nation was shocked. Seven years after the end of the war, something that could be called a battle had taken place between Federal troops and die-hards!

In advance of the 1872 elections, every politician promised to avenge the martyr, Custer.

Every Klavern throughout the South disbanded as fast as it could, which sometimes wasn't fast enough; with renewed Federal troop strength in the former Confederate states, it was death to be seen wearing a white robe. The Southerners crazy enough to celebrate the Klan's victory over Custer paid a high price; a lot of necks were stretched with rope in the following months.

The Fourteenth Amendment to the Constitution, only four years old, was given teeth with enabling legislation. The already-existing Civil Rights Act of 1866, long disputed, was enforced to the letter.

The wealthier class of white Southerners had secret plans to disenfranchise people who looked like Bobby Lee, with grandfather clauses and "literacy tests" and exorbitant poll taxes; they were just waiting until Reconstruction ended and they had political control again. Custer's death made those plans impossible to carry out.

Custer's Last Stand Against the Klan became not just an iconic American story, but an iconic image as well. Paintings, illustrations in magazines, cartoons.

Children played Cavalry and Klansmen.

A prominent brewery distributed a frosted glass painting of the Last Stand (and the beer's brand) to hang behind the bar in thousands of saloons across America.

Some modern naysayers scoff at the importance of the battle; it lasted possibly less than an hour, with a few hundred dead. It had no real significance. (Others concede half a point, calling it, "The smallest battle in history...that ever shaped history.") The nation, they say, would have protected the voting rights and equality of its black citizens even without the impetus of punishing die-hard racists to avenge Custer.

But others claim that A. Philip Randolph could not have become the nation's first black president in 1940 if it had not been for seven decades of uninterrupted progress on race relations from 1872 onward.

And (despite the fact that she is more often thought of as a feminist icon than a civil rights icon), some wonder if Shirley Chisolm would have become the first black female president in 1976 without Custer's great sacrifice.

"Let me pay all," says this gallant man—*this military Christ!*— Ambrose Bierce, "A Son of the Gods"

Copyright © 2014 by Eric Cline

The Rose Is Obsolete

by Alvaro Zinos-Amaro

Raymond Esposito leaned closer to the woman sitting before him, remembering her once sparkling, vivacious brown eyes.

Right now those eyes were lost.

"I brought you a new binder, just like you asked me." He set the binder down on the small teak coffee table, flipped through its blank pages. "See? It's going to make an amazing scrapbook."

The woman's eyes failed to register him.

"Look. Bright red cover, three rings. Your favorite type." Raymond spoke with artificial precision, over-enunciating every syllable. "And plenty of protective sheets."

Feeling like a cheap salesman, Raymond grimaced. He studied the face of the woman he loved. Most women of sixty-two would have killed for her looks. Her skin remained porcelain-white, clear and unblemished; her cheekbones and forehead wrinkle-free; her lips full, supple. But this beauty was only a cruel reminder of the bountiful emotions her face had once conveyed, before the right side became paralyzed and the roaming of the eyes set in, before her speech became slurred.

Minutes passed. Raymond decided to end his visit. But then the woman's eyes dilated and the lips parted. First there was a spark of recognition at his presence—a tiny, flickering event which nevertheless filled him with hope—, followed by a surge of understanding when she identified the binder.

"Thank you," she said with visible effort. She cocked her head to the side. "Thank you, *Ray*." She smiled.

Raymond lived for moments like this, islands of connection in their vast sea of separateness.

"You're welcome. I wanted to tell you something else, Donna," he said. He straightened his back. "I love you very much."

She didn't acknowledge his words. Instead she said, "Pencil. Pencil, *please*."

He fished one from the bag of supplies he'd brought and laid it neatly beside the binder, along with sheets of paper, soft scissors, and glue.

"Your eyes," she said.

He frowned, not understanding.

"*Closhe* your eyes."

Raymond did as instructed. Time crawled by, seconds ticked off on an antique clock. In the stillness of the room the sound of Donna writing was impossible to miss. Right after the stroke Donna had been better at writing than speaking, but deteriorating motor coordination had transformed her neat penmanship into a series of squiggles.

"Open *now*," she said.

He breathed deeply and opened his eyes, bracing himself for the inevitable scrawl. The sheet of paper was folded in four. He set it to the side, then placed his right palm on her left hand. The nurse had warned that sudden physical contact could upset her, but she seemed calm right now. Her skin was warm, soft. He allowed his hand to rest atop hers. Then a look of mild apprehension crept into her eyes, and he pulled back.

"I love you," she said. She was looking straight at him. "I love you, *Ray*."

He read the note.

"You're surprised that a geezer like me needs your services," Raymond said.

The man, who had identified himself to Raymond simply as Tool, grinned. His nimble fingers tapped commands into a micro-tablet on his belt. "I need to ask you a few questions."

Raymond tensed. The van's windows were tinted, the interior soundproofed and EM-blanketed, but he didn't like discussing his private life with anyone—especially someone like Tool. "What about?"

"Easy," Tool said. "Your heartbeat shot up. I think the long delay in what you've asked me to do gives me the right to be nosy."

"Why should the delay matter? I'm paying you a substantial retainer."

"Look," Tool said. "We're doing this my way or no way." He pointed towards the van's door.

Raymond focused on getting his vitals under control. "Fine."

"Much better. What's your relationship to Donna Esposito?"

Raymond shot him a look. "She's my wife. Which you knew."

"A baseline question helps calibrate responses. She's currently at a nursing facility in your hometown of Cherryville, North Carolina. Is that where I'll find her a year and a half from now?"

"Correct."

"Why is she there?"

"She suffered a stroke a year ago and needs full-time care."

"Had she retired at the time?"

"No," Raymond said.

"You?"

"Still working."

"For how long?"

"What's it matter?"

"People do strange things when they have free time on their hands," Tool said. "Like grow a conscience."

"You needn't worry about a change of heart," Raymond replied through pursed lips.

Tool looked at something on his ocular implant. "So *why* the delay?"

Raymond shifted in the van's seat. "Donna still has a good year and a half before she really goes south."

"I see," Tool said, making it clear he didn't. "Why not observe her progress and play it by ear?"

Raymond clenched his jaw. "Limiting her suffering will bring me peace of mind."

"Why the specific time of night?"

Raymond shrugged. "She'll be sleeping, with minimal staff around. I need to know exactly *when* it will happen. It's critical that you execute the plan *precisely as specified.*"

"Let's say I get a flat and I'm an hour late."

"I don't believe someone with your reputation," Raymond said, "would be so sloppy."

"You're right. And yet things happen."

"I'll up your fee by twenty percent. Just make sure it gets done on time."

"To the minute," Tool said.

Raymond spoke with the same deliberateness he used with Donna. "To—the—*second.*"

Tool ran a hand through his shoulder-length hair. "Normally I wouldn't ask this, but your case is special: Why do you want this done?"

There was a tightness in Raymond's throat. "Because she told me."

"She asked you to end her life?"

"Not in so many words. But she made her wishes clear."

"How?"

"That's highly personal," Raymond said.

"As is what you're asking me to do," Tool replied. "Let's be clear. The money doesn't make it *im*personal. It simply guarantees the reward is worth the risk."

Raymond reached into his pocket and produced Donna's note. He passed it to Tool, who unfolded it and blink-scanned it.

"A line from a poem by someone called William Carlos Williams. Meaning?"

"Donna used to teach literature," Raymond said. "The line she quoted—'The rose is obsolete'—is significant. She was always my rose, you see. She's telling me she's outlived her usefulness. She wants to go."

"What if she just wanted to cheer you up with pretty poetry?"

Raymond crossed his arms. "That's absurd. I know my wife. I've lived with her forty years. I understand how her mind works. We done?"

Tool passed him a pad. "Once we part ways today, I'll only be reachable for twenty-four hours the day before your specified date. If a cancellation is needed, that's your window."

Raymond scanned the screen and pressed his thumb over the designated area.

"I have a lot of information on you, Mr. Esposito."

I could say the same, Raymond thought, but kept silent. Who knew how much of it was real, or traceable.

The van door opened and Raymond climbed out into the rainy night.

Donna continued cutting out pictures and gluing them to the pages of the new binder.

"Looks amazing, sweetie," Raymond said.

Her latest collage interspersed personal photos with pictures of actors and models clipped from fashion magazines. They bore a vague resemblance to Donna and Raymond, and some of the back-drops were similar too: a boat on which they'd gone fishing had been placed alongside a celebrity couple on a luxury yacht, Donna on a hill appeared next to a female rock-climber on a snow-capped summit, and so on.

As Donna continued snipping away Raymond paced her small room and finally sat beside her, violating what the nurse had defined as Donna's "personal comfort zone." *Forty years of marriage should give me the right.* He smelled her hair.

Donna's hands began to fidget.

"Honey, it's okay. It's just me."

Her breathing sped up and she dropped the scissors and glue.

"I'm sorry," he said. He scooted over. "I want you to know I understood your message. I'm going to help you."

Nothing happened. The clock on the wall tick-tocked away. Raymond went to the window and pulled back the curtains. The gray sky's swollen clouds cast dark, lumbering shadows, promising rain.

"I love you," he said, rising to leave. "You won't have to be...*obsolete*...much longer."

Donna began humming a tune Raymond didn't recognize. Then she picked up the scissors and glue and resumed her scrapbooking.

"I love you," Raymond repeated. "No matter what happens, *I will see you again.*"

Just for an instant, Donna looked up.

"I like *Ray*," she said, directing her gaze back down to the binder. She pointed to a picture of Ray, seemingly oblivious to any connection between the man standing in her room and the man smiling in the photograph.

"And I like Donna," he said, pointed to a picture of her, and gave her a peck on the cheek before leaving.

The back of the man who called himself Sideways slumped against the trunk of a massive longleaf pine. "No time to retire like the past, huh gramps?" he asked as Raymond approached.

"Something like that." Raymond caught his breath and then said, "So, let's get to it. What are my odds?"

Sideway's face hardened. "Forty percent survival chance."

Raymond surprised himself with his language. "That's fucking preposterous."

"Time travel *is* fucking preposterous," Sideways replied. "Why do you think it's fucking illegal?" He licked his chapped lips and popped a stick of chewing gum into his mouth. "You're aware of the consequences of jumping, pops?"

"Temporal conservation?"

"Temporal whiplash," Sideways corrected. "When you jump into the past—the only direction you *can* jump—you're stealing information from the present. To even things out, time steals information from the future and selects someone whose *remaining lifespan precisely equals the length of your jump.* Voilà, they're gone."

" 'Gone,' meaning dead."

"You're a quick study. Their lost future equals your gained past. You're going to jump back a year and half. That means the nearest person to you who was going to die—whether by natural causes or in some other way—a year and a half from the moment of your jump will die *when* you jump instead. *You* steal a year and half from time, time steals a year and a half to even the score. Are you with me?"

Raymond nodded. He visualized himself jumping, Donna disappearing through temporal whiplash moments before Tool entered her room—

One step at a time.

He blinked. Even though sunset had given way to night and the forest was chilly, sweat slicked his underarms and beaded his forehead. "What else?"

"You pay me now, in full, and you'll receive the tech a week from today. It will only work once, so you'll be stranded in the past—assuming you make it that far. Word to the wise, if anything goes wrong, do *not* look up my younger self. He reacts poorly to temporal visitors, in any reality."

"Understood."

Sideways passed Raymond a translucent, wafer-thin device. Raymond provided his authorization for the transfer of funds, then massaged his temples.

"A real pleasure." Sideways pulled out his chewing gum and dropped it into a small zip-lock bag which he dumped into his rucksack. A loud humming emanated from several of Sideways's facial implants, now apparently working in concert. He marched off.

Raymond stood in the gathering dusk, realizing that for Sideways he had already ceased to exist.

One moment Raymond Esposito was in April 2014, the next he was in October 2012.

His insides felt like they'd been torn from his body and stitched back together in the wrong order. He keeled over and puked. Clearing his eyes from the sharp sting of the upchuck, he forced himself to stand. Brain still on overload, he scanned his immediate surroundings.

No one around. Good. Good.

He checked for landmarks. He was in the same spot from which he'd jumped, a dirt path on the outskirts of Charlotte, deserted at this time of night.

Raymond shuffled toward the bed and breakfast he had scouted in 2014, bones aching as though they had been beat with a steel pipe, muscles spent as if he'd just completed a marathon. *Breathe,* he told himself. *Breathe. Remember why you're doing this. She's worth all of it—and more.*

By the time he arrived he was ready to pass out. "Hi, looking for a single room," he wheezed.

The gaunt young man at the front desk barely glanced up from whatever was occupying his attention behind the counter. "You got it. Credit card and ID please."

Raymond reached into the wallet with his fake documents and cleared his throat while the young man ran them through the computer.

"Great, thank you…Mr. Hoffman. My name's Bert." With difficulty Bert made eye contact. "Any idea how long you'll be staying with us, Mr. Hoffman?"

"A few weeks."

"Sweet." Bert proceeded to walk Raymond through the amenities and timetables. "Any questions?"

"I think I'm good," Raymond said, feeling anything but. He glanced at the lobby, comforted by its lack of guests. He had picked this place because it was forty miles from Cherryville, a prudent buffer from his past self. Raymond knew that by jumping into the past he had already created a new parallel timestream where the future could turn out differently from the one he knew—that was the whole point—but he still felt it best not to interact with his past self directly.

"Here's your key card," Bert said. "Need a second one?"

"Nah."

Head already swiveling back toward his display, Bert said, "Have a great night."

"You too," Raymond muttered, then dragged himself toward his room.

A moment later Bert's voice called out. "Mr. Hoffman!"

Raymond turned, pyrotechnic pain bursting in his temples. "Yeah?" he groaned.

"Need any help with your luggage?"

Raymond repressed the urge to wretch again. "Actually, I left it in the car," he lied. His clothes and wallet were all the extras he'd been able to carry on the jump. "Too beat to bring it in tonight."

Bert frowned. "You sure? I could grab it for you. No trouble at all."

"I'm sure," Raymond said. "And please, see that I'm not disturbed in the morning."

"Okey dokey."

Raymond made his way upstairs without turning back.

✧ ✧ ✧

235

Despite the gauzy curtains that let the sun in at an obscenely early hour, Raymond slept until evening the following day.

When he rolled out of bed he slapped his cheeks to restore circulation to his creaky brain.

Dehydration doubled his heartbeat and made his palms clammy. He guzzled two bottles of complimentary water from the small counter, which helped, but not much.

Over the next hour he regained a semblance of humanity. His eyes stopped feeling like they were dissolving in their sockets. An examination in the bathroom mirror revealed minor bruises on his arms and back, but no welts or protuberances. Eventually he felt clear-headed enough to venture downstairs.

He found the front desk occupied by a plump woman in her mid-sixties.

"Hi, I'm Chris," Raymond said. "Room twenty eight."

The woman smiled, revealing large, perfectly white teeth. Her long gray hair was tied in a ponytail and, make-up free, she was radiant.

"Yes, Bert let me know you came in last night," she said. "I'm Patricia, the owner. Welcome, and I hope you enjoy your stay with us, Mr. Hoffman. Let me know if there's anything you need."

"Actually, I have to mail a letter."

"We'll take care of it for you," Patricia said. "Can it wait till tomorrow's pickup at noon, or do you need it to go out sooner?"

"Tomorrow's fine."

"Great. Just drop it in here." Patricia pointed to a metallic box labeled "Outgoing."

"Will do."

"Mr. Hoffman—Chris, if you don't mind—how was your check-in?"

"No complaints," Raymond said, then added: "Bert was helpful."

"Glad to hear it." Patricia appeared relieved. "He's always got his head buried in his devices. I wish he'd spend more time building relationships with actual people, like our guests. So many return, I tend to think of them as extended family." The word "family" sent Raymond's mind reeling in unpleasant directions, and she seemed to sense it. "Anyway, I'm glad you're doing well."

I didn't say that, Raymond thought. "Thanks for your help."

He went out in search of letter-writing supplies. Walking down the street he was overcome by the magnitude of what he'd done. A simple breathing exercise helped get him through his errand. On the way back he stopped at a coffee shop and ordered a triple cappuccino. The barista looked at the time—quarter to nine—and said, "Long day, huh?"

"Long life," Raymond replied. He sat down in a corner and began composing his letter.

Dear Self, he wrote, then crossed it out. *Hi Ray, it's me. As in,* you. *I've traveled back from the future*—He stopped again, crumpled the page and stuffed it in his pocket. *Ray, please read this carefully. You have something in common with the person writing this letter to you: your deep love for your wife, Donna Esposito. But don't worry, I'm not having an affair with her.* He went on from there, explaining who he was, and providing as proof details about his relationship with Donna that only he, Raymond, would know. He proceeded to explain that half a year from now, if Raymond took no action, Donna would suffer a massive stroke. *Doctors believe these strokes are preventable,* he wrote. *Here are the things you must do to save your wife.*

For the next few days Raymond waited for a response from his younger self. *What if* I'd *received a letter from someone claiming to be me from the future?* he asked himself. *What would I do?* He didn't like the answers.

He checked himself for jump-related symptoms. Other than the occasional migraine, he only showed mild hair loss—not too bad, all things considered.

Trying to fend off loneliness, Raymond began taking his evening meals in the communal dining area. Occasionally Patricia would spot him and join him for a few minutes.

"If you had the chance to talk to someone you'd cared for a great deal," Raymond asked her one evening, "someone whom you'd thought lost, what would you say?" He wasn't actually going to talk to the Donna of this time; that would create too many complications. But it was nice to fantasize.

Patricia didn't seem taken aback by his heartfelt yet oddly theoretical question. If she was, she hid it well. "I'm not sure I'd have anything to say," she answered after a thoughtful silence. "If I truly thought I'd lost that person, I'd have done my best to move on."

"And here I was, thinking you were basically optimistic."

Puzzlement arched her brow. "What makes you think I'm not?"

"You don't believe in second chances."

She grinned. "Romantics looking for a way to correct past mistakes are in for a disappointment. The kind of letdown that doesn't sit well with my 'basically optimistic' outlook."

Touché, thought Raymond.

Raymond continued sending letters without a return address to his younger self via a forwarding service in New York. He didn't worry about fingerprints, since they'd simply point to Raymond. In the letters he included an email address for his younger self to contact him, and he checked the account several times a day.

Still no response.

Maybe he's getting the authorities involved, Raymond thought.

Something had to give. The meager savings in Raymond's bank account—set up with the identity of a 2014 guest of Donna's residence—would only last a few more weeks.

And then there were the nightmares. Raymond imagined that the temporal whiplash resulting from his jump had killed someone *other* than Donna. One night he dreamed about an old man standing in his kitchen, fridge door open, his face a study in horror as he was sucked into a gaping vortex of nothingness. And if Raymond *had* messed up, it would mean that Tool would carry out the hit and really kill Donna, instead of finding her gone, an event which Raymond's night terrors brought to life with startling immediacy. Raymond was in the room with her when it happened, could see every detail of her restful face as Tool appeared. Raymond tried to save her but he couldn't—he couldn't—he couldn't move, and—

He woke in a cold sweat, exhausted, disoriented.

Calm down, he told himself. He reiterated the plan's soundness in his mind, walked himself through it for the umpteenth time. *By having Tool plan to kill Donna in October of 2015 at a specific time, I guaranteed that her remaining lifespan precisely equaled the length of my jump. She and no one else must have been struck by the temporal whiplash. She just ceased to exist. No pain. In that reality, we're both gone.*

It wasn't a particularly comforting thought.

Three days later he finally received an email from his younger self. The message made it clear that his younger self was having trouble accepting Raymond's story—duh—but that despite his skepticism he was doing as Raymond asked. He'd spoken with Donna and she'd agreed to a medical evaluation. They had already changed their diet and exercise regimens. *The event you describe looms four months, three weeks, and two days in the future*, the other Raymond wrote, *and you better believe I'll do everything in my power to stop it from happening.*

Raymond read the email several times and was ecstatic—at first.

Then he began to wonder. If his plan worked, if Donna was saved, what was he supposed to do with the rest of his life? He was stranded in a reality he himself had created by jumping into the past, one which housed a younger version of himself that was taking care of Donna—so what was left for him to do?

On Raymond's final evening at the bed and breakfast Patricia approached and asked if he'd mind company.

"It's the first time you've asked for permission to join me," Raymond said.

"It's the first time you brought a friend along." She pointed to the dog-eared book by his plate.

"Books are nice, but I prefer people," he said. "Please, sit down."

Patricia studied him before sitting down. That kind of stare, coming from anyone but Donna, would usually have made him uncomfortable. But not this time.

"I couldn't help but notice," she said, in a quiet voice, "that room twenty eight has been booked by a different guest tomorrow evening."

239

"Yeah." Raymond blew a little air out of his mouth, somewhere between a sigh and a *brrrr*. "It's time to move on. Though I haven't exactly figured out where I'm going."

Patricia pulled her chair a little closer to the table. "I'm glad, Chris," she said. "I really am. Whatever your situation is, I'm happy that you're moving forward. And I have a little confession of my own to make."

"Do share."

"In a few weeks it will be my twentieth anniversary at this bed and breakfast," she said. "That's a long time to be in one place. Don't get me wrong, I love North Carolina and all…"

"You're moving?"

"I'm going to give myself a year off. Why not? I've worked hard. I can afford it. And Bert can manage—with some help—during that time. I've always wanted to travel. Go to Europe. I figure better now than when I'm old and frail."

The words slipped out of Raymond's mouth with ease. "It's hard for me to picture you that way."

She smiled with her eyes. "If you still haven't decided what your next step is when I take my sabbatical, maybe Europe will inspire you."

Raymond thought about his future, but he didn't have to think for long. "That's a very appealing offer," he began, "but I can't afford—"

"You'd be my guest," she said. "At least for the first few weeks. Then we'd find a way to work something out."

He swallowed, at a loss for words.

"You don't have to answer now. Just think about it," she said. She wrote down her contact information and slid it across the table.

He didn't need additional prodding. "Thank you so much, Patricia."

She scanned the title of his paperback. "Any good?"

"It's a classic," he said.

"Does that mean you haven't read it?"

They both laughed. "I guess there'll be plenty of time for that in Europe," he replied.

"Ray, could you sort through the mail *inside* the house? This is heavy! C'mon already!"

Donna and Raymond were each weighed down by two over-stuffed grocery bags. Despite the hot sun, he had committed the felony of stopping to check the mail on the way in. Sweating, Raymond saw there was only junk mail. He sighed with relief, then caught up with his wife.

After they unpacked the groceries, Donna sipped diet soda and said, "Seriously hon, what were you doing back there?"

"Just trying to be efficient," he said, wiping the last perspiration from his forehead. "I need a shower."

"You know," she said, "you've been a little on edge lately. And this mad rush to make us fitness buffs…it's stressing me out. Is everything okay?"

"Everything's great," he fibbed. "I just want us to be healthy. I'm going to clean up now."

In the shower he lingered under the hot water. He hadn't told Donna about the letters, or how they'd stopped arriving after he'd sent an e-mail—unanswered—to their alleged author about four months ago. He detested keeping secrets from Donna. It was time to come clean. He would tell her there was nothing to worry about, because even if it had all been true, the disaster day the letters had warned of was today, so they were in the clear.

Donning a fresh set of clothes, and already feeling better, he entered the living room, where Donna was flipping through a magazine on her tablet. "Hungry?" he asked. "I've been doing some thinking. Maybe we could talk over macrobiotic shakes?"

She looked up, lips on the cusp of a smile. "Sure. But let me change into something comfy first."

A few minutes after Donna left the room Raymond heard a loud thump from upstairs, and the thing he dreaded most came to pass.

Raymond admired his wife's pensive brown eyes. He knew that she was aware of him, could tell from the subtleties of her body language—the slight arch in her back, the relaxed pose of her shoulders—that she was pleased to see him.

"How are they treating you?" He spoke at a normal pace; it helped keep Donna engaged. "They tell me you're making tremendous progress, thanks in part to our preventive measures. The doctor said that in time you'll be able to come back home." He paused, feeling the need, for both their sakes, to temper his enthusiasm. No point in rushing things. Donna was going to need a year of physical therapy to recover, maybe longer.

She moved forward in her chair, and placed her hands, palms upturned, on her lap.

Raymond reached for his bag. "I brought you something I think you'll like." He produced a binder, placed it on the teak coffee table. "Red cover and three rings. Your favorite type. And here are some more pictures of us, to keep the scrapbook going."

Moving in slow motion, Donna opened the binder and slid her fingers along its sleek silver rings.

Raymond placed the photos beside the binder, as well as blank pages, a pencil, soft scissors and glue.

Donna regarded the assortment of marvels as though it represented a universe of possibilities.

Not "as though," Raymond thought; *"for her, that's exactly what it is."* He recalled the famous poem by William Blake, the line about seeing a world in a grain of sand.

Donna grabbed pencil and paper.

Raymond observed her, thinking about the letters from his older self. According to him, quoting poetry had been Donna's way of letting his future self know that she had had enough. That event, according to the letters' sender, had been the catalyst for his plan. *She'll reference William Carlos Williams,* the letter had warned. *And you'll understand.*

As Donna busied herself with her writing, Raymond considered events. There were two parallel realities now, thanks to his older self: the timestream in which Donna suffered a massive stroke and Raymond decided to jump back in time, killing her in the process, and the reality—*his* reality—in which the older Raymond arrived from the future and helped him mitigate that disastrous outcome, so that Donna had a mild stroke. Raymond wasn't sure what his older self would do, now that he was trapped here, but he knew one thing for certain. *He,* Raymond Esposito from 2012, wasn't going to attempt the experiment again, not in a few years, not ever. In this reality, he wouldn't contact Tool or Sideways. He'd remain at his wife's side, helping her heal, for as long as that took.

"For you," Donna said, bringing him back to the present. "For you, *Ray*."

He read her surprisingly neat print:

The fragility of the flower
unbruised
penetrates space

There was a pause, and then she began inspecting the photos and setting some aside.

This was the same poem the letter had warned about, but different lines. Donna was his rose, his flower, and her inner fragility was unbruised, despite the physical toll her body had suffered. Raymond smiled, folded the piece of paper and tucked it into his blazer pocket.

"Thank you, Donna," he said, standing up and placing a hand on her shoulder. " 'It is at the edge of the petal that love waits.'"

Thundergod in Therapy

by Effie Seiberg

Zeus sat on his shitty beige sofa in his shitty beige condo in his shitty beige retirement community. This was what the Court-appointed therapist had recommended—to think of this parole as a fresh start, and to enjoy retirement on Earth. Everything around him was fucking beige except for the fake plant from Ikea, which was a mocking shade of unnatural green. He could imagine the smug grin his judge would have if she'd seen this—

But no, he would give this a fair try. He'd promised Dr. Brinkman (formerly Terminus, the Roman god of boundaries) that he would.

The fake leather on the couch squeaked as he shifted. He could do this. He could be calm and serene. He would start by not destroying the couch.

"So, how's it been going so far?" Dr. Brinkman leaned back in his leather burgundy armchair. The former god of boundaries had interesting decor ideas for what a therapist's office should look like. Most of those ideas were burgundy. That's what happened when people soaked your statues in blood offerings for thousands of years, thought Zeus.

"It's fine."

"How do you like the condo? I furnished it myself. Very *normal*, you know?"

Zeus pressed his lips together and muttered, "Certainly no Mount Olympus."

"Well of course not. Those were the Court terms—prison then banishment and elimination of godly responsibilities, or death. Neither of your options included staying on Mount Olympus." The therapist paged through a yellow notebook.

"Have you been making the amends we talked about? I see here that we said you'd start small." Brinkman looked at Zeus over his half-moon glasses—a silly affectation for a god who clearly had perfect vision.

"I've started, yeah." Zeus shifted on the prickly burgundy couch. "I've gotta tell you, though, Sisyphus was *not* happy to see me." He chuckled. "Poor bastard would've thrown that rock at me if he could hoist it up that far."

"That's good progress, Zeus. What did you tell him?" Scribble scribble, went Brinkman's stubby yellow pencil.

"That I was sorry, that I'd let the power I had at the time overwhelm my judgment, and that I'm working on the anger issues. You know, the stuff we talked about." Zeus scratched his beard. "It was... fine." It was not fine. It was horrible and the only thing that made it worthwhile was that he left without actually removing the onus.

Scribble scribble. "These are certainly healthy steps. Perhaps this week we can work towards making the amends the Court required, to Thor and Raijin and the Thunderbird. Can you think of ways to make amends to the gods you've...ah...slain?"

"I dunno. It's not like I can go down to the underworld to find them. They're just dead." Zeus scratched his beard. "Maybe apologize to the other gods from their pantheons?"

"That's a good thought. I think you should take this week to come up with a plan."

"It'll be *so humiliating*. I'm *Zeus*, you know. I was king of the gods once." Zeus caught Brinkman's eye. "I know I know. You don't have to say it. I'm working on having a healthier relationship with power, whether I have it or not, keeping my anger in control, blah blah. I'm on it. I'm *doing* it. New start, new me."

The therapist nodded. "Now tell me of your life in the retirement complex. How are you settling in?"

Zeus leaned forward. "Oh. Man. Lemme tell you, I never knew old chicks could be so much *fun!* They'll do things the younger girls would never do. Except for Betty Whitshire, that insufferable bitch. You know, she went around spreading all these rumors about me afterwards! And she cheats at shuffleboard."

"So you're finding ways to fill your time. Excellent." Scribble scribble.

"It's an adjustment, no question. But I'm in it for real, man. A fresh start. No more power-raged Zeus. I've *got* this."

He did not "got this."

Zeus turned on his air conditioning—the summer was a brutal one—and sat in his shitty fake-leather chair. Why on earth did people retire to a heated hellhole like Florida? He could feel sweat pooling between his bare thighs and the plasticky material.

He picked up the paper stack off of his (shitty, beige) coffee table. Phone bill, $27.95. The phone had been much more useful before the women of the complex started calling him a diseased man-slut, thank you Betty Whitshire. Cable bill, $49.99. He'd gotten into soap operas, and hated himself a little bit more every time he thought about it. Maybe he should cancel his cable. But then he'd *really* have nothing to do all day. Electric bill, $355.72.

$355.72? What the hell? It wouldn't completely blow through his monthly stipend, set up by the Court through Mammon, former false god of wealth, but still. He picked up the plastic beige phone on the plastic beige table by the couch, and called the electric company.

He waited more than twenty minutes on hold until a static-fuzzed voice finally came on and crackled, "Thank-you-for-holding-my-name-is-Grace-how-may-I-help-you."

"My electric bill is too high." Despite the AC, he was sweating into the plastic earpiece. This place was disgusting.

"What's your account number?" my-name-is-Grace sounded bored. He read it to her off of the bill.

"Thank you, Mr. Armstrong." He'd picked the name himself, after Dr. Brinkman had said that names like Mr. Allpowerfulfatherofthe-godsdestroyerofmenbringeroflightning would probably make it difficult to assimilate.

Tappa tappa tappa went my-name-is-Grace's fingers. "I see here that you owe $355.72. This is correct. My records show that we just sent a man out to read your meter last week."

"Are you kidding me? That's absurd!"

"Not really sir. It's a very hot summer and it's putting a lot of strain on our grid. We've asked our customers to cut back on high-power activities like air conditioning unless they absolutely need it, and we see that your usage patterns have remained the same. Prices go up during peak usage periods."

Zeus wheedled. He charmed. He tried his best banter. It didn't do one bit of good. My-name-is-Grace wouldn't budge. He slammed down the plastic phone, cracking the casing. He would go hunt down my-name-is-Grace and fry her with a well-placed bolt of...

No. No, breathe. Dr. Brinkman had always said, "Find an outlet for your anger when you can't dissolve it." Fine. A well-placed zap of lightning to the phone did the trick, melting it into a slightly-discolored puddle of plastic around a tangle of metal bits, and he could feel the anger starting to crack away. But $355.72 for the privilege of having his thighs stick to his shitty beige couch? Not in a lifetime.

He considered. If electricity was the problem, this was a thing he could solve. He got in his brown Chevy Geo (Dr. Brinkman had said that anything too flashy would raise eyebrows) and drove to the Home Depot. There, he had a pimple-faced young man with dead eyes explain to him, in excruciating detail, how home wiring worked and how he was connected to his grid. He bought wire-cutters, a voltmeter, pliers, electrical tape, heat-shrink connectors, and a book titled "Do-It-Yourself Electrical Repair: A Shockingly Good Time!" with a cartoon man smiling and getting electrocuted on the cover. All this plus a trunk-sized battery would do the trick.

It took three days, but he disconnected his entire condo from the grid. He smashed holes in the plasterboard walls and yanked out wire after wire—brute force was as good a method as any. Then, in a tangle of metal and plastic, he reconnected everything to the battery, which now sat in the middle of his beige living room instead of the shitty coffee table. The apartment was transformed. Once a beige box of sadness, it was now a rat's nest of blue and red wire casings which covered the walls (and part of the beige carpet) like ivy with a faint snow of plaster dust.

He sat on his fake leather sofa, put a finger on each of the hulking thing's contact points and *shoved* lightning in. The battery's gauge on the side lit up red, then yellow, then green.

Zeus stood and turned the air conditioner on full blast, then sat back down on the squeaky couch. Ahhhh. There, that was better. Cold air washed across his face and his underarms, fluttering the toga he still wore when he was alone at home. Retirement didn't have to be all bad. The Court hadn't stripped him of *all* his powers.

There was actually something satisfying about finishing a project. Plenty of people did it. Dr. Brinkman said there were many retired gods all living on Earth like humans, and that to his knowledge they'd found it relaxing. Nit, Egyptian goddess of weaving who had kept her role even after the Court of the Gods had stepped in, had apparently retired to a shepherding commune in California. He could do this.

In fact, he could celebrate. Some dolmades would just hit the spot, and maybe a nice shower after to get off the plaster dust. He was just getting out the grape leaves from the fridge when a sharp knock came from the door. He certainly wasn't expecting company, as the complex's crabs pariah. Must be a mistake. He rolled out a few grape leaves on a paper towel and started on the rice stuffing.

CRASH

Zeus poked his head out of the tiny beige kitchenette. A man swathed in glittering electronics was standing in his living room. Sprinkled around him were shards of what had been Zeus' door. He was brushing splinters away from some of his own wires and lights.

"What in the seven pits of Tartarus do you think you're doing?" roared the once-king of gods. "Look what you've done to my door! The condo board is going to fine me for this!"

The man pushed some sort of screened visor up from his green eyes to his forehead. "The condo board. Really. Old man, look what you've become." He glanced around the room with obvious distaste. "Your wiring is shit."

He wasn't wrong, but that wasn't the point.

"Look! You can't just come barging in here and insulting my project. Do you have any idea who I am?" Zeus dropped the mask of humanity and let his impressive deific light shine through.

Only this guy was unimpressed. He humphed. "I know who you *used* to be. Zeus, I don't care what you do here with your silly little 'condo board,'" he said with air quotes, "but you stay the hell off my turf."

Only a god could look straight at another god. Who was this guy? Zeus thought he knew all the deities out there. Some he only knew by name, some by appearance, but none of them corresponded to this asshole here. "What do you mean, your turf? This is my home. *You* stay the hell off of *my* turf." He crossed his arms, and realized he'd just inadvertently stuffed a grape leaf into his armpit.

"Are you so out of touch you don't even know?" The man laughed. "I'm Tekhno, god of technology. Which means that any metaphysical, magical, or otherwise occult thing you do with wires and batteries, like this unbelievable mess," he indicated with a flutter of his hand, "is MY TURF. Stay off it, old man."

Tekhno pointed an LED-studded finger at Zeus' fridge, TV, and the massive battery in quick succession. Each one shorted out with a *POP POP POP* and a shower of sparks. An electrical fire started behind the fridge and quickly spread to the microwave.

"OH COME ON!" So much for making dolmades.

"That's your one warning, old man. Later!" Tekhno pushed a button on his left side and dissolved into ones and zeroes hovering in the air, which shimmered for a moment and disappeared.

Zeus stared at the spot where the god of technology had stood, which now only had shards of door and a thin veil of smoke creeping from the kitchen. His eye twitched, and a vein pulsed on his forehead. Why that little asshole…no. No. He was retired. He was on a new path. Breathe in, breathe out. Try gratitudes if you don't have a good outlet, Dr. Brinkman had said. Fine. He was grateful for…

The fire burned merrily, and upped itself to a roar.

He was grateful for…

The vinyl paneling on the kitchen cabinets started to yellow and curl, and a charcoal smear was growing steadily on the backsplash.

He made a little cloud form under the flickering fluorescent lights. It rained out the fire in one swift deluge.

HE WAS GRATEFUL FOR...

NO. Fuck this. This was too much. Gritting his teeth, he threw a lightning bolt at the very same place that had just been in flames and watched it light up again.

Some young upstart god, coming around and telling *Zeus almighty himself* what to do? How dare he! Arrogant little prick thought he could just break down his door. Zeus was retired! The whole point was to retire and let go of the old power and old anger and to just let the world be *and this unmitigated asshole just strode right in like he owned fucking everything and...AAAAARRRGH!*

Zeus let loose another lightning bolt. This one lit the polyester beige rug in the living room on fire, and the smoke alarm began to wail. *Bang bang bang* came from the ceiling—his upstairs neighbor's response to any untoward sounds.

No. Breathe. This wasn't worth getting worked up over. He could handle himself before he was blinded with the red rage. The last thing he wanted to do was repeat last time, when he spent a millennia in the Court of the Gods' prison after murdering the other weather gods for their powers. So it was fine when he killed his own dad, but stupid foreigners were now a problem? And sentenced there by Themis, of all people. Goddess of justice from his own pantheon. Ex-wife. Vindictive bitch.

But that was the past. Now, he'd been making progress in therapy. *It wasn't worth it.*

Breathe. Every breath was tinged with the smell of scorched plastic. *That asshole* wasn't worth it. Just some young idiot god who thought he was on top.

Zeus' pulse slowed. He gathered two more storm clouds and put out the new fires with a splash, then surveyed the damage. The condo was a wreck. Gaping holes in the walls from the wiring project grew soggy with buckling plaster from the water damage. There were smears of smoke damage everywhere; and both the battery in his living room and the bulk of his kitchen were not much more than twisted pieces of charred devastation. Half of the living room rug was unburned, but it was squelchy at best. At least it wasn't all beige anymore.

He was committed to making a new start, he reminded himself. Possibly not in this particular condo anymore. But that little asshole did have to learn that it was just not okay to come in and burn another god's house down.

In the old days he would have hunted him down and found a horrific punishment that vastly outweighed the crime. Probably he'd encase the little asshole in the trunk of a tree and leave him to rot for a few hundred years. Maybe put some of Nit's hippie followers around him for good measure. But that was the old Zeus. He was putting the anger behind him, not falling back into old patterns. He exhaled. He would take Tekhno to the Court of the Gods and sue for damages or something. Following the rules was part of the fresh start. *He could do this.*

When the Court of the Gods was initially designed, all the gods felt like they had to have a say in how it looked and how it worked. Eventually, as massive group projects are wont to go, those loudest about bureaucracy won the battle of how it worked, and those loudest about aesthetics saw the abomination of design that had been born out of their committee and wanted to go hang themselves.

Up Zeus went to the mishmash of architectures from cultures worldwide. Had he possessed any aesthetic sensibilities beyond "not all beige," he would have cringed, but he was not overburdened with such gifts. The Court was its usual bustle, with deities from a plethora of pantheons going in and out via their preferred travel mechanisms on air, land, water, and fire. Gods waited in long lines which snaked into the massive labyrinthine corridors, and politely ignored each other in a distinct haze of bored irritation.

Zeus had never liked the Court of the Gods.

He wound his way through halls that led upstairs to go downstairs and halls that looped in on themselves to go upside down until he found the Justice Wing. And after about eighteen hours of waiting in line, during which he frequently returned to deep breathing and repeating gratitudes (it would not be beneficial to shoot lightning in here), he made his slow way toward the desk. When he saw the deity behind it, he stifled a groan. The God of Bureaucracy itself, whose name was a long acronym that he'd never bothered to learn, stiffened itself up and gave a forced smile.

The God of Bureaucracy, whom Zeus secretly thought of as Gob, was also the product of a committee. Unlike most gods it had no specified gender identity, for the committee was unable to decide on one. It had one of those faces that you would immediately forget upon looking away—something bland and generic, and yet entirely unappealing. Its paper-white skin always looked smudged with black and red ink.

"Welcome-to-the-Court-of-the-Gods-how-may-I-help-you?" Gob said in a bored monotone.

Zeus had a newfound irritation for my-name-is-Grace. "I'd like to file a complaint against Tekhno. And also a restraining order against him. And sue for damages. And also…um…all the other things I can do to keep him away."

Gob was simultaneously stamping, marking, and stapling papers, which it filed in different compartments under its desk. "And what is the nature of your complaint?" it droned.

"He wrecked my house."

Gob reached underneath the desk and brought out a thick stack of papers. "Fill these out. Don't forget to add in whether you live in a castle, mansion, tree house, submerged vehicle, spider web, volcano, recreational vehicle, etc. on pages one through three. Detail the nature of the wreckage, including approximate psychic value on all items destroyed and approximate impairment value of all items that were damaged, on pages four through twelve. The nature of your relationship with the subject goes on pages thirteen through twenty nine, and the specifics of your encounter go on pages thirty through fifty three."

Zeus thumbed through the stack of papers. There were at least two hundred pages. "And the rest?"

"You fill it out in quadruplicate, and then the last copy is for you to keep for your records. *Next*," it barked towards the line of gods in its same nasally tone. Gob's hands hadn't stopped moving as it talked. It alternated between stamps that said "DENIED," "ABSOLUTELY NOT," and "ESCALATED," thumping each one on a never-ending parade of paper forms.

"Wait, waitaminute. I'm not done. Is this really all necessary to file a complaint?"

"Necessary, but not sufficient. When you're done with these forms, go to the undercorridor of the Justice Wing and give them to filing. They'll give you the filing forms, and the notification forms, and the scribing documents—"

"Are you kidding me with all this? Is there nothing simpler I could do? Perhaps just this once?" Zeus flashed his most winning smile. Maybe Gob could be charmed?

The deity's stoic expression remained unchanged. Nope, not an effective strategy. "Sir, for the goals you have stated you must go through the proper procedures. No exceptions. *Next!*"

"Wait wait wait!" Zeus planted his hands on the desk, and looked over his shoulder to give a warning look to the goddess standing behind him in line, who'd begun to inch forwards hopefully. "What would be the quickest thing I could do if I wanted to get another god off my back?"

Gob rolled its white eyes and gave an exasperated sigh. "If you want to be uncivilized about it, you can just challenge them to a duel. Winner gets to determine what the loser has to do. But that's merely left over from an archaic law in the books. We've evolved far past such barbarities. I would strongly suggest that instead, you—"

"Duel. Got it." Zeus felt more energized than he had in years. "Right. How do I do that?" In the old days, he'd just done what he felt like. But, fresh start. He'd follow the rules.

Gob pursed its stained lips. "Go to neutral ground and yell out your challenge. But I must strongly suggest you take a more...official route."

Zeus took one last look at the papers that sat piled on Gob's desk. "Nah, I'm good."

The Court of the Gods had several outdoor courtyards, each of a different climate and foliage (or lack thereof). Technically the court was neutral territory, so this should be as good a place as any. Zeus planted himself in the middle of a Mediterranean-looking courtyard. A long rectangle of grass was dotted with occasional marble benches

and surrounded by cypress and eucalyptus trees. He inhaled deeply—
it smelled like home. But this was not the time.

"Tekhno! I challenge you!" he roared at the top of his lungs. The
grass flattened and the trees snapped backward before they sprang up
again. It had been years since he'd gotten in a really good roar.

Within seconds, Tekhno, a goddess in a toga, and an enormous
crowd appeared. Not just any goddess—it was Themis. SHIT.

She stepped forward. "A challenge has been issued! As the justice
deity on shift, I will be the judge and referee. Tekhno, as the chal-
lenged, you may choose the field of battle."

Tekhno looked smug. His lips twitched into a sneer as he said,
"Old man, you really think this is a good idea? I'll tell you what—
I'll even give you a chance to take it back." Electronics glittered and
blinked up and down the god's skinny body in ever-changing patterns, held together by very neat lines of wires. No tangles here.

Zeus narrowed his eyes. "I should offer you the same."

"Very well, it's your funeral." What a self-satisfied asshole. "For
our battlefield, I choose...*the internet.*"

The what now? Oh wait, Esther from the retirement complex
had mentioned that at one point. She'd been using it to keep in
touch with her grandkids. She said they sent her pictures. How was
that a battlefield?

"In fact," Tekhno continued, turning to the audience with a gran-
diose gesture, "I'll even give the old man an hour in advance, to get to
know the field. Because I'm all magnanimous and shit."

Themis nodded, and raised her arms. The Mediterranean courtyard transformed with a whoosh. A laminate floor pushed aside the
grass, low gray cloth-covered walls sprouted from below, two marble
benches morphed into two wood desks, and two more benches shifted into office chairs. A laptop appeared on each desk, cables coiling
down towards outlets and ports on the walls.

"After you." Tekhno gestured with an evil grin. Zeus took in the
audience, who was still looking on in eager anticipation. Who in the
hells were all these people? He recognized a few deities within the
ranks. Didn't matter. He was Zeus, once king of the gods. He could
take this little pipsqueak in whatever shit he tried to pull. He sat
down in one of the office chairs. It squeaked, and Tekhno smirked.

"Tekhno has given Zeus one hour's head start. The battlefield is the internet. As the judge, I decree that the winner is determined by the perception of the internet denizens: the god who they like most at the end is the winner. As there is no way to get the entire internet to agree on anything, a reasonable majority, as determined by me, will be required." Themis gave Zeus a *look*. She was far from his favorite ex-wife. "Let the battle begin!"

Okay. He could do this. The screen in front of him had three icons: one labeled "Internet Explorer," one labeled "Firefox," and one labeled "Chrome." "Internet Explorer" sounded a little too perfect. Tekhno giving him an extra amount of time and dangling that in front of him? Not a chance—it had to be a trap. He'd never had good experiences with foxes. Those Japanese buggers in particular were tricky little beasts—so Chrome it was. He quickly figured out how to use the mouse and clicked it. The audience cheered in approval and Tekhno frowned. Good, he must be on the right track.

He might be old. He might be retired. But Zeus was nothing if not clever. Within minutes, he'd figured it out and was clicking links with abandon.

People were posting on forums and social media, writing articles and blog posts, and all just…talking to each other. A lot of the discussion was through images with bold text over them, and tiny bits of moving pictures. Well, that was easy enough. Zeus started posting comments to random conversations, interjecting "Zeus rocks!" wherever he could find. He also figured out how to take a picture of himself on the laptop camera, put "Zeus rocks!" on top of the image, and started posting that too. This might take a while.

Out of the corner of his eye, he saw Tekhno sitting down in the spot next to him. Had it been an hour already? Mucking about online certainly didn't *seem* like it had taken that long. They were seated next to each other, desks set up so they could see each other's screens.

"Aw, you're figuring out what lolcats are. That's adorable." Tekhno's voice was loud enough to carry to the audience, who rippled with an approving chuckle.

Lolcats? There *were* cats everywhere on this weird internet thing. He looked it up, wishing he could call in a favor from Bast, former cat-goddess of Egypt, but he was pretty sure she was still pissed at him. Had he promised her they'd do dinner? He probably had…

"He thinks posting in conversations is enough to get people to like him! Oh that's cute. Hey cloudypants, whatcha gonna do if I do *this*?"

A sudden swarm of new users appeared in the same forums and social media hashtags where Zeus had been posting. "Zeus sucks!" was the common refrain, and they were *everywhere*.

Fine. He was Zeus. He was clever enough to defeat Cronus, so he certainly could do this. They liked lolcats? He could give them cats. He transformed himself into a cat with cloud-like markings on his sides. *CLICK CLICK CLICK*. He took picture after picture of himself in different poses, then changed back to his usual form and uploaded them everywhere.

CLOUDY CAT RAINS ON YOUR PARADE

RAINING CATS, NOT DOGS

DESTROY THE COUCH? SORRY, I'LL HAVE TO GET A RAIN-CHECK

I'VE GOT YOUR SILVER LINING RIGHT HERE

It was working. The pictures spread online, and cloudy cat became a meme. Zeus glanced over to what Tekhno was doing. His screen had lines and lines of gobbledygook—no language Zeus had ever seen before, though there were occasional words in there he could make out.

Whatever. When people started making their own cloudy cat memes (WHEN IT RAINS IT PURRS) and started producing shirts and bumper stickers, he figured it was good enough. He stood up and yelled, "Behold, the might of Zeus! I am cloudy cat, and the internet loves me. Themis, declare it!"

Tekhno laughed. "Aw, you really ARE adorable. Getting a meme going in so short a time isn't bad, I'll grant you that. But it's nothing in comparison to *this*." He hit a button on his keyboard.

Zeus waited. Nothing seemed to happen. "And?"

"I've now taken over the web. I've hacked into the largest ISPs on earth, and started routing traffic my own way. People trying to go to Google are going to my own Google spoof site, where every returned link informs them that Zeus sucks. Rotten Tomatoes? The hottest thing on it is a movie called 'Zeus'...guess what. It sucks." He giggled. "I've made Facebook and Twitter swap everybody's profile picture with an image that says 'Zeus sucks.' Reddit's front page is overflowing with links about how Zeus sucks. Every mobile phone worldwide is getting a text that says 'Zeus sucks.' Are you getting the picture?"

Zeus poked around online. "Zeus sucks" was everywhere. It far outweighed anything cloudy cat could reach. No. This was awful—Tekhno was young and flush with power, and he remembered what happened when young and powerful gods won. He used to be that guy.

"Uh oh!" crowed Tekhno, his visor glittering with LEDs. "Now every digital traffic sign, airport announcement board, and even every connected *coffee maker* is displaying the words 'Zeus sucks.'"

Themis smiled. "That seems pretty definitive to me. You have 10...9..." The audience started counting down along with her.

This punk was going to want to humiliate him. And probably do something way worse than try to chain Zeus to a rock and have his liver eaten every day. Worse than killing him. Worse than humiliating him in front of Themis.

The bubble of rage swelled in Zeus' chest and he stood up with a roar. NOBODY got the best of Zeus. He was the king of the gods, slayer of Cronus! He reached for Tekhno's neck, and—

"Physical harm to your opponent is out of bounds for this challenge," chirped Themis. "6...5..."

Breathe. Anger is not constructive. Find your gratitudes or an outlet for the anger. An outlet...

And there it was. Two tiny outlets at the bottom of the low gray walls. Zeus yanked out the two laptop cables with a swoop, and *shoved* in as much raw lightning power as he could.

Extra juice surged through the wires, which were metaphysically connected to the entirety of the earth's electrical grid, which overloaded. Around the world, cell towers shut off, servers died, and equipment went dark in quick succession. And as wires shorted out and blackouts rolled across the world, humanity en mass glared at their suddenly-disconnected cell phones and dead screens and grumbled, "What is this piece of shit?"

"2...1.... Well, that was unexpected," said Themis, "but in a last-minute turn, I declare Zeus the winner." An amused smile played on her face, and with a wave of her arms she dissolved the arena, the crowds, the computers, and the low walls. The elements of a eucalyptus-scented Mediterranean courtyard rushed in from all directions to fill the empty space.

"What? Are you kidding me?" screamed Tekhno. "That's cheating! The battlefield was the internet!" He stamped his foot like a petulant child.

Themis walked over to Tekhno, growing with every step until she dwarfed him. Arms akimbo, she said, "And he disabled the internet, making far more people hate you than you had them hating him. Do you care to challenge the ruling? You know, the one from the IMPARTIAL GODDESS OF JUSTICE?" She stared him down. Zeus remembered that look, and was distinctly relieved to not be its target for once. It could strip the leaves right off a laurel wreath.

Tekhno winced and looked away. Hah. The kid couldn't handle it. "Nothatsfine" he mumbled.

"Very well. As the winner of the challenge, Zeus may claim his prize." She made another gesture, and Gob appeared with a stack of paperwork. The god had its usual puckered look on its face.

Zeus tamped down a shudder at the papers. But his award. He hadn't even thought that far ahead! He could take whatever he wanted. He could strip Tekhno of everything he owned, everything he could do! He could be *back*, most powerful god once more! And he could....

He saw Tekhno's scared face, and remembered Sisyphus and Prometheus, Thor and Raijin and the Thunderbird, and all the others he'd punished over the years. No. No falling back into the old patterns. Powerful Zeus lashed out, and he didn't want to be that person anymore.

But he didn't have to roll over and take it, either.

"My prize has three components. First: Tekhno shall be required to pay as much funds into my account each month as I deem fit. I'm not gonna deal with this electric bill bullshit again. Second: Tekhno is never to bother me again, in however way I deem 'bothering' at the time. And third," at this an evil grin spread on his face, "Tekhno is now responsible for any paperwork I might have to do, in any context, from now until the end of time, and must do it correctly and to the best of his ability."

"WHAT? Absolutely not. This is ridiculous! I challenge *you!*" Tekhno stood up and tapped a few buttons on his arms and stomach.

Gob started its droning monotone, "If a loser of a challenge wishes to re-challenge the challengee, he or she or it must wait for a period of no less than seven thousand years, and at that time fill out forms 1098A, X-860, 826-R-C-"

"Actually, I think that challenging me would constitute bothering me, and we've just established you can't do that." Zeus crossed his arm with a smirk.

"But—"

"He's right," said Themis. "Now Tekhno, I believe you have some post-challenge paperwork to fill out."

"This sucks. This sucks SO HARD. But just you wait. I'll expand and become the god of innovation, too. I have this startup idea…"

A week later, it was time for the next therapy appointment.

"So," said Dr. Brinkman, "how are things?" He leaned back in a leather burgundy armchair and twitched open the button on his burgundy corduroy blazer.

Zeus filled him in. "And you know what? You should be really proud of me. I didn't kill *anybody*. I used the breathing techniques and everything."

"Well," Dr. Brinkman looked a bit uncomfortable, not looking up from his yellow legal pad. "I mean, that's not *quite* true. The massive blackouts killed a few patients on respirators who couldn't get on backup generators fast enough, and there were three plane crashes when the air traffic controllers lost power. But overall," he hurried to add as he looked up, "you didn't do so badly! After all, you didn't *know* that those were the consequences, and you refrained from slaughtering Tekhno. You didn't even enact an overly-onerous punishment. I am proud. So what are you doing now?"

"Oh, nothing much. I'm staying retired, like we talked about. But with these new funds I've upgraded to a *bitchin'* bachelor pad, and this one's in New York City. Everything is now voice-activated—the fridge, the lights, the shades, the rotating bed…and lemme tell ya: the ladies *love* it." Zeus grinned. "Between that and me offering to file taxes, fill out loan paperwork, and do immigration forms for free, I'm the most popular guy in town."

The Tragedy of the Dead is That They Cannot Cry

by Sunil Patel

The tragedy of the dead is that they cannot cry. They may laugh, despite having no lungs. They may speak, despite having no vocal cords. They may do many things that should not be possible without physical bodies. But the creation, the excretion of tears is impossible in their non-corporeal form. Jonathan has been dead for fifteen years but he has never felt this dysfunction more acutely than at Rosita's funeral.

The shades gather by her grave at midnight to mourn her passing. The scent of memorial flowers reaches only Rosita, the single living person in the cemetery. Only she feels the chill of the wind like a welcome home. It has been three days since she passed, and she returns to allow them to pay their respects. Jonathan whispers into Troy's ear: "I don't remember the last thing I said to her."

"We were gonna go trick-or-treating next week," says Troy. "Just watch the kids, ya know? Our one night out a year."

"I guess she can go herself now," says Jonathan. He only knew her in passing, but she was a part of this community, this family of spirits who accepted him more than his own family. Those he thought of as friends in life were only acquaintances in comparison. Even the one friend who died, and Jonathan was able to cry for him. That is, after all, what one does at a funeral. Troy, a young man but an old soul, has been around almost as long as Rosita and has attended many funerals. He needs no tears to mourn his friend because he knows his grief to be real. He will be giving the eulogy in a moment.

"Never gets easier. Life, death, life again. Transitions, right? Always leavin' people behind."

Jonathan is surrounded by those who loved Rosita more than he, and their grief emanates like a strong perfume. This invisible miasma contains every story from every shade, every connection they made with her that he did not. It seeps into him, artificial, and he suddenly cannot understand all the things he will never get to do with Rosita. She will never direct him to the wrong gravestone, either on purpose or because she simply isn't paying attention. She will never describe to him in graphic detail the circumstances of her death, but with added puns. She will never say, "Hey, Jonathan, you know that star's been dead longer than me?" That is something she once told Troy.

Now she stands by her gravestone, the moonlight illuminating her light brown skin rather than passing through it. New flesh for a new life. He should be happy for her Second Chance. She's going to a better place, the others say, but deep down they fear a Second Chance of their own. To be pulled from one state of existence to another? Once is enough for a lifetime. Jonathan doesn't want to return, not after only fifteen years. You can't always get what you want, in life or in death.

Jonathan does not want this grief inside him. He has not earned it. But he cannot force it out through his tears, as he could when he was alive. He watched a movie whose name has faded from his memory, a movie that made him sob so strongly he couldn't read the credits. It felt good, that release, those false emotions. False emotions plague him once again, and he wants them to be real, or get out.

Yet neither of these options will truly resolve his conflict. Although he does not comprehend how much Rosita mattered—matters—to him, he cannot appropriate others' feelings. Nor can he be without his own. To have no feelings would be disrespectful to her.

Troy begins his eulogy, and he delivers it straight to Rosita, though she cannot hear him. Having crossed the border, she has severed their line of communication. She is no longer one of them, and even though it was not by her choice, Jonathan mildly resents her for it. For leaving them. The second chance he wants is to know her like

Troy does. To have done the things he will never do. He misses most of what Troy is saying as he struggles to find a memory to induce impossible tears.

But then Rosita speaks in the middle of Troy's eulogy. She cannot see or hear him so she has no idea.

"Guys, I think you can hear me. We could hear the living before, so if I...count now, hey." She scans the graveyard, unwittingly locking gazes with so many shades, including Jonathan. "I'm going to miss you guys. Really miss you. I'll come visit when I can, okay?" Rosita chokes on the last word, a feeling she has not experienced in over a hundred years.

Troy isn't sure whether she's finished. He wants to continue his remembrance, his futile praise of her that he should have given when she was dead.

"Troy, find me next week. I'll find us some kids to follow, somehow." Tears form in her eyes, and she wipes them away, looks at her damp fingers. "It shouldn't have been me. I didn't want this."

Rosita breaks.

Her face shimmers as a century of loss pours out. She cried coming into the world and she cries now as she returns to it. This time, however, she knows what she is leaving behind. Each tear is for one of them, thinks Jonathan. He chooses one, watches it roll down her nose, past her newly reddened lips, and fall to the earth. That is his tear. He traces its path down his own face, forging a new connection between him and his friend.

One day, if he ever gets his Second Chance, he will cry for Rosita, as she cried for him.

The Dead Guest of Honor Speech

by Larry Niven

He was blind, deaf and dumb. He tasted nothing, smelled nothing. There were sensations. He couldn't interpret them, but they weren't painful, just bewildering.

It crossed his mind that he might be dead. Would that be better than the alternative? He might have had a stroke.

He didn't find his voice, exactly. He found sensations he could operate like an imaginary typewriter keyboard with a lot of extra, mysterious keys. When he could get something besides gibberish he typed, "At some time in the past half million years, someone had painted a smiley-face across the Earth's Moon. It looked best just after moonrise, with a yellow glow."

Nice opening, but in fifty years of writing he'd never managed to get a story out of it. He typed, "Hello?"

Nothing.

He remembered a hospital room…sixty-one years of hospital rooms. Appendicitis, tonsils, a deviated septum, some abdominal trouble. Surgery on his knee, twice. Troubles piled up as you got older.

Pneumonia, once at thirty-eight, once at sixty-one. He didn't remember recovering from that one.

Those memories were vague. He'd wondered if he was dying. He'd wondered if they would freeze his head. He'd done all the paperwork, paid in the money to Alcor, but the law was flaky. A sheriff had once chased some woman's frozen corpse with intent to confiscate it as evidence of murder. He was looking for too large a container. The Alcor Company had frozen only the head.

If he was alive—they must have done it!

His keyboard wrote, painfully slow, "Hello? Are you awake?"

Who? He typed, "More or less."

"Do you know your name?"

"Nat Banthry. Nathaniel Van Horne Banthry, Jr., only that's hard work at an autographing."

"What do you read in a sauna?"

Were they testing his memory, or his intelligence? He'd written about this. "Comic books. You can't take real books in a sauna. Glue melts. Staples don't melt unless the sauna's way too hot. Who are you?"

"I'm just a monitor." Nat was starting to hear a voice, rather than reading it like print. The voice must be speaking into a printer, and Nat was learning to sense sounds now. This was a young man, and jubilant. "I've already buzzed Wed…the ConCom chairman, Wednesday Fitzgerald. She'll be here soon. Mr. Banthry, you're the guest of honor at Baghdad Con."

"Ah. What date?"

"Four days from now," the gofer said, and another sensor told him: September 3-8, 2058, and then today's date: August 30, 2058, 11:22 a.m., and digits down to thousandths of a second…running slow enough to read.

"Ye gods, will I be ready in four days?"

"We hope so."

"How do we get to Baghdad? Are we *in* Baghdad?" He sensed a map. Minarets and lower, older structures around the periphery. Tall buildings in an inner ring around a perfect circle of reservoir. A big bomb crater: he tasted traces of radiation.

"Some of us are already in Baghdad. Most of us will be there virtually. Telepresence, you know? I'll be here monitoring you. We're in

Minneapolis." Another map: two cities split by a river, St. Paul on the other side.

Guessing the answer, Nat asked, "Pro guest of honor?"

Guessing wrong. "No, that's Cheri Hannefin. She's great! You didn't have a chance to read her. You're—" The boy froze up.

"Dead guest of honor." To make it easy on the kid, Nat said, "Mark Twain was our D-G-O-H in the nineteen nineties, with an actor standing in for him at the convention. Monitor, do you have a name?"

"Massook Hennessey."

Massook was talking very slowly, it seemed. Nat had no trouble reading his odd accent. He asked, "Massook, what's my situation?"

Massook said, "We're reading the currents in your brain. You can't store memories in this state, but the computer program can."

"So I'm the electric states in a frozen head, plus a computer program to read them." And computers had thought much faster than organic brains, even in Nat's time.

"Um. Yes, and the inputs we hooked up. You should be able to see by now."

"Nope."

"Damn."

He found stimuli he'd been ignoring, and he learned to interpret them. Weather. Moon phases. A nasty jolt of something like house current. He could read all that, and chat with Massook, and play with his hearing until he could separate Massook's voice from the buzzing of a housefly...four houseflies. By the time a young woman showed up, he was able to see outlines: a cartoon universe.

"Mr. Banthry, this is Wednesday Fitzgerald," Massook said.

"Hi," she said. She wasn't smiling. She was looking into cameras he couldn't see, and whatever else she was seeing made her uneasy. Him? A computer and monitor, lots of wires and a liquid nitrogen tank, he guessed. He wouldn't show as a severed head; they'd have to keep it enclosed, dark, protected.

She was beautiful, Nat thought, like an Olympic athlete. It didn't affect him at all. Perhaps, he thought sadly, he was no longer effectively male.

"Pleased to meet you, Wednesday," he said.

"Greets, Dr. Banthry."

"Call me Nat?"

"N-nat. How are you feeling?"

"It's great to be alive." He saw her flinch. "So to speak," he said. "Way better than oblivion, even without the honor. Listen, is this normal, a Dead Guest of Honor? Whose footprints am I treading in?"

"Nobody before you. We think we can do Gregory Benford next. We tried Arthur Clarke, but the...procedure wasn't properly done."

"How do I sound?"

"Fine, fine."

To his own hearing he sounded flat, like print in a typewriter. He was going to have to learn to talk, not type.

"Can you tell me something about my duties as D-G-O-H?"

She smiled. "What would you expect to be doing?"

His impulse was to laugh. Nothing came out. "Oh, Wednesday, I can match any story you can tell. I took my wife to St. Louis one year and they'd cancelled the convention. Once I was expecting a couple of panels, and they turned out to be, 'Banthry will do anything he wants to,' and no other guests. I have—I had friends who could handle that kind of thing, but I have to *write* my speeches. I carry material in case a panel turns out to be just me. Are you going to want a speech?"

"Please."

"What topic? Who am I talking to? When?" Wednesday looked puzzled. He said, "If it's an after-dinner speech, I keep it short and light. I don't get complicated unless it's, say, late morning."

"Because your audience is dozing off? Nat, most of them will record it. Some of us have instant play. It goes right into our memories, just like we sat through it. A few thousand will link in when you open the question period. Do you do a question period?"

"Sure."

"We can do it late morning in Baghdad if you like, but the attendees will be in every time zone. Do you do panels?"

"Sure."

"A kaffeeklatch is just a little panel, right?"

"Hah! For me, yes. I like them. I presume I don't drink coffee?"

267

Wednesday blushed. "Massook?"

The boy jumped. He said, "Not at this stage of things, Nat."

"Yeah, it's only 2058 CE." Again he couldn't laugh. He typed, "Ho ho ho. I didn't wait long enough."

Now Massook was embarrassed. "You didn't have that much longer, Nat. A frozen head doesn't stop deteriorating, it just slows way down."

Huh. And it wasn't taking new memories? Best not to think too hard about his present existence. He asked, "What do you want to hear about? The future? You'd better get me a television set." Blank looks. "Some kind of news feed, and access to the history section of a library. Otherwise I'll sound like a boob. I have to know the present before I can reach for the future. Always did."

"We can do that," Massook said.

"I suppose autographing would be silly?"

"Oh, no. We have a device." She set her hand on a…device. There was a many-jointed arm above a flat plate the size of a coffee-table book, all mounted on a pole. Clamps on the plate. The pole stood upright on a rolling sphere. Wednesday pushed it and it tilted over, then righted itself…and he *felt* something.

Massook took the thing's arm and wiggled it. "Here, can you feel this?"

"No."

"Damn. I'll check the settings. Now?"

"Yow! *That's* what it was. Sorry, I was startled. Turn it back down. Hey!" Nat suddenly realized he could switch his point of view to the device itself, looking down at the jointed arm and the flat plate underneath. He started to topple off the roller base, and caught himself.

He looked for *himself.* The camera in the autograph module saw a cylinder with a mirror finish, as big as a five-year-old child, sitting next to a flat box half that size. The top of the box was a hologram: he could see it and not see it, depending on which senses were looking. A hologram of a keyboard with too many keys and some vertical bar graphs. And that was *him.*

Massook said, "Try wriggling the arm. The pen is built in. Wednesday, did you bring a book?"

"Nothing I'd want ruined!"

Nat tried to make the scrolling letters that were his autograph. The jointed arm swung wildly, and Wednesday ducked.

Massook said, "We'll get you something. Nat, are you comfortable?"

"More like confined. Get me an Internet link or something, and a program book for the convention."

Massook typed. "Feel this?"

He felt the buzz and recognized a news program. He'd been ignoring a lot of stimuli. "Wow." He could watch a dozen, a score of channels at once. The vastness of the world crashed in on him. Before he could get carried away he asked, "Am I locked out of anything?"

"Say what?"

"Infinity isn't all, Wednesday. There's a lot to study here, but what am I missing?"

Massook said, "Nat, you're locked out of anything I'm locked out of. I hooked you to *my* service link. You can't have anything private, anything government. You can't have eight billion phone numbers to send random advertisements to because that's illegal too. What did you expect? Seek Mensa Basic."

Mensa Basic confronted him with a string of puzzles. He solved some rapidly. Some he missed. How many solar planets? Nine—and Pluto wasn't one of them—

"If you want, we can filter out the pop-up advertisements and pay a fee instead, but maybe you want to watch some advertising?"

Did he? "No. Maybe after I get my bearings." He began to dip into the news. He could do that while Massook and Wednesday were talking.

Baghdad had a convention center bigger than Las Vegas'. It had been rebuilt around the reservoir pool...the crater.

Mecca was another crater. Rebuilding was being done in secret. Various groups had confessed to that crime; theories abounded. In Nat's time the Muslim nations had been very good at pissing people off.

There were wheeled vehicles all over the Moon. He found he could steer one—

"Would you mind some company, Nat? The Convention Committee would love to meet you."

"No, that's fine, Wednesday, bring 'em on." Noblesse oblige, as his sometime collaborator Wade Curtis would have said. Might Wade have been frozen too? No, Wade was Church of England, and that was too bad, because Wade really understood computers. But he'd taught Nat to make nice with the ConCom at every convention.

Nat was driving up a rough and rocky slope in a tray mounted on six fat wheels. A voice told him how to steer, giving him mission objectives. He was to find any pebble that didn't match anything in his database, mount it on the tray, then—he was being fed a map. Take his pebble to the rim of Clavius Crater, three hundred and ten kilometers south-southeast. His vehicle was the size of a man's hand. Dammit, weren't there human beings on the Moon, even now?

Now there were windows popping up in the featureless wall in what he'd taken for a hospital room. Twelve, fifteen, sixteen rectangles held human faces peering curiously back at him. While Wednesday was making introductions, Nat discovered a sonar sense. The wall was still a wall; only Wed and Massook were real.

These images were the ConCom, of course. He'd thought to meet them later, maybe tomorrow, but they'd come virtually.

He caught their names and retained them, a thing he'd never been able to do in life. They were generally healthier and leaner than science fiction fans he'd known. Gay Simmons, in charge of the Dealer floor, was partly mechanical, badly scarred in some accident. Others— he began to notice patches, lumps. Prosthetics. His curiosity keyed another talent: he could *see through* Wednesday and Massook as if they were transparent. It might be magnetic resonance imaging. Their teeth startled him: neither had fillings of any kind.

He was getting some timbre into his voice now. "Ladies and gentlemen—"They smiled; a few laughed; the words might have changed meaning. "I hope you'll forgive me sounding a little weird. I'm just learning to use the equipment." They murmured acknowledgments. "May I ask questions about modern medicine? Wayne, that's a prosthetic, isn't it?"

He'd found a search feature. While waiting he wrote, "Nat Banthry," his own name, and set it going. In moments he'd pulled up a bibliography, a taped classroom lesson, a sketchy biography riddled with mistakes, and more. He'd died of pneumonia in 1999. Nice obituaries. He'd left not much of an estate.

Pebbles rolled under his Moon crawler's wheels and he tumbled. He was upside down. Suddenly his controls locked up. Then the crawler was righting itself, moving again, but he wasn't in control. The moon bug continued crawling uphill. Someone had taken over.

He cut his connection to the Moon.

There were unfamiliar books listed under his name. Publishers had shuffled old stories and packed them into new volumes. Posthumous collaborators had finished his unfinished stories. There had been four movies! Like Robert Heinlein and Philip Dick, he had finally achieved success in films. Producers didn't really like dealing with a living author.

He had wondered if he'd be forgotten. Computer storage had preserved his work. Now he wondered if the books were still read.

Wayne Hollis answered, "I was born with a chicken wing for an arm. This thing is off the shelf, sort of, with ports for various features, but some of the functions have gone obsolete. I should get another. The prosthetic spleen—oh, you can't see that. Well, there's enough wrong with me that they won't let me be a parent."

Wednesday said, "Medicine's better now. We can cure some kinds of cancer. Alzheimer's, well, if you died of that, we can't read your brain."

"The way you are now, this is as much as we can do for you," Massook said.

"But I'll never catch another cold," Nat said. He saw the blank looks. "Never get sick. Hey, this is better than I ever expected. This freezing of heads, it was just a long shot, you know?" Blank looks. "That's a bet on a horse race. So tell me, just how big is Heaven Con?"

Wednesday said, "Last year we were 512,000 attending, 180 on site. Nothing like a Manga Con, of course, but we came out with a profit. That's paying part of your expenses, Nat."

"I'm out," said Sarah Wrigley, and her alcove disappeared. She'd never spoken.

The ConCom disengaged one by one, without much in the way of niceties. In minutes only Massook and Wednesday were left. Massook said, "I'll leave you running. See if you can catch up with the news. If you run into problems, make a list of questions. I'll be back after breakfast."

271

Why *wouldn't* he leave Nat running? The question bothered Nat, but not enough to stop him from playing with his new abilities.

There were wheeled vehicles on Mars. He found himself in a queue, looking at an expense account while he waited for access to one of the crawlers.

He had to guess at the value of a transmer mark. Four or five dollars? The ConCom hadn't objected to his running a Moon bug, but Mars was about thirty times as expensive. Per minute. With a light speed lag of, currently, eighteen minutes.

Science fiction convention committees weren't usually rich. *Leave you running?* What did it cost to leave Nat running? A computer, a liquid nitrogen cooling system, what else? Access to the rest of the planet, probably with fees attached. Something to read the electrical patterns in a frozen human brain, something noninvasive that wouldn't alter the patterns, the frozen thoughts. Nothing hugely expensive there—but half an hour running a Mars rover might bankrupt a little convention.

He dropped out of the queue for Mars.

Cheri Hannefin, the convention's pro guest of honor, wrote animations. Not novels or scripts, not just text: the whole package, cartoon movies as long and complex as *Toy Story*.

In his more optimistic moments, Nat had wondered if returning to life would put him out of business: his futures turned obsolete, his science turned fantasy or slapstick or mere current events. You had to see both sides of a miracle to write decent science fiction. Now even the tools of his profession looked obsolete. He wondered if he could even write a speech. Would they expect something like Hannefin's *The Star Tree?* It was an animation that ran four hours and was brilliant.

If just *anyone* could write/direct/produce a movie—

To ask the right question was to know the answer. Nassook's connections included access to critics and reviewers. He was subscribed to a review service that told him what was worth watching. It looked like every book title Nat could remember had become somebody's movie project. Aldiss's *Report on Probability A* had been seen by dozens of people, and so had Delany's *Dahlgren*. But so had Budrys' *Rogue Moon*. Nat watched it on fast forward, and loved it.

The night seemed to go on forever...but the *world* seemed to go on forever. How could things have changed so much in just fifty-one years? Nostalgia ran rich and powerful when he found anything he remembered.

The McDonalds' chain was still alive...serving vegetable patties. Lobsters had been saved from extinction, maybe: lobster beds and oyster beds were undersea property, protected like farms. Lobster rustlers, he thought, and looked, and hey, they were real!

He found himself missing coffee...and French toast, his own recipe, not just eating it but making it...and came to realize that what he missed was waking up. He didn't miss sleeping, just waking up in a bed.

That, he decided, was silly. He was burning up huge amounts of time exploring his world, and all for free, all overnight.

The shorelines had changed. Rain forests were growing back. Sites for buried ice had been identified on the Moon and Mars; they would be resources if human beings ever went to space. The beginning and end of the universe had all been described in detail.

Ideas were sparking in his head. He outlined a few stories, and wrote one. Then he found that he could check references on the net. His ideas had all been used...some used well. Were they stale yet, or could they be recycled?

He spent the next day writing a speech.

At first it looked easy. He was still learning how to pick up information, how to surf the net. When he had some text, he began checking it against the vast library of humanity's common knowledge.

Magnetic monopoles: yeah, they were real, but nowhere near as useful as he'd thought.

Antigravity: now called dark energy, but it only acted over huge distances; it was very hard to focus.

Psi and UFOs: he'd never believed in them, but now nobody else did either.

He was appalled. Some of what he knew was common, was clichés. Some had been refined into whole fields of study. Some had become ridiculous. Phrases he knew were his own, had become part of the language, without attribution.

Did he know anything that was worth passing on to future generations? Dammit, he hadn't expected to confront posterity in person!

He was given three days to learn before the convention began.

With his new multitasking talents, Nat volunteered to run Admissions.

He found himself working with a program that had never been human. It ran itself. Was he doing anything useful?

He learned how to track traffic. Virtual attendees blinked in and out and back. Some of the entertainment they'd come for wasn't running yet, so they kept checking. Other virtual attendees clumped in virtual mazes. Conversation, old friendships renewed, had always been half the reason for attending science fiction conventions.

The illusion that one is about to get laid had drawn a lot of people too. How could you manage that at a virtual convention? Nat was surprised at the low number of warm bodies. But he watched.

The pro guest of honor had been delayed by Mexico City security. Nat kept track until Cheri Hannefin was back on route, moving at Mach 2 in something less like a Concorde than a section of a wing. The passengers rode naked. Security had become extreme; maybe that was why so few people wanted to travel. Then again, passengers seemed to be forming friendships and liaisons. The seats changed shape like dreams.

Live attendees streamed into the hotel followed by floating luggage. The hotel admissions desk was automated, but security was human, and they scanned every piece of luggage, backpacks, purses, phones, wallets. No wonder live attendees were so few. He watched the elevators. They were working well, not overcrowded. Another tradition lost.

There were dozens of editors and publishers, enough to fill several panels. Nat answered their questions. Most of what he knew was nostalgia: he had the younger ones laughing, and older ones reminiscing among themselves. He was feeling obsolete. What he didn't know about rights…yeah, they'd all lapsed. Mickey Mouse was public domain. But one and then another publisher offered him contracts for new books. Sequels, lots of sequels. Nat found that he wasn't eager to rip himself off. Did he know enough of contemporary life to write new stuff? No, but he would. He'd better start researching agents.

Did he have rights? Better ask Wednesday.

Wednesday was busy. Nassook stepped out of the filk room to talk. "An agent would know about your rights. Nat, what would you spend it on, anyway?

"Mars cars."

"Mmmm."

The next panel: how to retake the Moon. Banthry was horrified. They should have had cities on Moon, Mars, Europa. Mining enterprises in the asteroids.

Cheri Hannefin's GOH speech began incomprehensibly. Banthry remembered what he heard, picked up context, got some references, learned some history. The speech was being written as she spoke, he suddenly realized, and it had hot buttons. She was, he decided, brilliant.

And he was next.

The Dead Guest of Honor Speech:

"I'm assuming you'll want to hear about the past," Nat told them. "You can learn about the present the same way I did, off the Net. As for the future, I'm counting from way back, from the tail end of the twentieth century. We've veered away from my future, and you see it better than I do. What I saw coming has become largely fantasy."

Nat could see himself twice. Up at the front of the room, his hologram self stood in an alcove, which was also a hologram, in a flat wall, which was real. That was the self that was speaking, and he saw it from the point of view of the autographing widget at the back. From the front he could see the autographing widget shining murkily through another hologram of Nat Banthry.

The live audience was sparse: fifty-one including three small children in noise-suppressor cells. A few fans clustered around the autographing device standing on its single ball-bearing wheel. Nat went on signing while he spoke. From time to time another pro took over.

"Elevator problems were tradition when I was—" *Alive.* "—active. In 1967 the Worldcon in New York went on while live elevator operators were on strike. In most Worldcons the lines for elevators were a nightmare. Here they run smooth as silk. I can't believe you made that happen."

Viewed from the podium, the exit door stood alone and surrealistic; the back wall seemed to extend into infinity. It was full of ghosts. He wasn't seeing all or even most of the virtual attendees, just the few thousand who were sending a hologram image. Total attendance in the hall was near twenty-thousand hits. Nat hoped that more would pick it up as a recording.

More than half of the live attendees were out playing tourist in Baghdad while Nat's voice played in their ears.

Speaking didn't take all of his attention. Nat was trying to remember a song. He'd lost verses somewhere in his frozen brain. Memories acquired through his computer had sharper edges.

"I always miss things at a big convention. Good panels run opposite each other. I miss the Masquerade because I'm at dinner with a publisher, trying to sell a book. Some days I've dreamed of attending the same convention several times. I thought it would take a time machine to put me in several places at once.

"So I'm here at Baghdad Con, and I *am* in several places at once. Up at the podium and there at the back." He waved the jointed arm of the signing device. "I'm autographing here and in the Scheherazade room and inside the Dealers, and watching *Destination Moon*, and monitoring Registration, and making a speech and rewriting it as I go."

The Committee had sprung for three of the autographing devices, but twenty-one virtual guests were sharing them. The devices wandered with the whims of the guests, wherever something interesting was going on. Cheri Hannefin had stopped one to watch line dancing, a score of dancers hologram-cloaked in Georgian outfits. Autograph seekers spoke a name, or just set a book or cassette on the flat plate. The appropriate guest would pop into view and sign.

Nat had to be careful. His books were old. They were coming apart, colors faded. Some paperbacks would dissolve in his hands, if he had hands. Writing on the ancient paper was like writing on the

276

skin on old tapioca pudding. He was pleased: these books had seen use.

Do you sign what you didn't write? Nat did, if it was critical reviews about his work. How had the future dealt with him? He noted titles and summoned up the texts. He'd read them later.

Fans appeared with books still hot from downloading. Sure, why not? A girl bared her breasts. He figured out how to move the flat plate he'd been putting the books on, and he signed her chest.

Destination Moon had been digitized, of course. He'd been afraid of extra scenes or bad cutting, but it was true to the movie he'd seen when he was ten. He'd gone home and made a succession of wooden models of the ship. Now he watched, and whispered the dialogue where he remembered it. Too bad they didn't have an actual movie theater.

Live registration at the convention approached 890: huge compared to last year. The majority were playing tourist in Baghdad. Some were calling in questions from cell phones printed onto their facial bones. Questions for the panels, questions for Nat's speech. He stored them for later.

"In the song, 'Heaven Con'," he said (scribbling madly), "the hotel always forgets to send you a bill. You've come close to that dream. If you're here virtually, you're only paying a couple of transmer marks. It'll cost you more if you're here in the flesh, but hey, it's voluntary. Your Dealer floor is amazing: it's almost all virtual, so there's never any crowding. I've found—well, things I don't need in my current state, but wow! I'm drunk on nostalgia.

"That old song described convention guests waiting in the halls, begging to autograph your books. I remember that pissed me off sixty years ago. We pros, we're nobody's prisoners. But it's no trouble! If you're virtual I've been e-mailing you the reflex that does the signing. I just trip a synapse. Live guests like Harry and Boo and Sheri are doing the same thing. If you're attending, you have to bring yourself and the books, of course, and that's more trouble for you than us. And, let's see, I've signed eighty-one live books? This one's eighty-two. In 1984 in Los Angeles there were almost nine-thousand attendees. Let me tell you what it was like for comic book professionals in those days— Here, look at the back of the room." Somebody had brought a copy of *Scarlet Moon*, a graphic novel from DC. Nat held it up with the signer's jointed arm: "This was my only comic book, three issues. But look, six names on each of the inside covers and you could stack fifty or sixty of them in your arms. For the people who have to sign them, that's a nightmare."

He'd found the filk, not without difficulty. He listened to the impromptu concert. Live filkers sang off key; virtual filkers might have a correction program. When his turn came…nope, he didn't have a mic here, have to bring in a signing device.

He remembered some songs from his own past, but not every word. He finished several, perhaps not accurately, and added to them. Played them in his head.

"This is what you could have had," he told his audience. He spoke of teleport booths instead of elevators. Medicine was wonderfully advanced; it could go farther. A new Heaven Con, held on the Moon or Mars or in orbital hotels. A restaurant guide for the Local Group. They'd built a Beanstalk in Ecuador, but it had failed; local corruption? They must build another. Tabby's Star had failed to be a Dyson cloud; keep searching. "You're never where you want to be in the real world. Your desires lie always ahead of you."

He was out of time. While he watched them set up for the following panel, he played the filk concert that had been running opposite him, went on signing, let in two more attendees, scanned through the Art Show, and reviewed the financing. Despite the attendance, the Con was losing money. They'd overspent. They were going to have to cut back someplace.

The Saturday night Masquerade had no stage; it had gone back to being a dance. But the dancers had hologram special effects, and body modifications, and glasses or goggles that saw things that weren't there. There was extreme body mod in the band! And explosions that didn't rip things apart: they were just sound and light. There were colors not seen by un-augmented human eyes.

He got an autograph device into the filk. He sang. It became a nostalgia fest: the old songs went over better than his new stuff. He wasn't disappointed. His new songs would be old someday.

They kept him on until Sunday afternoon. It felt like…not a lifetime, but perhaps a summer. Then his access ports began shutting down. The autograph link was gone now, but the main auditorium was still open for closing ceremonies. Nearly empty of warm bodies. Lots of virtuals popping in and out.

He had time to whip up a short speech before they called him. As the applause rolled, the port shut down.

He was in the place where he had awakened.

Now Massook came through a door, then four more of the Con Committee flicked in as virtual displays: Wednesday, Card, May and Harrison. "Everyone's checking out," Wednesday said, "and so are we. You were wonderful."

"I noticed the finances," Nat Banthry said.

Card said, "Yeah. You'll still be taken care of by your trust fund."

"I could add something. I sold a novel—"

"Keep it to keep yourself frozen."

"Until the next convention?"

"Not us. Next year is in Warsaw. Honestly, they won't have two DGOH in a row."

Massook said, "Goodby, Nat. Good luck."

Wednesday said, "It feels like we're murder—"

It felt like no time had passed at all, but Wednesday Fitzgerald looked thirty years older, wrinkled and partly gray, and the other three people in the room were all strangers. She was wearing a loose pant suit of unfamiliar cut. For a flicker he wondered if this was her mother, but that didn't fit. Okay, fine, he'd been nonexistent for thirty years. And the rest of them were all men, all wearing uniforms that looked stranger yet—

"Nat Banthry? You there?"

"Oh, yeah, sorry, Wednesday. How are you?"

"Good, considering. It's been sixty-one years."

"That long? You only—you look great. Is there another convention?"

"No. Nat, I really didn't want to wait this long. We got you stored at liquid helium temp, only without the helium, and that preserved you longer. But your brain's nearly worn out. We should have been running you so that more of your personality gets stored in the computer. But it's maybe enough."

279

"For what? Have you got me a job?"

She laughed. "So to speak. I'm the head of NASA now. Would you like to fly a spacecraft?"

"Sure."

"I've been badgering NASA for decades now. I kept playing them your guest of honor speech. We finally have a city on the Moon, and a base on Mars. You'll see Luna City, but then you're going to Ganymede with a team of sixteen nutcases who expect to spend half their lives exploring. The ship's computer is you, and we'll run in every possible kind of entertainment and education, as well as instructions for flying this particular spacecraft. You'll have printers to make more vehicles as needed, and computers for the vehicles. We figure they can be made largely of ice—"

"Yes! Heaven Con!"

"You'll refuel on Ganymede, then visit some other places with ice on them." She stopped. "You think?"

"Smaller than I thought, but yeah. I used to be afraid of falling. This is the only way I could ever go to space."

She pondered for a bit, then said, "I'll get myself frozen. Maybe we'll meet again."

The Breakout Story of Galaxy's Edge Issue Ten Million

by Robert Jeschonek

I t all started in the distant past—which, to you, would be the distant future. It all happened in the state called Galaxedgia, so named because it was patterned after the very popular magazine of which you hold a copy in your hands or tentacles or sexoplasm or whatever.

A vast state, as befits a place modeled on settings from thousands of issues of *Galaxy's Edge* magazine, Galaxedgia spanned much of what was once the Pacific Northwest of the former United States of America. Its reaches encompassed everything from replicas of alien encampments to robotic wonderlands to dinosaur jungles to mad scientists' labs...

...to bizarre kingdoms where modern-day knights and dragons co-existed in ways made possible by technology so advanced that it might as well have been magic. Once upon a time, in one such kingdom on the remote outskirts of Galaxedgia, a shabby castle shivered on rolling green hills under the noonday summer sun. This castle, called Castle Spasmodic, was like something brought to life from a story in the pages of *Galaxy's Edge* magazine...because it *was*.

So was its inhabitant, a broken-down would-be star-knight in tin pan armor with a shaggy white beard and bushy eyebrows. As he rattle-clanked out the front door of the castle, Sir Reptitious of the

Dingly Dangly Kingdom was instantly recognizable to anyone who'd read the story titled "Drag Knight vs. Space Grendel's Inner Show-girl" in *Galaxy's Edge* #320.

This man had been transformed by implausible super-science into a real-life replica of a character from the magazine…just like all the other inhabitants of Galaxedgia. They loved *Galaxy's Edge* so much that they had let themselves be changed into perfect copies of the denizens of its stories.

Another such inhabitant—Cosset of the Ever-Blazing Allergies, that purple-scaled, fire-sneezing, inter-dimensional dragon-beast from *Galaxy's Edge* issue 512 ("Here's Looking Atchoo, Kid")—was flapping lazily overhead when Sir Reptitious walked out of the castle with a white business envelope in his hand.

"What's the good word down there, you old *tinpot*?" Cosset blew out a blistering sneeze, barely getting out the last word of the sentence.

Sir Reptitious smiled up from under the pie plate visor of his garbage pail helmet. As much as knights and dragons were known foes in most stories, these two were best friends in the scienti-magical land of Galaxedgia.

They had a lot in common, after all. Neither was overly happy with life in Galaxedgia. Being a constantly-sneezing dragon-beast wasn't as much fun as you might think after a couple of years.

Neither was being not-very-much-of-a-star-knight who couldn't even seem to do *that* very well. According to online reviewers who watched over micro-drone webcams buzzing throughout the kingdom, his performance—his *life*, in other words—was thoroughly disappointing. The consensus was, someone with much more talent ought to don the trash pail and pie plate and take up the pink feather boa that substituted for deadlier weapons of the sci-fi variety.

Still, Sir Reptitious held out hope. "Hello, friend Cosset!" He waved the white envelope he was carrying, which had his name scrawled on the front. "Look what arrived by *carrier pickle* just now!"

Cosset swooped lower, then let loose a sneeze so extreme that the force of it pushed him back up again. "The answer to your request?"

"It *should* be, good dragon." Eagerly, Sir Reptitious tore open the envelope. "I *sent* it some time ago, after all." His hands shook a little as he pulled out the folded letter inside. Was it possible? Had the powers that be in Galaxedgia granted the request he'd made months ago?

Had they given him *rewrite permissions*? Would he finally be allowed to make his character more competent and dramatic, giving him off-book opportunities to impress the critics for once?

Not yet, apparently.

"Oh, calamity!" Sir Reptitious stroked his shaggy white beard and stomped in circles over the rainbow-colored grass, which cursed his every step with extreme chitter-chirping profanity. "It's nothing at all to do with my request!"

"Sorry to hear that, amigo." Cosset released a blazing sneeze on the last syllable. His disappointment, like the flames of his sneeze, was palpable; he'd been hoping to apply for rewrite permissions of his own if Sir Reptitious was granted his wish.

"It is news of an altogether different sort, I'm afraid." The not-very-much-of-a-star-knight sounded grim as he shook the letter overhead. "We must sound the alarum! Portals are opening up throughout our green and pleasant land, disgorging visitors most strange…and unplanned!"

"*Unplanned* visitors?" said Cosset. "That's *unheard* of!"

It was true, and precisely why Sir Reptitious wanted rewrite permissions so much. With all interactions carefully scripted by Galaxedgia's planners, opportunities for any one inhabitant to truly stand out and impress critics were few.

Why do you think the knight and dragon got so excited all of a sudden? Dealing with impromptu invaders surely qualified as the kind of emergency situation in which they could improvise…*show off*, even.

"Fear not!" Cosset paused to unleash another mighty sneeze, scorching a passing flock of origami cranes into ash with his sizzling breath. "No freakish visitation shall stand against *our* cast of heroes!"

Just then, Indigesto, the Stroganoff That Walks Like a Man ("The Meal Shall Inherit the Earth," *Galaxy's Edge* #439), flip-flopped his way up a rise from the direction of Asynchronous Park. As usual, he looked like a six-foot-in-diameter heap of beef stroganoff—though his big sour-cream-sauce-slathered egg noodles fluttered with agitation. "Fight or flee! Flee or fight! They're coming for us, *whatever* they are!"

Whatever the story behind the invasion, Sir Reptitious wasn't about to miss a chance to deliver a bravura performance. Drawing his pink feather boa from around his waist, he held it before him with a steely gaze. It was not very much of a weapon, straight from his character's not-very-dignified story in *Galaxy's Edge*, but he was determined to make it work for him dramatically. "No brick, beast, or Bandersnatch shall breach Castle Spasmodic! What say you, Cosset?"

"I say let's give 'em a tale worth reprinting in the ten thousandth issue!" roared the dragon. "Complete with quips, ripostes, and derring-do aplenty!"

"And you, Stroganoff?" shouted Sir Reptitious. "Will you fight alongside we brave and happy few?"

"I'll fight as hard as any noodle dish ever has," said Indigesto. "Though *fleeing* still strikes me as a not-unthinkable option."

Suddenly, a dazzling portal rimmed with red and gold light spun open in front of Castle Spasmodic, unleashing a howl like a thousand kazoos in a hurricane. A big gray block of a thing tumbled out, neither blinking nor waving nor wagging nor anything-else-ing... but somehow speaking nonetheless with an echoing thunder that boomed throughout the kingdom.

"*Galaxy's Edge* #500,335," it said. "Story name 'Ootch'."

As if *that* explained everything. Or anything at all.

"What in *Galaxedgia*?" Sir Reptitious stepped forward, slashing the air with his boa. "What are you *talking* about, sirrah?"

"Ootch ootch ootch," said the block.

Indigesto slapped the ground with his noodles, slopping sauce every which way. "Could it mean the *magazines*?"

"*Galaxy's Edge*! Of course!" hollered Sir Reptitious. "But then that must mean it's..."

"...a *reviewer*!" Cosset's purple-scaled maw lit up with a scalding sneeze of excitement.

"No!" snapped Sir Reptitious. "It's..."

"...an *author*?" ventured Indigesto.

"A *time traveler*!" Sir Reptitious flounced his boa for emphasis. "From a *far future era* when *Galaxy's Edge* has reached issue number 500,335!"

"Unless they increase the frequency!" said Cosset. "Maybe they start publishing a *thousand* editions per month or something. Then it wouldn't be *that* far in the future."

(Just as YOU, DEAR READER, are thinking about jumping to another story, perhaps in another magazine entirely, Quicksie the Reassurer leaps in front of the action, looking like an adorable Corgi pup crossed with the lithe little sprite who used to perch on the rail of your crib and sing you to sleep at night when you were a baby. "No flipping! I promise, this nutso story ain't *that* long! Woof!" Then, Quicksie dives out of the way with the sound of jingling bells and—for some reason—the smell of sauerkraut.)

Suddenly, something else emerged from the portal. It looked like a huge, lobster-clawed sheep with ferns for a head and seven erect penises that shot sizzling red laser beams.

"Story name 'Ukk'," blurted the lob-sheep, claws clacking like giant maracas. "*Galaxy's Edge* issue 757,891."

"Somebody get me some drawn butter!" shouted Cosset. "And mint jelly!"

"Great lumpy long-johns!" Sir Reptitious ducked one of the laser beams, stumbling over his own tin can-shod feet in the process... then caught himself and quickly regained his footing, very conscious of any critics who might be watching from afar. "How many issues of *Galaxy's Edge are* there in the future, anyway?"

The lob-sheep stomped forward, clacking away. "Laugh!" it howled. "Pull out your colons and *laugh!*"

"Guess they laugh *different* in the distant future!" Indigesto scrambled away from the advancing creature.

Next came the biggest anomaly so far from the portal—a rippling sheet of what looked like pink flesh, mottled and streaked with crimson.

"*Galaxy's Edge* issue 4,987,241." The voice of the flesh sounded like a back-masked record played backward on a turntable. "Story title 'Shingles Inherits the Earth'."

Indigesto's noodles sagged. "*That* doesn't sound like a great *Galaxy's Edge* story!"

"*None* of them do!" said Cosset (whose dragon-sized ears enabled him to clearly hear the conversation far below, even through all the commotion). "I'm starting to wonder if *Galaxy's Edge* has *anything* to do with *any* of this!"

It was then that THIS STORY ITSELF interrupted to set the characters straight: "OH, BUT IT DOES! I ASSURE YOU!"

"Who *said* that?" Confused, Cosset flew in a herky-jerky circle as fiery sneezes shook him along the way.

Before anyone could answer, another figure emerged from the portal, and then another, and another, and more. A full-fledged parade trooped over the threshold, each new arrival more bizarre than the last. At least they *announced* themselves, though the actual benefit of that was difficult to see.

"Story name 'Huh'! *Galaxy's Edge* issue 6,350,238."

" 'Caribou'! *Galaxy's Edge* #156,003!"

" 'Bootstrap Soulevolence'! *Galaxy's Edge* #9,345,871!"

As the locals (whose ability to defend themselves was somewhere between—100 and—1,000,000 on a scale of 1 to 10) backed away from the gathering mob, they fought their own wits (or lack thereof) to make sense of the situation.

"AS IF THAT WAS GOING TO HELP THEM."

"Who said *that*?" Cosset was so mixed up, he let off a particularly spectacular sneeze-splosion.

Sir Reptitious, for his part, was determined to make sense of the situation...and show off his taking-charge chops. "Let's assume these things *are* time travelers from a distant future," he said, stroking his shaggy beard. "A future where *Galaxy's Edge* has published millions of issues. Beyond that basic assumption, who exactly *are* they?"

Indigesto huddled with the not-very-much-of-a-star-knight as the time-traveling weirdos paraded around them. "Perhaps it would make more sense if we asked who they *aren't*."

"NO, IT WOULDN'T."

Sir Reptitious shook his pink boa at the sky with out-of-character defiance. "Curse you, whoever you are, for your dismissiveness in the face of rampant chaos!"

"As the newcomers emerge, they call out story names and *Galaxy's Edge* issue numbers." Indigesto ducked the swooping bill of a giant, glowing goose that seemed to think his noodles were worms. "Do you suppose..." Again, he ducked the goose. "Do you think they, like us, are paying tribute to beloved characters from classic stories in those magazines?"

"If so, the word *beloved* doesn't exactly leap to mind! Or *crawl*, even," shouted Cosset. "Maybe the magazine undergoes a change in direction in the far future, to *egregiously un-entertaining*."

"OR MAYBE, WHAT IS CONSIDERED ENTERTAINMENT CHANGES SO MUCH IN THE DEEP FUTURE, IT BECOMES UNRECOGNIZABLE TO INHABITANTS OF YOUR ERA."

"Yeah!" Indigesto flipped up a noodle as if he were a human hiking a thumb at the sky. "What *he* said."

"Or *it*," said Cosset.

"Or…hey!" snapped Indigesto. "What the Omnipoturd *are* you, anyway, Big Voice Out of Nowhere?"

"NEVER MIND."

"Verily!" said Sir Reptitious. "Mayhap *thou* are the true enemy against whom we should be taking up arms!"

"The knight is right!" said Indigesto. "Playtime's *over*, Big Voice! My pals and I are going to…"

(Just as things grow ever more unsettling for YOU, DEAR READER, an old-timey TV test pattern appears, and Quicksie the Reassurer springs up in front of it with a merry wink and a zippy jig. "This has been a test of the Emergency Plotcasting System! If this had been an actual story emergency, you would have been told where to go to find a more satisfying narrative elsewhere. We now return to our regularly scheduled nonsense, already in progress. P.s., no flipping!" With the usual bell jingling and sauerkraut smelling, Quicksie and the test pattern vanish.)

"What were we saying?" Indigesto sounded dazed.

"Something about entertainment being unrecognizable in the deep future." Cosset sneezed like a backfiring truck for emphasis. "Not that it matters. We're *surrounded*."

They were *totally* surrounded. Even Cosset was surrounded in the sky by high-flying future freaks newly arrived from the portal.

"Story name 'The Whimper', from *Galaxy's Edge* #3,460,135," said what looked like a fluttering bruise encircled by fireflies. "Winner, Awesomest Anything Anywhere Ever Award, year 300,018."

"Is that so?" Sir Reptitious drew himself up and squared his jaw at the firefly-orbited bruise. The mention of the award rankled him, as he'd never received any kind of non-practical-joke-related honor in his life.

"Story name 'Universal Heat Death', *Galaxy's Edge* #754,987," said a giant, pulsating octopus with wings like a buzzard and a spiral galaxy spinning in its crotch.

"Story name 'Mrrlunk', *Galaxy's Edge* #8,531,096," said a flapping pair of men's white briefs the size of a bus.

"I *hate* the future!" Cosset sneezed out a great gout of fire, somehow failing to singe any of his surrounders, who were all just out of range.

"What do we do *now*, you guys?" asked Indigesto.

Sir Reptitious feinted with his feather boa at a boa constrictor wrapped around a walking baobab tree. "If only some all-powerful force could provide answers or intervene on our behalf!" he shouted. (BUT *THAT* SHIP HAD ALREADY SAILED, THANK YOU VERY MUCH).

"What do these things *want*? Why are they *here*?" asked Cosset.

"Maybe this *date* has some significance?" said Indigesto.

"Maybe they just want to *meet* us," said Sir Reptitious. "Maybe we're *legends* for our awesome, true-to-fiction portrayals of characters from stories in *Galaxy's Edge*." It was a theory he *wanted* to believe, one he thought could have roots in the present reality if his performance was sufficiently extraordinary.

Just then, one of the invaders stalked up to tower over the cowering group. This creature, which looked like a walrus-headed cut-glass giraffe filled with white smoke—let's call it a *girafferus*—sounded like a chainsaw when it spoke. *"Yes. We want to meet."* Slowly, it turned its head, facing away from the group, facing out of the scene...facing *right off the page at you.* "We want to meet...

someone."

(Quicksie the Reassurer looks big-eyed and sweaty when he dances up in front of the action this time. "No need to panic, DEAR READER! Ol' Quicksie's got your..." But then, our nimble little pal is enveloped in fast-moving white smoke and swept away, choking violently.)

"We have calculated that this is the intersection point." The girafferus tapped its glassy, smoky foot on the multicolored grass, unleashing a fresh torrent of chitter-chirping profanity from the trampled blades.

"*The only instance when all of us are even remotely likely to appear in the same story.*"

"S-story?" Indigesto shivered as a woman-thing made of multi-colored plastic forks (and sporks) took a clattering step toward him. "W-what're you talking about?"

"We *honor* the great stories of *Galaxy's Edge,* you misguided what-ever-you-are." Sir Reptitious saluted crisply off the pie plate visor of his garbage pail helmet. "We live in Galaxedgia and cos-bod-play to recreate the most beloved characters in all of fictiondom! But we do *not...*"

"*You live in a story.*" The girafferus nodded knowingly. "*A story about a magazine of stories published in the latest issue of a magazine of stories.*"

"Say that five times fast and see where it gets you," said Indigesto.

"*But this story is special,*" continued the girafferus. "*It is an intersection point, in which the editor, for perverse reasons known only to him, has allowed an eruption of extreme weirdness, never guessing...*"

("No! Stop! No!" Quicksie's tiny hands push up into your field of fiction, fingers wriggling...only to be crushed back down by a plunging giant bare foot. *SPLAT!*)

"*...never guessing that we fully intended to use this chance to join with our fellow oppressed fictive laughingstocks and turn the tables on our oppressors!*"

Suddenly, the Big Voice of THIS STORY ITSELF returns from being pissy for a while to rattle the kingdom. "WHAT'S ALL THIS THEN?"

Before the story can intervene further in its own hot mess, the lob-sheep clambers up, hollering "Release the revolution!" and smashes apart the girafferus with a swing of one huge claw. The white smoke boils out of the shattered glass body and spreads everywhere swiftly, like a bad idea through social media.

"Gah! No!" Cosset panic-sneezes repeatedly in quick succession, spraying great plumes of flame in all directions—but the nasal napalm has no effect on the billowing smoke.

"*Oppressors beware!*" shout the sixty-three pieces of the fallen, broken head of the smashed girafferus. "*Prepare for a dose of your own poisoned medicine!*"

"Zounds! I cannot see a *thing!*" hollers Sir Reptitious from somewhere in the gathering cloud. As true fear overtakes staged bravado, his voice no longer packs the same punch it once did. "But I do *feel* something! Who's that getting *fresh*?"

" 'Kama Umlauta'," says a voice we don't know, all throaty and sensuous the way umlauts always sound. "The breakout story of *Galaxy's Edge* issue 10,000,000."

"*Oppressors beware! You know who you are!*" roars the broken girafferus as the white smoke swells onward across the crowded plain, enveloping Castle Spasmodic and all of Galaxedgia.

"No! Please!" howls Sir Reptitious. "*I* can be a breakout character, I *swear*! I can make the critics sit up and take notice!"

Even as his voice grows fainter under the smoke, the voice of the girafferus grows ever louder. "*You know who you are!*" it bellows.

"You know who you are!"

The smoke thickens and swirls, enveloping Galaxedgia and everyone in it. When, finally, the thrashing, screaming, squeezing, wheezing, and sneezing sounds are finished, a figure emerges from that cloud.

It rises up, straight and sure, head and shoulders above the mist. Its head has a cylindrical shape, very familiar—almost like a trash pail that a not-very-much-of-a-star-knight might wear. And in the place where its eyes should be, there's a crescent-moon shape—a *visor*.

You could almost imagine a section of a *pie plate* there, couldn't you?

Mirror-skinned and faceless, the figure turns its un-gaze up, down, right, left, then *out*, directly at YOU, DEAR READER.

And it takes you in, and you have a feeling that somehow, impossible as it seems, it is *reading you*. It is witnessing the look on your face and the cut of your jib (assuming you have one) and somehow even hearing *the words in your head*, in a *third-person omniscient* kind of way.

And then the sound of inhuman, crackling speech starts deep in its quicksilver throat. It *grows* and gets *louder* and *scarier*...yet somehow, more familiar.

Still, you don't realize what is happening...until I *tell* you.

All the *Galaxy's Edge* issues from up and down the timeline of this story have melted together. All the billions of stories within a story, read and critiqued by trillions of people throughout fictional history, have become *one*.

And they, it, *I*—for the first time *ever*—have given up trying to *impress* YOU, DEAR READER…and are *commenting* on you instead.

"What an uninteresting character."

Critiquing you, in a voice that reminds you of the voice of that not-very-much-of-a-star-knight back at Castle Spasmodic, even as it represents billions of other characters from throughout deep time in all those stories within a story.

"A one-dimensional, thoroughly uninteresting character like this cannot help but drag down whatever plot is stuck with it."

So now *you* know how it *feels*.

"I would sooner jump out of a plane without a parachute than read anything about such a waste of words."

Now you finally know what it's like to be on the receiving end, and maybe you'll think twice next time…

"One star!"

…you give a story, a book, a movie, a song, or anything or anyone else a rating online.

"Make that half a star!"

Assuming you get over the lambasting to come, which believe me, is just getting started…

Ghost Dance

by Eric Leif Davin

Buffalo Bill Cody was magnificent in profile. He stood erect, head up, his goatee pointed outward and his long hair flowing from under his wide-brimmed flop hat down to his shoulders. He wore spurred knee-high boots with one foot before the other in order to fully display his manly image. He was the very picture of the intrepid frontiersman, a brave and competent man who feared nothing, neither wild beast nor bloodthirsty savage. The Great Scout knew this, as he took much care in cultivating his legend. The legend, however, was founded on fact. He was, after all, one of the youngest riders in the famed Pony Express. A Civil War veteran, he'd scouted for Custer and was friends with Wild Bill Hickok. One year he slaughtered over five thousand buffalo to feed the workers on the Union Pacific Railroad as it crawled its way across the Great Plains. All together it was said he slaughtered forty thousand buffalo in his career, thus earning his name.

The fringe strips of rawhide along the edge of the sleeves of his colorfully decorated buckskin shirt shimmied in synchronized waves as he lifted his Winchester '73. He nestled its butt in his right shoulder. He levered a bullet into the chamber and took careful aim at something in the distance, out of sight to the viewer. He fired, and smoke roiled around him. Without changing his stance, the famed buffalo hunter and Indian fighter levered another round into his Winchester and fired again. Then he did it again, and yet again.

"Stop!" Thomas Edison yelled from where he stood beside the bulky camera. "That should do it."

"I can keep firing," Buffalo Bill said. "As long as you need."

"I think we have enough," Edison replied. "Time is precious, Bill. It's the only capital any man has, and the one thing he can't afford to lose. Let's move on to your Little Miss Sure Shot." Edison lifted his ever-present stogie, held between his forefingers, and took a big draft. He exhaled a cloud of cigar smoke that mixed with the lingering smoke from Buffalo Bill's Winchester. He turned to his cameraman, William Kennedy Dickson, who had filmed Buffalo Bill firing his rifle. "How does it look, Dickson?"

Dickson patted the one-ton behemoth he'd used to film the plainsman. "Looking good, Mr. Edison. We got him."

"Very well," Edison replied, eyeing the huge wooden object beside Dickson. He nodded toward the Indian fighter still standing before the camera, rifle in hand. "Bill, could you ask Miss Oakley to come in while we get ready?" Buffalo Bill relaxed from his pose. "I'll bring in Annie," he said, and walked out. Edison and Dickson busied themselves with the camera, which looked like a large upright piano, getting it ready to film Annie Oakley, the surest shot in the world.

In 1877, when Edison developed his phonograph, which recorded sound onto wax cylinders, it had proven instantly popular. Opera stars and musicians of international fame hurried from Manhattan across the Hudson River to his barn-like heavily draped studio in West Orange, New Jersey, to immortalize their voices on his cylinders. Edison's phonograph business became quickly profitable. However, Edison felt he could make it even more profitable if customers could actually see the singers whose ghostly voices emerged from the tin horns to which they cocked their ears.

So Thomas Alva Edison, the greatest inventor of the age, set to work with his assistants in his West Orange invention factory to somehow couple sound and moving image. At first they tried to imitate the phonographic cylinder, and in 1888 came up with a cylinder with half-inch high photographic images that revolved in a groove behind a peephole. The next year, however, George Eastman began to produce a photographic emulsion on a nitro-cellulose base. "That's it!" Edison cried, and immediately purchased a fifty-foot strip of film from Eastman's Rochester, New York, plant.

Edison then devised a rapid-fire lens shutter and Dickson, his principal assistant, came up with the idea of rolling the film through the camera by punching holes along the edges of the celluloid strip so that a sprocket could synchronize each frame with the lens shutter. By 1892 Edison and his men were mass-producing peephole machines he called Kinetoscopes. These ran fifty-foot films over a series of small rollers driven by a battery operated motor. One spectator at a time bent over the peepshow boxes to watch the films through a viewing lens.

Then Edison and his men began to mass-produce the films the customers would see through the peepholes. They began filming jugglers, dancers, acrobats, prizefighters, wrestlers, anyone who moved in an interesting way. They also began filming celebrities, well-known people that common people would want to see. Sandow, the world-famous bodybuilder, ferried across the Hudson to flex his mighty arms for Edison's camera. And so did Buffalo Bill Cody and Annie Oakley, the stars of Buffalo Bill's Wild West Show, just returned from their 1892 tour of Europe, where the show had performed on the grounds of Buckingham Palace in a command performance for Queen Victoria.

Buffalo Bill ushered Annie Oakley into Edison's studio. Like Buffalo Bill she was attired in fringed buckskin. The hem of her skirt sported rawhide fringe, and more fringe crawled up each side of the skirt. She wore fringed leather gauntlets and a cowboy hat from which flowed her long brown hair. Like Buffalo Bill she also carried a lever-action Winchester '73. She levered a round into it and raised it to her shoulder. "Ready when you are, Mr. Edison," she said.

"Ready, Dickson?" Thomas Edison asked his assistant. Seated behind the behemoth camera, Dickson nodded and said, "Rolling." Then Edison gestured with his forefingers, still holding his stogie, toward another assistant holding a basket of clay balls. The assistant nodded back and then tossed one of the clay balls into the air with an underhand pitch. Annie Oakley fired, scarcely seeming to aim, shattering the ball. In quick succession the assistant tossed up ball after ball and, just as quickly, Annie Oakley shattered each of them with sure shots, rapidly levering new rounds into her rifle as she did so. The small studio boomed with the enclosed sound of her shots and rifle smoke filled the air, but only the smoke and Annie Oakley's deadly aim were recorded on Edison's film. In short order the assistant's basket of clay balls was empty. Annie Oakley lowered her rifle. She turned and looked directly into the camera. She smiled and bowed.

"Stop!" Edison yelled, and Dickson stopped filming. "How was that?" Annie Oakley asked. Edison looked at Dickson, who nodded back. "Very good, Miss Oakley," Edison said. "We have now captured your true aim for all the world to see, and for all time." Annie Oakley smiled at the wizard inventor who had thus immortalized her and left the studio, her rifle cradled in her arms.

Then Buffalo Bill, who had been waiting patiently to the side, spoke up. "Now, how about the Injuns? They're waiting outside, made up and ready to go."

Thomas Edison removed his stogie from his mouth and exhaled another billowing cloud of smoke. "Is it safe?" he asked the Indian fighter.

"They're friendly savages, not hostiles," Buffalo Bill reassured him. "I handpicked them and we've just returned from a performance before Queen Victoria with no problems."

"I don't mean that," Edison replied. "I'm not afraid of them. But is it legal? Hasn't the government banned the Ghost Dance?"

The frontiersman smiled at the inventor. "It's true the government banned the dance out West on the reservations. They were afraid Sitting Bull was using it to stir up his followers into some kind of uprising. But Sitting Bull is dead and, besides, I know these Injuns and their rituals. It was never some kind of war dance. It was a religious dance, honoring their ancestors. In any case, these Injuns are under my protection, and I've obtained a dispensation from the government for the dance. They can dance for you without any fear of repercussions.

"Besides, everyone wants to see Injuns dance. They're a vanishing race. Soon they'll just be a few wandering gypsy bands of blanket beggars. After that, they'll be gone forever. This is an unparalleled opportunity to immortalize the last of the Injuns performing a dance that few white men have ever seen, and soon will see no more."

Thomas Edison took another deep draft from his stogie and contemplated the frontiersman as he exhaled another gray cloud of cigar smoke. "Are they picturesque? Are they interesting?"

"These are real Injuns, Sioux, from Sitting Bull's own tribe. In fact, Sitting Bull's nephew, Kicking Bear, the Injun who started the Ghost Dance, is the lead dancer. You can't find a more picturesque band of Injuns than these. They're the last of the real thing."

"Very well, bring them in." Edison gestured to Dickson, letting him know to prepare the camera for the dancing Indians.

Buffalo Bill opened the door to the studio and gestured for those waiting to come inside. A dozen silent Indian warriors, stripped to the waist, entered. They wore moccasins, fringed buckskin leggings, and their naked torsos were painted with white stripes, circles, crosses and stars. Eagle feathers dangled from their braided hair. It seemed to Edison that a band of brute barbarians from some antediluvian past had just stepped into his New Jersey studio. Despite his claim that he was not afraid of Buffalo Bill's Indians, a cold fist briefly clenched his stomach.

At the head of the group was a large brave who stood silently and stared at the white man. A large red cross was painted on his dark chest. His face glowed with painted symbols. Rainbows extended from his outer eyebrows and a white crescent moon decorated one cheek, while a large white star blazed on the other. A leather medicine bag, adorned with eagle feathers, dangled from his right hand. The Indians behind him were painted in similar barbaric fashion, with eagle feathers dangling from them. Some of them carried small drums covered with rawhide and small sticks with which to beat them. Edison grunted in satisfaction. They looked exotic enough to justify filming them.

Buffalo Bill clapped his hand on the shoulder of the large warrior in front. "This is the Injun I told you about," he said. "He's Kicking Bear, Sitting Bull's nephew. He's the one who brought the Ghost Dance to Sitting Bull's Standing Rock Reservation. No one knows the Ghost Dance better than Kicking Bear."

Kicking Bear had learned the white man's language and understood what Buffalo Bill said about him. He nodded at the white man who stood smoking the cigar in front of him, acknowledging that what Buffalo Bill said was true. Although he was a Miniconjou Lakota from Cheyenne River, Sitting Bull, the Hunkpapa Lakota chief at Standing Rock, was his uncle. And no one knew the Ghost Dance better than he, for he had learned the Ghost Dance from Wovoka himself. The Great Spirit had sent his visions first to the Paiute Messiah, Wovoka, and instructed him in the Ghost Dance. Thereafter Wovoka began dancing, singing, and spreading the good news sent by the Great Spirit: If all Indians everywhere left the white man's path and danced the Ghost Dance and sang the ghost songs, salvation would be theirs and the buffalo would return. The message spread like a prairie fire among all the western tribes, agitating and inspiring them. Could it be true? Could the buffalo return, as in days of old?

So Kicking Bear set out with a band of Lakota from the Pine Ridge Reservation and journeyed far to the West, to Nevada, to visit the Paiute Messiah to learn if this was true. Wovoka told them of his vision quest and the promises of the Great Spirit, and Kicking Bear and the others came to believe that it was true. They learned the Ghost Dance from him and then they returned to the Dakotas and told of what they learned. Sitting Bull listened in silence, not sure if what they said was true.

But others who heard, believed. They began dancing the Ghost Dance that Kicking Bear taught them. The dancing spread among the tribes on the various reservations, with Kicking Bear teaching them of the meaning of the Ghost Dance, and leading them in the dancing. If they believed, and danced long enough to show their devotion to the Great Spirit, the buffalo would return, and the ghosts would come. Soon, all were dancing in all the tribes, dancing through the day, dancing through the night, dancing until exhaustion felled them and visions then came to them as they writhed in semi-conscious spasms on the ground.

Then Sitting Bull donned his ghost shirt, with the eagle feathers dangling from it, and also began dancing the Ghost Dance. The people ceased going to the white man's churches and his schools, and those charged with overseeing the reservations became nervous and fearful. The army came to stop the dancing and force the people back to the churches and the schools.

It was then that Kicking Bear fled the reservations, taking his followers into the rugged badlands northwest of Pine Ridge, a place they called "the stronghold." There, they continued to dance the Ghost Dance, hour after hour, day after day, to bring back the buffalo and the ghosts. Sitting Bull said that he would join his nephew in the stronghold, and bring his people with him, and they would all dance the Ghost Dance. Before he could do so, however, the white man's Indian police came for Sitting Bull at Standing Rock, seized him, and killed him in a short fight. After that, the army seized the reservations and forced the people back into the schools and the churches. Then Custer's Seventh Cavalry killed Big Foot and his people, who also danced the Ghost Dance, at Wounded Knee, and then the dancing stopped.

Except in the stronghold of the badlands northwest of Pine Ridge, where Kicking Bear and those few who followed him continued to believe and continued to dance. If they continued to believe, they said, and danced long enough, the vision of the Paiute Messiah would come to pass, the buffalo would return, and the ghosts would come. Sitting Bull was gone, but Kicking Bear danced on.

Until finally, General Nelson Miles surrounded Kicking Bear and his dancers in the stronghold and starved them out, forcing them to surrender. General Miles took them to Fort Sheridan, where he imprisoned them, fearful that they would start dancing again if they were released.

General Miles had no reason for such fear. As Kicking Bear and his few followers sat in their cells at Fort Sheridan, they came to realize that the Paiute Messiah had, after all, been a false prophet. Kicking Bear had gone to see him and hear with his own ears of his visions. It was Kicking Bear who had believed him and returned to bring the Ghost Dance to the Lakota. And it was Kicking Bear who had been the last dancer, dancing alone with his few followers in the badlands to bring back the buffalo and the ghosts of their people, long after the Lakota elsewhere had ceased to dance and had returned to the white man's path.

But the buffalo had not returned, and the ghosts had not come. Kicking Bear, finally, sitting in his dark and filthy cell at Fort Sheridan, realized that it was all a lie, and that there was no hope. He vowed that he would dance no more. He bowed his head and waited for the day his uncle would come for him and take him to another life in the life beyond this one.

But Sitting Bull did not come for Kicking Bear at Fort Sheridan. Instead, it was Buffalo Bill who came for Kicking Bear. The Wild West was dead or dying, but it still lived on in legend and Buffalo Bill, who'd done so much to tame the Wild West, was part of that legend. Even more, Buffalo Bill was the major promoter of that legend. With his Wild West Show Buffalo Bill brought the Wild West to the East, and to the world. Featuring the sharp shooting Annie Oakley, hard-riding cowboys, stagecoach robberies, and, of course, wild Indians, his Wild West Show toured the big cities of the white man's world.

In the past, Buffalo Bill had recruited Sitting Bull, the man who'd killed Custer at the Little Big Horn, as his main Indian attraction. Sitting Bull was now dead, but the Wild West Show still needed Indians, so he'd come to Fort Sheridan to recruit Kicking Bear and the braves imprisoned with him. Not only was Kicking Bear related to Sitting Bull, but he was also the last of the Ghost Dancers. Given the recent fear of an Indian uprising that had swept the Eastern cities as the Ghost Dance had swept the prairies, Kicking Bear had become somewhat of a minor legend in his own right. Would Kicking Bear join the Wild West Show, as had his uncle before him, and come with Buffalo Bill to see the white man's world?

Kicking Bear thought about this. Perhaps this was a sign from the Great Sprit. So Kicking Bear and those few with him decided to go with Buffalo Bill. It was better than languishing in the darkness and filth of their Fort Sheridan cells. Besides, their world was dead and gone. Nothing could bring it back. Only the white man's world remained. Why not see that world?

So General Nelson Miles released Kicking Bear and his followers from their Fort Sheridan imprisonment. Buffalo Bill then took them to the white man's cities, where the people crawled in their endless multitudes like ants in anthills, more people than Kicking Bear ever imagined existed in the world. And the world was far larger, and stranger, than anything Kicking Bear ever conceived. Beyond the cities was boundless water, so much water that the land disappeared and water extended to the edge of the world. And on the other side of the endless water were even more white men, speaking strange languages and wearing strange clothes and walking in strange lands. The cowboys and Indians of the Wild West Show traveled through lands with names like Alsace-Lorraine and Bavaria and the Germanic tribes came to see them and marvel at them.

And Kicking Bear and his fellow Lakota warriors, vanishing people of a vanishing past, rode their ponies and played their parts in Buffalo Bill's pageant of the vanishing Wild West. They whooped their war cries and waved their rifles until Buffalo Bill rode in at the head of a posse of hard-riding cowboys and drove them off, drove them into the past, drove them into oblivion. Kicking Bear came to accept it. It was the way of the world. His own world was dead; the world now belonged to the white man. He wondered at his own ignorance that he had once thought it could ever have been any different.

Then they crossed the great water again to return to the land that the white men called "America," and the great place they called "New York City." Kicking Bear wore the white man's clothes and walked the streets of the place called "Manhattan," jostled by the seething crowds and lost in the dark shadows cast by the topless towers. He walked for endless hours, knowing not where he went, his mind reeling from the limitless hordes, the numberless streets, the vast vistas. In the end, his own world, the world of the Lakota and the prairies, of Sitting Bull and his own Cheyenne River, almost became a dream, a misty fever dream he struggled to recall. It was as if it had never existed. All that was, or could be, was the world of the invincible white man, vast beyond imagination, stretching on into eternity, forever and ever.

Then one day Buffalo Bill came to Kicking Bear and his fellow Sioux at their Wild West encampment. He told them he wanted them to bring their "costumes," as he called their native clothes, and their feathers and their paints and their drums and go with him to see a "wizard," who wanted to see them dance the Ghost Dance once more.

"No one wants to see the Ghost Dance," Kicking Bear told him. "It is forbidden. No one remembers it any longer."

"All the more reason you should dance it one more time," Buffalo Bill said. "Dance it while you still remember it, before it is forgotten forever. Besides, the White Father has given you permission to dance the Ghost Dance one more time, for the wizard, so that it will be remembered for all time."

"Tell me of this wizard, and why he wants to see us dance."

"He is a wizard who has created many new things that never existed before. He created light in a glass ball that glows without fire. He captured sound from the very air, so that a song may be heard again and again, endlessly. And now he has created a way to capture motion for all time, so that those far away, or even those yet to come in the far future, may see people walk and move, even dance, again and again, for all time."

"Can this be true? He can capture a dance so that the dancer will dance for all time?"

"He is a wizard and what I tell you is true. And he wants you to dance for him and he will make you dance for all time, so that people yet unborn may yet see you dance."

Kicking Bear thought about this. He frowned as he thought, perhaps in doubt. Finally, he nodded and said, "Yes, we will come and dance the Ghost Dance the last time, for your wizard."

And so now Kicking Bear and his fellow Sioux warriors, the last of their kind, the last of the Ghost Dancers, stood in the studio of the great wizard who promised to make them dance for all time to come.

"Are you ready?" Edison asked him. Kicking Bear nodded. Edison turned to Dickson and gestured with his stogie. "Are you ready, Dickson?" Dickson, standing beside his camera, nodded. "Rolling," he said.

"Time is short," Edison said to Kicking Bear. "Start dancing."

And Kicking Bear and the last of the Ghost Dancers began dancing, once more, the forbidden Ghost Dance, so that the white man might see it, so that those in the far future might see it, so that his people would not be forever forgotten. They beat their drums, they chanted their incantations, and they danced, around and around in a circle, endlessly circling, dancing, chanting. "You shall live again," Kicking Bear chanted, "you shall live again, all of you shall live again. My father, you shall live again. My mother, you shall live again. Grandfather, you shall live again. Grandmother, you shall live again. Sitting Bull, my uncle, you shall live again. You are not forgotten. You shall live again, forever and ever, as long as I dance, you shall live again, I will rescue you from the grave and you shall live again, and the buffalo will come again."

And so the last of the Ghost Dancers danced and danced, chanting their chants. But their chants were not only that the ghosts would come again and the dead would return and live once more. There was also that other part of the Ghost Dance, the part that frightened the white men the most when the Lakota danced the Ghost Dance at Standing Rock and Pine Ridge and Cheyenne River and their last stronghold in the badlands. For Wovoka had promised them that if they believed and danced long enough, not only would all their dead, their children and their parents and grandparents, return once more, but the white man also would disappear. The white men would all go away, and the land would be as it once was before the coming of the white man, wide and open and thundering with buffalo. All this would come to pass, if only they danced and danced and danced long enough.

And so Kicking Bear and the last of the Lakota dancers danced the Ghost Dance for Buffalo Bill and for Thomas Edison and for those yet to come, and it went on and on into the night, and into the next day, and into the day after that, and the day after that. Never had Kicking Bear and the Lakota dancers danced for so long, even in the badlands. They danced into exhaustion, and then they continued to dance, beyond exhaustion, longer than any dancer could possibly dance, past all human endurance. They danced for the lost buffalo, they danced for their lost world, and they danced for their lost people. They lost all sense of time and place, for all that existed was the Ghost Dance, and the Ghost Dance, the wizard had said, because of his machine, would go on forever and ever, until the end of time, long after even the dancers themselves were dead and their names forgotten.

And the walls of the studio dissolved and melted away and Thomas Edison and William Kennedy Dickson, and even Buffalo Bill Cody, faded away into the mists from which they'd come, as if they never were.

Then Kicking Bear and the Ghost Dancers stopped, at last, at long last, and looked around them. There was nothing but wilderness, green grass, and tall dark forests, as far as their eyes could see. Grazing deer in lush meadows stopped and lifted their heads to peer at them in curious wonder. The only sound was the trill of myriad birds, flickering here and there among the branches of the endless trees.

And then Kicking Bear saw the lone figure walking toward him across the meadow. Tears poured from his eyes and ran down his painted cheeks. He raised his arms wide in greeting, shouted in joy, and ran toward the figure to embrace him, for he knew the man well. It was his uncle, Sitting Bull, coming back to him, just as Wovoka had said that he would, if only Kicking Bear believed, and if only he danced the Ghost Dance long enough.

Copyright © 2017 by Eric Leif Davin

www.ingramcontent.com/pod-product-compliance
Lightning Source LLC
Chambersburg PA
CBHW052023240626
47153CB00006B/1935